THE CIRCUS IN THE ATTIC
AND OTHER STORIES

The Circus in the Attic

and Other Stories

ROBERT PENN WARREN

A Harvest/HBJ Book
Harcourt Brace Jovanovich, Publishers
San Diego   New York   London

Copyright © 1947, 1946, 1945, 1943, 1941, 1937, 1936, 1935,
1931 by Robert Penn Warren
Copyright renewed 1975/1974, 1973, 1971, 1969, 1965, 1964,
1963 by Robert Penn Warren

Library of Congress Cataloging in Publication Data

Warren, Robert Penn, 1905–
   The circus in the attic, and other stories.

   (A Harvest/HBJ book)
   I. Title.
[PS3545.A748C6   1983]   813'.52   83-8461
ISBN 0-15-618002-2

Printed in the United States of America

A B C D E F G H I J

To

KATHERINE ANNE PORTER

Contents

For permission to reprint the stories in this collection the author wishes to thank the editors of *The Virginia Quarterly Review, Cosmopolitan, The Southern Review, Mademoiselle, Cronos,* and the Macaulay Company.

NOTE

The earliest story in this book was written in 1930, the latest in 1946, but the order here is not chronological.

THE CIRCUS IN THE ATTIC
AND OTHER STORIES

The Circus in the Attic

LET US assume that it is summer. Coming from the north, just at the brow of the ridge, you catch your first view of the valley and of Bardsville. There is the wide valley of Cadman's Creek, two miles below, opening sharp upon the river. To your right, to the west, there is the silver-green shine of the river and the green-silver shine of the rank corn in the bottom lands beyond, some miles away. But the sun-glazed highway spins off ahead of you, down the valley, like a ribbon of celluloid film carelessly unspooled across green baize. And at the end is the steel bridge over the creek.

Across the creek are the long, new, raw-brick structures of the war plant set in the gashed and still red-wounded clay, one of the tin-bright stacks still releasing unwaveringly the black smoke in a single column to an improbable height in the motionless, heat-benumbed air. And there are the dilapidated piles of the old furniture factory (which made ammunition boxes for the war), the coal yards on their patch of grimed earth, which glitters like mica, and the tracks, switches, and sidings exposed among the jumble, like a tangle of dissected nerves, to glitter, too, and quiver in the incandescent light. You cannot see the stone ruin of the old mill that stands at the other end of the bridge. But you do see, beyond the creek, flung down beyond the tracks, the shanties, trailers, and pre-fabricated houses of the war workers, and beyond that the shanties of nigger town which straggle up the hill, with washing here and there hanging abjectly on crazy lines like improvised flags of surrender among ruins. But all of that is not Bardsville. Bardsville is on the river bluffs beyond.

Cadman's Creek runs west to the river to make a big "V," and on the leg of the "V" toward the river, to the west, the land is high; for the worn limestone still holds there against the erosion of frost and flood, and every spring forces the swollen red river over the cornlands to the west. As you see it from the north, there are the steeples, the water tower, and the mauve and blue slate roofs with the color and shine of a pigeon's breast, embowered in the swollen and tufted greenery, with here and there the glimpse of sober red brick, or a white wall, or a white picket fence among the trees; and, now and then, a window, miles away on Rusty-Butt Hill, flashes the sun to you like a heliograph using some code which you cannot understand. That is Bardsville. It is the county seat of Carruthers County.

As you reach the brow of the ridge, and the valley and Bardsville fill your eye, you probably do not notice the little monument by the left of the highway. It is a single shaft of granite, about ten feet high, almost concealed in a riot of purple-tufted ironweed, flame-tufted milkweed, and sassafras growth. You have noticed, of course, the big road-sign to the right, advertising Carruthers House, "Southern Hospitality at Its Most Gracious," and a dining room recommended (before the war of 1941-45) by Duncan Hines, "Country Ham our *Specialitée.*" The sign stands on the old Sykes place, and the ruinous log-house up the lane beyond the sign, sagging and windowless, under the single scrofulous cedar, weathering to earth and surrendering to the clawing hands of vine and briar, is the old Sykes house, a refuge for field mice, a lone fox, and a couple of fat blacksnakes which like to sun themselves on the stone coping of the old cistern. Not even boys go there now.

Twenty-odd years ago, a nameless old tramp crawled up there and died. His body was not found for nearly a year, long after the buzzards had lost interest. For several years thereafter, boys would go to the Sykes house to whisper with delicious shudders in the sun-dappled gloom of the half-roof-less rooms and then listen to the sound of their own breathing. But the story died out of the folklore of Bardsville boyhood, even with the desperate addition of murder to spice the tale, and for another generation of boys the place was too near the highway to be romantic. Thicket and unchinked logs offered no defense, only a filter, against the whir of motors and the bleat of horns.

But Seth Sykes's name is on the monument, coupled with the name of Cassius Perkins, two heroes of Bardsville, who, as the inscription on the monument declares, gave their lives on this spot that their comrades might live and that the foot of the invader might not sully the soil of home. If you tear away the love vine from the gray granite (imported from Vermont), you can read the words. The monument was erected in 1917, as a curious backwash or eddy of the excitement and spirit of dedication evoked among the ladies of Bardsville by the coming of a new war, a war undertaken now by a united people to defend, beyond the seas, their liberty.

The new war had not yet become real in the summer of 1917. The bandages prepared at Red Cross meetings in the basement of the St. Luke's parish house or in the Sunday-school room of the Baptist Church seemed to have no more importance than the baskets prepared there for the poor before Christmas. The tears shed by mothers and sweethearts at the railroad station seemed to be no different from the tears shed when a boy went off to school or college. No armless khaki sleeve had yet appeared on the streets of Bardsville. So the tumescent, rich, meaningless emotionalism that ached sweetly in the breasts of the middle-aged ladies of the community found release and focus in the monument. The United Daughters of the Confederacy, the defenders of ancient pieties and the repositories of ignorance of history, undertook to raise the money. Bardsville had had heroes before, and it would have them again. Soon now. The monument would be an inspiration to the new heroes. So the monument appeared, and was dedicated, and while the mayor made a speech, a platoon of conscripts from a camp up in Kentucky, in untarnished khaki, with slick, scrubbed faces, stood stiffly by with the wooden embarrassment of boys trapped on the platform at high-school commencement.

Cassius Perkins and Seth Sykes had died on the old pike, on the brow of the ridge. It was the winter of 1861-62, when the Federal armies were coming down across Kentucky. The Yankees already held the towns across the Kentucky border. But Bardsville had its home guard, a few middle-aged men and a rag-tag-and-bobtail of young boys who could ride like circus performers and shoot anything that would hold powder and to whom the war was a gaudy picnic that their tyrannous mothers would not let them attend. Some of them did attend the picnic later. Some of them rode calluses on their rumps following Forrest across Mississippi and Tennessee and Alabama. Some of them huddled in the pits outside Vicksburg while the acid June sweat burned their eyes and made dewdrops on their silky boyish beards, and their shoulders ached with the interminable recoil of the rifle. But in December of 1861, Cassius Perkins was the only member of the home guard who really attended the picnic and stayed until it was over.

Cassius was one of a group of fifteen or twenty home guards who were encamped on the night of December 16, 1861, on the ridge north of Bardsville. They were on the lookout for Yankee cavalry patrols that had worked down a couple of times out of Kentucky. Their bivouac was in a grove of oaks, now gone, on top of the ridge. Their horses were tethered in a line under the trees. They had little fires and a keg of whisky. It was like a fishing trip or a hunting party, and already the spirit of Christmas was in the air. They felt very manly. And they felt perfectly safe. For they had sent two boys up the pike to watch. "Videttes" they had proudly learned to call them. The camp, very sleepy, totally confused, and half drunk, was surprised just at dawn. The videttes had been surprised and taken without a warning shot being fired. The home guards did manage to get to their horses, did mount, mill about for a moment on the pike, and then, after a brief exchange of shots, fall back to Bardsville. Later in the day, long after the patrol had withdrawn into Kentucky, they found the body of Cassius on the pike. Seth Sykes's wife had already dragged his body to their house. Nobody knew very clearly what had happened, but it was generally understood that they had saved Bardsville.

When the monument was erected, however, an old man, Jake Velie, who had been one of the boys, remembered the time. He was an old man now, past seventy, but he seemed older, in his greasy, tattered overalls, his chin and whiskers fouled with nicotine, the stub of his right arm standing out from his shoulder like a plucked chicken's wing (he had lost the arm twenty-five years before when he was a brakeman), a derelict and a reproach to the community, squatting against a maple in the court-house yard, exuding a miasma of dried sweat and rotgut whisky. "Yeah," he said, "yeah," and spat on the sparse turf with a quick, viperish outthrust of his tendoned, dirt-crusted neck, "putten up air-y monimint to Cash Perkins. I knowed him. I wuz thar. I wuz a home guard, lak all them little pukes. Oh, we wuz sojers, I hope to tell. Layen up thar on that-air ridge in them oak trees. Them trees is gone now, gone thirty year. Layen up thar lak hit wuz a coon hunt, eaten hog meat and drinken whisky, tellen what we wuz gonna do to them Yankees. Yeah, we done hit," he said, and spat, and sank back, silent for a moment, into the miasma of rotgut and time.

Then said: "Yeah. We done hit, in a pig's eye. Layen up thar drunk, and bout day them Yankees come. Half them pukes didn't wait to pick up no guns. But they didn't aim to fergit them hosses. They wuz homeward bound, I mean to say. They tuk out home. Cept Cash. He wuz drunk. Drunk and got the wrong hoss. Mike Stafford's mean sorrel hoss couldn't nobody ride but Mike. Cash wuz drunk, but ain't no man e'er been so drunk he would ride right at him a passel of Yankees single-handed. Bet Gin'l Lee ner none of them high-toned gin'ls e'er done hit. Cash didn't do hit. That sorrel hoss was runnen away."

Then said: "Them Yankees give him his'n. They didn't stay to hem ner haw. They give hit to him. They laid him down.

And none of them little pukes from town stopped to git his deathbed remarks. They wuz long-gone. And me, too."

Then, sitting under the maple, with the gray sparrow droppings staining the hot leaves above him, spat and said: "A monimint to Cash Perkins. Hit wuz an accidint. Mought as well put up air-y monimint to me fer gitten this here cut off." He waggled the stub of his arm shrouded in the hacked-off, blue shirt sleeve.

Then said: "Cash ne'er killed no Yankees. He was a likker-killer. Always wuz, time he wuz stout fer to draw a cork. Killed himsef a lot of likker that night, and got on the wrong hoss. A mean sorrel hoss. Mought as well put up that monimint with a jug of cawn whisky carved on top lak hit wuz a angel on a tombstone."

But nobody was there to hear him, under the maple. All of Bardsville was out on the ridge at the dedication. All but two little colored boys, and a collie dog panting sardonically with the heat, and another old derelict like Jake Velie who lay drowsing on the grass with a straw hat over his face. Nor would Bardsville, had Bardsville been there, have believed the truth, whatever truth it was, which Jake Velie uttered out of the candor and irony of age. Not even when he leaned forward off his haunches and savagely smote the sparse turf with the flat of his hand three times and croaked: "The truth. Hit is the Gawd's truth! I wuz thar. The truth!"

They would not have believed him or his truth, for people always believe what truth they have to believe to go on being the way they are.

But Jake Velie did not know all the truth. And all who did know it had been dead a long time, those who had known the truth about how Seth Sykes died. The men of the Yankee patrol and Seth Sykes's wife had known the truth, but they were dead.

Seth Sykes had a hundred acres of ridge land, where the rains ripped off the soil every year and bore it down the furrows, and the sun all summer baked the limestone. He lived in the log house with his wife and two children, and the place was his, and was the world. What happened in the wide and inimical world outside this world was nothing to him. Men spoke to him on the street in Bardsville and told him about the war. "Secesh ain't nuthin' to me," he said, and twitched his gaunt shoulders. "Niggers," he said, "niggers ain't nuthin' to me," he said. "Take 'em outer the country ain't nuthin' to me." They told him how the Yankees would come. "Yankees," he said, "they ain't nuthin' to me. Yankees ner niggers."

He had a fight, stomp and gouge, with a man on the street in Bardsville, and lost the fight, and went home streaked with blood. He had said he hoped the Yankees would come.

Then the winter fell, and Seth did not go to Bardsville any more, but holed up like a bear or a varmint in the log house on the ridge and ate the doled, haggled strips of hog meat off his razor-backs, which he had killed at the first good frost, and the squeezed and hand-weighed corn pone, and counted out the chunks of wood for the fire.

Then the Yankees came. Seth Sykes, leaning over the fireplace in the dawn to blow up the fire, heard the shots on the pike. By the time he got down to the foot of the lane, the home guards were beating it hell for leather down the ridge for town and the body of Cassius Perkins lay on the pike. Cassius Perkins was the man he had had the fight with in Bardsville.

Seth came out on the pike among the blue-clad troopers on the restless horses, nodding to them, saying good morning. He stood above the body of Cassius Perkins, flat, face-down, arms spread to clutch the pike to the bosom, and rubbed the toe of his brogan in the gravel, and said, "Secesh. What I told 'em."

He looked up at the young man with pale, silky mustaches, and said, "You the cap'n?"

"I am Lieutenant Wiggins," replied the young man, whose long-skirted blue coat seemed too big for him, and seemed to weigh too much, like a blanket thrown over a child's shoulders. The breath he uttered whitened on the still air above the yellow mustaches.

"You bossen these-here sojers?"

"I am in command," the young man said.

Seth Sykes looked down at the body on the pike. He fingered the scar along his jaw, scarcely healed, where the man on the street of Bardsville had kicked him as he lay. He took his eyes off the body and looked at the lieutenant. "You all hongry," he said, not as a question but as a statement. Then added, "I'll give you a piece of meat. You kin cook hit on a fahr." He nodded across the pike to the grove, where a little smoke yet rose from one of the campfires.

He turned up the lane, walking uneasily over the frozen, rutted ground with a rocking motion. The lieutenant followed, walking his horse at Seth's pace, the men following. They went up to the establishment. Seth Sykes went into his smoke house. One of the men dismounted and looked at the log crib by the barn. Before Seth Sykes had reappeared, he came back to the lieutenant and said, "They got corn."

"All right," the lieutenant said. "Use that wagon." He nodded to a wagon beside the barn.

When Seth Sykes came out of the smoke house, weighing a cured hog shoulder in his hands, he saw that they were spanning his mules to the wagon.

"What you doin'?" he demanded.

The lieutenant told him and added that he would be paid.

"Hit is my cawn," Seth Sykes stated without passion.

"You will be paid. I will give you an order for the money."

Seth Sykes looked at the lieutenant from head to booted and spurred heel. Then he turned deliberately, dropped the smoked shoulder, and approached the men at the wagon. He went straight up to the trooper who was holding the lead rope of the near mule. "Leave hit go," he said.

The trooper made no reply.

Seth Sykes took him by the arm and swung him round. The trooper struck him flat to the ground. Another trooper stood over him with a carbine. Seth Sykes lay there on the frozen ground, watching them put the mules in, and then load the wagon. Mrs. Sykes had run from the cabin at the noise. One of the troopers held her.

When the wagon was loaded, the lieutenant said, "Let him up." The cavalcade moved down the lane, the lieutenant in front, a trooper just behind him leading the horse which had been ridden by the trooper now driving the wagon. Two of the troopers rode behind the wagon. The wagon wheels groaned over the ruts.

They were almost at the foot of the lane when Seth Sykes rose from the ground. He ran down the lane after them. "Seth!" his wife called, "Seth!" Her voice was thin in the empty gray sky over the wide ridge.

He caught up with them just as the wagon drew onto the pike. He ran along the ditch by the pike toward the head of the column, the troopers all eyeing him incuriously. The lieutenant turned in his saddle. "Go back," he ordered sharply.

"Hit is my cawn!" Seth Sykes cried, and leaped out of the ditch to the pike and toward the lieutenant.

"Stand back!" the lieutenant cried, the authority in his voice cracking into querulousness.

Seth Sykes came on and the troopers watched him. He grabbed the lieutenant's near leg, the left leg, and shouted, "Hit is my cawn!"

The lieutenant leaned over and struck him about the head with his gauntleted fist. The horse shied and the lieutenant almost reeled from the saddle.

But the nearest trooper was on them now. He leaned from his saddle, seized Seth Sykes by the long, uncombed, matted hair, jerked his head back, and carefully put the muzzle of a pistol against the head, just above the ear, and pulled the trigger.

The body plunged, then sagged between the two horses like a dropped croker sack of nubbins.

The horses veered sharply apart, then stood. The eyes of the trooper who had fired the shot, gleaming from the crinkled, beefy face and black beard, met the eyes of the lieutenant, pale, astonished eyes above the yellow mustache.

"I didn't order you to do that," the lieutenant said uncertainly.

The bearded trooper made no reply. He looked at the body, and then sullenly replaced the weapon in its holster.

"Look!" the lieutenant cried with the tone of discovery, looking down at the blood and brains spattered on his trousers and boot. "Look!" he cried in pain and despair and outrage, and pointed with one finger at the fouled cloth and leather. "Look, you got it all over me!"

Then he leaned over the saddlebow and, in the blank morning, under the blank eyes watching him, vomited.

After the patrol had gone on, Seth Sykes's wife came out and dragged the body back to the cabin.

That was the truth about Seth Sykes and how he became a hero.

It was corn again, as it had been in the case of Cassius Perkins, and perhaps the monument should have been erected to corn, not just a carved jug, as Jake Velie had suggested, to commemorate Cash's corn whiskey, but on top of the shaft a carved jug set in the midst of a wreath of corn blades and of the spindling ears such as Seth Sykes had raised on his ridge farm. But such a monument with the jug and the wreath of corn would have been no disrespect to Seth Sykes and Cassius Perkins, nor to any hero who ever died. For perhaps Seth and Cash were no different from any other heroes, men who have been drunk on whiskey, or on something else as strong and heady, and have ridden runaway into the heart of the enemy, or have died defending a crib of corn, or something else, which they had sweated to make.

But the monument by the side of the dazzling concrete highway is only a simple shaft, with no jug or wreath, only the names and the inscription, which you will not stop to read. You will probably not even see the monument, for you will dip sharply over the ridge and take the long, tire-sizzling glide into the valley, over the Cadman's Creek bridge, by the Rotary Club's greeting sign, by the ruined mill, past the war plant, furniture factory, tobacco warehouses, and coal yards, and then swoop with purring motor up the rise through nigger town, where the dirt lanes fall away from each side of the concrete slab to wander among the shacks, and where a big-eyed, half-naked, chocolate pickaninny under a rose bush of red roses regards your hasty passage with the gravity of a philosopher.

You will go up the hill to the square, get gas and oil, and have lunch at the Carruthers House, overlooking the river, in the dining room where one shell from a Yankee gunboat landed in January, 1862, and made quite a mess. (The gunboats finally came up the river, were greeted with a spatter of small-arms fire from the home guard, lobbed three shells up the bluffs, and received the surrender of Bardsville.) Lunch will be served by a white girl wearing a green smock, a slash of lipstick, and an expression of indefatigable contempt; for the neat-handed, clairvoyant, grizzle-headed old colored waiters are there no more, thank you, sir. After lunch you will head out, out Chilton Avenue, up Rusty-Butt Hill and on out to hit Highway 83, and will whirl southward through the afternoon into the heart of Dixie.

Rusty-Butt Hill is the highest of the bluffs along the river, on the western leg of the "V" enclosing Bardsville. It was wooded once, great oaks and tulip trees, with a grassy glade on the western brow, above the cedars that clutched and grabbled into the limestone face, overlooking the wide river and the canebrakes beyond. One June afternoon, toward sun, about 1778 or '79, a man named "Lem Lovehart" entered the glade and, leaning on his long rifle, looked west over the river. He wore leather breeches, the fringed doeskin smock of the frontiersman, and a coonskin cap. A powder horn and knife hung at his side, and on his back was a leather-wrapped, thong-tied bundle. He had been born thirty-five years before in a cabin in the North Carolina Piedmont, had run away from home at fifteen with a couple of hunters, had been a trader with the Cherokees, and had worked his way into the great valleys beyond the mountains, driven by a hot restlessness and a dark compulsion that he had no name for. The previous winter he had spent holed up in a hut in what is now lower Middle Tennessee, alone, and with spring had started out northwestward, in a slow, aimless, zigzag track, like a journey in a dream. He was a rather short, chunky man, with some fat streaking his brawn, given to ready sweating. His leather garments had the rank odor of the winter den, and now, tired from his climb up the bluff, he stood at the edge of the glade and sweated with the sweat of the bear fat and venison which had built the padding over his stout bones.

He found a spring down the bluff, shot two squirrels, cooked them over a handful of fire, and ate his supper as sunset drew on and the light reddened and leveled across the miles of canebrake to the west. Then he lay down on the grass, in the great stillness, broken now and then by the liquid, somnolent ripple of a robin's note or a last, lost burst of birdsong from the cedars down the bluff, and for no reason his leathery heart suddenly softened and swelled in his breast and he wept.

He did not weep because he remembered home and the brief time of softness and affection before the years of loneliness and compulsion and hardship and violence and death began. As a matter of fact, he remembered nothing at that moment, and thought of nothing. His feeling was one of mild surprise that he should weep at all. But the tears came. Then he felt relaxed and happy, and, as night came on, slept like a child.

Three years later he led a party of settlers to the bluff. He built a cabin and married a fifteen-year-old girl, the daughter of one of the settlers. He had three children, two boys and a girl, and when the oldest was seven, was killed and scalped by a Chickasaw, seventy-five miles south, where he had gone to spy out the country.

Now his great-great-grandson, Bolton Lovehart, lives in an old brick house, halfway down the slope of Rusty-Butt Hill toward the square. The big houses of Bardsville, with the exception of a few new ones built in the flush times of the 1920's in a subdivision called Chilton Heights near the country club, are on Rusty-Butt Hill. They began to build the big houses on the hill more than a hundred years ago when the lucky sons among the sons of the pioneers were turning into land speculators and tobacco planters who shipped the leaf down the river. The first house up there was built in 1811 by Tolliver Skaggs, who had come as a big boy with the Lovehart party, who was a wild fellow known for his prowess with bottle and boot heel and knife until he got religion and became a savage Presbyterian, who prospered and lived forever, and in his old age, past ninety, said, "I come here early. I come 'mongst the first. I scalped me the first Indian. I shot the last bear. I run the first jug of whisky and I prized me the first hogshead of tobacco, and I reckin, by God, I brought civilization to Carruthers County." He told the truth, even about the Indian, and he had also built the first brick house on the hill, not a big house, but a square, solid structure among the oaks.

The other houses came during the next forty or fifty years, as the lucky grandsons of pioneers squeezed the unlucky ones off the good tobacco land or became bankers and squeezed the other lucky ones who had got good land. But none of the houses was a mansion. They were just big, solid, high-ceilinged houses, with white porticos where dogs lolled in summer and saddles and boots were flung on benches. Some time, in the thirties or forties, when the social structure of Bardsville had begun to harden, the people who lived near the square called the hill "Aristocrat Hill," with a mixture of envy and irony. And the name, in the mouths of those who lived, not near the square, but in the bottom near the creek, became "Ristycrat Hill," and then, without envy or irony, but with a great, hairy-lipped, stained-toothed, snag-toothed guffaw, "Rusty-Butt Hill." And "Rusty-Butt Hill" it has remained for all except realtors and the ladies who live in the old brick houses and see their husbands off every working morning to the insurance office, factory, office, bank, warehouse, or drug store.

Bolton Lovehart, the great-great-grandson of Lem Lovehart, lives in a house well down the hill, not one of the finest houses but safely situated on the hill. You will probably not notice the house, for it is not remarkable, except that its lawn has run to weeds and the gate is missing from the wrought-iron fence. And almost certainly you will not see Bolton Lovehart, a tall, emaciated man of sixty-seven, with no hair on his head, a gray, drooping mustache about his sweet mouth, no buttons on his wrinkled coat, and restless, clever, long-fingered hands, liver spots on the thin skin over the blue veins. You will not see him, for he, in all likelihood, will be in the attic, with the circus.

Bolton Lovehart was born in the house, the son of a man who had been a major in the Confederate Army and was, at the time of the birth, an Episcopalian minister, and of a woman whose disappointment in the marriage bed was almost forgotten in her passion for the Episcopal Church, her sickly, late-born son, and the name of "Bolton." Her passion for the first two was really an extension of her passion for the third, for only by contact with Bolton blood did the Episcopal Church (her father had been the local rector) and her son achieve their sanctity.

"Love" was not the name for her feeling for her child, which, with its very intensity of egotism, became a selfless and absorbing passion. But since there is no other name to give it and since the name, "love," has been applied to other passions equally dark and deep, it can be used for whatever it was that possessed her and possessed the child with a thousand invisible threads controlling the slightest movement of his limbs and lips and spirit like a clever puppet with beautiful chestnut curls and a lace collar on the velvet jacket.

On Sunday mornings in spring, neighbors saw the little boy, between the tall, black-garbed man and the bony, taut-faced, black-garbed woman, move down the brick walk, flanked by the rows of yellow jonquils under the oaks, moving toward the iron gate and the stone carriage block and iron hitching post surmounted by a horse's head. The little boy set his neat little booted feet (the little black boots had red buttons) on the moss-crusted bricks with the motion of prinking precision and appealing weakness, as if each step were in itself a new problem, considered and solved. The man and woman adjusted their pace to his, and it seemed forever down the thirty yards from the portico to the gate. As we look back on them, down the sixty years, they scarcely seem to move at all, to be fixed there in a photograph in an album to prove something sweet and sure about the past. But they finally reach the gate, which creaks on its hinges, and move, at the same rate, down the brick sidewalk toward St. Luke's Church.

The man, Simon Lovehart, moves with his eyes fixed down the street, as though unaware of his companions and of the street itself. He is, however, aware of them at times, in the middle of the night or on the spring street, aware of the powerful, vibrating, multitudinous web of life which binds the woman and child together, victor and victim (but which is which? he asks himself: is the present the victim of the past, or the past the victim of the present?), and when he is aware of that web and the million dark, pulsing tentacles, he feels that he stands at the end of something, on a promontory, lost, with a distant wind rushing somewhere in the night far behind him. He no longer has regrets as he stands there. He is past regrets. Should the wind blow upon him, he would draw up his coat and button it. When he brushes, by accident, against some single filmy strand of the web in his house, he stops dead still and quivers in every nerve.

He attributes his ill health to the old wound, the minnie ball that he carries in his thigh and that gives him his distinguished, scarcely disturbing limp. His left leg throbs in the night and he often lies awake for hours. When weather is brooding or the season moves into winter, the leg reminds him. The minnie ball, the size and shape of a man's thumbtip, long since washed lovingly clean by his blood, lies precious and heavy in its warm, secret purse of his innermost flesh like a talisman or jewel, and tells him what he needs to know. It absolves him and he is lucky. He is one of the lucky ones who carries with him the explanation of everything. Not every man can prod deep in his thigh and feel his truth the size and shape of a filbert, but heavy as lead. That fact consoles

Simon Lovehart for the shock which flung him from his horse late in the afternoon of the Battle of Franklin to lie and let the hurly-burly sweep monstrously past. Man wants to know the truth and if he knows the truth he can live past all passion, and Simon Lovehart has the truth. He has the minnie ball in his thigh and the prayer book in his hand, and as he walks down the street with his wife and son he knows what he needs to know. The minnie ball and the book, they are his rod and his staff and they comfort him.

The neighbors saw little Bolton Lovehart move down the walk with his mother and father, between the jonquils. They saw him, older, let us say nine years old, walk in the wide yard on a sunny autumn afternoon, the curls on his head more discreet now, wearing tight little blue serge trousers cut off at the knee, with three buttons on the outside seam of each leg, just above the bottom. He walked slowly about the yard, peering on the ground as though he had lost something there in the brittle carpet of tawny oak leaves. He scuffed the leaves with his feet, but ever so gently.

"No," his mother had said, "you cannot go to play at the Allston house."

"Why?"

"It is not for you to question your mother. But I will tell you. The Allstons are common."

"What is 'common'?"

"'Common' is what you must never be."

The neighbors saw him walk among the oak leaves, but they did not see him at those moments when Mrs. Lovehart would fling herself to her knees and suddenly seize him, driving her fingers into his thin back, and crush him to her bosom and crouch thus for minutes in the emptiness of one of the rooms where shadows depended like black gauze from the high ceiling. He has learned to accept this and stands patiently until she pushes him from her, rises abruptly, utters a gasp like pain, and takes her taut, yellow-tinted face from the room, into another room much like the first.

He was a good child, always obedient and studious. He

read a great deal. He read the Bible and history books which his father gave him or which he took from his father's study. He had a collection of flint arrowheads gathered along the bluff back of his house. He collected stamps and knew the names of the capitals of all the countries on the big map, and the colors which they were painted on the map. He sometimes thought of himself high in the sky and looking down like God on all the world to see the countries shining with those colors in the sun. He kept his treasures in a big attic room, with the cavalry saber which his father had once unbelievably worn and wielded, and the regimental flag, from which the blue and red had unevenly faded. His mother thought that he would be a minister.

He was a good child until the summer of 1892, just before he was twelve years old. Then, quite unexpectedly, even to himself, he committed the piece of misbehavior which brought scandal into the town and caused his parents such embarrassment. One of the sects of Baptists was having a revival down in the settlement along Cadman's Creek. On still August evenings the sound of singing, though fainter than a whisper, merely a kind of rhythmic pulse in the air, came up even as far as Rusty-Butt Hill. On the last Sunday afternoon in August, the revival concluded with a big baptizing in the creek, just above the settlement, where the community waste did not pollute the waters.

That Sunday afternoon Bolton Lovehart walked out of his gate and down the hill, through town, and down to the creek. He told himself that he wanted to hunt for arrowheads down by the creek. John Sanders, a schoolmate of his, had found a flint ax-head down there. When he got as far down as Gupton's Mill, already in the nineties an abandoned mass of stonework, he heard the singing upstream. But he could see nothing, for the thickets of cane and the big shaggy willows along the stream, and the shag-bark hickories on the flat ground just back from the creek bank. He walked upstream among the weeds in the old field beside the thicket and trees. An old dog, some kind of hound bitch, the yellow hide peeled-looking over the slat ribs, had followed him down from among the shacks at the foot of the rise, and now continued after him at a respectful distance. When the dog kept after him, he turned and shouted for it to go away. It stood, fifteen feet away, and looked mournfully, searchingly at him, like guilt. He shouted again, and took a few steps on his way. The dog followed. He stooped and gathered up several stones. He hurled them, one after another, at the animal. The animal did not turn or flinch, but stood there, tail down, head down, front legs bent, waiting for the stones. The last stone struck it on the head with a flat, wooden sound. The dog did not stir or whimper. It stood there before the boy like an image of medieval hunger and scabrous, slack-dugged humility and mournful, infinite forgiveness, and shivered in the blaze of August light.

The boy was almost sick with rage and hatred, and standing there, with the eyes upon him, he felt suddenly lost, bewildered, and friendless. He felt that he had no place to go in the wide world, that nobody knew his name. When he proceeded up the creek toward the sound of singing, he resolutely did not look back. The dog followed him no farther.

At a bend in the creek, where the willows broke, he saw the singers. A gravel bar ran out here into the stream, making a riffle where the water found its way across the narrows, and damming a wide pool above. The people stood on the bank and out on the gravel bar, singing. The boy approached them, almost unnoticed. If one pair of eyes had truly fixed upon him, he would have gone away, to wander in the world, his sense of lostness and friendlessness was so great. But nobody really noticed him. He came closer and moved along the edge of the group, noiseless as a thought, to the edge of the gravel bar where he could see.

The tall preacher stood waist-deep in the green water of the pool, which softly undulated even to the farther shore, lapping the drooping boughs of willows and tossing gently the bits of twig and the yellow leaves which floated out into the open. The preacher's black coat dripped and glittered in the sunshine, and to the shining black cloth a few gold willow leaves were stuck, here and there, like spangles. As Bolton Lovehart came out on the bar, a man was leading one of the saved out into the water, a thin girl of fourteen or so, wearing a droopy white dress too big for her. The girl hung back as the water lapped up to her thighs and made the white cloth billow about her like a dancer. The man drew her forward, not too gently. She took one faltering step after him, then turned her head back and swept a wild, wide, imploring look across the sky and field and world of the uplifted singing faces. But the faces, rapt in song, offered her no help or hope. The man's hand tugged at her, drawing her into the deeper water, and suddenly her resistance faltered, her body swayed toward him, and she was drawn forward while the crowd sang, "Let the nearer waters roll. . . ."

She tried with her free hand to force down the white cloth bouffant and wreathing upon the water, but did not entirely succeed.

The preacher took her and swung her so that she faced the people. He lifted one hand to heaven and called her name and said the ritual words in the sudden silence. Then he placed a hand between her shoulder blades for support and started to lower her backward. For an instant she refused to give over, and as he was about to place his other hand upon her face to save her from strangulation, she seized it desperately in both her own and clasped it to her breast. With that, all in one motion, she let herself go, arching her back somewhat, in surrender, and letting her head fall back, with her eyes wide to the sky, as she was plunged beneath the water.

The preacher drew her quickly up. The other man took her and led her toward the gravel bar. There a fat, stubby woman dressed in a respectable black dress waited with arms outstretched, making little whimpering sounds before the song lifted again. Then the woman stepped forward one step into the water, careless of her shoes, and clasped the girl to her, soaking the black dress, then stumbled back, drawing the girl, and sank to her knees still clasping the girl, and shouted above the song, "My baby's saved! My baby's saved! Glory to Jesus and bless His holy name!" The girl stood there in the embrace, the white cloth sticking to her thin, bony body, the wet hair stringing lankly at her neck and over her cheeks, the water running down her pinched, uncertain face.

Another candidate was being led forward, a hulking boy of eighteen or twenty, who marched boldly, step for step with his conductor. Then, later, others, an old man, two women, four or five big children. And then Bolton Lovehart was there at the very edge of the water, waiting, and the man's hand took him and led him forward in the midst of song.

Immediately after his baptism, Bolton Lovehart left the crowd at the creek. But he did not go home immediately. He wandered across the field, then back to the grove near the old mill. He was not yet dry, but he hid in the thicket, under the shag-barks, and waited, for what he was not sure. He could not bring himself to think of going home nor of the night coming on. He could not bear to think of being here alone all night, in the darkest darkness under the trees. He wished that he were dead.

But he did not die, and night did come. Just before dark, matted and damp, muddy to the knees with dust which had stuck to his wet legs, he turned in the gate of his house. He told his mother that he had fallen into the creek at the old mill. As soon as he had been bathed and dressed with clean clothes, his father was summoned to lecture him while his mother stood by with rigid face and clenched hands. By the time his father was ready to go to church for the evening service, the boy was running a high fever. Simon Lovehart had to go to church, but Mrs. Lovehart and Dr. Jordan stayed by the boy's bed.

The next day, Mrs. Lovehart learned the truth. It was all over Bardsville, over breakfast tables, at the groceries, on the humming telephone wires. But illness spared the boy his punishment, and he lay in his big bed, feeling weak and pure and sly, watching light grow on the windows in the morning and fade with evening. He did not want to die now, nor did he want to get well. He wanted to lie here forever, lapped in the long, soft rhythm of day and night, like a tide.

But he did get well, and did go back into the world, where the people were.

Just before Christmas, dressed in a new black suit with a starched white collar, he received his confirmation at St. Luke's.

"Yeah," old Ike Spackman said, leaning over his forge at the blacksmith shop, "yeah, you hear tell how they taken that boy in the 'Piscopal Church? Hear tell how his mammy bought herself the biggest lard kittle in Carruthers County and biled that-air brat a week a-forehand to git the Baptist creek water outen him 'fore them give him a bite and sup of that 'Piscopal Jesus." He slammed the glowing horseshoe in his tongs onto his anvil and gave it a couple of preliminary strokes of the hammer. "Yeah," he said, "but bet hit didn't do no good. You cain't bile a Baptist baptizen outer nobody. Once in grace, always in grace. Hit is gospel. Bet that brat right this minute is jist as Baptist as air-y mud cat."

But if Bolton Lovehart was as Baptist as any catfish in Cadman's Creek, he did not know it. His life fell back into the old pattern. He read his books and pored over his stamps and arrowheads. He now went to Professor Darter's academy for boys, where he studied hard. He was very good at his Greek and relished the praise which rewarded him.

Then, when he was sixteen, the circus came to town.

When it left, Bolton Lovehart went with it.

His flight, unlike his baptism, was carefully planned, not undertaken on impulse. He waited one afternoon until his mother was out, then brought down a suitcase from the storage room and packed it with a suit of clothes, three shirts, socks, and odds and ends of clothing, a few of his best arrowheads, and some bread and butter. He then carried the suitcase down to the river end of the Lovehart property, the pasture lot back of the unused carriage house, and hid it in a clump of elders and sumac. That night he wrote a strategic note to his mother, saying he was going to Nashville to start life for himself, and slipped downstairs after his parents were asleep (his month's allowance and a ten-dollar gold piece—a Christmas present—in his pocket), got his suitcase, and took the bluffside path to town. It was a starlight night, but he could have followed that hanging goat-track among the cedars and rotten limestone if it had been the darkest night of the year, his feet knew it so well. Not for nothing had he spent the long lonely afternoons back on the bluff, looking over the river.

If his flight, however, was carefully planned, behind that planning lay a necessity as powerful and as unanalyzed as that which had drawn him into the waters of Cadman's Creek. Or as unanalyzable; for if it had been analyzed and then its components in turn analyzed, would he not in the end have had to face, in the innermost darkness—beyond all plans, intentions, and justifications, beyond all the books ever written, the histories and sermons and prayers and the explanations of right and wrong or of heroism or cowardice—the blank-faced need swaying in the dark, coiled like the spring of his being, the unhooded, perpetual eyes gleaming imperially and giving forth the only light in that secret place, fixing deep into his own eyes with the pitiless hypnosis of destiny? But he did not try to analyze. He planned, packed the suitcase, and fled by night down the bluffside to the town, dodged the square, and found the spur track where the circus people were loading their tents, animals, and gear by the light of bonfires and flares.

He hung back, on the verge of the shadows, smelling the smell of smoke and rancid oil and stirred dust and the bold, compelling effluvium of great brutes, hearing the shouted orders and the grumbles and snarls of beasts, watching the tumult which was like a flame-streaked Dionysiac revelry or like the terror-stricken confusion of a barbarous tribe, rich in colored cloths and jangling metals and garish tinsel and savage, symbolic beasts, making ready to flee before the cosmic threat of fire or flood. When the activity had subsided somewhat, and the bonfires had burned out, he managed to hide himself in a car where he had seen men store canvas and crates. An hour later the train jerked and clanked, and undertook a grinding, jouncing motion that gradually evened out into the hum and clippety-clop of wheels on rails. When, fifteen minutes later, the locomotive whistle, far ahead and muffled, gave two blasts, he knew that it was blowing for Bedell's Crossing, ten miles from Bardsville. Shortly after that he fell asleep on the canvas and only awoke with broad day.

The train was motionless now. He sneaked from his hiding. There was nobody about the open space by the track except an old man wearing overalls, lop-sided high-heeled boots, and a sombrero, sitting on a box and eating a sandwich. The old man did not see him get off the car. Bolton could see that the train was on the edge of a city, for roofs and tall buildings were in the distance beyond the sheds on the other side of the cinder-packed loading area. He did not know the name of the city.

He went over to the sheds, walked in their cover on the other side of them from the man, up to a point which would make him seem, when he emerged, to come from the city. Then he approached the old man, said his name was "Joe Randall," and said he wanted a job. He was an orphan, he said.

"You're a God-blasted tom-fool," the old man said, eyeing him with bleared, squint eyes from under the sombrero.

"I want a job," the boy said, feeling strong and certain, and not afraid of the old man. He had never felt this way before. "Anything," he said. "I'll do anything."

"You don't look stout," the old man said, eyeing the stringy, tallish boy with the perspicacity and contempt of a horse trader inspecting an inferior animal.

"I'm stronger than I look," the boy said.

"You're a God-blasted fool," the old man said, "but you kin tote water fer the critters. You kin feed 'em."

The old man was one of the menagerie hands, nameless in the circus but for the name "Tim," old, chivvied about, broken. He saw a week, maybe two weeks ahead, a time in which he could boss the boy about, loaf a little on his job, before whatever happened that would happen about the tomfool kid who wasn't any more an orphan that he was the Angel Gabriel. Whatever happened, it would not be his fault. He didn't know anything. He hadn't said he would pay anything. There was always some grub, scraps from the mess car.

So Bolton Lovehart toted water and lugged baskets and buckets of food for the animals, bloody messes of meat or damp mixtures of stuff, and tossed hay, under the direction of the old man. The first day somebody stole his suitcase. He didn't care. He didn't care about anything, not even his sore back and aching arms or the nausea of fatigue. He ate scrap food which Tim provided and slept on straw in a boxcar.

On the afternoon of the second day, just before the show opened, a burly man in a gray tweed suit, with a cigar and diamond ring, came up to him. "What's your name?" he demanded.

"Joe Randall," the boy replied.

"You're a lying little snot," the man said. Then, "Look here, I want to know your name. I'm manager of this show and, by God, I'm not going to have any trouble with the cops on account of some lying little snot. What's your name?"

"Joe Randall," the boy said, and still felt the sweet, unaccustomed strength and certainty under his fear.

The manager was about to say something, but just then another man came hurrying up and spoke to him.

"I'll fix you later," the manager promised the boy, and turned away.

That afternoon after the show, the detective and Simon Lovehart came. The note about going to Nashville and Mrs. Lovehart's fear of scandal had delayed their arrival. But here they were, standing in the middle of the circus lot, among the tents and cages and bedlam, with Bolton Lovehart, no longer strong and certain, before them.

That evening they took the train out of Memphis to Bardsville.

Once back home, everything was as it had been before.

The boys at the academy that fall, it is true, tried to make him tell them about the circus. He was, for the moment, a kind of hero among them. But he could not even enjoy that. The memory was like an old sore healing slowly, or a broken bone retarding his motions, making him careful of gesture or speech. But there were his books. He could read the books, get the praise of teacher or parent, spend hours in the attic with the stamps and flag and saber and arrowheads (the best ones gone now, missing with the stolen suitcase), sit on the bluffside in the smoky autumn afternoons, walk wordlessly about the house, putting his feet down carefully on the betraying floor, or, when his parents spoke to him, answering dutifully, "Yes, Mother." Or, "Yes, Father." Or, "Yes, Mother, yes. I'm sorry I made you nervous. Yes, I'll sit still." He learned to sit very still, spying on her yellow-tinted face at the edge of the circle of lamplight.

He graduated from the academy, first in his class. His prize was a Greek Testament, delivered to him by Professor Darter up on the platform. His mother and father talked of sending him to college that fall, to the University of the South, the Episcopal university, up at Sewanee, Tennessee, in the mountains. He thought of the mountains. He had never seen mountains, only pictures—the Himalayas, the Matterhorn, Pike's Peak, Mt. Shasta, the Andes, pictures in books—great crags reared like masonry, the black pines, and beyond, the glittering, white Saturnian purity of the peak under the stars. He knew Sewanee would not be like that, but the picture was in his head, in his dreams. He knew that the mountains in East Tennessee were not like that, just big hills with trees on them, just bigger hills than the hills in Carruthers County. Sewanee was just more of Tennessee. But the picture was there and would not go away.

Then his father died. Simon Lovehart had a stroke as he walked one morning in early September up the brick walk to his house. He fell across the mossed bricks, among the few premonitory, tawny, brittle oak leaves and the now faded green spears of the jonquil plants bordering the walk. Mrs.

Lovehart saw him fall. She ran from the house and crouched by his side, under the oaks, lifting her head to utter wild cries of anguish that might have been wild cries of triumph. And in the sequel they were wild cries of triumph; for no one knows the meaning of the cry of passion he utters until the flesh of the passion is long since withered away to show the austere, logical articulation of fact with fact in the skeleton of Time.

The neighbors heard the cries, came to carry the man into his house, and laid him in his bed. Simon Lovehart revived and lay with his long limbs outstretched and his eyes closed. He had known it all before, long before on the field of Franklin, the shock that unhorsed him and flung him to earth under the thunder and tattered swirl of smoke and failing plunge of the banners. And he knew again, in the foreshortening and fusion of time, the pure, essential astonishment at the clap of peace out of fury. *Everything is so easy,* he thought, marveling, *everything in the world.* But he had known this a long time now. So he lay there for two more days and nights, dying with a decorous and cunning celerity like spilled quicksilver finding its way down a dark rat-hole.

Before he died, after strength enough for speech had come back to him, Bolton Lovehart came in to see him. The boy stood by the bed, waiting, hearing the grind and wheeze of breathing in the gloom. Then he said: "Father." Then: "Father."

"It—is—all right—son," the voice from the bed said, like a voice from a long way off and a long time back.

He knelt by the bed, holding one of his father's hands, cold and waxy to his touch. He thought his heart would burst, and mixed with his grief was a sense of discovery, the discovery of the man on the bed. A thousand questions leaped into his mind. He felt that he had to ask his father those questions, now, now before it was too late: *Father, what was the name of that old coon dog you had when you were a boy—I forgot his name, Father—Father, what was the name of the Wilcox boy, the boy you played with when you were little—Father, did it hurt when you were shot, Father—Father, what book did you like best when you were growing up—Father, did you ever talk to General Forrest—Father, did you hunt arrowheads when you were a boy—Father—* But he knew that it was too late, he would never know those things, for they were slipping through his fingers like a handful of water dropping onto dry sand, and he heard the distant voice again, saying: "Be good —to your mother—son. She is a—good woman—she means— everything—for your good—son—"

He listened to the voice, which was like a weary explanation, an apology, promised to be good, and left the room. An hour later Simon Lovehart was dead.

The boy did not go to Sewanee that fall. He lived the life he had lived before, except for the fact that he did not go to the academy now. He read a great deal, the books he thought the freshmen would be studying up at Sewanee. He walked along the bluffs. He sat in the evenings with his mother, the lamp between them on the living room table.

In June, Sam Jackson, a friend from the academy who had gone to Sewanee the fall before, came back to Bardsville. On the summer afternoons, Sam would sit for hours on the porch with Bolton, telling him about Sewanee, answering his questions. Then they would go up to the attic or out to the bluffs. Mrs. Lovehart, sitting in the shadows of the living room, just inside the open window, would listen to every word they spoke, and as she listened, her heart was like stone in her breast. But it was worse when they went off to the attic or wandered down by the bluffs where she could not follow them and hear.

One day at dinner she said to her son, "Son, don't you think you ought to begin to get ready to go?"

"Go where?"

"Why, to Sewanee. This fall."

She watched the flash of animation on the boy's face, saw the hand tremble with which he laid the fork on the plate. "Mother—" he managed to begin. "Mother, I didn't know— why, I—"

She briskly cut him off. "You must get ready to go," she said. "You must write for admission again. I must get your clothes ready. There are so many things. You must go." And added, with a quick glance at his face: "You must not think of me."

"Mother—" he began.

"You are young," she said. "You must not think of me."

They finished the meal in silence.

He went to Sewanee. At Christmas he came home. His mother gave him a party with Sam Jackson and some of the boys from the academy class and their girls. Sara Darter, daughter of Professor Darter, came as Bolton's girl. They drank grape-juice punch, and ate sandwiches and cakes, and sang Christmas songs. Bolton went to parties at the houses of the other boys and girls on the hill. And back home, late at night, his mother would wait up for him, to ask him questions about the party or about Sewanee and to tell him how happy and proud she was that he had done good work. He went back to Sewanee in January.

But he was back home again by the first of March. His mother had had a heart attack. She was never to be well again. Her bed was moved down to the little back sitting room on the first floor, with a table of medicine bottles, a Bible and a prayer book beside it. On good days she sat propped on pillows in a big basket chair, staring through the windows, if it was summer, or into the fire, if it was winter. Bolton spent much of his time with her. Almost always he prepared her medicine. "I don't mind it—I really don't," she would say, "when you give it to me." And she would smile up at him from the pillows. She had grown almost pretty after the heart attack, young-looking, fresh, and clear-eyed, the yellow hue gone from her complexion, with a shy virginal quality which she must have had as a very young girl when Major Simon Lovehart, the veteran with the distinguished limp, had come to court her.

Bolton went on with his studies, reading his father's books, borrowing books from Professor Darter, ordering books from

Nashville or Louisville. In the next summer, when Sam Jackson was home from Sewanee, he slyly interrogated him, and thought: *I've learned more than Sam. I know more than Sam.* He went to parties that summer, but he always came home early—to give his mother her medicine. And sometimes after he had given her the draught, he would go up to his room to read, or if the weather was not too hot, to the big attic, and he might hear music from beyond the trees or catch the flicker of Japanese lanterns strung across a lawn up the hill.

Late in the summer, his mother suggested that he go back to Sewanee. Not then, but the second term. "I want you to go," she said. "I want you to be happy. I went down into the Valley of the Shadow for you, son, and I want you to be happy."

"I know more than Sam Jackson," he said, and got up and left the room.

So the next four years passed, the parties fewer and fewer for him each summer and Christmas vacation, as the faces changed, as the boys and girls he had known married and settled down, or moved away. He could not talk to the younger boys, and the young girls were like strangers. And he was strange to them, a lanky young man with thinning black hair and very clean, unfashionable clothes that always looked awry on his nervous bones. He saw more of Professor Darter than of anyone else. And of Sara Darter.

He thought he was in love with Sara Darter. She was a thin, nervous girl, with big black eyes straining out of the dead white of her face. She might, in appearance, have been his sister. She was two years older than he. She knew how to make him feel at ease. He wrote poems and mailed them to her. And when they were alone together in Professor Darter's living room in the evening, before he had to go home to give his mother her medicine, they would clutch and cling, kissing with a desperate and sad excitement, waiting for the Professor's shuffling step in the hall.

He was writing a book. Or rather, he was getting ready to write a book. It was to be the history of Carruthers County.

"Bolton is writing a book," Mrs. Lovehart would confide to the Episcopalian ladies who dutifully came to call. And when the husbands of those ladies would say to their wives, "That Lovehart boy, he ought to be getting a job. The old lady is living off her capital, I bet. Simon was well fixed, but it won't last forever," the wives would say that Bolton was writing a book. That explained everything. He began to make talks to the Bardsville Ladies' Study Club and to the St. Luke's Men's Bible Class. The Bardsville *Gazette* recorded each event: "Mr. Bolton Lovehart, one of our most promising young authors . . ."

But Bolton did get a job. He got a job teaching in Professor Darter's academy. He taught there two winters. It was understood between him and Sara that they were to be married. When things got straightened out. Then Professor Darter died.

He left no money. Just the house and a mortgage on it and enough to put him decently underground. Bolton ran the academy for the rest of the year. Sara Darter wept often now, and Bolton tried to comfort her. But once when he put his arms around her and tried to kiss her, she struck him savagely on the chest, with clenched fists, and screamed at him with furious words which he could not interpret.

For a month after that she was very calm, submitting to his caresses when he came to see her, breathing shallowly and staring across the room. Then one night she said, "You've got to get a specialist to see your mother."

"But Dr. Jordan, he—"

But she cut him off. "If you don't do it," she declared, "I won't marry you."

He saw Dr. Jordan. "Son," the doctor said, "I don't mind you getting in anybody. I'm just an old country doctor, and it won't hurt my feelings. A heart's a funny thing, now. It's not like appendicitis or lockjaw or a gunshot. A heart is right in the middle of a man, or a woman for that matter, and in a manner of speaking it is them themselves. In a manner of speaking."

"What do you mean?" Bolton demanded.

The doctor studied the young man's face. Then he shrugged. "Nothing," he said. "It is just a manner of speaking. Of saying a doctor don't know much. Leastways, not an old country doctor like me, in a town like Bardsville."

"Will you get a specialist?"

"Son," Dr. Jordan said, "it won't hurt my feelings. That time I tried—I tried two or three times, now I recollect—your mother wouldn't hear of it. Nigh bit my head off. She said—"

"You tried?"

"Sure, son. Didn't you know?"

Bolton Lovehart stood there in the middle of the cluttered office, breathing the dusty odor of the worn horsehair furniture and the metallic tang of disinfectant, and his own heart took a leap and turn in his bosom like a bass when it strikes the barb. "You tried?" he demanded in a whisper.

"Sure, son."

"Do it!" Bolton Lovehart said with sudden authority, feeling the surge of strength and certainty that he had felt twelve years before, that morning when he had stood before the old circus roustabout and demanded a job.

"Son," Dr. Jordan said, studying him, "you get your mother's consent, and it suits me."

"I'll get it," Bolton declared.

It all seemed easy as he walked home down the familiar street in broad day. It was easy, and everything was going to be different. And it seemed easy that night, when, after he had given his mother her medicine, he stood by the bed and looked down at her. She seemed so frail and innocent, with that clear girlish quality, so will-less and trusting. It would be easy. So he told her, in detail, how he was worried that she got no better, that he had seen Dr. Jordan, that Dr. Jordan had agreed to having a specialist in, a big man from Nashville, from the university there.

It had been easy. She lay there perfectly silent while his reasonable voice went on, her clear eyes on him, and he almost thought that he detected a smile on her lips. So he smiled back and leaned as though to pat her hand.

He had almost touched her before he caught the words she was saying. She was speaking in a vibrant whisper through the lips that still seemed to smile, saying: "You—you, my son —to sneak behind my back. Oh, it is heinous! To sneak behind my back, like a thief. When I am ill. When I am the mother that bore you. That went down into the Valley of the Shadow. Oh, it is heinous. And you sneak and conspire—" The words came out, the vibrant, sibilant whisper, from the lips that still seemed to smile.

"Mother!" he exclaimed. "Mother!" And tried to take her hand.

But she heaved herself back in the bed, half rising. "Don't touch me!" she cried. "Oh, you are all against me. Everybody! Everybody! Don't touch me," she cried as he tried to take her hand. "It is the kiss of Judas! Oh, you want me dead, you want me to die!"

She swept her arm wide, knocking two bottles from the table, lunging back against the headboard as though to elude an attacker.

"Mother!" he exclaimed.

"Oh, you want me to die—flesh of my flesh, and you want me to die!" And she uttered again the wild, undecipherable, ambiguous, untranslatable cries which she had uttered by the fallen body of Simon Lovehart among the tawny oak leaves of autumn and the spears of jonquil plants.

Then she fell back, gasping and panting, pale as a sheet, clutching her bosom, seemingly unconscious, with the smile returned to her lips.

Dr. Jordan arrived. He worked over her a long time before she came to. Then her eyes fixed on her son. "Go," she said, in the same whisper as before, "go from my sight!"

He went and stood in the hall, waiting.

Dr. Jordan finally came out, closed the door softly behind him, and said, "She's in a bad way."

"Will she—" Bolton Lovehart began, "will she—" But he could not speak the word, "die."

"Will she die?" Dr. Jordan framed the question for him. He shook his head. "I don't know, son. I'm an old country doctor, and I don't know. But I do know this: we better get that specialist."

Bolton Lovehart could not speak. He could not say why he could not get the specialist. His lips worked, but he could not speak.

Dr. Jordan inspected his face under the hanging electric bulb of the back hall. (The house had been wired a few years before.) Then Dr. Jordan shrugged slightly. "Maybe," he said, "maybe it'll all come out all right." He turned and went into the front hall and picked up his flappy old panama from the table.

Bolton Lovehart still stood in the back hall, under the hanging bulb, long after the front door had closed.

Mrs. Lovehart was very sick for a long time, about a month. Then she sat again in her basket chair in the living room, looking across the lawn. Everything was as though nothing had happened, as though that night had been nothing but a bad dream now lost in the honest daylight. Neither ever said a word about it to the other.

Bolton Lovehart, however, had to say something to Sara Darter. After his mother was better, he told her exactly what had happened, or at least those parts which he could bear to tell, and apologized for withholding the truth earlier. "So you see, Sara," he wound up.

"Yes," she said, "I see." And patted his hand.

The next night when he came to see her, she seduced him with a cold, pertinacious, clumsy methodicalness based on dark hints and whispered lore and inept experiment, there on the red plush sofa in Professor Darter's parlor, under the portrait of Professor Darter and the serried eyes of dead grandfathers and grandmothers peering through the gloom, while from the room above came the faint rhythmic creak of the rocking chair of the old aunt who now lived in the house.

The next day Sara Darter left Bardsville. She had borrowed five hundred dollars from Mr. Dorrity, vice president of the bank, an old friend of her father. She went to Nashville, enrolled in a secretarial school, and later got a job in the city. The house was sold a few months after her departure, and every stick of furniture, every plate and cup, the pictures on the walls, the carefully mended linen in the drawers, the knickknacks and souvenirs from the mahogany whatnot. "Everything," the ladies of Bardsville whispered, "literally everything. Sold. Even her mother's wedding dress. I saw it at the auction. Thrown down like an old dust rag. That girl, she has no heart." And again: "Throwing her poor old aunt out in the world. After she had come to take care of her. That poor old woman. Not a place to lay her head, and that girl her nearest of blood."

Sara Darter did not hear the whispers or catch the sidewise glances, sharp as pins. She took her school course, got her job, and after a while married an insurance salesman, a widower, in the office where she worked. She had left Bardsville, and she never came back. The plan for her leaving, however, had come to her suddenly, like a revelation, the day before that last evening with Bolton Lovehart. That last encounter with him had not been part of the plan. Or if it was a part, it was a part that had not showed itself above the surface of the stream, where the trivial debris and drift moiled and spun in the light, but wallowed in the dark central depth of the current, like an old log, black and waterlogged, sucked up from the mud, and borne in secret to the rock-tossed, rapid narrows where the waters boiled over with a last fury into the placid reaches below, and where in that final, funneled rush the unwieldy inner burden heaved and lunged upward, black, blunt, big, and dripping, like a blind fish from a cave, hurled into light.

She had not planned the act, and once it was accomplished, she did not speculate about its meaning and motive. Once done, it seemed like something which had always had its existence, waiting not for her doing but for her recognition.

It was done, but it had always existed, even before her doing, an expiation *or* a vengeance or an expiation *and* a vengeance, inextricably interfused, the violent act caught like the very face of life between two mirrors, to be reflected, mirror within answering mirror, expiation and vengeance, vengeance and expiation, forever in opposite direction, forever toward the inwardness of self and forever toward the outwardness of the world, into twin infinities. But expiation for what? Vengeance on whom? Sara Darter did not have to answer those questions. Instead, she had to live, and she took the already packed suitcase out from under her bed the next morning, in the room grown suddenly strange, like the room where one stops overnight after a disaster, and caught the ten-forty train.

She was gone, and behind her were the voices, which say everything if we hear them, and which say nothing if we do not hear them. And Bolton Lovehart did not hear them. What he heard was nothing, and what he knew was a victory and a betrayal. One of those things is enough to live by, and if you have both, you can live, and he lived. He lived in the way people live, by finding life where he could find it. Which is always easy, for every act justifies itself like a flower, and every day, like the step of a child, is its own problem and its own solution. And years are nothing but so many days laid end to end. If you can live one day you can live forever.

In 1913 the first moving picture house in Bardsville opened. There had been moving pictures before, in tents, with the drone of the projecting machine and the tinkle of the piano like the moment in a revival meeting when the piano strikes a few notes, waiting in the eddy of silence for the singers to catch breath and drown the music, and now waiting for the locomotive to plunge forward, thunderless but for the frantic bass of the piano, or waiting for the horse and rider to come plunging across the screen with soundless hoofs. But now the moving pictures were to be in a real theater. It was the old opera house, where traveling companies had come to play *Thorns and Orange Blossoms* and *The Widowed Bride,* with preposterous stances and an excess of emotion. Now signs painted on canvas were hung out front, and there was a booth with a glass front where tickets were to be sold. Miss Lucile Mac-Intyre, who had taught music in Bardsville for thirty years, was to be at the piano. Bolton Lovehart got the job of collecting tickets at the inside door.

He collected tickets for two weeks, every evening except Sunday, and on Saturday afternoons. He stood in the cramped lobby, with his trousers too short on his bony shanks and his sleeves too short on the wrists, stooping forward to take the ticket with a kind of creaky ceremoniousness, like an old man being gallant to a young girl. (But he was not an old man, only thirty-three.) And when the face above the proffered ticket was one he had known on the hill from boyhood, he would say gravely, "Good evening, Miss Liza," or, "Good evening, Mr. Lawrence, I hope you enjoy the performance," with the air of an impresario. Then, when everybody was inside, and the show was on, he would slip to the door of the theater and stand in the shadow, and peer through a crack in the heavy red curtain at the screen, where Ben Hur whirled across in his victorious chariot or some dark-haired, full-busted beauty in a black dress, gorgeous with jewels and fringes, jerkily paced a rich room and wept or flung herself passionately into the arms of an obviously panting lover wearing a dress shirt, while Miss Lucile MacIntyre's piano defined, like a machine, the motion of the soul.

This lasted for two weeks.

One evening he came home after the show and went to his mother's room to give her the medicine. As he entered, he saw that she was propped up against the bare headboard of the bed, ignoring the pillows, staring at him. "Mother—" he said in alarm. "Mother, are you worse?"

"Yes," she replied, "I am worse. To know what I know."

"I'll call Dr. Jordan. Why didn't you ring for Marybelle to get him? I'll—"

But she stopped him with an abrupt gesture. "Come here," she commanded. And when he stopped at the foot of the bed,

she gestured again. "Closer," she said. And he came around
to the side where the medicine table was.

"Where have you been?" she asked.

"At the show," he said.

"Yes," she said, and echoed, "at the show."

He waited, stifling a crazy impulse to run from the room
from the house.

"At the show," she whispered. And whispered again, "No
shame. To lie to me. To go behind my back. Your own mother,
who gave you life. Who gave you suck. Have you no shame?"

"Mother—" he began.

"To bring shame on me. You, my son—a common ticket-
taker. Oh, your father would turn in his grave. A ticket-taker."

"I've got to do something," he burst out. "I'm thirty-three.
I've got to do something."

"You don't have to do that. And lie and sneak to do it. You
have your work. You have your book. You can finish your
book. And then I'll be proud of you."

"Yes," he said, "I can finish my book."

"Promise me," she said, keeping her eyes on him, "that you
will not go back there. That you will not shame me. That
you will let me live out my life and not spit on me as I bear
my cross. That you will not place thorns on my brow."

He did not speak for a moment.

"Promise me," she said, her voice again in a whisper.

"I promise," he said, whispering, too.

"Come closer," she said. "Give me your hand," she said.

He did so, and she drew him down. He sank to his knees
by the bed. "My son," she said, and placed her hand on his
head. It was light as a feather, but enough to make his head
sink against the covers, while she patted his head and toyed
with his hair and he felt the coldness of the fingers where she
touched the bald spot in the back.

Then she said, "Son, you are right. You must do something.
I'll take my affairs out of Mr. Dorrity's hands. You can manage
my affairs. Then you will be ready when I pass on to the Other
Shore. I shall pay you. I shall pay you well. You can manage

my affairs. And write your book. Then I can die happy. And
be proud that you are my son."

The voice went on and on, and the fingers toyed with his
hair.

The next day he went back to his book, the piles of notes
and the pages of manuscript written in a large, irregular, boyish hand, the history of Carruthers County—Carruthers
County, where Bardsville was and where Lem Lovehart, so
many years before, had lain down on the bluff amid the last
birdsong of a June evening and wept. But Bolton Lovehart
knew nothing of that, and in the chapter already written
about the founding of the town—called "The Coming of the
Fathers"—there was, of course, no mention of the episode.

He could not work in his room. Nothing would come right.
And so he moved his table to the attic.

That winter, just after Christmas, he began to make the
circus. One day in middle December he had gone to the square
on an errand, to talk with Mr. Dorrity at the bank, in fact,
and had seen the toy exhibit in the windows of Sellars' Hardware Store. He had stood there a long time before the window. In the middle of the window, dominating the exhibit,
was a circus. There were wooden animals, painted, with
jointed legs. The lions and tigers sat on little platforms. An
elephant reared on a tub. There was a ring master dressed
in black cloth, a girl acrobat with a stiff little skirt and a
painted smirk on her face and eyes far too large and blue, a
clown swathed in spotted cloth, balancing on top of a ladder,
held there by a slot in his wooden foot. After a while Bolton
Lovehart tore himself from the window and went on to the
Planter's Fidelity Bank to see Mr. Dorrity, whose friendly
burden of the Lovehart affairs had been doubled since Bolton
Lovehart had undertaken to handle them. Mr. Dorrity now
had to spend hours with him every month.

That same day Bolton Lovehart got some soft pine from the
lumber yard, and bought a strong jackknife and a set of water
colors. He laid those things on a shelf in his attic and did not
touch them for ten days. He worked at the book. But the wood

and paints and knife were there. The day after Christmas, late in the evening, long after he had given his mother the medicine and kissed her good night, in the timeless silence of the night, he began.

It took him a week to make the tiger. It was a silly-looking, stiff-legged thing, blunt-headed, not much like a tiger. When he tried to paint it, he found that the wood absorbed the water colors like a blotter and blurred all outlines. So he had to get oil paints. He had to order them from Nashville. He waited impatiently all the days before the package arrived. Then the colored girl, Marybelle, delivered it to the hand of his mother. He had to lie to her. He told her that he was going to make a map of Carruthers County. He felt no guilt about the lie and was surprised at himself.

The tiger was a poor thing, but when the color was on and it stood before him on his table, he felt, for a moment, the tremulous echo of the old excitement he had felt that night, years back, when he stood in the shadows and watched the flame-streaked, hoarse tumult as the circus was loaded.

The next animal, a lion, was better. And the elephant was better still. He had managed, after two weeks of experiment and effort, to make legs that would bend. By summer he had made a human figure, the ring master, and had dressed it, pricking his fingers at the unaccustomed sewing. He even gave the ring master a ferocious black mustache of a snippet of black yarn glued on. Then he made the girl acrobat, with blue eyes and a skirt of silk. That was his masterpiece.

But beside the masterpiece, the other things looked so sad and inept. He had to begin again. So night after night that summer, in the hot, dead attic air, he would lean over his table, with the sweat dripping from his face down on the wood or metal or cloth. The electric fan which he bought did little good. But he could not work downstairs. For nobody knew what went on up there, behind the always bolted door, in the big room where shadows and cobwebs massed in the corners and hung from the slanting, damp-ringed ceiling, where the arrowheads, long since washed clean of whatever hot blood had stained them, lay in orderly rows on sagging shelves with the albums of stamps, where the notes and books were stacked on a table, where the saber and the faded regimental colors of Simon Lovehart's regiment hung on the wall at the end of a gable. People going home late at night would see the light in the Lovehart attic, a faint gleam beyond the dense oak boughs, and would say, "That Lovehart boy's working on his book. He's a hard worker. Maybe he will amount to something."

Bolton Lovehart did still work at the book. Or at least he would read over the stacks of notes, or take new notes, or perhaps write a page now and then in his boyish script. This was before the time of the monument to Cassius Perkins and Seth Sykes, but he found out what he could about them from old men who gave him fragments of the official story. And he wrote a chapter called "The Battle of Bardsville." But all the writing went slowly. It was easier to gather material. Sometimes he spent whole days at the court house, fumbling through the dusty, sour-smelling papers in the vault of the clerk of the circuit court or of the county court clerk. Or he would hire a boy to drive him in a rig from the livery stable out into the country to talk with some old resident. But all of this was only in the daytime. The nights were his own.

So the months stretched into the year, and the year became another year, and his fingers grew cleverer and cleverer. And with the growth of skill, the passion for perfection grew to torment him. When he finished some new creature to add to the little throng which cluttered the shelves and floor, or devised some new apparatus for the circus, he felt for one moment, up there above the world, the peace and purity of spirit that comes when vision and cunning are commensurate. But next day, after he had risen early to go up to the attic to verify the happiness of the night before, he would spy, in the critical sunlight, some flaw, some ineptitude, and he would almost hate the thing he had made and his fingers would itch for the steady feel of the knife or awl and the softness of the wood. He could scarcely wait for night to come.

As the years grew and the painted eyes of animals and girl acrobats and riders and ring masters and clowns circled about him, so his world constricted to that orbit. He still made talks, but more and more infrequently, to the study club, and the Bardsville *Gazette* still recorded each event with the old phrases: "Mr. Bolton Lovehart, one of our most promising young authors . . ." He still worked at his book, but the words he wrote, like the words he spoke to the club, seemed more and more strange to him, more and more a penance he had to pay for an old crime or a price he had to pay for a new happiness. He went to church every Sunday. He still attended to his mother's affairs, wrote receipts for rent checks, arranged for painters and plumbers to repair, more and more infrequently, the little houses she rented, paid her taxes, and kept her accounts.

The war of 1917-18 came and passed. But it was not for him. He did not even read the papers. The bugles and uniforms were nothing to him, or the tears and kisses and speeches. When the news of the armistice came, when the whistles blew, and the bells rang and people ran out into the street, even there on the hill, and shouted, the noises scarcely reached him in the attic. He did not even bother to come down to find out what the tumult meant. That night, however, he did go down to the square to see the bonfire and hear the music and the speeches (made from a hastily erected platform at the foot of the Confederate monument in front of the court house) and the shouting and singing. The crowd sang:

> Smile a while, I've kissed you sad adieu,
> When the clouds roll by I'll come to you. . . .

There in the crowd he did experience a kind of happiness. He was happy in their happiness, with the happiness of a ghost who blesses out of his own steady peace the flickering joy of the living and wishes them well. He could afford to wish them well. He had his own victory.

Then he went back home to his victory, kissed his mother good night, and went up to the attic. The excitement of the night passed. The debris was cleaned from the square, and the platform in front of the monument knocked down. The wounded and the whole came home to listen to greetings on the streets of Bardsville, and then forgot, almost as quickly as others forgot, the event over which the skin grew back, leaving scarcely a scar.

As the years passed, he grew more and more attentive and tender with his mother. She seemed impervious to time, still fresh-cheeked, even though the flesh sagged a little and even though the color seemed to hint sometimes of the mortician's rouge applied with unusual subtlety, still bright-eyed, even though the eyes themselves sank a little more, year by year, into the delicately arched sockets. She lived as though sustained in the heart of a timeless peace, lying among embroidered counterpanes (grown slightly yellow), propped among lace pillows (artfully mended), smiling in benediction. The long lie he lived, the secret locked in the attic and never suspected by a breathing soul, gave him the right to love her perfectly at last. For he hugged a dear truth to him: you can only love perfectly in terms of a great betrayal.

Then she died. She woke up in the middle of the night with a stab of pain and a sudden suffocation, and with astonishment knew that it was her heart. With that first astonishment came the black fear, brute fear like a tremendous maw opening before her. And with the fear were the words in her mind, like the words of another self: *Oh, I won't do it. I won't go, they can't make me go, not now when I've got everything fixed like I want it, when I'm happy, oh, so happy, oh, I won't go. I won't go, they can't make me go!* But she knew she was going. The fangs of that great black maw were closing on her, dripping with cold saliva. Then, suddenly, fear and refusal were lost in the simple sense of outrage, a stupendous outrage, at the deceitful, sneaking little heart. Oh, it was heinous! It had lain there inside her all those years, doing her will, pretending to love her, giving her instant obedience, and planning this, this, this. Like the kitten she had had as a child, that had lain on her knee, purring, and then had scratched her, and she had felt this same outrage and had flung the nasty thing from her, out of the second-story window, to thud on the bricks of the drive. Now she clawed at her breast to tear out the treacherous, sneaking little beast of a heart and fling it away. Oh, she would fix it! She would never again have a sneaking little heart like this. Oh, this was worse than the kitten that scratched her. This was worse than the son, flesh of her flesh, who had sneaked behind her back and tried to betray her. This was worse than anything, for this was her own dear heart, herself, herself, doing this to herself, doing this to Louise Bolton, to pretty little, nice little Louise Bolton. Oh, she would tell her father!

Then it did it.

That was in 1934, when Mrs. Lovehart was eighty-seven years old. But next morning when her son found her, she did not, even then, look her age. In the last instant her face had relaxed, and except for the paleness, she looked herself, the pretty little old lady who might smile any moment.

The doctor came, not Dr. Jordan (dead now for years), but a young man, sun-tanned from the links, full of confidence. "She probably died very quickly," he said, by way of comfort, snapping his case shut.

"She died," Bolton Lovehart echoed, musingly, wonderingly, almost in a whisper as to himself. Then to the doctor, out loud, "She died—look, she died in here, all alone, at night, by herself at night—"

"It was probably very sudden," the doctor said, with a faint hint of irritation. "Very little pain, probably. And at her age—"

"She died," Bolton Lovehart whispered, "at night—all by herself."

And he saw himself alone. Forever alone, in the house. And he would die alone in one of the dark rooms, at night, or in the attic, falling to the floor among the hateful, painted eyes of the creatures he had made.

He was alone in the house now. The Negro woman came and cooked his meals, and passed a dust cloth wearily over furniture in a kind of ritualistic incompetence, and slammed the back door and went away at first dusk. Bolton Lovehart tried at first to keep on with the old routine, but he found himself sitting there in the attic at his table, doing nothing, brooding into emptiness. The reason for his occupation was gone. The old pleasure was gone, the compulsion. There was no need to lie any more. He wandered the house at night, from room to room, in a blaze of electric light, all the lights turned on. Or he sat in the living room, in the dark, staring out of the window. On some nights he fell asleep in the basket chair and was there all night.

Now and then, the necessity for attending to his affairs would draw him out into the world. He would wander down to the bottoms where the rental houses were, little better than shacks now, falling paintlessly to pieces, and knock at the doors to meet the sullen face of a man or the bitter face of a woman, children peering like animals from about her skirts, and ask for the rent. Sometimes they gave him a little like grudging alms. Sometimes they began to talk in whining or bullying voices, but he could never attend properly to the words they said. Sometimes they said nothing, just looked at him and shut the door, or looked at him, wordlessly, until he wandered off like a man who has been caught in a shameful act. Mr. Dorrity was dead now, and there was nobody to tell him what to say, what to do. But there was a little bank stock left, and that, even in the bad times of the thirties, kept him going.

The bank stock and the church kept him going. The bank stock gave him something to eat. The church gave him a reason for eating. He was no more religious than before, but he went there, to every service. He had not gone much in the last years of his mother's life, but at the funeral people had been kind, even people whose names he had forgotten. The church was a place to go, away from the house, away from the attic, away from himself and all the years.

If it had not been for the church he would never have met Mrs. Parton.

Mrs. Parton was the daughter of a poor, scratch-living farmer in the county just south of Carruthers County, a lean country full of bare limestone and blackjack oak and sassafras, with moonshine stills, even in the days before Prohibition, back in the cedar thickets. She had married Mr. Parton when she was just a girl and he was a drummer for a wholesale hardware company, working that district. But back about 1920, Mr. Parton had got the agency for a cheap automobile in Bardsville and had prospered, begotten a son, and had died, leaving Mrs. Parton with a fair bank account to make her way as best she could in the life of Bardsville.

Mr. Parton had been no asset to Mrs. Parton's ambitions. He had been definitely common, with his chewed cigar, his back slapping, his country drummer's manner. But pretty little blond Mrs. Parton had caught on fast. Out of the corner of her innocent, china-blue eyes she watched what people were like, and her tight little mind snapped up and ticketed away every bit of old gossip or new scandal, every tone of contempt or admiration. In the end she knew Bardsville better than Bardsville knew itself. And knowledge is power.

Knowledge is power and patience can move mountains. Mrs. Parton was nothing if not patient. She could wait. She never obtruded herself. She never took a step before she was sure of her footing. She was willing and unresentful and agreeable, and she carried her head modestly. She had seen every rung of the ladder, every stage of the ascent, but nobody suspected her knowledge. She joined the PTA when her child was in school, and was active in the Presbyterian Church. Then she learned to play "five hundred" and joined a card club. She watched her grammar. She subscribed to a national organization which sent her a good book every month, and she sometimes read the book. She had gone in for color on her clothes when she first came to Bardsville, but the right magazines and the sight of certain ladies on the streets had modified her ideas. By 1930 she was a member of the Episcopal Church, but the transition from Presbyterianism had been so gradual that people scarcely noticed it. By 1934 she had learned to drink cocktails. "Just one," she would say, "just one. Oh, no, thank you, I only take one." And she never took but one, or at most two, in public, though now and then, safe at home, in the evening, she would pull the shades and make herself a shakerful and drink it and go to bed and lie hot and dizzy and shaking in the dark, and feel her body flow tinglingly away from her. But she knew what she wanted. There was still a long way to go from her pleasant little brick house, tastefully decorated according to the magazines, at the foot of Rusty-Butt Hill.

She married Bolton Lovehart, and moved into the house. In one sense, though neither she nor Bolton Lovehart knew it, she had as much right to be in the house as he did. For Lovehart blood was in her veins, too. She, too, was descended from old Lem Lovehart, by the daughter he had left when the Chickasaw scalped him. That daughter had married a settler of Bardsville who then pioneered into the scrub country to the south, where the recollection of Lovehart was lost and only the secret blood in the veins remained.

Mrs. Parton was then in her late thirties, still prettyish, a little full in the body, but with the innocent china-blue eyes and good ankles. Bolton Lovehart was fifty-nine. That was in 1939.

She made few changes in the Lovehart house except to bring order and cleanliness. The old furniture and knick-knacks, shabby and battered as they were, kept their places. She was too smart to be caught in that trap. Changes could come later, if there were changes to be made. She knew that the attic room was always locked with a good padlock, but after the first questions she held her peace. Her husband had said that that was where he kept his books and papers, his "work," his "book," and that he didn't want anything disturbed. A few times when he was out of the house, she did try to open the lock with a batch of old keys she had found, but without success. It was a good lock. And she had no reason to disbelieve her husband. He did go up there sometimes and stay for a while. And she knew he was cranky and set in his ways. Everybody had always said he was cranky. So she could wait. She had waited to satisfy more important longings than curiosity.

Her son, Jasper Parton, came to live in the house, too. He was about nineteen then, a well-built, brawny lad, with the undefinable promise, however, of fat and slackness. He had curly brown hair, a wide, heavy mouth, full of good teeth which he showed often in an expectant smile when he looked around after he had made some remark. He laughed readily, and most readily at his own words. He would say something and roll his large brown eyes like a comic stallion, and then laugh. He had the habit of rubbing his hands together, or pulling at his fingers to crack the knuckles. He called his mother "Old Girl," or "My Little Chickadee," and was accustomed to slap her on the rump in playful good spirits. He soon got the habit of slapping Bolton Lovehart on the shoulder, and calling him "Pop," or "Pop, Old Boy." His mother was disturbed by this at first, but she soon saw that her husband didn't mind, that he really seemed to like it.

Bolton Lovehart did like it. He liked everything about the new life. He liked the friends his wife brought home (though she brought few people, for she was gradually preparing to drop some of them), and even tried to learn to play bridge. And he especially liked Jasper's girl, Janie Murphy, a good-looking, well-mannered girl, with few words but a nice, direct look at you out of her gray eyes. Bolton Lovehart sank into the new happiness with a sense of perpetual surprise. He had not even suspected that things might be this way.

Mrs. Lovehart did not like Janie Murphy. Or rather, she did not like or dislike Janie Murphy: she disliked the idea of Janie Murphy. Janie Murphy would not do. Not with old Tom Murphy for a father. And a Catholic to boot. But she could wait, and wait in perfect confidence.

So when in the fall of 1940 her son was drafted for military service, she was almost glad. He would forget Janie. She was sure of that. And the war was far away. It was far away across the ocean where it belonged.

Bolton Lovehart was almost happy, too, when the draft came. He liked Jasper, but the event gave him a sense of excitement, of having his finger somehow on the pulse of the world. He went to the station with the boy when he left. "Good-bye, Pop," the boy said with good-humored contempt, and rolled his eyes. "Take care of yourself," he said, and slapped the old man on the shoulder. Bolton Lovehart wanted to say something, he didn't know what, but something which was swelling in his heart. "My boy—" he began, "my son—" Then he fumbled for words.

"Tootle-oo, Pop," the boy said, and swung up to the platform of the coach, grinned over all of Bardsville, and disappeared from sight.

Bolton Lovehart got the habit of going downtown early for the morning paper. He began to read magazines and books about Europe and the war. He got the habit of stopping on street corners or in the post office to talk with men about the situation. "In so far as I have been able to inform myself," he would begin, and clear his throat, then proceed. About any other subject in the world, the men would not have listened. But the war was coming and they listened. And after Bolton Lovehart had left, one of them would say, "You know, Old Lovehart has got a head on him. He's read all those books."

Another might say, "Yeah, he might as well have read 'em. He never did a damned thing else all his life. Me, I had to get out and chase the almighty dollar. Give me nothing else to do and I'd sit on my tail and read me some books."

But they listened. And one day Bolton Lovehart was asked to speak to the Kiwanis Club on the European situation. He became the town authority on the subject. He made speeches to all the clubs in town, and at the high school. Whatever he had been waiting for all his life now seemed to be his. He was happy.

When the war came, what had been happiness was transformed almost overnight into a kind of bliss, of excitement, which even on the dullest day glowed unwinkingly in his bosom. Sometimes it surprised him, the sense of lightness and meaning inside him, and he would stop about his occupation or stand in the street and demand of himself, *Is this me, is it me?* He was busy all the time now. He had to read all the books and magazines and newspapers and take notes. Somebody had to find out things and tell people, explain to them. Somebody had to work for paper collection and rubber collection. Somebody had to work for bond drives and Red Cross drives.

He lived for the morning paper and the radio broadcasts. The long story of the early defeats, detail by detail, wrenched him to the core, but in the pain was the stab of life, a clean quickening and a dedication. He was walking up the street from town, where he had gone for the morning mail, hoping for a letter from Jasper, when he heard the news of Bataan. Mr. Sullivan, who lived down the hill, stopped him and said, "They just surrendered. Bataan has surrendered. I just heard it on the radio."

"Thank you," Bolton Lovehart murmured, and after Mr. Sullivan had gone on, stood there in the street steadily breathing the sweet spring air, letting the tears run down his cheeks, feeling the exquisite sensation in his bosom. He reached out, timidly, to touch the bark of the old maple which grew between the pavement and the street. The coarseness of the bark was a vibrant delight to his fingers. He touched it humbly. He looked up at the tree, at the tinted, waxy beginnings of buds, then swung his gaze over the street, the houses, the trees, the springing lawns, and up at the great, rain-washed, glowing sky. It was all real. It was real.

In the scrub county just south of Carruthers County a big army post had been established, and a new concrete road, straight as a knife edge, had been driven through the red clay and limestone hills, a white slab over which the red clay bled streakingly down in wet weather from the cuts where clay and limestone looked like a gigantic side of beef brutally slashed open. In the evenings the lost boys, bulging or scrawny in khaki, wearing big clumsy shoes like plow boys, wandered the streets of Bardsville, or hung around the restaurants and drug stores and pool rooms. They got drunk and shouted in the streets or went down to the bottom to the whores or stood in wordless groups on street corners, staring with a wistful and penal humility out of their strange world into a strange world.

The town had to take care of them, and every one was a hero and precious in the early months before they became a curse and a burden. The town turned an old hall into a recreation center. Church people had a soldier to dinner every Sunday. People gave parties for them on Saturday night. Bolton Lovehart worked indefatigably on the recreation committee of St. Luke's. And the Loveharts gave parties. They filled the big old living room with boys and a scattering of regular army non-coms, leather-faced, mature men, who gorged on sandwiches and cake and coffee and beer, and made the house rock with laughter, and the blare of the radio turned up full. Sometimes in the racket two or three of the regular army non-coms would go into the back parlor and talk to Mrs. Lovehart and drink beer with her. Occasionally, with a show of giggling and theatrical furtiveness, she would give them a drop of something stronger than beer.

Bolton Lovehart could afford to buy sandwiches and beer for the boys. The pinch of the 1930's was over. He had sold, for a handsome figure, a strip of his property down in the bottom. The war plant stood on it. And the parties were his delight.

The best parties occurred when Jasper came home on his infrequent leaves, brawny and laughing, a lieutenant now. They then had the girls in and they danced to the radio, shaking the house, making the room dizzy with smoke. That was the best. Bolton Lovehart sat by the wall, watching everything, his whole being absorbed into everything, and the bliss in his bosom glowed white and hot like a live ember when the blast from the bellows hits it.

Among the girls who came to these parties was Janie Murphy. There was nothing Mrs. Lovehart could do about that if Jasper wanted it. But she was still confident. When word came that Jasper was to be sent overseas, there was a hard kernel of satisfaction in the middle of her grief. Everything would be all right now. He would forget that Janie.

Jasper came home on his last leave. And he married Janie Murphy. They eloped up into Kentucky, in the middle of the night. It had happened on the spur of the moment. Jasper had had no intention of marrying Janie Murphy, or anybody else. But she adored him. Every glance, every gesture, her hands clinging to him, flattered his vanity. And the excitement of going overseas roused an unexpected sentimentality in his nature. He thought about having a dear little wife back home. And having Janie Murphy as his wife was the only way to get Janie Murphy. He had found that out. Even the excitement of the last leave hadn't changed that fact. She wept and clung to him, but she was a good little Catholic girl. She was a good little Catholic girl, but when, on impulse late one evening, he proposed that they elope, she let her scruples be overruled. She loved him so. They were married by a bleary justice of the peace, sleepy and half-dressed, whom they had roused from bed. Jasper promised that they would get married by a priest later.

They went on up into Kentucky and had a three-day honeymoon and saw a horse race, and up in the hotel room she even drank whisky with him, she loved him so much. They would get married by the priest when they got home to Bardsville, he said. When they got back, there was no time—or at least not enough time—for Jasper had new orders to report immediately.

"Oh, you might take time, it won't take much time," she begged him.

But he said, "Kiddo, look here. Orders is orders. This is the army, kiddo. And, chicken, you and me, we are married good as anybody. Don't let 'em tell you different."

"But, Jasper—you—"

"Sure, kiddo. When I get back. Sure, and don't you love me?"

On the train he leaned back and propped his feet up. For the moment he was almost glad to get away. Just for a sort of a breath of fresh air, you might say. Sure, she was the stuff. Sure, he loved the kid. She was his little wife and she sure had what it took, no matter what those priests had told her. He'd knock that nonsense out of her.

He leaned back and drowsed. He thought how he would have something to tell the fellows, how he had got married. He'd laugh and say with mock woe how she had thrown the hooks into him. *But, boy,* he would say, *boy, I tell you, it is easy punishment. What she has got. Listen here, let me tell you, she* . . . He could scarcely wait to get to camp and tell the fellows.

Mrs. Lovehart made the best of the situation. She did not lose hope. The event was passing almost unnoticed in Bardsville. So many strange things happened every day now, with the war on, and new people, and people acting funny and doing things they had never done before, behaving the way they had never expected to behave. So she put the best face possible on the marriage, and referred to it as little as possible. But her husband could talk of little else. He wanted to stop people on the street and tell them about it. She could have strangled him. Sitting alone, thinking of him down the street telling somebody, she could have coldly strangled him with her bare hands. Her hands clenched, her breath came quick, and she thought of doing it. She suddenly loathed him, everything about him, everything, everything. She had always loathed him. It rose up inside her. She suddenly knew it. The thought filled the room, like light.

Bolton Lovehart's excitement about the marriage, however, did not last long. There was the war itself, the committees and drives, and the letters from Jasper. When one of the rare letters came, he would read parts of it to anybody in town whom he could stop on the street. "You know my boy Jasper," he would say, "you know Jasper. He's a lieutenant. In Sicily now. I know you'd like to hear what he has written. I find it very informative." Then he would read the letter.

He wrote often and sent Jasper money, more money than he could afford.

Jasper Parton was killed in Italy. It was a great blow for Mrs. Lovehart. It shook her confidence in the world, and in all she had learned, and in herself. It was, at first, an even greater shock for Bolton Lovehart, but even the grief was absorbed into life, into his occupations, the conversations on the street: "My son—you remember my boy Jasper, who was killed in Italy—" And there were the other boys. Nothing would be too good for them now. And then he got his great idea.

One of the ladies' organizations of St. Luke's was having a bazaar to raise money for the Red Cross. The bazaar was to fall on December 5th, when Christmas was already on the way. It was Christmas that made him think of it, for it had been the Christmas-toy display in the hardware store long ago which had started the whole thing. He would give his circus to the bazaar to be sold for toys. He said nothing to his wife about the matter, but began to spend all his days and evenings in the attic. He was retouching such of the poor creatures as needed retouching, replacing costumes that had faded, packing them in neat boxes. Then they were all carried to the church, where, the night before the bazaar, he worked for hours in the recreation room, arranging them in a great circus, setting up tight ropes and bars and trapezes, sprinkling finely ground sawdust in the rings, adjusting the animals on their stands. He did not finish until after two o'clock.

The circus was a great success. It was the hit of the bazaar. Children were crazy about it. Broken up and sold piece by piece it brought nearly two hundred dollars for the Red Cross. And for Jasper. The Bardsville *Gazette* ran a photograph of Mr. Lovehart standing beside the circus: "Prominent Citizen Has Secret Hobby. Gives proceeds to Red Cross." The death of Jasper had brought the secret circus out into the world to live, to be enjoyed, to be used and broken in the end. There was some kind of atonement in this, Bolton Lovehart felt, for the long lie, for all the past, and he felt resigned now even to the death of Jasper.

Jasper Parton was killed on the banks of a swift river—what would pass for nothing better than a creek back home in Tennessee—under the shadow of snow-stung rocks in the Apennines. He had crossed the stream, with two companies, on an unsteady pontoon bridge, by the ruins of a stone bridge, under machine-gun fire from Germans above the little road, up in the rocks. A couple of planes got through the murk and knocked out the position. Just in time, too, for the clouds were thickening, lower and lower. The men strung out up the little road, in the mountain quiet, and spread up the ridge, feeling it out. It was very quiet, except for gunfire, far to the west. Then the Germans hit. Two other machine guns, which had remained silent during the crossing, opened on the men who had remained near the bridge. Then the troops appeared, out of the earth, among the rocks, ready to rush the bridge. It was an effective surprise.

The Americans up the road began piling back, but it was a good distance. They were cut off. It was Jasper and two of the other men near the bridge who blocked the rush and held it. They managed to get a machine gun placed in the lee of an outcropping of rock. One of the men was killed. Jasper was hit, but not badly. It was Jasper who, at the last minute, sent the survivor back, and stayed until the grenades got him. He had stayed long enough.

Jasper Parton was awarded the Congressional Medal.

His wife, Janie Murphy Parton, was to go to Washington to receive the medal.

"To think," Mrs. Lovehart said in her bitterness, "to think that he named her his next of kin. To think—that girl—and he was only married to her four days. Four days before he went away." It was cruel. It was too cruel, she decided.

"You go to Washington, too," Bolton Lovehart comforted her. "You'll go, my dear."

"I'll not go! Not with that girl. I'll not go. She can have it. She got Jasper and now she can have that medal."

"You must go," her husband urged. "I'll take you. You must go for Jasper's sake."

She swore that she would not go. But she went to Washington, and saw that girl receive the medal. She had, however, her own satisfactions. Great men shook her own hand and murmured their congratulations and sympathy. Only when, back in the hotel room, she saw the picture in the paper, the picture of that girl with the medal, and herself in the background, did the bitterness surge up so powerfully that nothing else mattered. She tore the paper across and flung herself on the bed. She had been robbed of everything.

It was better back in Bardsville. People back in Bardsville at least knew the difference between Mrs. Bolton Lovehart and that Murphy girl. So when the celebration occurred in Bardsville, that girl did not crowd her out. She sat on the platform next to the mayor, with her husband, who was to speak a few words, the rector of St. Luke's and Colonel Malcolm, from the army post down in the forgotten county of her birth. That girl was up there, too, but far over to one side, looking frightened and lost. Mrs. Lovehart could see her out of the corner of her eye. She was pleased with what she saw. *She has no composure,* she thought. *She can't keep her hands still, she is picking one of her nails,* she thought. She surreptitiously spread her own small, well-shaped, well-manicured fingers in her lap and studied them, her head slightly bowed in her characteristic modest way.

Bolton Lovehart's speech was the most successful of his life. His words were slow and halting at the beginning, his gestures cranky and unsure. For the first few minutes his voice droned along, saying what people expected him to say, but what they strained forward to hear above the muffled coughs and the cautious scraping of feet. Then, still uncertain, in that dry, pedantic voice of a schoolteacher or Sunday-school superintendent, he said, "We do not come here tonight to honor Jasper Parton. We cannot honor him. That medal—the highest recognition this country can give a citizen—does not honor him. Or any man who died, far away in a foreign land.

He does not need any honor. We come here tonight because we are to be honored. By him. Because one morning in a foreign land, he did us honor. He did honor to Bardsville, and to all of us. We grieve for him. I grieve for him. He was not my son. You all know that. I have no son. But I want to think of him as my son. I want to think of him and of all who went away as my sons. For they are all our sons—every one of them is the son of each of us—I want to think of him—as my son— for they all—they all—"

He could not continue. He did not break down. He showed no emotion. He simply stopped and the words would not come any more. For a moment he looked out to the people, and then turned and sat down stiffly in his chair.

There was music after that. They stood and sang the national anthem.

At the reception afterwards, he stood quietly, almost somnambulistically, beside Mrs. Lovehart, and the people came to shake their hands.

But Janie Murphy had slipped away. She had walked across the square and down the dark streets beyond, not able to hold the tears any longer, down to one of the side streets, to the house of old Tom Murphy.

The newspapers, the radio reports, the conversations were full of victories now. The final victory was certain. Housewives, waiting their turn in the butcher shop, grumbled a little now. Sometimes soldiers from the camp to the south would wait on the edge of the highway just out of town with lifted arms, late at night, and watch the cars whizz past. Not many got invited to Sunday dinner any more. People knew that these boys would never get overseas, would never fight in jungles or in icy mountains or ruined towns. They would never die in foreign lands. They would stay here in the camp a while and then be sent home. They were a nuisance, a burden, and little more. Even the merchants and café owners were tired of them. But Bolton Lovehart was not tired. He would do what he could for them. There were still the parties up at the Lovehart house, the free beer, sandwiches, and cigarettes, and the loud radio.

He still went to committee meetings, still tried to arrange entertainments for the soldiers, still worked at bond selling and in Red Cross drives. He still stopped people on the street to tell them something he had read about, to refer to Jasper Parton: "You know Jasper—my boy that was killed in Italy— well, he used to say, he used to predict—" But people did not listen closely to him any more. Their eyes wandered from his face and they moved restlessly.

One night he went to a bond meeting in a village some ten miles from Bardsville. He got home late, long after midnight. Mr. Simmons, the rector, let him out of the car at the gate and drove away. Bolton Lovehart saw that the light was on in the living room. He assumed that his wife was waiting up for him, though that would have been unusual. As he opened the front door, he saw two men's hats lying on the table. Then, once in the hall, he saw the men waiting for him, standing in the middle of the living room. One of the men he recognized as Milt Suggs, the sheriff. The other man he did not know, but he looked like the kind of man a sheriff would have with him.

The sheriff apologized: "We just come in." Then: "Didn't nobody answer, and the door was open, so we just come in. Hope you didn't mind."

"Of course not," Bolton Lovehart said, his face, however, showing his question.

The sheriff was uneasy, shifting from foot to foot. "Mr. Lovehart," he finally managed, "it's—it's about Mrs. Lovehart."

"What?"

"It's Mrs. Lovehart," the sheriff said, and stopped again.

"Tell me," Bolton Lovehart ordered. "Tell me!"

"Well," the sheriff said. "Well—" Then he got himself together. "She's dead," he said. "Done killed."

Mrs. Lovehart was killed that night in an accident on the highway. She and a certain Captain Cartwright, who had been at the wheel, had driven at high speed into the back of a heavy truck parked on the shoulder of the highway ten miles south of town. They had both been drinking. Bolton Lovehart knew Captain Cartwright, a big, red-faced, burly man, fiftyish, who had been a sergeant in the regular army for years before the war and had received a commission for distinguished service in action and had been sent back to the training camps. He had come to the Lovehart house now and then. He and Mrs. Lovehart were killed instantly in the collision. Both bodies were severely mangled.

The last victories came. The last blood was shed in the ruined streets of Berlin. Half the world away, American fleets lifted some dream island in the morning light and the bombardment began, while landing craft skeetered crazily shoreward like water insects and the planes poured steadily overhead. People in Bardsville knew how it was. They could see it in the newsreel after the feature. Then the bomb fell on Hiroshima.

It meant nothing, however, to Bolton Lovehart. For some time now, all day long and far into the night, he had sat in the attic, leaning over his table, where lay the block of soft pine, the glue pot, the wire, the awl, the knife, the paint tubes and brushes, the bits of cloth and needles and scissors. Finally, he had found his way back.

Some of the forward-looking business men of Bardsville have formed a corporation and have bought the war plant, where small arms ammunition was made. Plastics will now be manufactured there. The old furniture factory is operating day and night since the strike has been settled. New houses are going up in the bottoms to replace some of the more decrepit shacks occupied by the war workers. Many of those workers will stay, the Chamber of Commerce confidently predicts, people drawn from the red clay hills to the south, the banks of sluggish, stippled, moccasin-drowsing creeks over toward the Mississippi, the cross-roads settlements, and the slums of Memphis. Bardsville now has nearly twenty thousand people.

Janie Murphy Parton has just married again. She went through a period of great anguish. It was anguish not only for the loss of Jasper Parton, whom she had loved so much, but an anguish of guilt. She felt that she was the cause of his death. She had sinned in marrying him outside the church, and her punishment had been to lose him. For a long time she could scarcely keep from killing herself, especially after the trip to Washington and the medal, which was the public mark of her guilt. She resisted that impulse, and then it seemed that she would die. Nobody could feel such anguish, day and night, and live. Nothing she could do and nothing Father Donnelly could say seemed to help her.

But she lived. And she has married Murray James, a fore-man at the furniture factory, a man ten years older than she, a big, quiet man, very strong and very kind. He satisfies her in every way much better than Jasper Parton ever did, and she loves him better, even, than she ever loved Jasper Parton. She knows this, and she knows that now, at last, in this way she has truly killed poor, vain, cheap, laughing, eye-rolling, heroic Jasper. Knowing this, she sometimes wakes up in the night and out of this new guilt in her happiness, she weeps silently and sweetly a while and then reaches over to take the big, coarse hand of Murray James and hold it between both her own and listen to his breathing.

This occurs less frequently in recent weeks, and soon now she will let Jasper go. He will go away where he belongs, to join the circus in the attic. He will join Seth Sykes and drunken Cash Perkins and all the heroes who ever died for all their good reasons, and old Lem Lovehart, who laid himself down amid birdsong at dusk and was scalped by a Chickasaw, and Simon Lovehart with the wound and the prayer book as his truth, and Louise Bolton Lovehart with her dear, treacherous heart in her bosom, and the kitten little Louise Bolton flung from her window to thud on the paving bricks, and the blood-less arrowheads and the fading flag of Simon Lovehart's regiment, and the song, "Let the nearer waters roll," which they sang at the baptizing and the song they sang in the square the night of the armistice in 1918, and the painted animals carved from wood and the sinister ring master and the girl acrobat with the frivolous skirt and round blue painted eyes, and all the things by which Bardsville had lived, and found life worth living, and died. And Jasper will be at home there.

Blackberry Winter

To JOSEPH WARREN *and* DAGMAR BEACH

IT WAS getting into June and past eight o'clock in the morning, but there was a fire—even if it wasn't a big fire, just a fire of chunks—on the hearth of the big stone fireplace in the living room. I was standing on the hearth, almost into the chimney, hunched over the fire, working my bare toes slowly on the warm stone. I relished the heat which made the skin of my bare legs warp and creep and tingle, even as I called to my mother, who was somewhere back in the dining room or kitchen, and said: "But it's June, I don't have to put them on!"

"You put them on if you are going out," she called.

I tried to assess the degree of authority and conviction in the tone, but at that distance it was hard to decide. I tried to analyze the tone, and then I thought what a fool I had been to start out the back door and let her see that I was barefoot. If I had gone out the front door or the side door she would never have known, not till dinner time anyway, and by then the day would have been half gone and I would have been all over the farm to see what the storm had done and down to the creek to see the flood. But it had never crossed my mind that they would try to stop you from going barefoot in June, no matter if there had been a gully-washer and a cold spell.

Nobody had ever tried to stop me in June as long as I could remember, and when you are nine years old, what you remember seems forever; for you remember everything and everything is important and stands big and full and fills up Time and is so solid that you can walk around and around it like a tree and look at it. You are aware that time passes, that there is a movement in time, but that is not what Time is. Time is not a movement, a flowing, a wind then, but is, rather, a kind of climate in which things are, and when a thing happens it begins to live and keeps on living and stands solid in Time like the tree that you can walk around. And if there is a movement, the movement is not Time itself, any more than a breeze is climate, and all the breeze does is to shake a little the leaves on the tree which is alive and solid. When you are nine, you know that there are things that you don't know, but you know that when you know something you know it. You know how a thing has been and you know that you can go barefoot in June. You do not understand that voice from back in the kitchen which says that you cannot go barefoot outdoors and run to see what has happened and rub your feet over the wet shivery grass and make the perfect mark of your foot in the smooth, creamy, red mud and then muse upon it as though you had suddenly come upon that single mark on the glistening auroral beach of the world. You have never seen a beach, but you have read the book and how the footprint was there.

The voice had said what it had said, and I looked savagely at the black stockings and the strong, scuffed brown shoes which I had brought from my closet as far as the hearth rug. I called once more, "But it's June," and waited.

"It's June," the voice replied from far away, "but it's blackberry winter."

I had lifted my head to reply to that, to make one more test of what was in that tone, when I happened to see the man.

The fireplace in the living room was at the end; for the stone chimney was built, as in so many of the farmhouses in Tennessee, at the end of a gable, and there was a window on each side of the chimney. Out of the window on the north side of the fireplace I could see the man. When I saw the man I did not call out what I had intended, but, engrossed by the strangeness of the sight, watched him, still far off, come along the path by the edge of the woods.

What was strange was that there should be a man there at all. That path went along the yard fence, between the fence and the woods which came right down to the yard, and then on back past the chicken runs and on by the woods until it was lost to sight where the woods bulged out and cut off the back field. There the path disappeared into the woods. It led on back, I knew, through the woods and to the swamp, skirted the swamp where the big trees gave way to sycamores and water oaks and willows and tangled cane, and then led on to the river. Nobody ever went back there except people who wanted to gig frogs in the swamp or to fish in the river or to hunt in the woods, and those people, if they didn't have a standing permission from my father, always stopped to ask permission to cross the farm. But the man whom I now saw wasn't, I could tell even at that distance, a sportsman. And what would a sportsman have been doing down there after a storm? Besides, he was coming from the river, and nobody had gone down there that morning. I knew that for a fact, because if anybody had passed, certainly if a stranger had passed, the dogs would have made a racket and would have been out on him. But this man was coming up from the river and had come up through the woods. I suddenly had a vision of him moving up the grassy path in the woods, in the green twilight under the big trees, not making any sound on the path, while now and then, like drops off the eaves, a big drop of water would fall from a leaf or bough and strike a stiff oak leaf lower down with a small, hollow sound like a drop of water hitting tin. That sound, in the silence of the woods, would be very significant.

When you are a boy and stand in the stillness of woods, which can be so still that your heart almost stops beating and makes you want to stand there in the green twilight until you feel your very feet sinking into and clutching the earth like roots and your body breathing slow through its pores like the leaves—when you stand there and wait for the next drop to drop with its small, flat sound to a lower leaf, that sound seems to measure out something, to put an end to something, to begin something, and you cannot wait for it to happen and are afraid it will not happen, and then when it has happened, you are waiting again, almost afraid.

But the man whom I saw coming through the woods in my mind's eye did not pause and wait, growing into the ground and breathing with the enormous, soundless breathing of the leaves. Instead, I saw him moving in the green twilight inside my head as he was moving at that very moment along the path by the edge of the woods, coming toward the house. He was moving steadily, but not fast, with his shoulders hunched a little and his head thrust forward, like a man who has come a long way and has a long way to go. I shut my eyes for a couple of seconds, thinking that when I opened them he would not be there at all. There was no place for him to have come from, and there was no reason for him to come where he was coming, toward our house. But I opened my eyes, and there he was, and he was coming steadily along the side of the woods. He was not yet even with the back chicken yard.

"Mama," I called.

"You put them on," the voice said.

"There's a man coming," I called, "out back."

She did not reply to that, and I guessed that she had gone to the kitchen window to look. She would be looking at the man and wondering who he was and what he wanted, the way you always do in the country, and if I went back there now she would not notice right off whether or not I was barefoot. So I went back to the kitchen.

She was standing by the window. "I don't recognize him," she said, not looking around at me.

"Where could he be coming from?" I asked.

"I don't know," she said.

"What would he be doing down at the river? At night? In the storm?"

She studied the figure out the window, then said, "Oh, I reckon maybe he cut across from the Dunbar place."

That was, I realized, a perfectly rational explanation. He had not been down at the river in the storm, at night. He had come over this morning. You could cut across from the Dunbar place if you didn't mind breaking through a lot of elder and sassafras and blackberry bushes which had about taken over the old cross path, which nobody ever used any more. That satisfied me for a moment, but only for a moment. "Mama," I asked, "what would he be doing over at the Dunbar place last night?"

Then she looked at me, and I knew I had made a mistake, for she was looking at my bare feet. "You haven't got your shoes on," she said.

But I was saved by the dogs. That instant there was a bark which I recognized as Sam, the collie, and then a heavier, churning kind of bark which was Bully, and I saw a streak of white as Bully tore round the corner of the back porch and headed out for the man. Bully was a big, bone-white bull dog, the kind of dog that they used to call a farm bull dog but that you don't see any more, heavy chested and heavy headed, but with pretty long legs. He could take a fence as light as a hound. He had just cleared the white paling fence toward the woods when my mother ran out to the back porch and began calling, "Here you, Bully! Here you!"

Bully stopped in the path, waiting for the man, but he gave a few more of those deep, gargling, savage barks that reminded you of something down a stone-lined well. The red clay mud, I saw, was splashed up over his white chest and looked exciting, like blood.

The man, however, had not stopped walking even when Bully took the fence and started at him. He had kept right on coming. All he had done was to switch a little paper parcel which he carried from the right hand to the left, and then reach into his pants pocket to get something. Then I saw the glitter and knew that he had a knife in his hand, probably the kind of mean knife just made for devilment and nothing else, with a blade as long as the blade of a frog-sticker, which will snap out ready when you press a button in the handle. That knife must have had a button in the handle, or else how could he have had the blade out glittering so quick and with just one hand?

Pulling his knife against the dogs was a funny thing to do, for Bully was a big, powerful brute and fast, and Sam was all right. If those dogs had meant business, they might have knocked him down and ripped him before he got a stroke in. He ought to have picked up a heavy stick, something to take a swipe at them with and something which they could see and respect when they came at him. But he apparently did not know much about dogs. He just held the knife blade close against the right leg, low down, and kept on moving down the path.

Then my mother had called, and Bully had stopped. So the man let the blade of the knife snap back into the handle, and dropped it into his pocket, and kept on coming. Many women would have been afraid with the strange man who they knew had that knife in his pocket. That is, if they were alone in the house with nobody but a nine-year-old boy. And my mother was alone, for my father had gone off, and Dellie, the cook, was down at her cabin because she wasn't feeling well. But my mother wasn't afraid. She wasn't a big woman, but she was clear and brisk about everything she did and looked everybody and everything right in the eye from her own blue eyes in her tanned face. She had been the first woman in the county to ride a horse astride (that was back when she was a girl and long before I was born), and I have seen her snatch up a pump gun and go out and knock a chicken hawk out of the air like a busted skeet when he came over her chicken yard. She was a steady and self-reliant woman, and when I think of her now after all the years she has been dead, I think of her brown hands, not big, but somewhat square for a woman's hands, with square-cut nails. They looked, as a matter of fact, more like a young boy's hands than a grown woman's. But back then it never crossed my mind that she would ever be dead.

She stood on the back porch and watched the man enter the back gate, where the dogs (Bully had leaped back into the yard) were dancing and muttering and giving sidelong glances back to my mother to see if she meant what she had said. The man walked right by the dogs, almost brushing them, and didn't pay them any attention. I could see now that he wore old khaki pants, and a dark wool coat with stripes in it, and a gray felt hat. He had on a gray shirt with blue stripes in it, and no tie. But I could see a tie, blue and reddish, sticking in his side coat-pocket. Everything was wrong about what he wore. He ought to have been wearing blue jeans or overalls, and a straw hat or an old black felt hat, and the coat, granting that he might have been wearing a wool coat and not a jumper, ought not to have had those stripes. Those clothes, despite the fact that they were old enough and dirty enough for any tramp, didn't belong there in our back yard, coming down the path, in Middle Tennessee, miles away from any big town, and even a mile off the pike.

When he got almost to the steps, without having said anything, my mother, very matter-of-factly, said, "Good morning."

"Good morning," he said, and stopped and looked her over. He did not take off his hat, and under the brim you could see the perfectly unmemorable face, which wasn't old and wasn't young, or thick or thin. It was grayish and covered with about three days of stubble. The eyes were a kind of nondescript, muddy hazel, or something like that, rather bloodshot. His teeth, when he opened his mouth, showed yellow and uneven. A couple of them had been knocked out. You knew that they had been knocked out, because there was a scar, not very old, there on the lower lip just beneath the gap.

"Are you hunting work?" my mother asked him.

"Yes," he said—not "yes, mam"—and still did not take off his hat.

"I don't know about my husband, for he isn't here," she said, and didn't mind a bit telling the tramp, or whoever he was, with the mean knife in his pocket, that no man was around, "but I can give you a few things to do. The storm has drowned a lot of my chicks. Three coops of them. You can gather them up and bury them. Bury them deep so the dogs won't get at them. In the woods. And fix the coops the wind blew over. And down yonder beyond that pen by the edge of the woods are some drowned poults. They got out and I couldn't get them in. Even after it started to rain hard. Poults haven't got any sense."

"What are them things—poults?" he demanded, and spat on the brick walk. He rubbed his foot over the spot, and I saw that he wore a black, pointed-toe low shoe, all cracked and broken. It was a crazy kind of shoe to be wearing in the country.

"Oh, they're young turkeys," my mother was saying. "And they haven't got any sense. I oughtn't to try to raise them around here with so many chickens, anyway. They don't thrive near chickens, even in separate pens. And I won't give up my chickens." Then she stopped herself and resumed briskly on the note of business. "When you finish that, you can fix my flower beds. A lot of trash and mud and gravel has washed down. Maybe you can save some of my flowers if you are careful."

"Flowers," the man said, in a low, impersonal voice which seemed to have a wealth of meaning, but a meaning which I could not fathom. As I think back on it, it probably was not pure contempt. Rather, it was a kind of impersonal and distant marveling that he should be on the verge of grubbing in a flower bed. He said the word, and then looked off across the yard.

"Yes, flowers," my mother replied with some asperity, as though she would have nothing said or implied against flowers. "And they were very fine this year." Then she stopped and looked at the man. "Are you hungry?" she demanded.

"Yeah," he said.

"I'll fix you something," she said, "before you get started." She turned to me. "Show him where he can wash up," she commanded, and went into the house.

I took the man to the end of the porch where a pump was and where a couple of wash pans sat on a low shelf for people to use before they went into the house. I stood there while he laid down his little parcel wrapped in newspaper and took off his hat and looked around for a nail to hang it on. He poured the water and plunged his hands into it. They were big hands, and strong looking, but they did not have the creases and the earth-color of the hands of men who work outdoors. But they were dirty, with black dirt ground into the skin and under the nails. After he had washed his hands, he poured another basin of water and washed his face. He dried his face, and with the towel still dangling in his grasp, stepped over to the mirror on the house wall. He rubbed one hand over the stubble on his face. Then he carefully inspected his face, turning first one side and then the other, and stepped back and settled his striped coat down on his shoulders. He had the movements of a man who has just dressed up to go to church or a party—the way he settled his coat and smoothed it and scanned himself in the mirror.

Then he caught my glance on him. He glared at me for an instant out of the bloodshot eyes, then demanded in a low, harsh voice, "What you looking at?"

"Nothing," I managed to say, and stepped back a step from him.

He flung the towel down, crumpled, on the shelf, and went toward the kitchen door and entered without knocking.

My mother said something to him which I could not catch. I started to go in again, then thought about my bare feet, and decided to go back of the chicken yard, where the man would have to come to pick up the dead chicks. I hung around behind the chicken house until he came out.

He moved across the chicken yard with a fastidious, not quite finicking motion, looking down at the curdled mud flecked with bits of chicken-droppings. The mud curled up over the soles of his black shoes. I stood back from him some six feet and watched him pick up the first of the drowned chicks. He held it up by one foot and inspected it.

There is nothing deader looking than a drowned chick. The feet curl in that feeble, empty way which back when I was a boy, even if I was a country boy who did not mind hog-killing or frog-gigging, made me feel hollow in the stomach. Instead of looking plump and fluffy, the body is stringy and limp with the fluff plastered to it, and the neck is long and loose like a little string of rag. And the eyes have that bluish membrane over them which makes you think of a very old man who is sick about to die.

The man stood there and inspected the chick. Then he looked all around as though he didn't know what to do with it.

"There's a great big old basket in the shed," I said, and pointed to the shed attached to the chicken house.

He inspected me as though he had just discovered my presence, and moved toward the shed.

"There's a spade there, too," I added.

He got the basket and began to pick up the other chicks, picking each one up slowly by a foot and then flinging it into the basket with a nasty, snapping motion. Now and then he would look at me out of the blood-shot eyes. Every time he seemed on the verge of saying something, but he did not. Perhaps he was building up to say something to me, but I did not wait that long. His way of looking at me made me so uncomfortable that I left the chicken yard.

Besides, I had just remembered that the creek was in flood, over the bridge, and that people were down there watching it. So I cut across the farm toward the creek. When I got to the big tobacco field I saw that it had not suffered much. The land lay right and not many tobacco plants had washed out of the ground. But I knew that a lot of tobacco round the country had been washed right out. My father had said so at breakfast.

My father was down at the bridge. When I came out of the gap in the osage hedge into the road, I saw him sitting on his mare over the heads of the other men who were standing around, admiring the flood. The creek was big here, even in low water; for only a couple of miles away it ran into the river, and when a real flood came, the red water got over the pike where it dipped down to the bridge, which was an iron bridge, and high over the floor and even the side railings of the bridge. Only the upper iron work would show, with the water boiling and frothing red and white around it. That creek rose so fast and so heavy because a few miles back it came down out of the hills, where the gorges filled up with water in no time when a rain came. The creek ran in a deep bed with limestone bluffs along both sides until it got within three quarters of a mile of the bridge, and when it came out from between those bluffs in flood it was boiling and hissing and steaming like water from a fire hose.

Whenever there was a flood, people from half the county would come down to see the sight. After a gully-washer there would not be any work to do anyway. If it didn't ruin your crop, you couldn't plow and you felt like taking a holiday to celebrate. If it did ruin your crop, there wasn't anything to do except to try to take your mind off the mortgage, if you were rich enough to have a mortgage, and if you couldn't afford a mortgage you needed something to take your mind off how hungry you would be by Christmas. So people would come down to the bridge and look at the flood. It made something different from the run of days.

There would not be much talking after the first few minutes of trying to guess how high the water was this time. The men and kids just stood around, or sat their horses or mules, as the case might be, or stood up in the wagon beds. They looked at the strangeness of the flood for an hour or two, and then somebody would say that he had better be getting on home to dinner and would start walking down the gray, puddled limestone pike, or would touch heel to his mount and start off. Everybody always knew what it would be like when he got down to the bridge, but people always came. It was like church or a funeral. They always came, that is, if it was summer and the flood unexpected. Nobody ever came down in winter to see high water.

When I came out of the gap in the bodock hedge, I saw the crowd, perhaps fifteen or twenty men and a lot of kids, and saw my father sitting his mare, Nellie Gray. He was a tall, limber man and carried himself well. I was always proud to see him sit a horse, he was so quiet and straight, and when I stepped through the gap of the hedge that morning, the first thing that happened was, I remember, the warm feeling

I always had when I saw him up on a horse, just sitting. I did not go toward him, but skirted the crowd on the far side, to get a look at the creek. For one thing, I was not sure what he would say about the fact that I was barefoot. But the first thing I knew, I heard his voice calling, "Seth!"

I went toward him, moving apologetically past the men, who bent their large, red or thin, sallow faces above me. I knew some of the men, and knew their names, but because those I knew were there in a crowd, mixed with the strange faces, they seemed foreign to me, and not friendly. I did not look up at my father until I was almost within touching distance of his heel. Then I looked up and tried to read his face, to see if he was angry about my being barefoot. Before I could decide anything from that impassive, high-boned face, he had leaned over and reached a hand to me. "Grab on," he commanded.

I grabbed on and gave a little jump, and he said, "Up-see-daisy!" and whisked me, light as a feather, up to the pommel of his McClellan saddle.

"You can see better up here," he said, slid back on the cantle a little to make me more comfortable, and then, looking over my head at the swollen, tumbling water, seemed to forget all about me. But his right hand was laid on my side, just above my thigh, to steady me.

I was sitting there as quiet as I could, feeling the faint stir of my father's chest against my shoulders as it rose and fell with his breath, when I saw the cow. At first, looking up the creek, I thought it was just another big piece of driftwood steaming down the creek in the ruck of water, but all at once a pretty good-size boy who had climbed part way up a telephone pole by the pike so that he could see better yelled out, "Golly-damn, look at that-air cow!"

Everybody looked. It was a cow all right, but it might just as well have been driftwood; for it was dead as a chunk, rolling and roiling down the creek, appearing and disappearing, feet up or head up, it didn't matter which.

The cow started up the talk again. Somebody wondered

whether it would hit one of the clear places under the top
girder of the bridge and get through or whether it would get
tangled in the drift and trash that had piled against the upright girders and braces. Somebody remembered how about
ten years before so much driftwood had piled up on the bridge
that it was knocked off its foundations. Then the cow hit.
It hit the edge of the drift against one of the girders, and hung
there. For a few seconds it seemed as though it might tear
loose, but then we saw that it was really caught. It bobbed
and heaved on its side there in a slow, grinding, uneasy
fashion. It had a yoke around its neck, the kind made out of
a forked limb to keep a jumper behind fence.

"She shore jumped one fence," one of the men said.

And another: "Well, she done jumped her last one, fer a
fack."

Then they began to wonder about whose cow it might be.
They decided it must belong to Milt Alley. They said that he
had a cow that was a jumper, and kept her in a fenced-in
piece of ground up the creek. I had never seen Milt Alley,
but I knew who he was. He was a squatter and lived up the
hills a way, on a shirt-tail patch of set-on-edge land, in a cabin.
He was pore white trash. He had lots of children. I had seen
the children at school, when they came. They were thin-faced,
with straight, sticky-looking, dough-colored hair, and they
smelled something like old sour buttermilk, not because they
drank so much buttermilk but because that is the sort of smell
which children out of those cabins tend to have. The big
Alley boy drew dirty pictures and showed them to the little
boys at school.

That was Milt Alley's cow. It looked like the kind of cow
he would have, a scrawny, old, sway-backed cow, with a yoke
around her neck. I wondered if Milt Alley had another cow.

"Poppa," I said, "do you think Milt Alley has got another
cow?"

"You say 'Mr. Alley,' " my father said quietly.

"Do you think he has?"

"No telling," my father said.

Then a big gangly boy, about fifteen, who was sitting on a scraggly little old mule with a piece of croker sack thrown across the saw-tooth spine, and who had been staring at the cow, suddenly said to nobody in particular, "Reckin anybody ever et drownt cow?"

He was the kind of boy who might just as well as not have been the son of Milt Alley, with his faded and patched overalls ragged at the bottom of the pants and the mud-stiff brogans hanging off his skinny, bare ankles at the level of the mule's belly. He had said what he did, and then looked embarrassed and sullen when all the eyes swung at him. He hadn't meant to say it, I am pretty sure now. He would have been too proud to say it, just as Milt Alley would have been too proud. He had just been thinking out loud, and the words had popped out.

There was an old man standing there on the pike, an old man with a white beard. "Son," he said to the embarrassed and sullen boy on the mule, "you live long enough and you'll find a man will eat anything when the time comes."

"Time gonna come fer some folks this year," another man said.

"Son," the old man said, "in my time I et things a man don't like to think on. I was a sojer and I rode with Gin'l Forrest, and them things we et when the time come. I tell you. I et meat what got up and run when you taken out yore knife to cut a slice to put on the fire. You had to knock it down with a carbeen butt, it was so active. That-air meat would jump like a bullfrog, it was so full of skippers."

But nobody was listening to the old man. The boy on the mule turned his sullen sharp face from him, dug a heel into the side of the mule and went off up the pike with a motion which made you think that any second you would hear mule bones clashing inside that lank and scrofulous hide.

"Cy Dundee's boy," a man said, and nodded toward the figure going up the pike on the mule.

"Reckin Cy Dundee's young-uns seen times they'd settle fer drownt cow," another man said.

The old man with the beard peered at them both from his weak, slow eyes, first at one and then at the other. "Live long enough," he said, "and a man will settle fer what he kin git."

Then there was silence again, with the people looking at the red, foam-flecked water.

My father lifted the bridle rein in his left hand, and the mare turned and walked around the group and up the pike. We rode on up to our big gate, where my father dismounted to open it and let me myself ride Nellie Gray through. When he got to the lane that led off from the drive about two hundred yards from our house, my father said, "Grab on." I grabbed on, and he let me down to the ground. "I'm going to ride down and look at my corn," he said. "You go on." He took the lane, and I stood there on the drive and watched him ride off. He was wearing cowhide boots and an old hunting coat, and I thought that that made him look very military, like a picture. That and the way he rode.

I did not go to the house. Instead, I went by the vegetable garden and crossed behind the stables, and headed down for Dellie's cabin. I wanted to go down and play with Jebb, who was Dellie's little boy about two years older than I was. Besides, I was cold. I shivered as I walked, and I had goose-flesh. The mud which crawled up between my toes with every step I took was like ice. Dellie would have a fire, but she wouldn't make me put on shoes and stockings.

Dellie's cabin was of logs, with one side, because it was on a slope, set on limestone chunks, with a little porch attached to it, and had a little whitewashed fence around it and a gate with plow-points on a wire to clink when somebody came in, and had two big white oaks in the yard and some flowers and a nice privy in the back with some honeysuckle growing over it. Dellie and Old Jebb, who was Jebb's father and who lived with Dellie and had lived with her for twenty-five years even if they never had got married, were careful to keep everything nice around their cabin. They had the name all over the community for being clean and clever Negroes. Dellie and Jebb were what they used to call "white-folks' niggers." There was a big difference between their cabin and the other two cabins farther down where the other tenants lived. My father kept the other cabins weatherproof, but he couldn't undertake to go down and pick up after the litter they strewed. They didn't take the trouble to have a vegetable patch like Dellie and Jebb or to make preserves from wild plum, and jelly from crab apple the way Dellie did. They were shiftless, and my father was always threatening to get shed of them. But he never did. When they finally left, they just up and left on their own, for no reason, to go and be shiftless somewhere else. Then some more came. But meanwhile they lived down there, Matt Rawson and his family, and Sid Turner and his, and I played with their children all over the farm when they weren't working. But when I wasn't around they were mean sometimes to Little Jebb. That was because the other tenants down there were jealous of Dellie and Jebb.

I was so cold that I ran the last fifty yards to Dellie's gate. As soon as I had entered the yard, I saw that the storm had been hard on Dellie's flowers. The yard was, as I have said, on a slight slope, and the water running across had gutted the flower beds and washed out all the good black woods-earth which Dellie had brought in. What little grass there was in the yard was plastered sparsely down on the ground, the way the drainage water had left it. It reminded me of the way the fluff was plastered down on the skin of the drowned chicks that the strange man had been picking up, up in my mother's chicken yard.

I took a few steps up the path to the cabin, and then I saw that the drainage water had washed a lot of trash and filth out from under Dellie's house. Up toward the porch, the ground was not clean any more. Old pieces of rag, two or three rusted cans, pieces of rotten rope, some hunks of old dog dung, broken glass, old paper, and all sorts of things like that had washed out from under Dellie's house to foul her clean yard. It looked just as bad as the yards of the other cabins, or worse. It was worse, as a matter of fact, because it was a surprise. I had never thought of all that filth being under Dellie's house. It was not anything against Dellie that the stuff had been under the cabin. Trash will get under any house. But I did not think of that when I saw the foulness which had washed out on the ground which Dellie sometimes used to sweep with a twig broom to make nice and clean.

I picked my way past the filth, being careful not to get my bare feet on it, and mounted to Dellie's door. When I knocked, I heard her voice telling me to come in.

It was dark inside the cabin, after the daylight, but I could make out Dellie piled up in bed under a quilt, and Little Jebb crouched by the hearth, where a low fire simmered. "Howdy," I said to Dellie, "how you feeling?"

Her big eyes, the whites surprising and glaring in the black face, fixed on me as I stood there, but she did not reply. It did not look like Dellie, or act like Dellie, who would grumble and bustle around our kitchen, talking to herself, scolding me or Little Jebb, clanking pans, making all sorts of unnecessary noises and mutterings like an old-fashioned black steam thrasher engine when it has got up an extra head of steam and keeps popping the governor and rumbling and shaking on its wheels. But now Dellie just lay up there on the bed, under the patch-work quilt, and turned the black face, which I scarcely recognized, and the glaring white eyes to me.

"How you feeling?" I repeated.

"I'se sick," the voice said croakingly out of the strange black face which was not attached to Dellie's big, squat body, but stuck out from under a pile of tangled bedclothes. Then the voice added: "Mighty sick."

"I'm sorry," I managed to say.

The eyes remained fixed on me for a moment, then they left me and the head rolled back on the pillow. "Sorry," the voice said, in a flat way which wasn't question or statement of anything. It was just the empty word put into the air with no meaning or expression, to float off like a feather or a puff of smoke, while the big eyes, with the whites like the peeled white of hard-boiled eggs, stared at the ceiling.

"Dellie," I said after a minute, "there's a tramp up at the house. He's got a knife."

She was not listening. She closed her eyes.

I tiptoed over to the hearth where Jebb was and crouched beside him. We began to talk in low voices. I was asking him to get out his train and play train. Old Jebb had put spool wheels on three cigar boxes and put wire links between the boxes to make a train for Jebb. The box that was the locomotive had the top closed and a length of broom stick for a smoke stack. Jebb didn't want to get the train out, but I told him I would go home if he didn't. So he got out the train, and the colored rocks, and fossils of crinoid stems, and other junk he used for the load, and we began to push it around, talking the way we thought trainmen talked, making a chuck-chucking sound under the breath for the noise of the locomotive and now and then uttering low, cautious toots for the whistle. We got so interested in playing train that the toots got louder. Then, before he thought, Jebb gave a good, loud *toot-toot*, blowing for a crossing.

"Come here," the voice said from the bed.

Jebb got up slow from his hands and knees, giving me a sudden, naked, inimical look.

"Come here!" the voice said.

Jebb went to the bed. Dellie propped herself weakly up on one arm, muttering, "Come closer."

Jebb stood closer.

"Last thing I do, I'm gonna do it," Dellie said. "Done tole you to be quiet."

Then she slapped him. It was an awful slap, more awful for the kind of weakness which it came from and brought to focus. I had seen her slap Jebb before, but the slapping had always been the kind of easy slap you would expect from a good-natured, grumbling Negro woman like Dellie. But this was different. It was awful. It was so awful that Jebb didn't make a sound. The tears just popped out and ran down his face, and his breath came sharp, like gasps.

Dellie fell back. "Cain't even be sick," she said to the ceiling.

"Git sick and they won't even let you lay. They tromp all over you. Cain't even be sick." Then she closed her eyes.

I went out of the room. I almost ran getting to the door, and I did run across the porch and down the steps and across the yard, not caring whether or not I stepped on the filth which had washed out from under the cabin. I ran almost all the way home. Then I thought about my mother catching me with the bare feet. So I went down to the stables.

I heard a noise in the crib, and opened the door. There was Big Jebb, sitting on an old nail keg, shelling corn into a bushel basket. I went in, pulling the door shut behind me, and crouched on the floor near him. I crouched there for a couple of minutes before either of us spoke, and watched him shelling the corn.

He had very big hands, knotted and grayish at the joints, with calloused palms which seemed to be streaked with rust with the rust coming up between the fingers to show from the back. His hands were so strong and tough that he could take a big ear of corn and rip the grains right off the cob with the palm of his hand, all in one motion, like a machine. "Work long as me," he would say, "and the good Lawd'll give you a hand lak cass-ion won't nuthin' hurt." And his hands did look like cast iron, old cast iron streaked with rust.

He was an old man, up in his seventies, thirty years or more older than Dellie, but he was strong as a bull. He was a squat sort of man, heavy in the shoulders, with remarkably long arms, the kind of build they say the river natives have on the Congo from paddling so much in their boats. He had a round bullet-head, set on powerful shoulders. His skin was very black, and the thin hair on his head was now grizzled like tufts of old cotton batting. He had small eyes and a flat nose, not big, and the kindest and wisest old face in the world, the blunt, sad, wise face of an old animal peering tolerantly out on the goings-on of the merely human creatures before him. He was a good man, and I loved him next to my mother and father. I crouched there on the floor of the crib and watched him shell corn with the rusty cast-iron hands, while he looked down at me out of the little eyes set in the blunt face.

"Dellie says she's might sick," I said.

"Yeah," he said.

"What's she sick from?"

"Woman-mizry," he said.

"What's woman-mizry?"

"Hit comes on 'em," he said. "Hit just comes on 'em when the time comes."

"What is it?"

"Hit is the change," he said. "Hit is the change of life and time."

"What changes?"

"You too young to know."

"Tell me."

"Time come and you find out everthing."

I knew that there was no use in asking him any more. When I asked him things and he said that, I always knew that he would not tell me. So I continued to crouch there and watch him. Now that I had sat there a little while, I was cold again.

"What you shiver fer?" he asked me.

"I'm cold. I'm cold because it's blackberry winter," I said.

"Maybe 'tis and maybe 'tain't," he said.

"My mother says it is."

"Ain't sayen Miss Sallie doan know and ain't sayen she do. But folks doan know everthing."

"Why isn't it blackberry winter?"

"Too late fer blackberry winter. Blackberries done bloomed."

"She said it was."

"Blackberry winter just a leetle cold spell. Hit come and then hit go away, and hit is growed summer of a sudden lak a gunshot. Ain't no tellen hit will go way this time."

"It's June," I said.

"June," he replied with great contempt. "That what folks say. What June mean? Maybe hit is come cold to stay."

"Why?"

"Cause this-here old yearth is tahrd. Hit is tahrd and ain't gonna perduce. Lawd let hit come rain one time forty days and forty nights, 'cause He wus tahrd of sinful folks. Maybe this-here old yearth say to the Lawd, Lawd, I done plum tahrd, Lawd, lemme rest. And Lawd say, Yearth, you done yore best, you give 'em cawn and you give 'em taters, and all they think on is they gut, and, Yearth, you kin take a rest."

"What will happen?"

"Folks will eat up everthing. The yearth won't perduce no more. Folks cut down all the trees and burn 'em cause they cold, and the yearth won't grow no more. I been tellen 'em. I been tellen folks. Sayen, maybe this year, hit is the time. But they doan listen to me, how the yearth is tahrd. Maybe this year they find out."

"Will everything die?"

"Everthing and everbody, hit will be so."

"This year?"

"Ain't no tellen. Maybe this year."

"My mother said it is blackberry winter," I said confidently, and got up.

"Ain't sayen nuthin' agin Miss Sallie," he said.

I went to the door of the crib. I was really cold now. Running, I had got up a sweat and now I was worse.

I hung on the door, looking at Jebb, who was shelling corn again.

"There's a tramp came to the house," I said. I had almost forgotten the tramp.

"Yeah."

"He came by the back way. What was he doing down there in the storm?"

"They comes and they goes," he said, "and ain't no tellen."

"He had a mean knife."

"The good ones and the bad ones, they comes and they goes. Storm or sun, light or dark. They is folks and they comes and they goes lak folks."

I hung on the door, shivering.

He studied me a moment, then said, "You git on to the house. You ketch yore death. Then what yore mammy say?"

I hesitated.

"You git," he said.

When I came to the back yard, I saw that my father was standing by the back porch and the tramp was walking toward him. They began talking before I reached them, but I got there just as my father was saying, "I'm sorry, but I haven't got any work. I got all the hands on the place I need now. I won't need any extra until wheat thrashing."

The stranger made no reply, just looked at my father.

My father took out his leather coin purse, and got out a half-dollar. He held it toward the man. "This is for half a day," he said.

The man looked at the coin, and then at my father, making no motion to take the money. But that was the right amount. A dollar a day was what you paid them back in 1910. And the man hadn't even worked half a day.

Then the man reached out and took the coin. He dropped it into the right side pocket of his coat. Then he said, very slowly and without feeling: "I didn't want to work on your —— farm."

He used the word which they would have frailed me to death for using.

I looked at my father's face and it was streaked white under the sunburn. Then he said, "Get off this place. Get off this place or I won't be responsible."

The man dropped his right hand into his pants pocket. It was the pocket where he kept the knife. I was just about to yell to my father about the knife when the hand came back out with nothing in it. The man gave a kind of twisted grin, showing where the teeth had been knocked out above the new scar. I thought that instant how maybe he had tried before to pull a knife on somebody else and had got his teeth knocked out.

So now he just gave that twisted, sickish grin out of the unmemorable, grayish face, and then spat on the brick path. The glob landed just about six inches from the toe of my father's right boot. My father looked down at it, and so did I.

I thought that if the glob had hit my father's boot something would have happened. I looked down and saw the bright glob, and on one side of it my father's strong cowhide boots, with the brass eyelets and the leather thongs, heavy boots splashed with good red mud and set solid on the bricks, and on the other side the pointed-toe, broken, black shoes, on which the mud looked so sad and out of place. Then I saw one of the black shoes move a little, just a twitch first, then a real step backward.

The man moved in a quarter circle to the end of the porch, with my father's steady gaze upon him all the while. At the end of the porch, the man reached up to the shelf where the wash pans were to get his little newspaper-wrapped parcel. Then he disappeared around the corner of the house and my father mounted the porch and went into the kitchen without a word.

I followed around the house to see what the man would do. I wasn't afraid of him now, no matter if he did have the knife. When I got around in front, I saw him going out the yard gate and starting up the drive toward the pike. So I ran to catch up with him. He was sixty yards or so up the drive before I caught up.

I did not walk right up even with him at first, but trailed him, the way a kid will, about seven or eight feet behind, now and then running two or three steps in order to hold my place against his longer stride. When I first came up behind him, he turned to give me a look, just a meaningless look, and then fixed his eyes up the drive and kept on walking.

When we had got around the bend in the drive which cut the house from sight, and were going along by the edge of the woods, I decided to come up even with him. I ran a few steps, and was by his side, or almost, but some feet off to the right. I walked along in this position for a while, and he never noticed me. I walked along until we got within sight of the big gate that let on the pike.

Then I said: "Where did you come from?"

He looked at me then with a look which seemed almost

surprised that I was there. Then he said, "It ain't none of yore business."

We went on another fifty feet.

Then I said, "Where are you going?"

He stopped, studied me dispassionately for a moment, then suddenly took a step toward me and leaned his face down at me. The lips jerked back, but not in any grin, to show where the teeth were knocked out and to make the scar on the lower lip come white with the tension.

He said: "Stop following me. You don't stop following me and I cut yore throat, you little son-of-a-bitch."

Then he went on to the gate, and up the pike.

That was thirty-five years ago. Since that time my father and mother have died. I was still a boy, but a big boy, when my father got cut on the blade of a mowing machine and died of lockjaw. My mother sold the place and went to town to live with her sister. But she never took hold after my father's death, and she died within three years, right in middle life. My aunt always said, "Sallie just died of a broken heart, she was so devoted." Dellie is dead, too, but she died, I heard, quite a long time after we sold the farm.

As for Little Jebb, he grew up to be a mean and ficey Negro. He killed another Negro in a fight and got sent to the penitentiary, where he is yet, the last I heard tell. He probably grew up to be mean and ficey from just being picked on so much by the children of the other tenants, who were jealous of Jebb and Dellie for being thrifty and clever and being white-folks' niggers.

Old Jebb lived forever. I saw him ten years ago and he was about a hundred then, and not looking much different. He was living in town then, on relief—that was back in the Depression—when I went to see him. He said to me: "Too strong to die. When I was a young feller just comen on and seen how things wuz, I prayed the Lawd. I said, Oh, Lawd, gimme strength and meke me strong fer to do and to in-dure. The Lawd hearkened to my prayer. He give me strength. I was in-duren proud fer being strong and me much man. The Lawd give me my prayer and my strength. But now He done gone off and fergot me and left me alone with my strength. A man doan know what to pray fer, and him mortal."

Jebb is probably living yet, as far as I know.

That is what has happened since the morning when the tramp leaned his face down at me and showed his teeth and said: "Stop following me. You don't stop following me and I cut yore throat, you little son-of-a-bitch." That was what he said, for me not to follow him. But I did follow him, all the years.

When the Light Gets Green

MY GRANDFATHER had a long white beard and sat under the cedar tree. The beard, as a matter of fact, was not very long and not white, only gray, but when I was a child and was away from him at school during the winter, I would think of him, not seeing him in my mind's eye, and say: He has a long white beard. Therefore, it was a shock to me, on the first morning back home, to watch him lean over the dresser toward the wavy green mirror, which in his always shadowy room reflected things like deep water riffled by a little wind, and clip his gray beard to a point. It is gray and pointed, I would say then, remembering what I had thought before.

He turned his face to the green wavy glass, first one side and then the other in quarter profile, and lifted the long shears, which trembled a little, to cut the beard. His face being turned like that, with his good nose and pointed gray beard, he looked like General Robert E. Lee, without any white horse to ride. My grandfather had been a soldier, too, but now he wore blue-jean pants and when he leaned over like that toward the mirror, I couldn't help but notice how small his hips and backsides were. Only they weren't just small, they were shrunken. I noticed how the blue jeans hung loose from his suspenders and loose off his legs and down around his shoes. And in the morning when I noticed all this about his legs and backsides, I felt a tight feeling in my stomach like when you walk behind a woman and see the high heel of her shoe is worn and twisted and jerks her ankle every time she takes a step.

Always before my grandfather had finished clipping his beard, my Uncle Kirby came to the door and beat on it for breakfast. "I'll be down in just a minute, thank you, sir," my grandfather said. My uncle called him Mr. Barden. "Mr.

Barden, breakfast is ready." It was because my Uncle Kirby was not my real uncle, having married my Aunt Lucy, who lived with my grandfather. Then my grandfather put on a black vest and put his gold watch and chain in the vest and picked up his cob pipe from the dresser top, and he and I went down to breakfast, after Uncle Kirby was already downstairs.

When he came into the dining room, Aunt Lucy was sitting at the foot of the table with the iron coffee pot on a plate beside her. She said, "Good morning, Papa."

"Good morning, Lucy," he said, and sat down at the head of the table, taking one more big puff off his pipe before laying it beside his plate.

"You've brought that old pipe down to breakfast again," my aunt said, while she poured the bright-looking coffee into the cups.

"Don't it stink," he always said.

My uncle never talked at breakfast, but when my grandfather said that, my uncle always opened his lips to grin like a dog panting, and showed his hooked teeth. His teeth were yellow because he chewed tobacco, which my grandfather didn't do, although his beard was yellow around the mouth from smoking. Aunt Lucy didn't like my uncle to chew, that was the whole trouble. So she rode my grandfather for bringing his pipe down, all in fun at first before she got serious about it. But he always brought it down just the same, and said to her, "Don't it stink."

After we ate, my uncle got up and said, "I got to get going," and went out through the kitchen where the cook was knocking and sloshing around. If it had rained right and was a good tobacco-setting season, my grandfather went off with me down to the stable to get his mare, for he had to see the setting. We saddled up the mare and went across the lot, where limestone bunched out of the ground and cedar trees and blue grass grew out of the split rock. A branch of cold water with minnows in it went through the lot between rocks and under the cedar trees; it was where I used to play before

I got big enough to go to the river with the niggers to swim.

My grandfather rode across the lot and over the rise back of the house. He sat up pretty straight for an old man, holding the bridle in his left hand, and in his right hand a long hickory tobacco stick whittled down to make a walking cane. I walked behind him and watched the big straw hat he wore waggle a little above his narrow neck, or how he held the stick in the middle, firm and straight up like something carried in a parade, or how smooth and slow the muscles in the mare's flanks worked as she put each hoof down in the ground, going up hill. Sassafras bushes and blackberry bushes grew thick along the lane over the rise. In summer, tufts of hay would catch and hang on the dry bushes and showed that the hay wagons had been that way; but when we went that way in setting time, just after breakfast, the blackberry blooms were hardly gone, only a few rusty patches of white left, and the sassafras leaves showed still wet with dew or maybe the rain.

From the rise we could look back on the house. The shingles were black with damp, and the whitewash grayish, except in spots where the sun already struck it and it was drying. The tops of the cedar trees, too, were below us, very dark green and quiet. When we crossed the rise, there were the fields going down toward the river, all checked off and ready for setting, very even, only for the gullies where brush was piled to stop the washing. The fields were reddish from the wet, not yet steaming. Across them, the green woods and the sycamores showing white far off told where the river was.

The hands were standing at the edge of the field under the trees when we got there. The little niggers were filling their baskets with the wet plants to drop, and I got me a basket and filled it. My Uncle Kirby gave me fifty cents for dropping plants, but he didn't give the little niggers that much, I remember. The hands and women stood around waiting a minute, watching Uncle Kirby, who always fumed around, waving his dibble, his blue shirt already sticking to his arms with sweat. "Get the lead out," he said. The little niggers filled faster, grinning with their teeth at him. "Goddam, get the lead out!" My grandfather sat on his mare under the trees, still holding the walking cane, and said, "Why don't you start 'em, sir?"

Then, all of a sudden, they all moved out into the field, scattering out down the rows, the droppers first, and after a minute the setters, who lurched along, never straightening up, down the rows toward the river. I walked down my row, separating out the plants and dropping them at the hills, while it got hotter and the ground steamed. The sun broke out now and then, making my shadow on the ground, then the cloud would come again, and I could see its shadow drifting at me on the red field.

My grandfather rode very slow along the edge of the field to watch the setting, or stayed still under the trees. After a while, maybe about ten o'clock, he would leave and go home. I could see him riding the mare up the rise and then go over the rise; or if I was working the other way toward the river, when I turned round at the end, the lane would be empty and nothing on top the rise, with the cloudy, blue-gray sky low behind it.

The tobacco was all he cared about, now we didn't have any horses that were any real good. He had some silver cups, only one real silver one though, that his horses won at fairs, but all that was before I was born. The real silver one, the one he kept on his dresser and kept string and old minnie balls and pins and things in, had 1859 on it because his horse won it then before the War, when he was a young man. Uncle Kirby said horses were foolishness, and Grandfather said, yes, he reckoned horses were foolishness, all right. So what he cared about now was the tobacco. One time he was a tobacco-buyer for three years, but after he bought a lot of tobacco and had it in his sheds, the sheds burned up on him. He didn't have enough insurance to do any good and he was a ruined man. After that all his children, he had all girls and his money was gone, said about him, "Papa's just visionary, he tried to be a tobacco-buyer but he's too visionary and not practical." But he always said, "All tobacco-buyers are sons-of-bitches, and three years is enough of a man's life for him to be a son-of-a-bitch, I reckon." Now he was old, the corn could get the rust or the hay get rained on for all he cared, it was Uncle Kirby's worry, but all summer, off and on, he had to go down to the tobacco field to watch them sucker or plow or worm, and sometimes he pulled a few suckers himself. And when a cloud would blow up black in summer, he got nervous as a cat, not knowing whether it was the rain they needed or maybe a hail storm coming that would cut the tobacco up bad.

Mornings he didn't go down to the field, he went out under the cedar tree where his chair was. Most of the time he took a book with him along with his pipe, for he was an inveterate reader. His being an inveterate reader was one of the things made his children say he was visionary. He read a lot until his eyes went bad the summer before he had his stroke, then after that, I read to him some, but not as much as I ought. He used to read out loud some from Macaulay's *History of England* or Gibbon's *Decline and Fall*, about Flodden Field or about how the Janizaries took Constantinople amid great slaughter and how the Turk surveyed the carnage and quoted from the Persian poet about the lizard keeping the courts of the mighty. My grandfather knew some poetry, too, and he said it to himself when he didn't have anything else to do. I lay on my back on the ground, feeling the grass cool and tickly on the back of my neck, and looked upside down into the cedar tree where the limbs were tangled and black-green like big hairy fern fronds with the sky blue all around, while he said some poetry. Like the "Isles of Greece, the Isles of Greece, where burning Sappho loved and sung." Or like "Roll on, thou deep and dark blue ocean, roll."

But he never read poetry, he just said what he already knew. He only read history and *Napoleon and His Marshals,* having been a soldier and fought in the War himself. He rode off and joined the cavalry, but he never told me whether he took the horse that won the real silver cup or not. He was with Forrest before Forrest was a general. He said Forrest was a great general, and if they had done what Forrest wanted and cleaned the country ahead of the Yankees, like the Russians beat Napoleon, they'd whipped the Yankees sure. He told me about Fort Donelson, how they fought in the winter woods, and how they got away with Forrest at night, splashing through the cold water. And how the dead men looked in the river bottoms in winter, and I lay on my back on the grass, looking up in the thick cedar limbs, and thought how it was to be dead.

After Shiloh was fought and they pushed the Yankees down in the river, my grandfather was a captain, for he raised a cavalry company of his own out of West Tennessee. He was a captain, but he never got promoted after the War; when I was a little boy everybody still called him Captain Barden, though they called lots of other people in our section Colonel and Major. One time I said to him: "Grandpa, did you ever kill any Yankees?" He said: "God-a-Mighty, how do I know?" So, being little, I thought he was just a captain because he never killed anybody, and I was ashamed. He talked about how they took Fort Pillow, and the drunk niggers under the bluff. And one time he said niggers couldn't stand a charge or stand the cold steel, so I thought maybe he killed some of them. But then I thought, Niggers don't count, maybe.

He only talked much in the morning. Almost every afternoon right after dinner, he went to sleep in his chair, with his hands curled up in his lap, one of them holding the pipe that still sent up a little smoke in the shadow, and his head propped back on the tree trunk. His mouth hung open, and under the hairs of his mustache, all yellow with nicotine, you could see his black teeth and his lips that were wet and pink like a baby's. Usually I remember him that way, asleep.

I remember him that way, or else trampling up and down the front porch, nervous as a cat, while a cloud blew up and the trees began to rustle. He tapped his walking cane on the boards and whistled through his teeth with his breath and kept looking off at the sky where the cloud and sometimes the lightning was. Then of a sudden it came, and if it was

rain he used to go up to his room and lie down; but if it came
hail on the tobacco, he stayed on the front porch, not trampling any more, and watched the hail rattle off the roof and
bounce soft on the grass. "God-a-Mighty," he always said,
"bigger'n minnie balls," even when it wasn't so big.

In 1914, just before the war began, it was a hot summer
with the tobacco mighty good but needing rain. And when
the dry spell broke and a cloud blew up, my grandfather
came out on the front porch, watching it like that. It was
mighty still, with lightning way off, so far you couldn't hardly
hear the thunder. Then the leaves began to ruffle like they
do when the light gets green, and my grandfather said to me,
"Son, it's gonna hail." And he stood still. Down in the pasture,
that far off, you could see the cattle bunching up and the
white horse charging across the pasture, looking bright, for
the sun was shining bright before the cloud struck it all at
once. "It's gonna hail," my grandfather said. It was dark, with
jagged lightning and the thunder high and steady. And there
the hail was.

He just turned around and went in the house. I watched
the hail bouncing, then I heard a noise and my aunt yelled.
I ran back in the dining room where the noise was, and my
grandfather was lying on the floor with the old silver pitcher
he dropped and a broken glass. We tried to drag him, but he
was too heavy; then my Uncle Kirby came up wet from the
stable and we carried my grandfather upstairs and put him
on his bed. My aunt tried to call the doctor even if the lightning might hit the telephone. I stayed back in the dining
room and picked up the broken glass and the pitcher and
wiped up the floor with a rag. After a while Dr. Blake came
from town; then he went away.

When Dr. Blake was gone, I went upstairs to see my grandfather. I shut the door and went in his room, which was almost
dark, like always, and quiet because the hail didn't beat on
the roof any more. He was lying on his back in the feather-
bed, with a sheet pulled up over him, lying there in the dark.
He had his hands curled loose on his stomach, like when he

went to sleep in his chair holding the pipe. I sat on a split-bottom chair by the bed and looked at him: he had his eyes shut and his mouth hung loose, but you couldn't hear his breathing. Then I quit looking at him and looked round the room, my eyes getting used to the shadow. I could see his pants on the floor, and the silver cup on the dresser by the mirror, which was green and wavy like water.

When he said something, I almost jumped out of my skin, hearing his voice like that. He said, "Son, I'm gonna die." I tried to say something, but I couldn't. And he waited, then he said, "I'm on borrowed time, it's time to die." I said, "No!" so sudden and loud I jumped. He waited a long time and said, "It's time to die. Nobody loves me." I tried to say, "Grandpa, I love you." And then I did say it all right, feeling like it hadn't been me said it, and knowing all of a sudden it was a lie, because I didn't feel anything. He just lay there; and I went downstairs.

It was sunshiny in the yard, the clouds gone, but the grass was wet. I walked down toward the gate, rubbing my bare feet over the slick cold grass. A hen was in the yard and she kept trying to peck up a piece of hail, like a fool chicken will do after it hails; but every time she pecked, it bounced away from her over the green grass. I leaned against the gate, noticing the ground on one side the posts, close up, was still dry and dusty. I wondered if the tobacco was cut up bad, because Uncle Kirby had gone to see. And while I looked through the gate down across the pasture where everything in the sun was green and shiny with wet and the cattle grazed, I thought about my grandfather, not feeling anything. But I said out loud anyway, "Grandpa, I love you."

My grandfather lived four more years. The year after his stroke they sold the farm and moved away, so I didn't stay with them any more. My grandfather died in 1918, just before the news came that my Uncle Kirby was killed in France, and my aunt had to go to work in a store. I got the letter about my grandfather, who died of flu, but I thought about four years back, and it didn't matter much.

Christmas Gift

THE BIG white flakes sank down from the sagging sky. A wet gray light hung over everything; and the flakes looked gray against it, then turned white as they sank toward the dark earth. The roofs of the few houses along the road looked sogged and black. The man who sat in the wagon that moved slowly up the road wore an old quilt wrapped around his shoulders and a corduroy cap pulled down to his eyes. His ears stuck out from under the cap, thin as paper and lined with purplish veins. Before him, vanishing, the flakes touched the backs of the mules, which steamed and were black like wet iron.

When the man spoke to the boy on the seat beside him, the ends of his mustache twitched the amber drops that clung to it. "You kin git off at the store," he said.

The boy nodded his head, which looked tight and small under the rusty-felt man's hat he wore.

The hoofs of the mules cracked the skim ice in the ruts, and pale yellow mud oozed up around the fetlocks. The wagon wheels turned laboriously, crackling the ice with a sound like paper.

The man pulled on the reins, and the mules stopped, their heads hanging under the sparse downward drift of flakes. "Whoa," he said, after the mules had already stopped. He pointed his thumb toward the frame building set beside the road. "You kin git off here, son," he said. "Most like they kin tell you here."

The boy climbed over the side of the wagon, set his foot on the hub, and jumped. His feet sank in the half-frozen, viscous mud. Turning, he took a step toward the building, then stopped. "Much obliged," he said, and started on. For a moment the man peered after him from small red-rimmed eyes.

He jerked the reins. "Giddap," he said, and the mules lay against the traces, their hoofs crackling the skim ice.

The boy mounted the steps to the sloping boards of the porch and put his sharp gray clawlike fingers on the latch bar. Very quietly he pushed the door inward a little space, slipped through the opening, and closed the door, letting the latch back down without a sound. He looked down the shadowy corridor of the store between the shelves of cans and boxes and the clothing hung on racks against the other wall. At the end of the corridor some men sat, their bodies in huddled outline against the red glow of the stove.

With hesitant steps the boy approached them, stopping just behind the circle. A big man, whose belly popped the broad leather belt he wore, let his chair come forward to rest on the floor, and surveyed him. "What kin I do for you today, buddy?" he said.

The tight skin of the boy's face puckered grayly toward the lips, and his Adam's apple twitched up his throat. The big man kept on looking at the boy, who stood dumbly beyond the circle, the oversize mackinaw hanging to his knees, and shook his head at the big man.

"You wanter git warmed up?" the big man said.

The boy shook his head again.

"Naw, sir," he managed.

"You look cold," the big man said. "You come round here." He motioned to the open space in front of the stove.

Eyes fixed in question on the big man's face, the boy obeyed the gesture. He came round, carefully stepping over a man's outthrust leg. He stood inside the circle, about six feet from the stove, and spread his hands out to it.

"Git up closter," the big man said. "Git yore bottom up to hit."

The boy moved forward and turned his back to the stove, his hands behind him working weakly toward the warmth. The men kept looking at him. Steam from the mackinaw rose up against the stove, with the sick smell of hot, wet wool.

"Now ain't that better?" the big man demanded.

The boy nodded at him.

"Who are you, pardner?" one of the men said.

The boy turned toward him. He was a short stocky man, bald and swarthy, and he sat with his booted legs bunched under him like an animal ready to spring.

"I know who he is. I've seen him," another man said. "He's one of Milt Alley's kids."

Another man beyond the stove leaned forward, bucking his chair nearer to the boy. "Now ain't that nice," he said. "Pleased ter meet you. So you're one of Milt's little bastards."

The bald swarthy man glared at him. "Shut up!" he ordered abruptly.

The other man leaned elaborately back and studied the ceiling, whistling softly between his teeth.

"In doing yore Satiday trading?" the bald swarthy one said.

The boy shook his head. Then he looked at the big man. "I wanter git the docter."

"That's what he's for," the big man admitted and blinked at the stove.

"Yore folks sick?" the bald swarthy man said.

"My sister," the boy said, "she's gonna have a baby."

The man who was whistling stopped. "Yore little sister, buddy?" He addressed the ceiling in mock solicitude and shook his head. "Them Alleys allus did calf young."

"Hit's my big sister," the boy said to the bald man. "She come up here last summer. She ain't nuthin' but my sister on my ma's side."

"Well, well," said the man who was looking at the ceiling. He let his chair thump down on the front legs and spoke to no one in particular. "So they's gonna be another little bastard out to Milt's place."

The bald swarthy man stared glumly across at the speaker. "Bill Stover," he commented with no feeling, "you gonna make me stomp hell outer you 'fore sun."

The boy glanced quickly from one to the other. The bald swarthy man stared across the space, his legs bunched under him. The other man grinned and winked sidewise.

"I oughter do it now," the bald swarthy one said as if to himself.

The other stopped grinning.

"If you want the doc," the big man said, "you go up the road four houses on the right-hand side. It ain't no piece. That's where Doc Small lives. They's a office in his front yard right smack on the road, but you go up to the house, that's where he is."

"Hit's a chicken office," one of the men said. "That's where the doc keeps his chickens now going on twenty years."

"You ain't gonna miss hit," the big man said.

The boy came out of the circle and stopped before the big man. He looked up with a quick, furtive motion of the head. "Much obliged," he said. He pulled his mackinaw about him, taking up the slack in the garment, and moved down the corridor toward the door.

"Wait a minute," the big man called after him. He got up ponderously to his feet, hitched his belt up on his belly, and went forward to the single glass showcase. The men watched him, craning their necks, all except the bald swarthy one, who crouched and stared at the red bulge of the stove.

The big man reached into the glass showcase and took out a half dozen sticks of red-striped candy. He thrust them at the boy, who, looking suspiciously at the objects, shook his head.

"Take 'em," the man ordered.

The boy kept his hands in the pockets of the mackinaw. "I ain't got nuthin' ter pay fer it with," he said.

"Here, take 'em, buddy," the man said.

The boy reached out his hand uneasily, all the while studying the man's face, which was without expression. The fingers, scaled gray by cold like a bird's claw, closed on the candy, jerked back, clutching the sticks. The hand holding the candy slipped into the loose mackinaw pocket.

"Beat it," the big man said, "afore they beat hell outer you at home."

The boy slipped out the door, quick and quiet as a cat.

The big man came back to the stove and sank morosely into his chair. He tilted it back and put his arms behind his head, on which the thin brown hair was slickly parted.

"You sick, Al?" one of the men said to him.

He did not answer.

"You must be sick, giving something away just offhand like that."

Bill Stover again leaned forward, wet his lips, and winked at the man who spoke. He himself seemed about to speak. Then he saw the face of the bald swarthy man, whose dark eyes burned with a kind of indolent savagery.

"You go straight to hell," the big man was wearily saying.

The snow had almost stopped. It was getting colder now. The flakes were smaller now, drawing downward breathlessly like bits of white lint. They clung to the soaked grass by the road and lay on the frozen mud. The boy's feet cracked the skim ice on the mud, then, in withdrawal, made a sucking sound.

Two hundred yards up the road he came to the place. Jutting on the road, the one-room frame building stood beside a big cedar. A tin sign, obscured by rust and weather, was nailed to the door, carrying the words: *Doctor A. P. Small, Office.* The boy turned up the path by the cedar, whose black boughs swooped down toward the bare ground. The house was set far back from the road, half hidden by trellises to which leafless, horny vines clutched and curled. The windows of the house gave blankly, without reflection, on the yard where grass stuck stiffly up from dirty ice-curdled pools at the roots. The door had a glass pane in it; behind the glass a lace curtain hung like a great coarse cobweb.

He tapped the paintless wood of the door.

It was a woman who at last opened the door.

"What do you want, boy?" she said.

"I wanter git the docter," he said.

She said, "Clean your feet and come in," and abruptly turned down the low hall. He scraped his shoes, stooped to wipe them with his fingers, and then, wringing the mud from his hands, wiped them on the mackinaw. He followed her, with quick secret glances from one side to the other. She was standing before a door, her thin arm pointing inward. "You come in here," she ordered. He stood back from the hearth while the woman thrust her hands nervously at the blaze. She was a little woman, and while she warmed her hands she kept looking over her shoulder at him with a wry, birdlike asperity. "What's the matter?" she said.

"My sister's gonna have a baby," he said.

"Who are you, boy?"

"Sill Alley's my name, m'am," he said, looking at her little hands which approached and jerked from the bright blaze.

"Oh," she said. She turned fully at him, inspected him sharply from head to foot. "You ought to take off your hat when you come in the house, boy," she said.

He took the big hat off his head and, standing before her, held it tightly in both hands.

She nodded at him; said, "Wait a minute"; and was gone out the door.

With a dubious, inquiring step, as on suspected ice, he went across the straw matting toward the hearth and put his back to the fire. He looked at all the objects in the room, covertly spying on them as though they had a life of their own: the gilt iron bed covered by a lace counterpane, the unpainted rocking chairs with colored pillows on the seats, which were pulled up to the hearth, the table on which stood a basket full of socks rolled up in neat balls. The fire spat and sputtered in mild sibilance, eating at the chunks of sawn wood on the hearth. And the clock, its face supported by plump cupids of painted china, ticked with a small busy sound. The boy laid his hat on the yellow cushion of one of the chairs and put his hands to the fire. Against the plump little cushion, its color so bright, the hat was big and dirty. With hands still stretched out, the boy regarded it. It was soggy black with wet flecks of mud clinging to it; at the creases it was worn through. The boy took it quickly off the chair.

With that neat industrious sound the clock kept ticking.

"Hello, son," the man at the door said.

The man was buttoning up a brown overcoat that dropped to his ankles. Beneath the coat his small booted feet stuck out. The woman slipped in past him and came to the fire, put her hands toward the blaze again, jerked them back, all the while looking at the boy. The man pulled a black fur cap on his head and turned down the ear flaps. "Let's go," he said.

The woman went up to him, touching his breast with a quick indecisive motion as when she spread her hands to the fire.

"Don't wait up for me," he said.

He put his face down, a sharp expressionless face that seemed inconsequential under the big fur cap; and the woman kissed his cheek. Her kiss made a neat, dry sound, like a click.

"Let's go," he said.

He went into the hall, the boy following to the door of the room, where the woman stood aside to let him pass. He paused an instant at the threshold. "Much obliged," he said to her and slipped down the hall after the man like a shadow.

A horse and buggy, the curtains up, stood beyond the cedar at the corner of the office. The powdery flakes of snow drifted cautiously downward, were lost in the dark branches of the tree, on the road where the horse stood, head down in patience.

"You get in," the man said and went around to the driver's side. The boy climbed into the buggy, slipping under the curtain. The man got in and bent to fasten the curtain flap on his side. "You fix 'em over here," he said and picked up the reins. The boy fumbled with the metal catch, the man, reins in hand, watching him. "Don't you know nothing, son?" he said.

"I ain't never fixed one afore," the boy said.

The man thrust the reins into the boy's hands, leaned across his knees to latch the curtain, straightened up, and took the reins as though lifting them from a peg. "You pull that rug off the seat back of you," he said, "and give it here."

The boy obeyed, unfolding the rug. The man took an end, jabbed it under his thigh and wrapped it around the outside leg. "Now fix yourself up over there," he ordered. He shook out the reins through the slit in the curtain.

The horse swung into the road, the front wheel groaning and scraping with the short turn, the buggy jerking sidewise over the ruts. The buggy straightened out and drew more easily. The hoofs crunched and sloshed, the wheels turning.

"That's right, ain't it?" the doctor said. "We go outer the settlement this-a-way?"

"Yes, sir," the boy said.

"I thought I recollected it so."

They drew past the store. A man went down the steps and started to walk up the road, walking with a plunging, unsteady stride, plowing the mud. His high shoulders hunched and swayed forward.

"John Graber." The doctor jerked his mittened thumb toward the man. "He better be gitting on home, his woman sick like she is." He shook his head, the sharp features without expression. "A mighty sick woman. Kidneys," he said.

"Yes, sir," the boy said.

"Graber'll be cooking his own supper 'fore long."

They passed the last house, a small gray house set in the open field. Yellow gullies ran across the field, bald plateaus of snow-smeared sod between gully and gully. A mule stood close to the barbed-wire fence which separated the field from the road, and the fine flakes sank in the field and the gullies. From the chimney of the house a line of smoke stood up very still amid the descending flakes.

"Graber's house," the doctor said.

The boy sat up straight and peered through the isinglass panels at the house and smoke and the gutted field.

"Do I turn off up the creek?" the doctor asked.

"Yes, sir."

They crossed the wood bridge, where the timbers creaked and rattled loosely with the turning wheels. Beneath it the swollen water plunged between limestone rocks, sucking the yellow foam. The flakes touched the spewing foam, the water plunging with a hollow constant sound.

"What's your pappy doing now?" the doctor said.

"My pappy's croppin' on a place fer Mr. Porsum, but hit ain't no good."

"Uh-huh," the man grunted. He looked through the isinglass front. They had turned off the main road up the road by the creek. On one side the limestone stuck out from the bluff side, thin gray icicles hanging from the gray stone among the shriveled fern fronds. The creek below the dead growth of the gorge on the other side made its hollow sound.

"Hit ain't worth nuthin'. Cain't even grow sassafras on hit."

"Uh-huh," the man said.

"We be leaving this year. We ain't gonna have no truck no more with Mr. Porsum, that ole son of a bitch. He ain't done nuthin' like he said. He ain't—"

"That's what your pappy says," the man said.

"My pappy says he's a goddam sheep-snitchin' son-a-bitch."

The man stared through the isinglass pane, his sharp nose and chin sticking out in front, his head wobbling with the motion of the buggy. Then he opened his mouth: "I reckon Jim Porsum's got something to say on his side."

The boy stole a glance at the man's face, then relapsed to the motion of the buggy. Out of the red mess of the road, limestone poked, gray and slick like wet bone, streaked with red mud. The wheels surmounted the stone, jolting down beyond on the brittle mud. On the bluff side the cedars hung. Their thick roots thrust from the rotten crevices of stone, the roots black with moss, garnished with ice; their tops cut off the light.

The man handed the reins over to the boy. "Hold 'em," he said.

The boy drew his hands from under the rug and held the reins. He grasped them very tight with both hands, the knuckles chapped and tight, and peered through the isinglass panel at the horse; the head of the horse, under the cedars, bobbed up and down.

Clamping his mittens between his knees, the man rolled a cigarette. His breath, as he licked the paper, came frostily out from his mouth in a thin parody of smoke. He lighted the cigarette; then, as he reached for the reins, he found the boy observing him, observing the twisted paper that hung from his lips. He did not put the tobacco sack in his pocket, but, after a moment of hesitation, held it toward the boy. "All right," he said, "go on and take it."

The boy shook his head, watching the sack.

"Aw, hell," the man said and dropped the sack on the boy's lap.

The boy took the sack without assurance, adjusted the paper, poured tobacco into it. Biting the string with his teeth, big square teeth irregularly set in the tight mouth, he pulled the sack together and dropped it. Then he lifted the paper to his lips; the tip of his tongue darted out between his lips, strangely quick from the stolid, pinched face, and licked the edge of the paper. With that delicacy of motion, with the sharp gray fingers bunched like claws together to hold the bit of paper to his mouth, the boy, crouching there in the dim interior, looked at that instant like a small coon intently feeding.

He took a deep drag of the smoke, the end of the cigarette shriveling with the sucking coal, and his thin chest expanded under the cloth of the mackinaw.

Balancing the sack in his mittened hand, the doctor regarded the process. The smoke drifted colorless from the boy's nostrils, which were red and flattened. "You ought not to do it," the doctor said, "and you just a kid like you are."

"I'm ten," the boy said.

"It's gonna stunt your growth all right."

"Hit never stunted my pappy's growth none, and he's been a-smokin' ever since he was eight. He's big. Ain't you never seen him?"

The doctor looked at the lips which puckered grayly to the twist of paper, the pale eyes set close together under the man-size hat. The cigarettes, the man's and the boy's, glowed indecisively in the shadow. "I've seen him all right," the man said at length.

"He's a plenty strong son-a-bitch," the boy said.

The man pushed his cigarette through a crack in the curtain and sank back. His torso, swathed in the heavy overcoat, rolled and jerked to the impact of rut or stone like some lifeless object in uneasy water. Down the gorge, like the sound of wind driving through woods, the creek maintained its hollow constant plunging. "I didn't know Milt Alley had any girl big enough to be having babies yet," the man said.

"He ain't. Not I knows anything about."

"You said your sister, didn't you?"

"She's my sister on my maw's side. That's what she says and that's what my maw says."

The live cigarette, burned almost to the very end, hung at the corner of the boy's lips, glowing fitfully and faintly with his speech. It hung there, untouched by his hands, which were thrust under the rug. He no longer drew the smoke in; it seemed to seep in without conscious effort on his part, drifting from his nostrils thinly with his breath.

"She just come up here last summer," the boy said. "I never knowed nuthin' 'bout her afore that. Maw was glad ter see her, I reckin. At first, I reckin."

"Uh-huh," the man said absently, his sharp features fixed forward apparently without attention.

"But pappy warn't, he just raised holy hell fer sartin. She just worked round the house and never said nuthin' ter nobody. 'Cept ter me and the kids. Then Pappy got so he didn't pay her no mind ter speak of."

The cigarette burned close to the lip, the paper untwisting so that bits of red ash slipped from it and fell toward the rug. The boy withdrew one hand from beneath the rug and, with thumb and forefinger pinched together, removed the cigarette. The paper had stuck to the flesh of the lip; he jerked it free, licking the place with that strange darting motion of the tongue tip. The tongue was pink and damp against the dry gray flesh of the lips. "Then she up and got sick and she's gonna have a baby," he said.

"So that's why she's up here," the man said.

The boy shook his head. "I dunno," he said. "She just come."

In the gloom of the buggy, their bodies, one long and lax against the back of the seat, the other short and upright, jerked and swayed.

The road climbed a little. The bluff wall lost its steepness, falling to heaps of detritus among boulders. No cedars showed here, only stalks of weeds and the wiry strands of vine showing on the broken surface. Then the road went down again, swinging away from the creek. There was no further sound of water.

At the foot of the slight grade the bottom spread out: bare cornfields with stubble and shocks that disintegrated to the ground, rail fences lapped by the leafless undergrowth. Away to the left a log house stood black under bare black trees. From it the somnolent smoke ascended, twined white and gray against the gray sky. The snow had stopped.

Beyond the bottoms the knobs looked cold and smoky. From them, and from the defiles, fingers of mist, white to their blackness, crooked downward toward the bare land. The horizon rim, fading, sustained a smoky wreath that faded upward to the space without sun.

They drew toward the lane that led to the log house.

"You go on past here," the boy said. "Hit's up them knobs."

The boy, almost surreptitiously, took a stick of candy from his pocket, broke off half, and stuck it between his lips. He looked at the man's sharp expressionless profile. Then he held out a piece to him. Without a word the man took it and stuck it between his lips, sucking it.

They moved forward between the empty fields.

Goodwood Comes Back

LUKE GOODWOOD always could play baseball, but I never could, to speak of. I was little for my age then, but well along in my studies and didn't want to play with the boys my size; I wanted to play with the boys in my class, and if it hadn't been for Luke, I never would have been able to. He was a pitcher then, like he has always been, and so he would say, "Aw, let him field." When he was pitching, it didn't matter much who was fielding, anyway, because there weren't going to be any hits to amount to anything in the first place. I used to play catcher some, too, because I had the best mitt, but he pitched a mighty hard ball and it used to fool the batter all right, but it fooled me too a good part of the time so I didn't hold them so good. Also, I was a little shy about standing close up to the plate on account of the boys flinging the bat the way they did when they started off for first base. Joe Lancaster was the worst for that, and since he almost always played on the other side, being a good hitter to balance off Luke's pitching, I had to come close, nearly getting scared to death of him braining me when he did get a hit. Luke used to yell, "For Christ sake get up to that plate or let somebody else catch for Christ sake that can!"

Joe Lancaster wasn't much bigger than I was, but he was knotty and old-looking, with a white face and hair that was almost white like an old man's, but he wasn't exactly an albino. He was a silent and solemn kind of boy, but he could sure hit; I can remember how he used to give that ball a good solid crack, and start off running the bases with his short legs working fast like a fox terrier's trying to catch up with something, but his face not having any expression and looking like it was dead or was thinking about something else. I've been back home since and seen him in the restaurant where he works behind the counter. I'm bigger than he is now, for he never did grow much. He says hello exactly like a stranger that never saw you before and asks what you want. When he has his sleeves rolled up in the summertime, and puts an order on the counter for you, his arms are small like a boy's, still, with very white skin you can see the veins through.

It was Joe hit me in the head with a bat when I was catching. Luke ran up toward the plate, yelling, "You've killed him!"—for the bat knocked me clean over. It was the last time I played catcher; the next time I came out bringing my mitt, which was a good one, Luke said, "Gimme that mitt." He took it and gave it to another boy, and told me to go play field. That was the only thing I didn't like about Luke, his taking my mitt.

I stayed at the Goodwood house a lot, and liked it, even if it was so different from my own. It was like a farmhouse, outside and inside, but the town was growing out toward it, making it look peculiar set so far back off the street with barns and chicken yards behind it. There was Mr. Goodwood, who had been a sheriff once and who had a bullet in his game leg, they said, a big man one time, but now with his skin too big for him and hanging in folds. His mustache was yellow from the chewing tobacco he used and his eyes were bloodshot; some people said he was drinking himself to death, but I'll say this for him, he drank himself to death upstairs without making any fuss. He had four boys, and drink was their ruination. They say it was likker got Luke out of the big league, and none of the Goodwoods could ever leave the poison alone. Anyway, the Goodwood house was a man's house with six men sitting down to the table, counting the grandfather, and Mrs. Goodwood and her daughter going back and forth to the kitchen with sweat on their faces and their hair damp from the stove. There would be men's coats on the chairs in the living room, sometimes hunting coats with the old blood caked on the khaki, balls of twine and a revolver on the mantel-piece, and shotguns and flyrods lying around, even on the spare bed that was in the living room. And the bird dogs came in the house whenever they got good and ready. At my house everything was different, for men there always seemed to be just visiting.

Luke took me hunting with him, or sometimes one of his big brothers took us both, but my mother didn't like for me to go with the grown boys along, because she believed that their morals were not very good. I don't suppose their morals were much worse than ordinary for boys getting their sap up, but hearing them talk was certainly an education for a kid. Luke was as good a shot as you ever hope to see. He hunted a lot by himself, too, for my folks wouldn't let me go just all the time. He would get up before day and eat some cold bread and coffee in the kitchen and then be gone till after dark with his rifle or his shotgun. He never took anything to eat with him, either, for when he was hunting he was like they say the Indians were in that respect. Luke reminded you of an Indian, too, even when he was a boy and even if he was inclined to be a blond and not a brunette; he was long and rangy, had a big fine-cut nose, and looked to be setting his big feet always carefully on the ground, and came up on his toes a little, like a man testing his footing. He walked that way even on a concrete walk, probably from being in the woods so much. It was no wonder with all his hunting he never did study or make any good use and profit of his mind, which was better than most people's, however. The only good grades he made were in penmanship, copybooks still being used then in the grammar school part of school. He could make his writing look exactly like the writing at the top of the page, a Spencerian hand tilted forward, but not too much like a woman's. He could draw a bird with one line without taking the pencil off the paper once, and he'd draw them all afternoon in school sometimes. The birds all looked alike, all fine and rounded off like his Spencerian writing, their beaks always open, but not looking like any birds God ever made in this world. Sometimes he would put words coming out of a bird's bill, like "You bastard," or worse; then he would scratch it out, for he might just as well have signed his name to it, because the teachers and everybody knew how well he could draw a bird in that way he had.

Luke didn't finish high school. He didn't stop all at once, but just came less and less, coming only on bad days most of the time, for on good days he would be off hunting or fishing. It was so gradual, him not coming, that nobody, maybe not even the teachers, knew when he really stopped for good. In the summer he would lie around the house, sleeping out in the yard on the grass where it was shady, stretched out like a cat, with just a pair of old pants on. Or he would fish or play baseball. It got so he was playing baseball for little town teams around that section, and he picked up some change to buy shells and tackle.

That was the kind of life he was living when I finished school and left town. We had drifted apart, you might say, by that time, for he didn't fool around with the school kids any more. I never found out exactly how he broke into real baseball and got out of what you call the sand lot. My sister wrote me some big man in the business saw Luke pitch some little game somewhere and Luke was gone to pitch for a team up in Indiana somewhere. Then the next year he got on the sport page in the papers. My sister, knowing I would be interested in the boy that was my friend, you might say, used to find out about the write-ups and send me clippings when the home paper would copy stories about Luke from the big papers. She said Luke was making nine thousand dollars playing for the Athletics, which was in Philadelphia. The papers called him the Boy Wizard from Alabama. He must have been making a lot of money that year to judge from the presents he sent home. He sent his mother a five-hundred-dollar radio set and a piano, and I admired him for the way he remembered his mother, who had had a hard time and no doubt about it. I don't know why he sent the piano, because nobody at his house could play one. He also fixed up the house, which was in a bad shape by that time. Mr. Goodwood was still alive, but according to all reports he was spending more time upstairs than ever, and his other three boys never were worth a damn, not even for working in the garden, and didn't have enough git-up-and-git to even go fishing.

The next year Luke pitched in the World Series, for the team that bought him from the Athletics, in Philadelphia, and he got a bonus of three thousand dollars, plus his salary. But he must have hit the skids after that, drink being the reason that was reported to me. When he was home on vacation, my sister said he did some fishing and hunting, but pretty soon he was drunk all the time, and carousing around. The next year he didn't finish the season. My sister sent me a clipping about it, and wrote on the margin, "I'm sure you will be sorry to know this because I know you always liked Luke. I like Luke too." For a matter of fact, I never saw a woman who didn't like Luke, he was so good-looking and he had such a mixture of wildness and a sort of embarrassment around women. You never saw a finer-looking fellow in your life than he was going down the street in summer with nothing on except old khaki pants and underwear tops and his long arms and shoulders near the color of coffee and his blondish hair streaked golden color with sunburn. But he didn't have anything to do with girls, that is, decent girls, probably because he was too impatient. I don't suppose he ever had a regular date in his life.

But the next year he was back in baseball, but not in such a good team, for he had done some training and lived clean for a while before the season opened. He came back with great success, it looked like at first. I was mighty glad when I got a clipping from my sister with the headlines, *Goodwood Comes Back*. He was shutting them out right and left. But it didn't last. The drink got him, and he was out of the big-time game for good and all, clean as a whistle. Then he came back home.

It was on a visit home I saw him after all that time. I was visiting my sister, who was married and lived there, and I had taken a lawn mower down to the blacksmith shop to get it fixed for her. I was waiting out in front of the shop, leaning against one side of the door and looking out in the gravel street, which was sending up heat-dazzles. Two or three old men were sitting there, not even talking; they were the kind of old men you find sitting around town like that, who never did amount to a damn and whose names even people in town can't remember half the time. I saw Luke coming up the road with another boy, who didn't strike me as familiar right off because he was one of those who had grown up in the meantime. I could see they were both nearly drunk, when they got under the shade of the shed; and I noticed Luke's arms had got pretty stringy. I said hello to Luke, and he said, "Well, I'll be damned, how you making it?" I said, "Fine, how's it going?" Then he said, "Fine."

After they stood there a while I could see the other boy wasn't feeling any too good with the combination of whisky and the heat of the day. But Luke kept kidding him and trying to make him go up to the Goodwood house, where he said he had some more whisky. He said he had kept it under a setting hen's nest for two weeks to age, and the other boy said Luke never kept any whisky in his life two days, let alone two weeks, without drinking it up. It was bootleg whisky they were drinking, because Alabama was a dry state then, according to the law, even after repeal; Luke must have been kidding too, because he ought to know if anybody does, whisky don't age in glass whether it's under a setting hen or not. Then he tried to make the boy go up to Tangtown, which is what they call nigger town because of the immoral goings-on up there, where they could get some more whisky, he said, and maybe something else. The other boy said it wasn't decent in the middle of the afternoon. Then he asked me to go, but I said no thanks to the invitation, not ever having approved of that, and Tangtown especially, for it looks like to me a man ought to have more self-respect. The old men sitting there were taking in every word, probably jealous because they weren't good for drinking or anything any more.

Finally Luke and the other boy started up the road in the hot sun, going I don't know where, whether to his house or off to Tangtown in the middle of the afternoon. One of the old men said, "Now, ain't it a shame the way he's throwed away his chances." One of the others said likker always was hard on the Goodwoods. Luke, not being any piece off and having good ears even if he was drinking, must have heard them, for he stooped down and scooped up a rock from the road like a baseball player scooping up an easy grounder, and yelled, "Hey, see that telephone pole?" Then he threw the rock like a bullet and slammed the pole, which was a good way off. He turned around, grinning pretty sour, and yelled, "Still got control, boys!" Then the two of them went off.

It was more than a year before I saw him again, but he had been mentioned in letters from my sister, Mrs. Hargreave, who said that Luke was doing better and that his conduct was not so outrageous, as she put it. His mother's dying that year of cancer may have quieted him down some. And then he didn't have any money to buy whisky with. My sister said he was hunting again and in the summer pitching a little ball for the town team that played on Saturday and Sunday afternoons with the other teams from the towns around there. His pitching probably was still good enough to make the opposition look silly. But maybe not, either, as might be judged from what I heard the next time I saw him. I was sitting on the front porch of my sister's house, which is between the Goodwood house and what might be called the heart of town. It stands close up to the street without much yard like all the houses built since the street got to be a real street and not just a sort of road with a few houses scattered along it. Some men were putting in a concrete culvert just in front of the house, and since it was the middle of the day, they were sitting on the edge of the concrete walk eating their lunch and smoking. When Luke came along, he stopped to see what they were doing and got down in the ditch to inspect it. Although it was getting along in the season, there were still enough leaves on the vine on my sister's porch to hide me from the street, but I could hear every word they said. One of the workmen asked Luke when the next game would be. He said Sunday with Millville. When they asked him if he was going to win, he said he didn't know because Millville had a tough club to beat all right. I noticed on that trip home that the boys talked about their ball club, and not their ball team. It must have been Luke's influence. Then one of the men sitting on the curb said in a tone of voice that sounded righteous and false somehow in its encouragement, "We know you can beat 'em, boy!" For a minute Luke didn't say anything; then he said, "Thanks," pretty short, and turned off down the street, moving in that easy yet fast walk of his that always seemed not to be taking any effort.

It was a couple of days later when I was sitting in my sister's yard trying to cool off, that he came by and saw me there and just turned in at the gate. We said hello, just like we had been seeing each other every day for years, and he sat down in the other chair without waiting to be asked, just like an old friend, which he was. It wasn't long before he got out of the chair, though, and lay on the grass, just like he always used to do, lying relaxed all over just like an animal. I was a little bit embarrassed at first, I reckon, and maybe he was, too, for we hadn't sort of sat down together like that for near fifteen years, and he had been away and been a big league pitcher, at the top of his profession almost, and here he was back. He must have been thinking along the same lines, for after he had been there on the grass a while he gave a sort of laugh and said, "Well, we sure did have some pretty good times when we were kids going round this country with our guns, didn't we?" I said we sure did. I don't know whether Luke really liked to remember the times we had or whether he was just being polite and trying to get in touch with me again, so to speak.

Then he got to talking about the places he had been and the things he had seen. He said a man took him to a place in some city, Pittsburgh I believe it was, and showed him the biggest amount of radium there is in the world in one place. His mother having died of cancer not much more than a year before that day we were talking must have made him remember that. He told me how he shot alligators in Florida

and went deep-sea fishing. That was the only good time he
had away from home, he said, except the first year when the
Athletics farmed him out to a smaller team. I was getting
embarrassed when he started to talk about baseball, like you
will when somebody who has just had a death in the family
starts talking natural, like nothing had happened, about the
departed one. He said his first year in Pennsylvania he got
six hundred dollars a month from the club he was pitching
for, plus a little extra. "Being raised in a town like this," he
said, "a fellow don't know what to do with real money." So
he wrote home for them to crate up his bird dogs and express
them to him; which they did. He leased a farm to put his dogs
on and hired somebody to take care of them for him, because he couldn't be out there all the time, having his job
to attend to. Then he bought some more dogs, for he always
was crazy about dogs, and bought some Chinese ring-neck
pheasants to put on his farm. He said that was a good time,
but it didn't last.

He told me about some other pitchers too. There was one
who used to room with him when the club went on the road.
Every time they got to a new city, that pitcher made the
rounds of all the stores, then the boxes would begin coming
to the hotel room, full of electric trains and mechanical auto-
mobiles and boats, and that grown man would sit down and
play with them and after the game would hurry back so he
could play some more. Luke said his friend liked trains pretty
well, but boats best, and used to keep him awake half the
night splashing in the bathtub. There was another pitcher
up in Indiana who went to a roadhouse with Luke, where
they got drunk. They got thrown out of the place because that
other pitcher, who was a Polak, kept trying to dance with
other people's women. The Polak landed on a rock pile and
put his hand down and found all the rocks were just the
size of baseballs, and him a pitcher. He started breaking
windows, and stood everybody off till the cops came. But
Luke was gone by that time; so the police called up the hotel
to tell Luke there was a guy needed two thousand dollars

to get out of jail. So he and three other players went down and put up five hundred apiece to get the fellow out, who was sobered up by that time and wanted to go to bed and get some rest. Luke didn't know that fellow very well and when the Polak went off with the team to play some little game and Luke didn't go, he figured his five hundred was gone too. The fellow didn't come back with the team, either, for he had slipped off, so he figured he had really kissed his five hundred good-bye. But the night before the trial, about three o'clock in the morning, there was a hammering on the hotel-room door and before Luke could open it, somebody stuck a fist through the panel and opened it. And there was the Polak, wearing a four-bit tuxedo and patent-leather shoes and a derby hat, and his tie under one ear, drunk. He fell flat on the floor, clutching twenty-three hundred dollars' worth of bills in his hands. That Polak had gone back to the mines, having been a miner before he got in baseball, and had gambled for three days, and there he was to pay back the money as soon as he could. Luke said he wouldn't take money from a man who was drunk because the man might not remember and might want to pay him again when he got sober; so he got his the next morning. The fine and expense of fixing up the road-house wasn't as much as you'd expect, and the Polak had a good profit, unless a woman who got hit in the head with a rock and sued him got the rest. Luke didn't know how much she got. He said all pitchers are crazy as hell one way or another.

He told me about things that he saw or got mixed up with, but he said he never had a good time after he had to give up the farm where he had the dogs and the Chinese ring-neck pheasants. He said after that it wasn't so good any more, except for a little time in Florida, shooting alligators and fishing. He had been raised in the country, you see, and had the habit of getting up mighty early, with all that time on his hands till the game started or practice. For a while he used to go to the gymnasium in the mornings and take a work-out, but the manager caught on and stopped that because he wouldn't be fresh for the game. There wasn't anything to do in the mornings after that, he said, except pound the pavements by himself, everybody else still being asleep, or ride the lobbies, and he didn't have a taste for reading, not ever having cultivated his mind like he should. Most of the boys could sleep late, but he couldn't, being used to getting up before sun to go fishing or hunting or something. He said he could have stood the night drinking all right, it was the morning drinking got him down. Lying there on the grass, all relaxed, it didn't look like he gave a damn either.

He had his plans all worked out. If he could get hold of a few hundred dollars he was going to buy him a little patch of ground back in the country where it was cheap, and just farm a little and hunt and fish. I thought of old Mr. Bullard, an old bachelor who lived off in a cabin on the river and didn't even bother to do any farming any more, they said, or much fishing, either. I used to see him come in town on a Saturday afternoon, walking nine miles in just to sit around in the stores looking at people, but not talking to them, or, if the weather was good, just standing on the street. But Luke probably liked to hunt and fish better than Mr. Bullard ever did in his life, and that was something for a man to hold on to. I told Luke I hoped he got his farm, and that now was the time to buy while the depression was on and land was cheap as dirt. He laughed at that, thinking I was trying to make a joke, which I wasn't, and said, "Hell, a farm ain't nothing but dirt, anyway."

After lying there some more, having about talked himself out, he got up and remarked how he had to be shoving on. We shook hands in a formal way, this time, not like when he came in the yard. I wished him luck, and he said, "The same to you," and when he got outside the gate, he said, "So long, buddy."

About six months later he got married, much to my surprise. My sister wrote me about it and sent a clipping about it. His bride was a girl named Martha Sheppard, who is related to my family in a distant way, though Lord knows my sister wouldn't claim any kin with them. And I reckon they aren't much to brag on. The girl had a half-interest in a piece of land out in the country, in the real hoot-owl sticks, you might say, where she lived with her brother, who had the other half-share. I guessed at the time when I read the letter that Luke just married that girl because it was the only way he could see to get the little piece of ground he spoke of. I never saw the girl to my recollection, and don't know whether she was pretty or not.

I have noticed that people living way back in the country like that are apt to be different from ordinary people who see more varieties and kinds of people every day. That maybe accounts for the stories you read in papers about some farmer way back off the road getting up some morning and murdering his whole family before breakfast. They see the same faces every day till some little something gets to preying on their mind and they can't stand it. And it accounts for the way farmers get to brooding over some little falling-out with a neighbor and start bushwhacking each other with shotguns. After about a year Martha Sheppard's brother shot Luke. My sister wrote me the bad blood developed between them because Luke and his wife didn't get along so well together. I reckon she got to riding him about the way he spent his time, off hunting and all. Whatever it was, her brother shot Luke with Luke's own shotgun, in the kitchen one morning. He shot him three times. The gun was a .12-gauge pump gun, and you know what even one charge of a .12-gauge will do at close range like a kitchen.

The Patented Gate and the Mean Hamburger

YOU HAVE seen him a thousand times. You have seen him standing on the street corner on Saturday afternoon, in the little county-seat towns. He wears blue jean pants, or overalls washed to a pale pastel blue like the color of sky after a shower in spring, but because it is Saturday he has on a wool coat, an old one, perhaps the coat left from the suit he got married in a long time back. His long wrist bones hang out from the sleeves of the coat, the tendons showing along the bone like the dry twist of grapevine still corded on the stove-length of a hickory sapling you would find in his wood box beside his cookstove among the split chunks of gum and red oak. The big hands, with the knotted, cracked joints and the square, horn-thick nails, hang loose off the wrist bone like clumsy, home-made tools hung on the wall of a shed after work. If it is summer, he wears a straw hat with a wide brim, the straw fraying loose around the edge. If it is winter, he wears a felt hat, black once, but now weathered with streaks of dark gray and dull purple in the sunlight. His face is long and bony, the jawbone long under the drawn-in cheeks. The flesh along the jawbone is nicked in a couple of places where the unaccustomed razor has been drawn over the leather-coarse skin. A tiny bit of blood crusts brown where the nick is. The color of the face is red, a dull red like the red clay mud or clay dust which clings to the bottom of his pants and to the cast-iron-looking brogans on his feet, or a red like the color of a piece of hewed cedar which has been left in the weather. The face does not look alive. It seems to be molded from the clay or hewed from the cedar. When the jaw moves, once, with its deliberate, massive motion on the quid of tobacco, you are still not convinced. That motion is but the cunning triumph of a mechanism concealed within.

But you see the eyes. You see that the eyes are alive. They are pale blue or gray, set back under the deep brows and thorny eyebrows. They are not wide, but are squinched up like eyes accustomed to wind or sun or to measuring the stroke of the ax or to fixing the object over the rifle sights. When you pass, you see that the eyes are alive and are warily and dispassionately estimating you from the ambush of the thorny brows. Then you pass on, and he stands there in that stillness which is his gift.

With him may be standing two or three others like himself, but they are still, too. They do not talk. The young men, who will be like these men when they get to be fifty or sixty, are down at the beer parlor, carousing and laughing with a high, whickering laugh. But the men on the corner are long past all that. They are past many things. They have endured and will endure in their silence and wisdom. They will stand on the street corner and reject the world which passes under their level gaze as a rabble passes under the guns of a rocky citadel around whose base a slatternly town has assembled.

I had seen Jeff York a thousand times, or near, standing like that on the street corner in town, while the people flowed past him, under the distant and wary and dispassionate eyes in ambush. He would be waiting for his wife and the three tow-headed children who were walking around the town looking into store windows and at the people. After a while they would come back to him, and then, wordlessly, he would lead them to the store where they always did their trading. He would go first, marching with a steady bent-kneed stride, setting the cast-iron brogans down deliberately on the cement; then his wife, a small woman with covert, sidewise, curious glances for the world, would follow, and behind her the towheads bunched together in a dazed, glory-struck way. In the store, when their turn came, Jeff York would move to the counter, accept the clerk's greeting, and then bend down from his height to catch the whispered directions of his wife. He would straighten up and say, "Gimme a sack of flahr, if'n you please." Then when the sack of flour had been brought, he would lean again to his wife for the next item. When the stuff had all been bought and paid for with the grease-thick, wadded dollar bills which he took from an old leather coin purse with a metal catch to it, he would heave it all together into his arms and march out, his wife and towheads behind him and his eyes fixed level over the heads of the crowd. He would march down the street and around to the hitching lot where the wagons were, and put his stuff into his wagon and cover it with an old quilt to wait till he got ready to drive out to his place.

For Jeff York had a place. That was what made him different from the other men who looked like him and with whom he stood on the street corner on Saturday afternoon. They were croppers, but he, Jeff York, had a place. But he stood with them because his father had stood with their fathers and his grandfathers with their grandfathers, or with men like their fathers and grandfathers, in other towns, in settlements in the mountains, in towns beyond the mountains. They were the great-great-great-grandsons of men who, half woodsmen and half farmers, had been shoved into the sand hills, into the limestone hills, into the barrens, two hundred, two hundred and fifty years before and had learned there the way to grabble a life out of the sand and the stone. And when the soil had leached away into the sand or burnt off the stone, they went on west, walking with the bent-kneed stride over the mountains, their eyes squinching warily in the gaunt faces, the rifle over the crooked arm, hunting a new place.

But there was a curse on them. They only knew the life they knew, and that life did not belong to the fat bottom lands, where the cane was head-tall, and to the grassy meadows and the rich swale. So they passed those places by and hunted for the place which was like home and where they could pick up the old life, with the same feel in the bones and the squirrel's bark sounding the same after first light. They had walked a long way, to the sand hills of Alabama, to

the red country of North Mississippi and Louisiana, to the
Barrens of Tennessee, to the Knobs of Kentucky and the scrub
country of West Kentucky, to the Ozarks. Some of them had
stopped in Cobb County, Tennessee, in the hilly eastern part
of the county, and had built their cabins and dug up the
ground for the corn patch. But the land had washed away
there, too, and in the end they had come down out of the
high land into the bottoms—for half of Cobb County is a
rich, swelling country—where the corn was good and the tobacco unfurled a leaf like a yard of green velvet and the
white houses stood among the cedars and tulip trees and
maples. But they were not to live in the white houses with
the limestone chimneys set strong at the end of each gable.
No, they were to live in the shacks on the back of the farms,
or in cabins not much different from the cabins they had once
lived in two hundred years before over the mountains or,
later, in the hills of Cobb County. But the shacks and the
cabins now stood on somebody else's ground, and the curse
which they had brought with them over the mountain trail,
more precious than the bullet mold or grandma's quilt, the
curse which was the very feeling in the bones and the habit
in the hand, had come full circle.

Jeff York was one of those men, but he had broken the
curse. It had taken him more than thirty years to do it, from
the time when he was nothing but a big boy until he was
fifty. It had taken him from sun to sun, year in and year out,
and all the sweat in his body, and all the power of rejection
he could muster, until the very act of rejection had become
a kind of pleasure, a dark, secret, savage dissipation, like an
obsessing vice. But those years had given him his place, sixty
acres with a house and barn.

When he bought the place, it was not very good. The land
was run-down from years of neglect and abuse. But Jeff York
put brush in the gullies to stop the wash and planted clover
on the run-down fields. He mended the fences, rod by rod.
He patched the roof on the little house and propped up the
porch, buying the lumber and shingles almost piece by piece

and one by one as he could spare the sweat-bright and grease-slick quarters and half-dollars out of his leather purse. Then he painted the house. He painted it white, for he knew that that was the color you painted a house sitting back from the road with its couple of maples, beyond the clover field.

Last, he put up the gate. It was a patented gate, the kind you can ride up to and open by pulling on a pull rope without getting off your horse or out of your buggy or wagon. It had a high pair of posts, well braced and with a high cross-bar between, and the bars for the opening mechanism extending on each side. It was painted white, too. Jeff was even prouder of the gate than he was of the place. Lewis Simmons, who lived next to Jeff's place, swore he had seen Jeff come out after dark on a mule and ride in and out of that gate, back and forth, just for the pleasure of pulling on the rope and making the mechanism work. The gate was the seal Jeff York had put on all the years of sweat and rejection. He could sit on his porch on a Sunday afternoon in summer, before milking time, and look down the rise, down the winding dirt track, to the white gate beyond the clover, and know what he needed to know about all the years passed.

Meanwhile Jeff York had married and had had the three towheads. His wife was twenty years or so younger than he, a small, dark woman, who walked with her head bowed a little and from that humble and unprovoking posture stole sidewise, secret glances at the world from eyes which were brown or black—you never could tell which because you never remembered having looked her straight in the eye—and which were surprisingly bright in that sidewise, secret flicker, like the eyes of a small, cunning bird which surprise you from the brush. When they came to town she moved along the street, with a child in her arms or later with the three trailing behind her, and stole her looks at the world. She wore a calico dress, dun-colored, which hung loose to conceal whatever shape her thin body had, and in winter over the dress a brown wool coat with a scrap of fur at the collar which looked like some tattered growth of fungus feeding on old wood. She wore black high-heeled shoes, slippers of some kind, which she kept polished and which surprised you under that dress and coat. In the slippers she moved with a slightly limping, stealthy gait, almost sliding them along the pavement, as though she had not fully mastered the complicated trick required to use them properly. You knew that she wore them only when she came to town, that she carried them wrapped up in a piece of newspaper until their wagon had reached the first house on the outskirts of town, and that, on the way back, at the same point, she would take them off and wrap them up again and hold the bundle in her lap until she got home. If the weather happened to be bad, or if it was winter, she would have a pair of old brogans under the wagon seat.

It was not that Jeff York was a hard man and kept his wife in clothes that were as bad as those worn by the poorest of the women of the croppers. In fact, some of the cropper women, poor or not, black or white, managed to buy dresses with some color in them and proper hats, and went to the moving picture show on Saturday afternoon. But Jeff still owed a little money on his place, less than two hundred dollars, which he had had to borrow to rebuild his barn after it was struck by lightning. He had, in fact, never been entirely out of debt. He had lost a mule which had got out on the highway and been hit by a truck. That had set him back. One of his towheads had been sickly for a couple of winters. He had not been in deep, but he was not a man, with all those years of rejection behind him, to forget the meaning of those years. He was good enough to his family. Nobody ever said the contrary. But he was good to them in terms of all the years he had lived through. He did what he could afford. He bought the towheads a ten-cent bag of colored candy every Saturday afternoon for them to suck on during the ride home in the wagon, and the last thing before they left town, he always took the lot of them over to the dogwagon to get hamburgers and orange pop.

The towheads were crazy about hamburgers. And so was his wife, for that matter. You could tell it, even if she didn't say anything, for she would lift her bowed-forward head a little, and her face would brighten, and she would run her tongue out to wet her lips just as the plate with the hamburger would be set on the counter before her. But all those folks, like Jeff York and his family, like hamburgers, with pickle and onions and mustard and tomato catsup, the whole works. It is something different. They stay out in the country and eat hog-meat, when they can get it, and greens and corn bread and potatoes, and nothing but a pinch of salt to brighten it on the tongue, and when they get to town and get hold of beef and wheat bread and all the stuff to jack up the flavor, they have to swallow to keep the mouth from flooding before they even take the first bite.

So the last thing every Saturday, Jeff York would take his family over to Slick Hardin's *Dew Drop Inn Diner* and give them the treat. The diner was built like a railway coach, but it was set on a concrete foundation on a lot just off the main street of town. At each end the concrete was painted to show wheels. Slick Hardin kept the grass just in front of the place pretty well mowed and one or two summers he even had a couple of flower beds in the middle of that shirttail-size lawn. Slick had a good business. For a few years he had been a prelim fighter over in Nashville and had got his name in the papers a few times. So he was a kind of hero, with the air of romance about him. He had been born, however, right in town and, as soon as he had found out he wasn't ever going to be good enough to be a real fighter, he had come back home and started the dogwagon, the first one ever in town. He was a slick-skinned fellow, about thirty-five, prematurely bald, with his head slick all over. He had big eyes, pale blue and slick looking like agates. When he said something that he thought smart, he would roll his eyes around, slick in his head like marbles, to see who was laughing. Then he'd wink. He had done very well with his business, for despite the fact that he had picked up city ways and a lot of city talk, he still remembered enough to deal with the country people, and they were the ones who brought the dimes in. People who lived right there in town, except for school kids in the afternoon and the young toughs from the pool room or men on the night shift down at the railroad, didn't often get around to the dogwagon.

Slick Hardin was perhaps trying to be smart when he said what he did to Mrs. York. Perhaps he had forgotten, just for that moment, that people like Jeff York and his wife didn't like to be kidded, at least not in that way. He said what he did, and then grinned and rolled his eyes around to see if some of the other people present were thinking it was funny.

Mrs. York was sitting on a stool in front of the counter, flanked on one side by Jeff York and on the other by the three towheads. She had just sat down to wait for the hamburger—there were several orders in ahead of the York order—and had been watching in her sidewise fashion every move of Slick Hardin's hands as he patted the pink meat onto the hot slab and wiped the split buns over the greasy iron to make them ready to receive it. She always watched him like that, and when the hamburger was set before her she would wet her lips with her tongue.

That day Slick set the hamburger down in front of Mrs. York, and said, "Anybody likes hamburger much as you, Mrs. York, ought to git him a hamburger stand."

Mrs. York flushed up, and didn't say anything, staring at her plate. Slick rolled his eyes to see how it was going over, and somebody down the counter snickered. Slick looked back at the Yorks, and if he had not been so encouraged by the snicker he might, when he saw Jeff York's face, have hesitated before going on with his kidding. People like Jeff York are touchous, and they are especially touchous about the womenfolks, and you do not make jokes with or about their womenfolks unless it is perfectly plain that the joke is a very special kind of friendly joke. The snicker down the counter had defined the joke as not entirely friendly. Jeff was looking at Slick, and something was growing slowly in that hewed-cedar face, and back in the gray eyes in the ambush of thorny brows.

But Slick did not notice. The snicker had encouraged him,

and so he said, "Yeah, if I liked them hamburgers much as you, I'd buy me a hamburger stand. Fact, I'm selling this one. You want to buy it?"

There was another snicker, louder, and Jeff York, whose hamburger had been about half way to his mouth for another bite, laid it down deliberately on his plate. But whatever might have happened at that moment did not happen. It did not happen because Mrs. York lifted her flushed face, looked straight at Slick Hardin, swallowed hard to get down a piece of the hamburger or to master her nerve, and said in a sharp, strained voice, "You sellen this place?"

There was complete silence. Nobody had expected her to say anything. The chances were she had never said a word in that diner in the couple of hundred times she had been in it. She had come in with Jeff York and, when a stool had come vacant, had sat down, and Jeff had said, "Gimme five hamburgers, if'n you please, and make 'em well done, and five bottles of orange pop." Then, after the eating was over, he had always laid down seventy-five cents on the counter— that is, after there were five hamburger-eaters in the family— and walked out, putting his brogans down slow, and his wife and kids following without a word. But now she spoke up and asked the question, in that strained, artificial voice, and everybody, including her husband, looked at her with surprise.

As soon as he could take it in, Slick Hardin replied, "Yeah, I'm selling it."

She swallowed hard again, but this time it could not have been hamburger, and demanded, "What you asken fer hit?"

Slick looked at her in the new silence, half shrugged, a little contemptuously, and said, "Fourteen hundred and fifty dollars."

She looked back at him, while the blood ebbed from her face. "Hit's a lot of money," she said in a flat tone, and returned her gaze to the hamburger on her plate.

"Lady," Slick said defensively, "I got that much money tied up here. Look at that there stove. It is a *Heat Master* and they cost. Them coffee urns, now. Money can't buy no better. And this here lot, lady, the diner sets on. Anybody knows I got that much money tied up here. I got more. This lot cost me more'n . . ." He suddenly realized that she was not listening to him. And he must have realized, too, that she didn't have a dime in the world and couldn't buy his diner, and that he was making a fool of himself, defending his price. He stopped abruptly, shrugged his shoulders, and then swung his wide gaze down the counter to pick out somebody to wink to.

But before he got the wink off, Jeff York had said, "Mr. Hardin."

Slick looked at him and asked, "Yeah?"

"She didn't mean no harm," Jeff York said. "She didn't mean to be messen in yore business."

Slick shrugged. "Ain't no skin off my nose," he said. "Ain't no secret I'm selling out. My price ain't no secret neither."

Mrs. York bowed her head over her plate. She was chewing a mouthful of her hamburger with a slow, abstracted motion of her jaw, and you knew that it was flavorless on her tongue.

That was, of course, on a Saturday. On Thursday afternoon of the next week Slick was in the diner alone. It was the slack time, right in the middle of the afternoon. Slick, as he told it later, was wiping off the stove and wasn't noticing. He was sort of whistling to himself, he said. He had a way of whistling soft through his teeth. But he wasn't whistling loud, he said, not so loud he wouldn't have heard the door open or the steps if she hadn't come gum-shoeing in on him to stand there waiting in the middle of the floor until he turned round and was so surprised he nearly had heart failure. He had thought he was there alone, and there she was, watching every move he was making, like a cat watching a goldfish swim in a bowl.

"Howdy-do," he said, when he got his breath back.

"This place still fer sale?" she asked him.

"Yeah, lady," he said.

"What you asken fer hit?"

"Lady, I done told you," Slick replied, "fourteen hundred and fifty dollars."

"Hit's a heap of money," she said.

Slick started to tell her how much money he had tied up there, but before he had got going, she had turned and slipped out of the door.

"Yeah," Slick said later to the men who came into the diner, "me like a fool starting to tell her how much money I got tied up here when I knowed she didn't have a dime. That woman's crazy. She must walked that five or six miles in here just to ask me something she already knowed the answer to. And then turned right round and walked out. But I am selling me this place. I'm tired of slinging hash to them hicks. I got me some connections over in Nashville and I'm gonna open me a place over there. A cigar stand and about three pool tables and maybe some beer. I'll have me a sort of club in the back. You know, membership cards to git in, where the boys will play a little game. Just sociable. I got good connections over in Nashville. I'm selling this place. But that woman, she ain't got a dime. She ain't gonna buy it."

But she did.

On Saturday Jeff York led his family over to the diner. They ate hamburgers without a word and marched out. After they had gone, Slick said, "Looks like she ain't going to make the invest-mint. Gonna buy a block of bank stock instead." Then he rolled his eyes, located a brother down the counter, and winked.

It was almost the end of the next week before it happened. What had been going on inside the white house out on Jeff York's place nobody knew or was to know. Perhaps she just starved him out, just not doing the cooking or burning everything. Perhaps she just quit attending to the children properly and he had to come back tired from work and take care of them. Perhaps she just lay in bed at night and talked and talked to him, asking him to buy it, nagging him all night long, while he would fall asleep and then wake up with a start to hear her voice still going on. Or perhaps she just turned her face away from him and wouldn't let him touch her. He was a lot older than she, and she was probably the only woman he had ever had. He had been too ridden by his dream and his passion for rejection during all the years before to lay even a finger on a woman. So she had him there. Because he was a lot older and because he had never had another woman. But perhaps she used none of these methods. She was a small, dark, cunning woman, with a sidewise look from her lowered face, and she could have thought up ways of her own, no doubt.

Whatever she thought up, it worked. On Friday morning Jeff York went to the bank. He wanted to mortgage his place, he told Todd Sullivan, the president. He wanted fourteen hundred and fifty dollars, he said. Todd Sullivan would not let him have it. He already owed the bank one hundred and sixty dollars and the best he could get on a mortgage was eleven hundred dollars. That was in 1935 and then farmland wasn't worth much and half the land in the country was mortgaged anyway. Jeff York sat in the chair by Todd Sullivan's desk and didn't say anything. Eleven hundred dollars would not do him any good. Take off the hundred and sixty he owed and it wouldn't be but a little over nine hundred dollars clear to him. He sat there quietly for a minute, apparently turning that fact over in his head. Then Todd Sullivan asked him, "How much you say you need?"

Jeff York told him.

"What you want it for?" Todd Sullivan asked.

He told him that.

"I tell you," Todd Sullivan said, "I don't want to stand in the way of a man bettering himself. Never did. That diner ought to be a good proposition, all right, and I don't want to stand in your way if you want to come to town and better yourself. It will be a step up from that farm for you, and I like a man has got ambition. The bank can't lend you the money, not on that piece of property. But I tell you what I'll do. I'll buy your place. I got me some walking horses I'm keeping out on my father's place. But I could use me a little place of my own. For my horses. I'll give you seventeen hundred for it. Cash."

Jeff York did not say anything to that. He looked slow at Todd Sullivan as though he did not understand.

"Seventeen hundred," the banker repeated. "That's a good figure. For these times."

Jeff was not looking at him now. He was looking out the window, across the alleyway—Todd Sullivan's office was in the back of the bank. The banker, telling about it later when the doings of Jeff York had become for a moment a matter of interest, said, "I thought he hadn't even heard me. He looked like he was half asleep or something. I coughed to sort of wake him up. You know the way you do. I didn't want to rush him. You can't rush those people, you know. But I couldn't sit there all day. I had offered him a fair price."

It was, as a matter of fact, a fair price for the times, when the bottom was out of everything in the section.

Jeff York took it. He took the seventeen hundred dollars and bought the dogwagon with it, and rented a little house on the edge of town and moved in with his wife and the towheads. The first day after they got settled, Jeff York and his wife went over to the diner to get instructions from Slick about running the place. He showed Mrs. York all about how to work the coffee machine and the stove, and how to make up the sandwiches, and how to clean the place up after herself. She fried up hamburgers for all of them, herself, her husband, and Slick Hardin, for practice, and they ate the hamburgers while a couple of hangers-on watched them. "Lady," Slick said, for he had money in his pocket and was heading out for Nashville on the seven o'clock train that night, and was feeling expansive, "lady, you sure fling a mean hamburger."

He wiped the last crumbs and mustard off his lips, got his valise from behind the door, and said, "Lady, git in there and pitch. I hope you make a million hamburgers." Then he stepped out into the bright fall sunshine and walked away whistling up the street, whistling through his teeth and rolling his eyes as though there were somebody to wink to. That was the last anybody in town ever saw of Slick Hardin.

The next day, Jeff York worked all day down at the diner. He was scrubbing up the place inside and cleaning up the trash which had accumulated behind it. He burned all the trash. Then he gave the place a good coat of paint outside, white paint. That took him two days. Then he touched up the counter inside with varnish. He straightened up the sign out front, which had begun to sag a little. He had that place looking spick and span.

Then on the fifth day after they got settled—it was Sunday —he took a walk in the country. It was along toward sun when he started out, not late, as a matter of fact, for by October the days are shortening up. He walked out the Curtis-ville pike and out the cut-off leading to his farm. When he entered the cut-off, about a mile from his own place, it was still light enough for the Bowdoins, who had a filling station at the corner, to see him plain when he passed.

The next time anybody saw him was on Monday morning about six o'clock. A man taking milk into town saw him. He was hanging from the main cross bar of the white patented gate. He had jumped off the gate. But he had propped the thing open so there wouldn't be any chance of clambering back up on it if his neck didn't break when he jumped and he should happen to change his mind.

But that was an unnecessary precaution, as it developed. Dr. Stauffer said that his neck was broken very clean. "A man who can break a neck as clean as that could make a living at it," Dr. Stauffer said. And added, "If he's damned sure it ain't ever his own neck."

Mrs. York was much cut up by her husband's death. People were sympathetic and helpful, and out of a mixture of sympathy and curiosity she got a good starting trade at the diner. And the trade kept right on. She got so she didn't hang her head and look sidewise at you and the world. She would look straight at you. She got so she could walk in high heels without giving the impression that it was a trick she was learning. She wasn't a bad-looking woman, as a matter of fact, once she had caught on how to fix herself up a little. The railroad men and the pool hall gang liked to hang out there and kid with her. Also, they said, she flung a mean hamburger.

A Christian Education

MR. JIM NABB, who was a successful farmer and highly respected in our section, had about three hundred and fifty acres of first-rate land, a couple of big red barns, a big house painted red with the same kind of paint used on the barns, a big fat wife and a boy who wasn't right bright. He was a good man, everybody used to say, and from all reports I reckon he was. He was superintendent of the Sunday school at the Methodist church in town, and I can recollect the time when I was a boy and used to go to church and recollect him there every Sunday up in front leading the singing or making the announcements about how the Epworth League would meet that night at seven o'clock and would all the members please come because it would be an interesting meeting. He was almost what you might call a little man, but he stood up straight in his Sunday suit and he had a wide face too big for his body, his face being smooth and pink like a boy's, even if his clean-looking mustache was getting grayish. He didn't have either the bullying kind of voice or the tearful kind of voice like most people have who get up and talk a lot in public to show off, especially in church, and when he led the singing his voice would get up mighty high like a woman's or get swallowed up in the noise the other people made. But when he talked or made his announcements everybody listened close, even if his voice wasn't very strong, because he was so well respected in the community.

Mr. Nabb never smiled, that is, to speak of, but always had a sort of sad look on his face. He didn't have a sour look, just sad and resigned like he was carrying his cross, as the saying goes. Looking back now, I reckon he had that sad look on account of his boy not being very bright, which must be enough to make a man sad, especially when you've got a good piece of land and a house like his and money in the bank, but nobody to leave it all to when you pass on to the better world. I guess he wanted another child mighty bad, somebody who could take up where he left off, so to speak, and protect the one who wasn't very bright. I can remember the ladies talking about how Mrs. Nabb just couldn't get in a family way no matter what she tried, and her health wasn't too good anyway like it frequently isn't with those big fat women who ail all the time and are inclined to cry if you look at them. Mrs. Nabb used to start getting tearful in church sometimes at the least little thing, and sometimes just for nothing you could notice. Anyway, it took Mr. Nabb eleven more years before he got any results and there was another baby, which was a boy, too. Mrs. Nabb told the ladies it was just an answer to prayer and was like a miracle, and my mother told my father, and my father, sitting there at the dinner table, told her not to go talking about him that way if she ever got another child because it wasn't very flattering to Mr. Nabb.

When the second baby came Mr. Nabb didn't lose that sad look like you might think, even if now he did have what he had been praying for for such a long time. His face had probably just grown that way by that time, or maybe he wasn't sure the new one would turn out to be right bright either, for you can't tell when they're little, and he didn't want to be counting his chickens before they hatched. And by the time the new one, Alec Nabb, had got any size on him and you could tell he had good sense, something else happened to make Mr. Nabb look sad again.

Everybody always felt sorry for Mr. Nabb because he was a good man and tried to practice what he preached. A Christian education, he said, was the greatest thing in the world. And he tried to give his boy, the one who wasn't bright, a good raising, and it must be pretty hard to try to give a nitwit a good Christian education, when they look at you that way and are liable to slobber. When they look at you that way, you must feel like you are just pouring something valuable down the drain.

Silas Nabb wasn't really an idiot, he just wasn't right bright. He was in the same Sunday school class I was in, and got promoted when the time came, even if he couldn't answer questions. He could say the Golden Text sometimes, though, if he got a little prompting from his mother, who taught the class. When he got it all out, she used to look mighty pleased, and when he didn't and began to stare off at something else, the tears would start running down her cheeks. But he didn't get promoted in school after the first year or two, and after he was in the second grade for about three years his father took him out of school, which likely is the only advantage in being a nitwit.

But Silas learned one thing his people tried to teach him about being a good Christian. Mrs. Nabb used to try to teach us boys in Sunday school about a soft answer turning away wrath and about turning the other cheek when somebody was mean to you and about the meek inheriting the earth. That and about giving your money to the poor was what she tried hardest to hammer into us, but since we didn't have any money anyway, being just kids, we didn't have much trouble learning the second thing. What money our people gave us for Sunday school, we had to put in the collection anyway, for we would have caught hell if we hadn't. Silas always brought a dime to Sunday school, and he used to put it in his mouth and suck it until his mother made him stop. After a while she got so she would put it in his shirt pocket and pin up the pocket with a safety pin; then he would have trouble getting the pin out when the collection came and she would have to help him half the time. But he learned better than anybody about turning the other cheek.

The boys used to pester him a little bit just because they knew he wouldn't do anything about it or fight back. They never hit him or were real mean to him. They would just push him off the sidewalk out in front of the church when we were waiting for Sunday school to start; or maybe they would rub their knucks in his head a little, which if you ever had done to you, you know how unpleasant it is. It don't hurt, but it sure makes you mad. It is called the Dutch shampoo.

We used to get to Sunday school early because the only fun in going was to horse around outside before things got started. We would stand around out there in front in our good clothes, somebody sneaking up to pull somebody else's tie or mess somebody's hair up. Then somebody would see the Nabbs come driving up the street and everybody would straighten up and look innocent.

Mr. Nabb would be sitting up in front holding the reins, with Mrs. Nabb by his side. Silas would be on the back seat, leaning against the back and looking behind at the dust they raised. Mrs. Nabb would say good morning to all of us, calling us by our names, and then she would say to Silas, "Silas, don't you want to play with the boys?" Then she would leave him out there.

The boys weren't really mean to Silas. They just pestered him. They would push him off the sidewalk and make him step in the deep dust and get his shoes full of dust, or full of mud, if it was muddy. He would just say, "Don't," and come back on the sidewalk, and somebody would push him off again. Even the little kids would push him and I remember kids not more than four or five years old going up to push Silas when he was ten or twelve and big for his age. That was the funniest. Then somebody would say, "Silas, why don't you lam somebody for pushing you? I wouldn't let nobody push me like that." And maybe he would say, "God says not to fight." That is, if he said anything.

And somebody would say, "Did God say that? You know I didn't hear Him say nothing, or maybe I just misunderstood Him."

But nobody ever got any rise out of Silas, except maybe to make him cry. If he cried, everybody would get afraid he would tell and they would wipe his nose and comfort him to make him stop. I used to get plain disgusted sometimes, and after I got any size on me, I never pushed him myself because I got so I didn't approve of it somehow. But it was funny when the real little kids pushed him. But sometimes I used to wish Silas would knock hell out of somebody.

There used to be a big Sunday school picnic every summer. All the women would fix up stuff to eat, fried chicken and boiled ham and deviled eggs and beaten biscuits and lemon pie and chess pie and salt-rising bread and tea in fruit jars. And they would carry a lot of ice wrapped up in tow sacks to make iced tea and to keep the ice cream good.

The summer that Silas was about thirteen or fourteen years old, Mr. Nabb asked them to have the picnic out at his place, which for a matter of fact was a right good place for a picnic. There was a big pond or sort of lake on his place, not just a stock pond with mud and manure tramped around the edges, but one with nice trees and some thickets you could hide in, and there was good grass all around the pond. And there was a good rowboat people used for fishing, though Mr. Nabb himself didn't fish any. He just kept the boat there for people who liked to fish, which was one of the things that made Mr. Nabb so highly respected in the community.

We had the picnic out there under the trees. It was July and hot, but it was cool in the shade with a nice breeze. After the ladies got everything fixed out nice on the tables, we all came up and stood around while Mr. Nabb returned thanks for the blessings God had bestowed upon us. Then we got paper plates and paper napkins and the ladies gave us helpings of everything. We ate all we could hold, but there was always a lot left over, because no lady likes to have people think she's stingy. Mr. Nabb always suggested they ought to give what was left to the poor, which they did.

We ate all we could, and then we lay around a little letting it settle. But it don't take long for food to settle on a kid's stomach, and so pretty soon we got to horsing around and playing games, playing "high spy" in the thickets and behind the trees. Then somebody, Joe Sykes I believe it was, said to me. "Let's go out in that boat." So some of us pushed the boat out and got in. Then Silas Nabb came down and wanted to go too. Mrs. Nabb didn't want him to go, but Mr. Nabb came down and said it would do Silas good to go, and asked us very politely did we mind. It being Mr. Nabb's boat, what could we say? So we said, "Sure."

We rowed around out there in the pond some, but rowing around in a pond never is as much fun as you think it is before you start, unless you're fishing or something. And the sun was bearing down too. The trouble was there just wasn't anything to do sitting out there in a boat in the sun, so the boys got to telling Silas dirty jokes like they did sometimes or teaching him dirty words. They would ask him dirty questions and no matter what he said, whether he said yes or no or what, it would sound funny, coming from a nitwit that way. Then the smallest boy in the boat, Ben Tupper, who was about nine years old maybe, got to pestering Silas. He was sitting behind Silas in the boat and he would pull the short hair on the back of Silas' neck a little or take his shirttail out behind. We told him to stop, but it just made him worse. And all the time we were drifting around out there in the hot sun.

Little Ben Tupper wouldn't stop, so one of the bigger boys said, "Ben, I'm gonna slap your teeth down your throat if you don't stop." But after a minute he kept right on. He would pull out Silas' shirttail and say, "Silas, what does God say?" But Silas never said anything the whole time.

I guess it was the sun bearing down and Silas being so crowded up with people in the boat that made him do it. And that boat was too full anyway. But Ben Tupper kept on pestering him, and saying, "Silas, what does God say?" All of a sudden I noticed Silas had a little pocketknife in his hand, which his father didn't have any better sense than to give him one Christmas. So I yelled, "Ben!" But it didn't do any good, for just that second Ben was jerking at the short hair on the back of Silas' neck again. And Silas swung round with that knife open to make a pass at Ben. One of the big boys up front near Silas made a grab for his arm, and got stabbed in the hand, and yelled, "God damn you!" And little Ben Tupper, just scared to death, jumped up and fell back to get out of the way. Mrs. Nabb way back on shore must have seen something was up, because I can remember hearing her voice coming across the water saying, "Silas! Silas!" Maybe she caught the sunshine on that knife. But one of the other boys made a grab for Silas and maybe hit him accidentally or something, or maybe it was because little Ben started the boat to rocking so bad, but all of a sudden Silas hit the water and splashed everybody in the boat wringing wet.

You know how it is when somebody dives out of a boat, it sends the boat away a piece, too. Well, Silas fell out of the boat the same way, and by the time we stopped the boat rocking we were more than fifteen feet away. Silas came back up to the top of the water and began to yell and splash, and I saw he couldn't swim. I was a pretty good swimmer, and I always figured I would like to save somebody's life sometime and be a hero, but when I saw him go down again, I just didn't move a muscle even if I did hear a voice in my head plain as day, saying, *He's going to drown.*

One of the oars was lost and was floating around near Silas, but he didn't see it or didn't have sense enough to grab it, though somebody yelled to him to grab it. We paddled with the other oar and with our hands trying to get to him, but the boat was heavy, and we didn't make it. We just sat there looking at the place a minute. Then somebody said, "He's drowned." And the Tupper kid began to cry.

We got the other oar and started back to the shore. That was all we could do, and while we rowed in we could hear Mrs. Nabb's voice screaming, "Silas! Silas!" We didn't look at her as we rowed in.

By the time we got there she had fainted and they had dragged her back from the shore a piece, and the ladies were working on her. But there was Mr. Nabb and the other men standing there around him on the shore, watching us come. One of the men walked out in the water toward us and said: "Boys, get outer that boat. We got out, and the men climbed in, Mr. Nabb too. Then one of the men said to me, "Get your pants and shirt off and get in here." And I did, though for just a minute I couldn't think what for. Then I knew I was going to have to dive for that body. That man knew I could swim and dive pretty good. So we rowed back out to the place as near as we could tell, Mr. Nabb sitting on the seat in the boat, gone mighty white in the face and not saying anything and not crying. One of the men said, "If we can get him up right quick maybe there's some breath in him." But Mr. Nabb said, "No, it's God's will."

When we got out there, one of the men said: "Is this the place?"

I said, "I reckon so."

"All right," he said. He didn't say for me to dive, he just said, "All right." So I stood up, feeling the sun hitting me on the back of my neck and between my shoulder blades, and got ready to dive. I didn't look at Mr. Nabb. The men held the oars in the water to steady the boat, and I dived. I was so nervous or something I didn't get a good breath before I hit the water, and so I didn't get to bottom before I had to come up. One of the men helped me climb in the boat. None of them said a word, just sitting there in the sun.

The next time I got bottom. I went down fast, swimming breast stroke down, and I felt my hand touch bottom, for it was so deep it was dark. The bottom of a pond is the softest place in the world and dark deep down, not water and not mud, just like velvet in the dark, only softer, and when my hand touched bottom that time, just for a split second I thought how nice it would be to lie there, it was so soft, and look up trying to see where the light made the water green. Then I got scared, and I swam for the top and popped out of the water with my ears roaring and the light sudden like an explosion.

I kept on diving. I likely dived near fifty times I guess, and I got bottom a lot of times. One time I touched the body on the face, and I made a grab for something to hold to, but I missed, and I couldn't see in the dark. When I touched that face, I felt like screaming, but you can't scream under water but once. When I missed, I came back on up.

After a while I got so tired out I couldn't get in the boat hardly. The last time, they had to pull me in and I couldn't move. I said I would dive again in a minute, but Mr. Nabb said, "No. And thank you, Son."

They rowed back in and took me out of the boat. Somebody had telephoned town, and some big boys and men had come on out to get the body. A young fellow named Spooner dived down and got it. He got it on his third try, but that was just luck to get it so soon. I was sick at my stomach and my head was about to pop open from diving so much. In a way I was glad I didn't get the body, for if I had been the one to get it up, Mr. Nabb might have thought I was good enough to save Silas when he fell in. I was so sick I didn't even see them carry the body to the house. I just heard voices, but I didn't care. After a while people wrapped me up in a blanket they got and carried me home.

It was mighty hard on Mr. and Mrs. Nabb having a tragedy like that in the family, I reckon. In some ways I reckon it is worse to have a nitwit die on your hands than somebody with good sense, because you feel more responsible. But some people said it was a blessing in the long run, Silas being afflicted like he was. And the Nabbs had Alec, who wasn't but about three years old then.

Alec turned out to have good sense, all right. And they never tried to teach him about turning the other cheek like they did Silas. Somebody must have told them how the boys imposed on Silas because Silas never hit back. Alec turned out to be a terror. He wasn't very big, taking after his father, but he was a terror. He wouldn't take anything off nobody, and he always had a chip on his shoulder. The older he got, the worse he got that way. And he kept fast company too. When he was about twenty-two he got in a row and shot a man with a .38. The man died. Alec is over in Nashville in the pen now, and I guess he'll be there a good long time.

The Love of Elsie Barton:
A Chronicle

SHE WAS SO still and withered that no one who saw her now walking up the street of the little town ever bothered to remember. Morning and evening, she went back and forth between her own house, the house where she had been born fifty years before, and Mr. Allen's feed store, where she kept the books, a small woman wearing a baggy man's sweater, her feet making a quick and incongruous clacking sound on the pavement, her small head, with its tight knot of hair at the back, thrust a little forward, her face peculiarly still with the stillness of water carried in an old pail, miraculously without a glint or quiver despite the quick step. Sometimes, but not often, when somebody spoke to her on the street, saying, "Howdy-do, Miss Elsie," the surface might lighten and riffle a little as though the pail had been tapped or jostled, but even at the moment, the stillness returned and she passed on, going to the store or, if it was evening, going home, to enter the house which nobody else had entered in nearly fifteen years.

Once there, she would shut the door and draw the shades, and all anybody passing could see would be the little line of light around a shade. If it was summer, they wouldn't even be able to see that, for the house would be dark except for the few minutes when she was preparing for bed. But people passing would know that Miss Elsie was sitting on her porch behind the screen of moonvine. What she did behind the moonvine or in the house, they didn't know or think about.

Except for one thing. They knew that she ate standing up. "She eats out of cans," they said, "and never a decent meal. Just stuff out of cans."

But that was the women, for that particular kind of comment was beneath a man's dignity. The women said it with a mixture of pity and censure due to any woman who was so aimless or lazy or thriftless as to fail to perform the rite of preparing a proper meal, hungry or not, alone or not. They knew that she would stand in her kitchen and eat something out of a can with a spoon, or would stand by the safe, perhaps without bothering to turn the light on, and eat a piece of bread with butter on it. Light bread, too, they said, out of the store, for Miss Elsie never made bread at home or baked biscuits. "Just light bread," they would say, "and stale as like as not, a loaf laying up there as long as it'd take her by herself to eat it."

That was the only thing worth commenting on about her now: the kind of bread she ate. For everything else had been forgotten, or if not forgotten, it had been so covered by the detritus of all the subsequent life of the town that only the very old and the very idle had the patience to shuffle it up from its depth. People scarcely remembered that she had been Elsie Barton, and they had called her "Miss Elsie" so long now that they had almost forgotten that she was, in fact, Mrs. Beaumont, and had almost forgotten who Benjamin Beaumont was, who had come to the town, had married Elsie Barton, had prospered for a time, and then gradually had taken to drink and loose women, and had died of a stroke, in a hotel room over in Nashville, where he had gone, as the rumor had it, "to have him a high old time, and you bet it wasn't the first one, neither." The body had been brought back to the town, the funeral had been preached, with emphasis on mercy rather than justice, the grave had been filled in, and the widow's face had been as expressionless as wax as she stood by the grave, clutching the hand of the weeping ten-year-old daughter (who favored the father, people said).

So Benjamin Beaumont, who had come to the town from up in Kentucky, and into Elsie Barton's life, was gone, and the weeds grew ranker, year by year, on his grave, for she never tended it. "Never even a flower," they said, "and him her husband, even if he did kick up dirt in her face." They said that, for it was, in a fashion, a kind of warped and back-hand glory for a woman to put flowers on the grave of a husband who had kicked up dirt in her face. But that fact, too, was forgotten with the years. And it was as though there had never been a Benjamin Beaumont, just Miss Elsie and the little girl.

And then all at once the little girl was a big girl, with the plain school dress tight across her new breasts and long curly brown hair and a sudden way of looking straight into your eyes which took you by surprise like a blow, for the girl had always been a quiet one, like her mother, and had walked with eyes down on the pavement. "Just like her pappy," they said now, "she's got her pappy's look"; for suddenly with the girl grown up among them, like spring come all at once after the last cold spell, they remembered how Benjamin Beaumont had had that straight look. So Benjamin Beaumont lived again briefly in the town's memory because the girl had that straight, surprising look.

Then the girl was gone. There was no real reason for her to go. It was true that half the boys and young men had been wild over her, there was no doubt about it, but after any party, and she did not go to many, she always went straight home, and the boy was left standing at the gate when she went in to join her mother behind the moonvine, if it was summer, or behind the drawn shade, if it was winter. It was true, too, that she had taken up with that Frank Barber, who was nearly fifteen years older than she and whose pay as the railroad detective never bought that big black car he drove, and who was, they said, mixed up some way in bootlegging. But nobody really had anything on him, and certainly, nobody had anything on her, though there was some loose talk that winter and spring when she was still in high school that she was going for rides with Frank Barber in the big car. People said they bet he was making some time and he wasn't riding out in the country to see how the crops were coming.

But in early summer she suddenly stopped going with him. It was clear that she had thrown him over and he hadn't thrown her over, for a couple of times people saw him try to pick her up in his car when she was walking down the street. Then one evening about dusk in July, he stopped her on the main street and argued with her and when she wouldn't come, he took her by the arm. She jerked away and almost ran the thirty yards to Mr. Allen's feed store, where her mother was working late.

Old Mr. Dick Bailey saw it. He was sitting under the iron awning of the drug store with another man, taking the cool, not twenty feet from where Frank Barber and Helen Beaumont were standing. He came over to Frank Barber and said, "Frank, you ever bother that girl again and I'll pump your guts full of lead. So help me God." Old Mr. Bailey was one of those big, rocky old men that time slows down but doesn't dent. He never was a man for saying much, but he owned three good farms and a lot of bank stock, and had a name for meaning what he said when he got around to saying something. So Frank Barber never bothered the girl again, and as for other people, since old Mr. Bailey was the man he was, what he said had the effect of shutting up talk and of adopting Helen Beaumont back into the town.

She stayed on the rest of the summer, but she never had any more dates, not with anybody. The boys and the young men tried to take her out, but she turned them all down. She was by herself at home behind the moonvines, or somewhere back in the dark house with her mother. Then, just as the leaves began to turn, she left. There was no reason, but suddenly, without warning, she left on a night train, and never came back. Her mother did not even go to the station with her. The people in Charlestown never knew why she left.

So the mother, Elsie Beaumont, was left alone at last. The letters from St. Louis, from Chicago, from Detroit, from Buffalo, came less and less frequently. People ceased to ask her on the street how Helen was getting along. The girl had had jobs in the far-off cities. The girl had married. A child had been born to her. They had learned those things and then forgotten them. Then they forgot the girl. They forgot Benjamin Beaumont again. They had long since forgotten the scandal about Elsie Beaumont herself. For one reason, seeing her as she was passing them down the street, the small woman in a man's sweater, no one could believe the old story even though he knew it to be true. The truth had to be untrue, for this woman could have no story. Nothing could ever have happened to her. She was obviously invulnerable and immortal. If she had a story it was the fact that she had no story. So the life of Elsie Beaumont, who had been Elsie Barton, slowly achieved its perfect form, like a crystal growing, according to its ineluctable pattern, in a solution kept in a still bottle. That was all.

Mrs. Beaumont, who had been Elsie Barton, did not differ in origin from the other women who had been summoned to happier and fuller destinies in the community of Charlestown, Tennessee. She was of good stock, men and women who, generally speaking, had been healthy, vigorous, honest, moderately intelligent, and moderately literate. Her father, a native of Georgia, had risen from the ranks to be brevet colonel on the late, blundering, bloody, and wasteful battlefields out of Atlanta. After the war he had come as far north as Charlestown, Tennessee, where he finally opened a store, married a local girl, and lived the remainder of his life without recrimination or bitterness, amiable and somewhat baffled to the end. Occasionally, toward the twilight of his life when his prosperity, never beyond the ordinary scale of the community, began to wane, he might remark, "Maybe I oughter gone on farther north to get a start. It looks like folks does better farther north. But hind sight is better'n foresight."

He was a clean old man, loving his daughter and his wife, who died some time before him of a tetanus contracted from the cut of a rusty butcher knife, an old man with few regrets and few memories. His amiability survived even the disgrace and marriage of his daughter. It was, as a matter of fact, scarcely a disgrace, at least not in any public sense. It was merely that his daughter had married suddenly and unexpectedly, under peculiar circumstances, and had not come back to

Charlestown for more than a year afterwards. She had then come back with her baby, the pretty baby named Helen—had almost slipped back, unnoticed, into the life of the town; for that was her way to enter even a room, her feet not making any noise and her shoulders turned a little sidewise as though to offer less of a target for whatever eyes might be leveled at her.

She might, in fact, have slipped in unnoticed, if it had not been for a drummer who worked the north Tennessee territory for a wholesale hardware company up in Louisville, a drummer who knew Benjamin Beaumont and who knew another drummer who worked the territory up in Kentucky where Benjamin's father lived. He had picked up some garbled bit of news about the birth of a baby long before the return to Charlestown. That started the talk. But the talk might have started anyway, sooner or later, for the old women of Charlestown could give one searching look at a baby and tell its age to the week with the same certainty with which they could estimate to the ounce the weight of meat on a leg of lamb at the butcher shop.

There was talk, but it was not quite public talk, and old Mr. Barton did not have to face it. He could surmise what was said. He could catch the curious glances that fixed on the bowed head of his daughter between him and her husband in church. He could almost hear the stillness that fell over a group when he approached. But the disgrace was not public. It was not public because the menfolks were a little afraid of trouble with Benjamin Beaumont. They sensed, behind his easy good humor and jaunty air, a cold capacity for violence. And they liked old Mr. Barton. So they restrained their righteous wives and their envious daughters, and the disgrace was not public. Elsie Beaumont simply came home to live, for a time, in a limbo of whispers, a land of sidelong glances. And though that was all, old Mr. Barton took some comfort from the fact that his wife was dead. She would have worried about things, but he could stand them.

In the remaining two years of his life he went to his store

as usual every day except Sunday, and in the evening fell
asleep in his chair or went to his daughter's rented house,
where, not talking much, he held his infant granddaughter on
his lap and felt, as he smoothed the silky hair beneath his
stubby, gnarled fingers, that all that had ever happened to
him had been a sad, somehow sweet dream, not very clearly
remembered. Once or twice, when left alone with the child,
he wished it were old enough for him to talk seriously to it.
He felt that he had something to tell it.

He died, however, before the child was old enough to understand what he might have to tell, what prop and wisdom
he might have to leave, even if he could have found words for
it. He died and left his daughter, with her child and husband, to live out her life in Charlestown.

There was every reason why Mrs. Beaumont should have
been like the other women in Charlestown. As a girl she could
not tell that her people were different from their people.
Whether clean old men or not clean, richer or poorer than her
father, older or younger, amiable or soured, their fathers were
like her father, the same kind of people. And their mothers,
too, were like her mother. As a girl she lived the same kind of
life the others lived, going to school with them, wearing the
same kind of dresses they had, going to the Baptist Church
with her parents and then, when she was older, sitting with
the other girls during the sermon. When she was seventeen,
her parents put her in a girls' seminary in a town up in Kentucky, a school run by the Baptist Church with the president
a retired preacher who wore well-pressed black suits and had
a combed white beard, and who prayed in chapel every
morning and told the girls that they were on the threshold of
life. Since it was the first time she had ever been away from
home, she did not like the new existence at first, but after a
time the routine seemed so natural and appropriate that she
could conceive of nothing else. She woke to the sound of a
bell, went to the cold chapel, went to her classes, went downtown with other girls and a woman teacher, studied in the
evenings the books she did not understand, and walked up

the dingy hall arm in arm with her room-mate, whom she did not really like very much but whom she kissed every night before she put on her white cotton nightgown and got into the hard and chilly bed.

Going away to school was the only thing that set her off from the girls she knew at home, for only one other girl, Emmeline Tupper, had gone away like this. Her own father could not really afford it, but it seemed to him the proper symbol of his love for her. Then the summer after her first year in the seminary, her mother died of the cut from the rusty butcher knife, and she did not go back to school, but stayed to keep house for her father. She ran the house competently, made dresses for herself, went to Nashville every spring and fall when her father went to buy stock for the store, visited the girls in town, but had no intimates among them, and occasionally attended the picnics or parties given by the young people. It was a period of unlaborious order in her life, and of small excitements, excitements long since swallowed in time except for the random recollections now and then provoked by the presence of some article in the house that had survived from those days. She was not a sentimental person, and when the echo of some old excitement or pleasure came to mind, she automatically put it from her, never seeking to probe into the lost context and never pondering on what forfeited era of content and innocence it might represent. She was not sentimental, but the instinct was strong in her never to relinquish to its proper and immediate fate any physical object or possession that had once been in her hands. The dresses she had made for herself, after being thriftily refashioned once or twice, were always consigned to boxes that now, after thirty years, reposed in her garret, and letters she had received from her parents during the year at school were filed away in some semblance of order to await the predictable end, the bonfire in the backyard after her death. She never inspected the dead lumber and drift of her life that she had thus accumulated in the garret under the dry roof.

At eighteen Elsie Barton was not precisely a pretty girl. But she was small and delicately formed and her arms and legs, though thin, were not ungraceful. Her hair was brown and somewhat curly, her eyes brown and wide, and her face in repose wore habitually an expression of gravity and a certain gentle confusion. There was never any amount of positive gaiety in her nature, and probably for this reason she was not popular with the young men of the town; but she liked to go to parties to see the movement and hear the laughing and talking. She wanted to please people, trying to laugh with them and act as they did, but generally, even after the parties where she had enjoyed herself most, she felt more cut off from other people than before. She felt that all of them possessed a secret which would never be hers.

Thomas Adams was the only young man who consistently came to see her and escorted her to church, the church picnics, and the parties. His earnestness, his timidity, his gentleness, perhaps even his confusion, were like her own, and she responded to them, feeling comfortable with him and at home with him; but when she was absent from him, she did not miss him and never thought of him. In the summer evenings, while, back in the house, Mr. Barton slept in his chair beside a table that bore a lighted lamp, she sat on the porch with Thomas Adams, hearing his voice but not able to make out his face on account of the darkness. It was as if he were but a voice, a voice talking earnestly, timidly, gently in the warm darkness and lulling her into a happy security from which the disorders, the speculations, the dust, and the stridencies of daytime were cleansed. He might be talking about himself and how he was studying, for he was reading law in spare time from his job in Mr. Taylor's drug store. When he talked about himself and his plans, as he often did in that indecisive voice of his, she never resented it; the talk reassured her, coming to her, perhaps, as a kind of flattery, although half the time she neither listened to nor cared what he was saying.

He rarely touched her. Sometimes, it was true, he sat beside her and held her hand lightly with his sharp, dry fingers;

but on those occasions he did not talk, and in the silence she always felt alone, as much alone as sometimes at night when she crawled into bed and pulled up the clean, soap-smelling sheet. At times he even kissed her. She endured the groping, unclinging contact of his lips, half understanding that this was some kind of obligation on her part, remembering the things the girls had said about kissing and what it was like, but the contact left her somewhat humiliated, somewhat betrayed. Sometimes, rarely, he told her he loved her. To this she never replied anything. But she thought she might marry Thomas Adams. She had never consciously decided this. She had simply realized that it would probably come to pass, like growing old, like the turn of a season. She would marry him; and there was a kind of modest comfort and satisfaction in the thought. He would be good to her. And she would be good to him.

Upon this routine obtruded the figure of Benjamin Beaumont, the tobacco buyer, a tallish man with blue eyes and a brown mustache, a skin like fine oiled leather, and a dignified good humor for everybody. People said that he came from up in Kentucky and that his father was a successful farmer, highly respected in his county. Benjamin Beaumont was about thirty years old, wore good clothes with a jaunty unkemptness, had a good horse and rig, and made good money at his business. He stopped in the stores and talked to the older men in a serious voice about politics and business; rode around the country seeing farmers and inspecting their crops; played poker with the loose fellows at the livery stable where he kept his horse; went to Nashville sometimes for as long as a week at a time; was popular with the girls in town, talking and jollying with them at their parties; and sang in a fairly good baritone at church. Old Mr. Barton liked him. When he came to sit on the Barton porch at night, Mr. Barton usually came out for a while, too, and Benjamin Beaumont, in his serious man's voice, would talk about politics and business and ask Mr. Barton's opinion. Then Mr. Barton would go back into the house, and, sitting in his chair, fall asleep.

Thomas Adams, finally, did not come any more. She did not miss him, for she had never missed him in his absence. From the presence of Benjamin Beaumont she extracted a new and keener pleasure than any she had ever had, the pleasure of vanity, because she was aware that the other girls, who had never wanted Thomas Adams and had been a bit scornful of him, wanted Benjamin Beaumont. They teased her about him, not entirely in fun, and she would sit silent in the midst of the teasing with a secret, sweet thought in her head, like the piece of candy a child holds on its tongue and secretly sucks in school or church, and a little spot of color would glow in either of her cheeks. The thought of Benjamin Beaumont was sweetest to her then, in the teasing, for it was then that he established her in the world with the girls around her who twined their arms on each other's shoulders and leaned their heads together.

It was the late summer of 1899 when Benjamin Beaumont began to come to see her, and all during the following winter he took her to parties, where the eyes of the other girls upon him and their laughter with him at his jokes fed her new vanity. She liked that even better than when she was alone with him. But, even alone, he could make her smile and feel warm, with a warmth like the recollection of the pleasure at a party. And she liked for him to call her "Kitty." That was her father's pet name for her, and Benjamin Beaumont had, without so much as a by-your-leave, taken it up, too. The first time he had called her "Kitty," it had shocked her profoundly and powerfully. Her face must have shown the magnitude of the shock, for, laughing, Benjamin Beaumont had said, "Hey, look at yourself! A rabbit must've jumped over your grave." But she grew to like to hear him call her "Kitty." It made her feel warm and safe. It was like a good promise.

Only many months after the relationship began did Benjamin Beaumont kiss her. In the midst of laughing at some joke, suddenly, irrelevantly, he stooped and kissed her directly on the mouth. Then he said. "How did you like that, Kitty?" And when she did not answer, he patted her on the head, again laughing. She had not liked it, the rough skin, the hot, strong breath, with the odor of cigars, but she did not tell him so. His other kisses, which came infrequently during the succeeding months, she accepted in the same fashion, not resisting them, not inviting them, even liking them a little but not exactly in the way the talk of the other girls had led her to believe you liked kisses. The expression of gentle puzzlement on her face after he withdrew his lips usually made him want to laugh; and sometimes he did laugh, saying as he had said the first time, "How did you like that, Kitty?" But once or twice, seeing her face with that expression, he felt a blank fury, quickly snuffed out, stir in the depth of his being.

He did not understand himself, really; or why he came to see Elsie Barton at all. He was, as a matter of fact, an unspeculative, careless, good-natured young man, enjoying laughter, whisky, and talk, the kisses the nice girls in town gave him and the embraces of women he took to his hotel room when he went to Nashville on his trips. Elsie Barton was not exactly his style. But he continued to see her. In the spring and summer evenings he sat beside her in the porch swing, while the old man dozed inside the house, and held her against him with her head on his shoulder and listened to her light breathing and felt as though he were drifting luxuriously down a broad, gentle, sweetly flowing stream with the far banks on either side swathed in darkness. Then, occasionally, he would wonder in a cold, detached way what it would take to make that light breath come quick and strong, and would slip his hand farther under her arm to lie on her breast. "No," she would whisper, "no," and he would feel her body stiffen against him. Then the breath would come lightly and evenly as before. The truth was that Elsie Barton, in her gentleness, her childlike confusion, flattered him in a way more subtle than that to which he had been accustomed; she flattered him and unconsciously challenged him; and more, she touched some obscure, thin, and pure spring of sentiment in his make-up.

One hot afternoon, toward the middle of August in 1900,

Benjamin Beaumont drove up Tolliver Street, the street on which the Bartons lived, on his way out to the country to see a farmer on business. Beyond the maples in the Barton yard he could see Elsie sitting on her front porch, apparently sewing. Without reflection, on the mere impulse of the moment, he pulled his roan up, hitched him, walked up to the porch, and asked her to ride out to the Turner place with him because he had to see Mr. Turner. Ordinarily, she would never have done such a thing; riding with him on Sunday afternoon, on invitation, was one thing, but to ride with a man out in the country on a week-day, when he was going on business, fell outside all her categories of propriety. But she said she would go, hearing in a distant, lackadaisical surprise her own voice giving consent. With the still air enveloping the world, with the houses around shuttered for the afternoon, with the silence and the hypnotic pulsation of the heat, that day was, perhaps, the one day in her entire life when she would have said yes, and gone with him. She stuck the needle neatly into the white cambric she had been sewing, and went inside to get her hat.

They did not talk as they rode between the dry fields. The pastures were brown and lusterless, the corn laid by, the tobacco rank. Not a breath of air was stirring. The plops of dust raised by the roan's hoofs billowed dully as high as the animal's belly. Three miles from town they turned off the pike up the lane leading to the Turner place. The house itself stood off the main road, in the middle of the farm, on a slight knoll up which the lane, shaded on each side, ran straight between the empty pastures. The roan pulled very slowly up the knoll, his coat looking black with sweat and a few flecks of foam hanging from the bit. But under the cedars which surrounded the Turner house, the lawn looked cool, and the house, a two-story log structure weatherboarded over and painted white, looked cool and dignified among the black, heavy boughs of the evergreens. They drew to the stone carriage block under the nearest cedar, and Benjamin Beaumont got down and hitched. "I'll be back in a minute," he said,

opened the wooden gate set in the stone wall of the yard, and
proceeded up the path, which was marked by large, flat slabs
of limestone. He knocked several times at the front door, but
receiving no response, shouted to arouse a possible sleeper
within, and then walked around to the back and shouted
again. A large shepherd dog, chained to a tree, gave a couple
of perfunctory barks at him before settling again in the dust
by the cedar bole. The place was deserted. He walked back
to the rig. "Nobody home," he said.

"It's too bad you had to come all this way," she said.

"It don't matter," he said. Then: "I'm gonna get me a drink
of water, do you want one?"

"Thank you," she said.

"I'll bring you one from the well," he said. He went to the
well house in the side yard, but returned almost immediately.
"The dipper's chained," he said.

Before he could help her, she had got down from the rig
and stood beside him at the gate.

The well house was large, really a kind of summerhouse
with a table in it, a rickety rocking chair, an old couch with
the springs poking out under the bottom. There were signs
of domestic use, a sewing basket on the table, a rag doll in
the chair, and a bench made of rough wood. The well was in
one corner, a dipper chained to a staple set in a joint of the
stonework by the little hand pump.

"See," he said, pointing with a kind of vindication, "the
dipper's chained."

"Yes," she said.

He got her a drink, then took one himself, the water cold
and of a mineral flavor. Standing in the middle of the summer-
house, he put an arm around her, carelessly as around a
child's shoulders, and kissed her. He saw that expression of
gentle puzzlement on her face. Then, without premeditation,
really without passion, but from the depth of the blank fury
which once or twice before had stirred in him at that look
on her face and which now took possession of him, he thrust
her to the dilapidated couch with a violence which was un-

necessary, for she did not struggle, and there assaulted her. Against the violence and the pain she did not struggle, though her hands were up to his chest in a position of automatic and futile protest. She thought, or rather she heard the very words in her mind: *He oughtn't do this, he oughtn't, I'm Elsie Barton, Elsie Barton, Elsie Barton.* And her name, "Elsie Barton," filled her mind, over and over, like remote and muffled bells, with that dull asseveration of her identity.

After it was over, he stood in the middle of the summer-house, and barely stifled the impulse, the crazy impulse, to laugh and say, as he had said before, "And how did you like that, Kitty?" He went quickly outside and wandered, very slowly, back and forth under the big cedars, looking down the rise at the empty lane between the heat-ridden fields. After a while she came out, walked past him without looking in his direction, and got into the rig.

On the long and silent ride back to town, his dissatisfaction took the form of remorse, a remorse conventional enough in the way it presented itself to him, for those were the only terms he knew. He said to himself that he had ruined her, maybe. A sense of loss suffused him: he did not realize that it was because he had dried up that obscure and thin, but pure spring of sentiment that Elsie Barton had provoked in him. He had lost that, and the flattery and complacency it had entailed, without feeding his vanity on the grosser diet to which it was otherwise accustomed, without even gaining the moment's pleasure. He did not realize, quite naturally, that if he had gained the pleasure he would not now suffer the remorse, or rather, suffer those confused things, loss, dissatisfaction, and unfulfilled vanity, which appeared to his mind in the vocabulary of remorse. First, he blamed himself, and then be began to make excuses for himself. If only the dipper had not been chained, he thought, then it would never have happened. So he began to curse the dipper.

In the middle of the ride he suddenly realized that she had not said a thing to him, that she had not even offered him accusation, tears, and recrimination. He looked sharply at her, at the still face. "Go on!" he burst out harshly. "Go on and say it. Damn it, say it!"

She turned her pale face and gazed at him with the large, brown, defenseless eyes.

"My God!" he roared. "My God! So that's the way it is."

He did not know what was the way it was exactly, but he lashed the big roan, not once but several times in quick succession, savagely, and the animal lunged in the shafts and plunged ahead and the white dust billowed and plumed down the pike behind them. But in the heat the pace quickly flagged. Benjamin Beaumont held the whip numbly in his hand, but he did not strike again. He did not know exactly what he had said, or why.

Back in town, at home, when he stopped at the Barton gate, she got quickly down and went to the house without saying a word to him. He had wanted to tell her he was sorry—and somehow the crime uppermost in his mind now was the fact that he had screamed at her on the way home and had lashed the horse—but looking into her face, he had not been able to find the words to say how he felt. Now he saw her mount the steps of the porch, and then pause, in the most natural way in the world, and go over and pick up the sewing in the swing. And that pause and that gesture of picking up the sewing, which under ordinary circumstances would have been so natural, seemed to be a monstrous attack upon himself. She had stopped for that sewing—that damned sewing, he muttered. Then he rode on down the street, under the drying and pock-leafed maples, hating himself and hating her.

He did not know how she felt or what she thought. Not really knowing her, and having no talent for speculation or power to cast himself imaginatively into another person's being, he could not even guess. And in the end it was this that brought him to her again, for it was necessary for him to know. To return to her was like the impulse to pick a scab, to feel the twitch and the pain; and his vanity could not rest without knowledge. On several other occasions during the autumn he possessed her, always without premeditation, always with the same self-defeating violence, always with the same distress of spirit in consequence. Her passivity, her silence which he could not force her to break, her acquiescence, her clenched hands thrusting him away after consummation, all in all, the undecipherable compound she presented to him left him always baffled and confused in self-hatred, hatred of her, and loss.

Toward the middle of December she told him that she was going to have a baby. She had been pregnant for three months. The information came to him with no shock of surprise, for it seemed the proper and ironical end. Everything, everything in the world, was a God-damned mess. But the positive news intensified in him the rebellion that had been growing. Already he was flirting with another girl in town. His stock of patience was run through, or rather the capacity for self-torture in his robust and amiable nature. He thought that he would go away, probably to Oklahoma, to a new place just opened up. For a week he neither saw her nor communicated with her. On Christmas Eve, while her father stayed late at the store for the Christmas trade, she sat at home alone, thinking, while the rain made its somnolent drumming on the roof and sluiced down the panes, that it was right to be alone, that this was best.

The next day, however, the present came, a silver-backed toilet set with her initials on it, but Benjamin Beaumont did not come. She did not really suffer from the insolence of the gift in his absence, even when her father admired it, for she was still wrapped in that security, that sense of inner harmony, of the past evening. She took the articles from their plush-lined case and placed them on her dresser. The next day her father told her, both question and disapproval in his tone, that Benjamin Beaumont had been drunk down at the livery stable Christmas and had played cards all day and half the night with the men down there.

Four days later he married her.

He had been incompetent to his rebellion. White in the face, the fumes of liquor still strong upon him, small beads of

sweat gathering on his temples, red streaks of fresh mud on
the bottom of the trousers of his best black suit, he stood in
the parlor of the parsonage and heard, as from a considerable
distance, the words of the marriage ceremony. The faces about
him in the dingy, over-heated, cramped parlor were strange
to him, for he had brought Elsie Barton up to a little town
across the Kentucky line for the marriage, driving up in his
buggy through rain and red mud in which the horse's hoofs
sank to the fetlock. The marriage took place just at dusk.
That night he lay on a bed in the little hotel of the town,
while his wife put cold cloths to his forehead and while far
off in the rain firecrackers exploded to celebrate the season.

Applying the cloths, looking down at the burly form on
the bed, she thought: *It's him, it's my husband. I've got to
love him. I've got to do my duty by him.* But the thought
seemed to belong to somebody else, a stale echo of phrases
heard long ago, uttered by the leaning, whispering faces of
the women who had once sat in her mother's parlor when
her mother was alive. The faces had said the words: "husband," "love," "duty." Now those words came into her mind,
and she heard them with a slow marveling, trying to fathom
them. Oh, she had always been told to be good and she
wanted to be good and do what was right. But the room was
strange to her, not like her neat little room at home. And the
man was strange to her. And the woman was strange to her,
too, the woman she was. She felt as though she were trapped
in that alien body as she was trapped in the alien room.

The next day, still weak from his long debauch, Benjamin
Beaumont took his bride back to Charlestown to get their
clothes and to wind up some pressing business. Then he set
out for his father's house, in central Kentucky, where, pre-
sumably, they would be safe from gossip and prying eyes,
to wait for the birth of the child. The house, a big white
structure, with a limestone chimney at each gable end, stood
on a rise, in the middle of five hundred acres of well-culti-
vated, well-watered, rolling land, backed by the blue knobs
to the west. Inside, it was like a sty. Old Mr. Beaumont, an

old, somewhat shrunken, more violent, more profane Benjamin, lived there in rooms cluttered with newspapers, saddles, shotguns, liniment and whisky bottles, and used dishes. The old Negro woman who did the cooking for him made only the feeblest gesture toward order in the house. In the twenty-five years since Mrs. Beaumont's death, the Negro woman had forgotten the old discipline which had once made everything "nice," and had gradually discovered the depth to which the widower, in his violent, hard-working, sporting, lonely life, was willing to sink.

"So Benjy's gone and done it, huh?" the old man demanded as he greeted her in the big house, leaning toward her, inspecting her. "And I don't blame him, durn him, not a mite, little lady," he added, leaning the hairy face down to her, peering at her with the bleared but cunning old blue eyes which seemed to be peering from ambush. Then he reached out to touch her cheek with a blunt forefinger which grated on her skin like the end of a sawed stick.

He was kind to her in his way. He made the Negro woman go through the motions of cleaning one of the rooms upstairs, and put her there. She was ill much of the time, and the old man would often come up and stir the fire, or heave on a fresh chunk of wood. "They'd let you freeze to death, durn 'em, warn't fer me," he would boom out. She would thank him politely, then he would lean by the door jamb and talk. She never asked him to sit down. Or he would come up at breakfast and boom out, "Now how's the pretty little lady this morning?" Then, while she sat up in bed, her hands holding the edge of the covers, and while the coffee got cold and the bacon stiffened in its dish of grease, he stood there and talked on in his hearty way, telling her she would be all right and have a fine little bugger soon, and how his wife always had an easy time with hers, nothing to it, or telling her dirty jokes to cheer her up.

The child, a girl, was born in early June. In the middle of winter they moved back to Charlestown. On a cold, brilliant January day, she stood on the front porch and Old Man Beau-

mont kissed her good-bye on both cheeks, carefully brushing
back his whiskers before he did so. "Bring the little bugger
back to see me some time," he told her. Quite suddenly, she
burst into tears, because she knew that she would never see
him again. It was merely that, not because she liked him. As
a matter of fact, she had never liked him; she had heard, day
after day, his foot on the stair, or heard his voice rasping and
booming downstairs, and had felt trapped and tied before
some blind, brutish force which in its passage would trample
her and pound her until there was nothing left. But now the
tears came; it was the first time she had cried since she was
married. Old Man Beaumont, very much embarrassed, followed out to the surrey which was to take them to the station.
"If Benjy's ever mean to you," he said, "just write me a letter
and I'll come down and shoot the son-of-a-bitch."

Then he went into the house, and they drove off into the
enormous world which she would never understand.

Testament of Flood

SO DRY, so withered, she appeared as she went up and down the street that the boy, meeting her, could scarcely believe her the subject of those narratives inconclusively whispered now and then by ladies who came to see his mother. What did they say? They said: *No shame, staying here all these years. She didn't love him. What did she marry him for then? What did she do the other for then? She didn't love him, dead ten years and never even a flower on his grave. Wait, that girl will be off the old block.* They said: *Never even a flower.* Meeting her in the street, he remembered what they said. So dry, she was like those bits of straw or trash lodged innocently in the branches of creek-bottom sycamores as testament of long-subsided spring flood—a sort of high water mark of passion in the community.

Dry, but the boy must believe the story and speculate about the details he seemed never able to learn, because there was a more convincing memento of its verity than Mrs. Beaumont, who walked up and down the street. It was the girl. On a winter evening the girl would probably be hurrying to the grocery, walking with quick prim steps through the cold air; in summer, loitering with other girls on the way to the drug store for ice cream; or going, winter or summer, to the post office with a letter in her hand.

The hand that held the white rectangle would be ungloved, at least in his recollection always ungloved. The stamp would show on the white paper, a single splotch of red. And when her shoulder pushed open the office door, the brown curls which hung without precocity at her neck would shake. He never happened to be in the office when she consigned the letter to its slot, but he felt as if he had observed the act: the little push of the fingers projecting the letter, which she herself might have written, on its way to someone he would never know; the metal click of the box.

So long as the letter remained between the fingers, it was intimate and part of herself. When the letter plunged into the black cavity and the lid clicked, the inscribed sentiments were abstracted, only connected with her being by a signature which he might recognize in precise backhand like the "Helen Beaumont" on her school papers. The letter with the signature "Helen" would no longer belong to her; it would belong to the world, to almost anybody, to that person he would never know. But it never belonged to him. His recollections, however, were always of her carrying the letter to the post office rather than sitting in the schoolroom where now, since he had skipped a grade and was a senior, he saw her almost every day.

"Helen Beaumont," Mr. Griffin said, tapping with his chalk the chart of lines and triangles drawn on the blackboard, "can you tell me why this angle is commensurate to this?"

Mr. Griffin's fingers twisted the chalk, tapped the blackboard. He was a very tall young man who lifted a bony hand to his mouth when, ashamed and guilty, he coughed. He was trying to earn money to go back to college, or maybe out West. Sometimes the boy and a friend would go to Mr. Griffin's boarding house at night. Under the green lamp, papers were stacked on the table beside the geometry book and *Caesar's Gallic Wars*. Mr. Griffin talked about the University of Tennessee. On a frame by the wall hung a set of old chest weights which he showed them how to use. Seriously, he worked the handles back and forth, one-two, one-two-three, while the boys regarded him. The flanges of his big pointed nose twitched in time to the count, and on his forehead little beads of sweat, almost imperceptible, gathered. "It'll put hair on your belly," Mr. Griffin said. "It'll make a man outer you." He took a deep breath, pulling the handles.

"Helen Beaumont," Mr. Griffin said, "can you tell me?"

She fixed her eyes on him, on the twisting chalk, as if to rebuke the creature of straight lines and cold angles for ob-

truding himself on another world whose lines all curved
voluptuously toward some fulfillment he could not possibly
understand.

"You don't know," Mr. Griffin remarked in some asperity.

"No, sir," she said.

It was always the same. When Mr. Griffin asked her a question, the boy did not look at her, but through the window
across the fields where winter rain distantly fell on the sodden
corn stalks. Far beyond the fields, the woods appeared, a
depthless misty smudge no less remote than the sky which
sagged gray and soundless like a damp drumhead. One could
walk beneath the black boughs out yonder with no noise ever
given from the tread of foot on the sopping mat of leaves.

It was always the same. Someone else would answer the
question. It did not matter; she was such a fool. If Mr. Griffin
asked him—"Steve Adams, can you tell me?"—he would answer
the question. But once as he opened his lips to answer, he
found her gaze, mild and satirical, directed at him. "I don't
know," he said.

The swollen bulb of the stove glowed all day. The windowpanes sweated, obscuring the printed world. At noon recess
the older girls sat near the stove to eat their lunches. Heat
flushed their cheeks and their voices harbored a subdued excitement. Sometimes Steve ate at his desk, eating soberly,
after each bite regarding the arc his teeth had made in the
bread. He heard the voices of the girls, and turned some
phrase over in his mind, regarding it soberly as he regarded
the mark of his teeth on the bread. He heard Helen Beaumont's voice: ". . . Frank said, but I said, 'It don't matter to
me.'" He carefully crushed the lunch paper in his hands.

"Steve," Sibyl Barnes said, "want some cake?" She was a
thin dark girl, shrewish and bitter when she did a kindness,
as though ashamed to be ensnared in common weakness.
"Take it," she said sharply, "it's good devil-food."

He went over and leaned with one hand on her desk while
he reached for the cake.

"Lord," she said, "that's a filthy wart you've got."

He held the cake in midair, looking down at the hand which touched the desk. The wart, fat and encrusted, clung rottenly beside the nail of his forefinger. He watched the finger bend slowly backward to concealment of the palm, leaving the stub of knuckle like the stub on the hand of Luke Smith, who worked in his father's sawmill.

"Lemme see it," Sibyl commanded.

"It's nothing," he said.

She took the finger, holding it dubiously. "You can get 'em off," she said.

"It's nothing," he said.

He jerked the hand loose and sat again at his desk. The chocolate tasted dry and bitter in his mouth. He heard the voices, Helen Beaumont's voice: ". . . Frank said, but I said, 'It don't matter to me.' "

Naked that night he stood in front of the washstand mirror and lifted the hand against his body. In the mirror the hand against the white flesh was gray and clutching like a great spider, the wart monstrous. He did not see his face in the mirror. He put on his nightshirt quickly, then crouched on the tile hearth and stared at the disintegrating embers. He heard his mother's voice from the next room.

"Go to bed, son," the voice said.

The stove all day glowed hotly. The windowpanes sweated like melting frost, hiding the fields of old corn stalk. Toward three o'clock, the red of the stove-belly dulled, the slumberous gray of iron encroached, mottled the subsiding tint of rose. Old spittle and orange pulp resumed their outline, mottling the iron. The minute hand of the clock climbed painfully, and in the dead pause of Mr. Griffin's voice, the sound of the clock ticking its certainty filled the room.

At three the pupils went out, first the grade children walking in line with their teachers, then the high school pupils in random parties. The older girls, ashamed to wear overshoes, picked their way as hens do in a wet barnyard. The boys slogged across the bald squashy sod; or if the day was cold and bright, they charged, clattering, over the frozen surface and called each other's names in voices empty and shrill like kildees.

It was a cold bright day and the boys called to each other when the big new Hudson for the first time came easing down the grade, crunching and spattering like gravel the skim ice in the ruts. It stopped at the corner of the school lot, and Frank Barber let down the glass and put his head out, smiling like brittle, unclear ice. Frank Barber had been to France in the army, in 1918, and now was the railroad detective, though they said he never bought the biggest car in town on his salary. He hung around the station hotel in daytime, and late at night people heard his cutout throbbing away from town. They turned over and said: *That's Frank Barber out again.*

While the little children passed, dirty-nosed and awkward as turnips, he leaned out the window of the new Hudson and smiled. The big girls came by, walking in tight groups. Helen Beaumont stopped, said something to the others, and went over to the Hudson. She got in beside Frank Barber, and he closed the glass. The car slithered away down the hill, bright in the sun, cutout roaring.

It was a late spring, wet without sun. Afternoons the boy eyed the glowing iron of the stove, its live red duller day by day as the new green thickened and curdled over the sodden ground. Or he eyed the window which framed vistas of old corn stalk arched over pools between the rows. It was like a print which had been dropped in water so that the splotchy colors ran, merging, and outlines decayed. Only the crows that beat somnambulantly over the fields had life. He could not hear, but knew, the yellow beaks opening against the wind to utter —caw—their ironic negation. The thin repercussion of the call hung in his mind above the voices as he waited for the clock to point three and the big black car to come down the grade. Once or twice when it did not come, he went home moodily, feeling numbed and heavy with disappointment. But waiting for three o'clock, he had hoped it would not come.

When going home, if he went out of his way a little down Front Street, he might see the car before Mr. Allen's hay and feed store, where Mrs. Beaumont worked as bookkeeper. Frank Barber would lean over the glass talking to a man who stood on the pavement, but their voices were always too low for him to hear a word. Or if alone, Frank Barber, inside the sweating glass, sat with both hands on the wheel and looked down the street while smoke rose straight up from the cigarette stuck in his face. On one occasion the girl ran out of the store and drove off in the Hudson just before Steve got even with the spot. As he walked by, he recognized Mrs. Beaumont's face in the gloom beyond the glass of the door. She, staring down the street where the car had vanished, did not see him. For a minute he thought he might go in and talk to her, though the only words he had ever in his life spoken to her were, "Good morning, Mrs. Beaumont."

The stove in the schoolroom was cold. Beyond the window a man followed a plow, seeming in the false perspective rather to ascend the pane than retreat across the field toward the green haze of woods. Behind the man the earth split open like a ripe melon. Solemnly, crows stood along the furrow. "It shore is one late spring," Jake Miles had said, a good old country boy who rode in every morning to school on a savage leering horse with one white eye. "Ain't nobody gitting any plowing done," Jake Miles had said, "'cept that Frank Barber. I reckin I might learn ole Snakebite to carry double, then I could git my spring plowing done like him." Steve glanced over at Jake Miles, who hulked above his desk with lips that moved stiffly as he read. He turned away and watched the man retreat toward the woods, the earth, dark, unfold. He fixed his eyes on his book.

He fixed his eyes on the page before him. *After Shakespeare there developed a drama which, in comparison with the broad sympathy and humanity of the great bard, rightly deserves the name of decadent. But John Webster is sometimes capable of real poetic feeling, if not scope, as in the Duchess of Malfi*

(1616) when the brother looks at the sister slain to avenge the family honor:

Cover her face: mine eyes dazzle: she died young.

His lips, moving stiffly like the lips of Jake Miles, formed the words. *Cover her face: mine eyes dazzle: she died young.* Did he really speak the words out loud; he could never remember. His stomach went cold. He felt the veins of the neck throb, and heard, in his ears, the mounting blood that roared, then gradually diminished as when one rides away from the sea. And in the resultant quietude he discovered that he felt himself far away from her, and much older; older than Frank Barber; older than Mr. Griffin; older, even, than her mother's face behind the glass door. Then as he turned stealthily in his seat to look at the girl, he felt that she, so much younger than himself, had already, somehow, inherited the strict and inaccessible province.

The Confession of Brother Grimes

IT MAY depend on what you mean by crime. You say the Lord fits the punishment to the crime, and the Lord's ideas on crime and my ideas might not be exactly the same. I don't go so far as to state right out that my ideas and the Lord's ideas on the subject don't fit. That's just one way of looking at it, you might say, for the sake of argument. And then, there's another question, who is on the receiving end of the punishment, and who did the crime he is getting punished for? The night Archie Munn tried to drive a new Ford coupe through the back end of a parked truck that didn't have any lights on out on that new concrete road toward Morgansville the punishment was distributed right liberal.

Archie's wife he'd been married to six months, her name being Sue Grimes before she married him, was the most sensational performer, when it come to taking punishment. That truck had a pole sticking out behind, and it just went through that Ford, including Sue Grimes, like the toothpick through a club sandwich. But Sue didn't hog all the punishment, there being plenty to spare. They found Archie bunched up in a field with so many bones sticking out of him they said he looked like a mad porcupine. Mrs. Grimes never got over the shock when she heard the news, and died pretty soon, her heart never having been any good to speak of anyway, and you might add her liver-and-lights for that matter, considering the time she always spent in bed complaining. Then there was Brother Grimes, as good and kind a man as you ever hope to see and a preacher to boot, brought down in sorrow and white hair to a lonely old age, all by consequence. The punishment was pretty general, not to mention a nigger on top the truck who got thrown off and skidded on the place where some people claimed his face had been, but you couldn't tell it, and if they made a death mask of it like they did of Napoleon it would have looked like a statue of a fallen omelet.

The Lord's ways are mysterious, Brother Grimes said in his sermon as soon as he was able to preach, which was after the accident, but before his wife gradually died. But they move in perfect justice, he said. The church was packed to gunnel, for people wanted to hear what he would say after his tribulation and they were sorry for him too. He always was a fine-looking man, even if he was about sixty-five, a big strong fellow with flashing eyes and a mop of long black hair on his head, not a gray hair in it. He had a wonderful voice. He had such a fine voice they said he could bring tears to your eyes when he gave thanks in front of a platter with three fried chickens on it. Up in the pulpit he would shake his big fine head like a lion with all that black mane of hair, and that voice would come rolling out and he would gesture with both arms out like a man swimming the breast stroke. Every Sunday he was like William Jennings Bryan, the Great Commoner, getting ready to let go with that Cross of Gold speech that made him famous. Brother Grimes said that the Lord's ways move in perfect justice, which was one of his favorite sayings, and if he said it again that Sunday you might reckon he really believed it. There wasn't a dry eye in the house.

But it raised the question. Not that there was much question about Archie Munn not deserving what he got, for there wasn't any meanness this side of murder and robbery he hadn't been up to. He was a likker head, and no woman who prized her reputation more than rubies and fine gold would be caught out with him, and no man who wanted to stay out of the hospital would ride in a car with him on account of the way he drove. Every time they built a new stretch of concrete road anywhere in ten counties Archie had to go over and christen it like they christen a ship. Only he wouldn't bust a bottle of champagne on that concrete, not being a hand to waste likker, he'd just go bust up a car and maybe some bones, his or somebody else's. He was God's gift to dealers in spiritous likkers, Henry Ford, and the medical profession. Only the medical profession didn't quite get the break with the others, because there usually wasn't much left, even if Archie did spend a lot of time in the hospitals. He spent four months after the time he killed Sue Grimes, and he hasn't paid for it yet. That was the fellow Sue Grimes married. Marrying him must have been her crime, if you figure you have got to figure out her crime that close. It's the only one anybody ever figured out for her, for nobody even lifted a tongue against her in any other respect. That being her crime, and her a young girl to boot, the punishment seemed to fit with considerable to spare around the edges. There was some to hang over the edges in fitting the punishment to the crime for Mrs. Grimes, too, who was according to all reports a good but complaining woman, and some to spare in fitting the punishment to the crime of Brother Grimes even after he figured it out and confessed it before God and man. There might have been a little to spare in fitting the punishment to the crime of the nigger, too, but you couldn't tell, because nobody knew anything about what you might call the nigger's private life.

In the end Brother Grimes figured out his own crime to his own satisfaction and said it just went to prove what he always said, the Lord's ways moved in perfect justice and the punishments fit the crime. But he never wasted any energy trying to figure out the crime for Sue. He got inconsistent enough to name her in his sermon as his stainless daughter, and then caught himself up quick and said, "O Lord, forgive us, for no one of Thy children is stainless in Thy sight." Anybody could see how his mind was running on her being stainless and how that dropped a stitch in the way he argued. But he just passed it over and said the Lord in His justice and mercy had used her death for an instrument, as you might say, to remove the scales from our eyes. That sounded all right, maybe, but nobody at that time could see exactly how it helped his argument.

But he kept on saying, almost every Sunday in some connection, even if it looked like he dragged it in by the tail, the Lord's ways move in perfect justice. Then Mrs. Grimes died, or "died" may be too strong a word for what she did, since it didn't seem she had even been alive proper during the ten years since they came to town. Brother Grimes preached the funeral himself, even if he looked like he was ready to fall down by the grave he looked so bad. It was the last hot weather before the summer breaks, and a drought too, and the sweat ran down his face. His face was white as paper and his long black hair was plastered to his head with sweat. He said: "O Lord, we believe in Thy justice."

He went home that afternoon, walking by himself all the way from the burying ground in the hot sun. He shut himself up and wouldn't see anybody. He fired his cook. The first day or two some women in the church tried to get in, but he told them to go away, he was going to wrestle with the angel by himself. People knew he was alive because he would telephone the store and have them leave some groceries on his back porch. Some said he was losing his mind. Nobody laid eyes on him. Then one Saturday he telephoned Deacon Broadbent he was going to preach the next day. When he came in to do the preaching his hair was white as snow.

Archie Munn went to live with Brother Grimes. They would sit out on the front porch of an evening, Archie with the crutch he still had to use, and talk. Nobody knows what they talked about, but everybody knew Archie was a reformed character, because he had promised his wife to reform just before he killed her in that Ford car. Brother Grimes said it had all happened just to save Archie's soul and bring him to his senses and that now he could lean on Archie, and that Sue Grimes and Mrs. Grimes would be glad to have it that way. Either he had forgotten the nigger or he wasn't so sure how the nigger would feel about it.

Anybody could have guessed what would happen. Archie threw that crutch away, got hold of some whisky and a car, and went out and killed two white men and a horse in broad daylight. The horse was hitched to a buggy and the men were in the buggy, that is, up to the time Archie hit. Then the buggy and the men and the horse were all separated from each other. Archie was lucky that time, not being hurt a bit. They put him in the penitentiary.

You could tell it was about the last straw for Brother Grimes, but he didn't say a word till the Sunday after Archie got sentenced. Then, up in the pulpit, he said the punishment was fitted to the crime. He wasn't talking, he said, about the punishment of that poor misguided boy. He was talking about his own punishment, for he felt responsible, he said. He had lived a lie, and the Lord moved in His great justice. Then his poor wife had been taken and he had ceased to live a lie, but he didn't have the courage to stand up and confess before God and man. His crime, he said, had been pride, pride and sinful vanity, and pride was the crime the angels fell out of Heaven for. But now he was going to confess before God and man. He had, he said, used black hair dye for twenty years.

Her Own People

FISHILY, he stared at the high ceiling, where gray plaster, delicately ringed by marks of old damp, was still shadowy, although bright sunshine struck into the room between cracks in the drawn, blue curtains. Between the cracks in the curtain small waxy leaves were visible, brushing against the windowpane.

"Get up," the voice beside him said without much friendliness.

"I've got a slight head," he complained, still looking at the ceiling. A single fly, torpid, clung to the gray plaster directly above him, and he watched it.

"Last night you said it was the best corn we'd had."

"Did I say that?" He threw back the covers and let his feet drop to the floor, while he lay on his back, looking up. "I made a mistake then. And it's Sunday."

"If I'm doing the cooking from now on," the voice said, "you've got to help some."

"I'll help," he said and got up. He stood in the middle of the big room, surveyed the room once helplessly, and pulled off his pajama jacket. He was not very tall, but thick in the body. A purplish scar ran diagonally down the relaxed stomach, which pressed against the pajama string, and lost itself in the crisp black hairs. Meditatively he slipped his short forefinger along the scar. "My appendix is getting better. It doesn't look so much like bad blue carbon on yellow back-sheet any more."

"It's better"—there was a stir from the bed—"but you're getting a stomach. If you get a stomach, you've got to move out. There will be no stomachs in my house."

"It's because the muscles haven't knitted up yet," he said, and fingered the scar. "You haven't got any sympathy." He crossed to the dresser and studied himself in the mirror. "I can take it off right away," he said, patting it.

"Spading up the rest of the garden will take it off."

"I can't spade today. I'm paid to dish political dirt for the *Advocate*, not spade gardens. Spading is a luxury."

"You can spade an hour," she said.

"Look at my eyes," and he squinted closer to the mirror; "you can tell I've got a head."

"Spading will help your head."

He got a pair of corduroy trousers and a sweat shirt from the big walnut wardrobe in the corner, and put them on. For a minute he regarded the hump of bedclothes from which a few strands of blond hair strayed out on the pillow. "Aren't you getting up?" he said. "I want some breakfast."

"You start the fire in the stove."

Without haste he hunted for something about the room, standing in the middle of the floor to look all around, then on hands and knees peering under the bed. One hand touched the blue dress that lay on the floor by the bed and he picked it up. Under it the bedroom slippers lay. "You hid my slippers with your dress," he said, holding out the sky-blue dress, which dangled from his large hairy hand. "You ride me about not hanging my things up, and you go and throw your dress on the floor. On my slippers."

"Well," the voice said, "whose fault was it I threw it down last night?"

"Well," he said, and put on the slippers, and went out the door.

When he came back from the garden, grasping the new wet lettuce in his hands, she was ready to put slices of ham into a skillet on the stove. She wore a green gingham dress, her hair, yellowish in the sun from the kitchen windows, falling loose and uncombed over the crisp green cloth. Her bare feet were stuck into dirty buckskin oxfords, from which the untied laces trailed out. He leaned over the sink, washing the lettuce, leaf by leaf, then laying it on a towel. She stood beside him for an instant, too slender, almost skinny, and as tall as he was; then she turned to the stove with the bowl of eggs.

When it was ready they carried the food on platters into the dining room, where bright sun pouring from the open windows showed the full disorder. The split-bottom chairs were scattered about, one on its side. Dishes on the table held remnants of anchovy sandwiches, about which, without much interest, a fly buzzed. All sorts of glasses cluttered the sideboard, the mantelpiece, and the uneven stone hearth before the dead fireplace. "My God," she breathed, balancing the platter of ham, "my God, why do people have parties?" Then, with nervous, angular gestures, she set the platter down, swept off one end of the table, and laid two plates.

She ate hungrily, he slowly in dull, dutiful distaste. While she ate, she kept looking about her at the objects of the room, examining them with a resentful, curious glance. "We just can't have any more parties," she finally said.

"Suits me fine," he said.

"Not with all this mess next morning."

He looked about him with an air of discovery. "We might get some new friends. Some nice refined lady and gentlemen drinkers who wouldn't make a mess. I might run an ad in the *Advocate*."

"The friend I want this morning," she said, and glared at the old anchovy sandwiches, "is Viola. My God, why did she have to up and leave right now?"

"Once a nigger goes sour, it's all up. I told you that."

"I suppose you're right. And I'm worn out with all my lover's quarrels with her."

"She'll want to come back in a week," he said. Then, critically surveying the room, "And you'll take her back, all right."

"I told her if she went, it was the last time."

"We ought never brought her up here from Alabama," he said in gloom. "I told you at the time too." He got up from the table and crossed to the fireplace. From the mantel, among the clutter of glasses, he picked up a pipe, and lighted the half-burned tobacco in its bowl. Smoke from his short thick nostrils spun out in the sunlight.

Mournfully, she looked at him. "She was the cleanest nigger I ever saw," she said in some reproach. "She was so clean that when she was a little girl, she says she wouldn't sit on the ground with the other little niggers, she sat on a plate."

"She was fine in Alabama, but she's not worth a damn in Tennessee. She ought to go back to Alabama and sit on a plate."

"She *is* going home. She can't stay here with that old hussy of Jake's wife charging her nine dollars for a week's board and room while we went off, and it's the only place she can stay. Nine dollars, when we only pay her six! God, it makes me furious. I told the milk boy I was furious just so he'd tell Jake's wife."

"You needn't take it out on me," he said, regarding her outthrust nervous hands and her flushed cheeks. "You look like you were mad at me."

"I'm mad at that bitch," she said, suddenly more composed. "She's just trying to drive Viola off because she's jealous of that beautiful Jake of hers. She just doesn't like Viola. And she doesn't like me. You ought to hear the things Viola says she says about me."

Not answering, he turned to the open window. Beyond the rail fence of the yard, where strands of buckberry bushes exhibited the faintest tracery of green, the little valley fell sharply away. The lane went down the valley, bordered on one side by trees; the new flat leaves hung very still and bright. "The trouble is," he finally said, "that Viola is a white-folks' nigger."

"She's ashamed of her nigger blood, all right."

"She hasn't got too much nigger blood in her to be ashamed of. I bet she's cousin to a long line of drunken Alabama statesmen."

"She says niggers are dirty."

"Well," he said amiably, "aren't they?"

She rose abruptly from the table, glanced in despair at the articles on it and at his broad stubby back, then straightened herself. "I wish I had a dirty nigger here right now." She seized a plate in each hand and started for the kitchen. "Come on," she ordered, "you too."

He picked up two plates and followed her. Returning, he got two more, but paused as he passed the window. "Hey, Annabelle," he called, "here comes Jake! He's got on his Sunday clothes, too."

"Let him come."

There was the sound of water running in the kitchen. He stood by the window, holding the plates, and looked down the valley. Below him the tall black-coated figure moved slowly up the lane, moving with unhurried dignity beside the new-leafed trees. He watched until the figure had passed out of vision from the window, then he went through the kitchen, where she bent over the steaming sink, and out the back.

Standing on the top of the back steps, he said, "Hello, Jake."

"Good morning, Mr. Allen," the Negro said, and approached the steps in his slow dignified pace. He stopped at the bottom of the steps, took off his black felt hat, and smiled gravely. "Kin I speak to Miz Allen?" he said.

"I'll see." He went inside.

"What does he want?" she demanded.

"He says he wants to talk to you."

"Bring him in the dining room."

He put his head out the kitchen door and called, "Jake, you come on in here."

The Negro man came in through the kitchen, bending his head at the door frame, treading very softly on the faded blue carpet on the dining room floor.

"Good morning, Jake," she said to him, and sank down in a chair at the table, laying her damp bony hands out on the cloth before her.

"Good morning, Miz Allen," he said.

She waited, looking at him. He stood carefully in the exact center of the open space between the table and sideboard, holding his hat decorously in his hand. He wore jean pants, pale blue from washings, and a black Prince Albert coat drooping from his high shoulders. A big gold watch chain hung across the black vest, which was too loose for him and not long enough. "Miz Allen," he said oratorically. Then he smiled, again gravely, but with no apology. "Miz Allen, I ain't accustomed to mess in no woman's affairs, but they's something I oughter tell you."

"All right, Jake," she said.

"Hit's this girl, Viola. She done said a lie about my wife and me. She done said to you we charged her nine dollars that week you and Mr. Allen went off and she ate down there with us."

"That's what she said," she agreed in some weariness. "And I gave her three dollars extra, I felt so sorry for her."

"That girl, Viola, she ain't said the truth. My wife never charged her no nine dollars," he said sadly. "We'se charged her seventy-five cents a week for that room, Miz Allen, that's ev'y God's penny. And when she eat there, my wife done said thirty cents a day, that oughter be enough." He stood patiently in the open space, his brown face, with the silky drooping mustache, decorous and unexpectant.

"So she lied to me," the girl at the table said after a little.

"Yassum," he said, "she lied. I dunno what else you might call hit."

"She wanted me to give her that three dollars, and I gave it to her."

"Yassum, she wanted that three dollars, I reckin." He hesitated, and cleared his throat. "Miz Allen." He shifted his hat to the other hand and continued, "I reckin I know what she wanted hit for."

"Yes?"

"She got herself a new coat. The other day she brought hit to the house and showed my wife hit. A gray coat what's got fur on hit, too."

"A new coat!" She got up from the table, jarring the dishes that remained there. "My Lord, a new coat. She didn't need a new coat. And she lied to me to get three dollars. After all the clothes I've given her this year. Jake, you've seen those clothes, haven't you?"

"I seed 'em," he said. "She brought 'em to the house."

"I gave her a coat too."

"Yassum, she didn't need no more clothes. She doan never go nowhere I knows of no way. She just comes in er-nights and gits herself all dressed up in them clothes you give her and combs her hair. She doan go nowhere, she just sets there in that room a time, then she gits in the bed."

"She hasn't got any friends, I know," she said.

"She doan ack like she wants no friends," Jake said.

The young white man, who leaned against the kitchen door, took the pipe from his mouth and wagged it at them. "The trouble," he said morosely, "is that we ought never brought her from Alabama away from her people."

The Negro pondered a moment, stroking his silky long mustache with a forefinger. "Maybe so," he admitted, "maybe she might do right well with her people. But she ain't my wife's and my kind of people. You ast anybody round here. We tries to do the fair and God-fearing thing towards ev'y-body, be he white or black. You ast anybody."

"I'm glad to know you all didn't charge her that nine dollars," she said.

"No, ma'm. And we never wanted her nohow. We owns our house and lot and I gits plenty work carpentering and bricklaying to git along. We ain't never wanted her. But I says to my wife, she's a girl a long way from home amongst strangers in a strange country. But we never wanted her." He intoned the words like a speech memorized, holding his black felt hat in his hands, looking straight out from his height over the head of the woman who stood before him. "She cain't stay no longer, lying like she done."

"She quit me last night, Jake. When some people were coming to a party, too," she said bitterly. "And I won't take her back this time either like I did before."

"She cain't stay at my house no more. I reckin she better go."

"I reckon so," she said.

He backed toward the kitchen door, sliding his flat heels

soundlessly over the carpet, saying as he did so, "She better git back to her own people, wherever she come from." In the kitchen he paused and fumbled with his hat as if trying to remember just one more thing to say.

"Jake," the woman said, her face suddenly hard and pointed, "you tell Viola to come up here. Right away this morning."

"Yassum."

"Don't tell her what for, just send her up here."

"Yassum."

"All right, Jake."

He lingered in the kitchen a moment, still deliberating. Then he said, "Good morning, Miz Allen," and walked out the back way, shutting the porch door very gently behind him.

At the almost inaudible sound of the door closing she seemed to relax a little, sinking again into the chair by the table. "My God," she said, "the fool goes and spends all her money for a coat. When she's got a coat, and when I've been trying all winter to make her save."

"Niggers," he remarked with some unction, and stood straddle-legged in the space by the sideboard. "Niggers"—he paused to give the pipe a precautionary suck—"know how to live. Just like the good book says, 'Man does not live by bread alone.' Now Viola works all winter and you teach her to save money and when she gets it saved, she knows what to do with it."

"Oh, hush up, Bill." Distraught and unhappy, she sat at the table, working her bony fingers back and forth on the rough cloth.

"She got herself a new coat. Now that nigger's got a sense of values."

"She's got a sense of values all right. She got three dollars out of me."

"My little philanthropist," he said, and scized a dish of mangled crumby sandwiches and stamped toward the kitchen.

"Your little sucker," she said, and followed him.

He was sitting on the side porch off the dining room, lean-ing an elbow by the typewriter on the big unpainted table, when she came up the lane. When she passed just a little distance below him, her beanpole-thin, crooked legs work-ing methodically over the rough ground, her body bent for-ward and her hands at her breast as if poked into an invisible muff, he pretended not to see, putting his face down toward the typewriter. His wife came out on the porch, a cigarette in her hand.

"There she is," she said.

"I saw her all right," he said. "She's got her new coat on."

"What'll I say to her?"

"Hell fire, you got her up here. I didn't."

"What'll I say?"

"Tell her she's a thief and a liar, and that you love her like a sister and want her to wash the dishes."

The old plowpoints hanging as weights for the gate chinked as the gate fell to. The Negro woman stood just inside the gate and regarded the porch with a gaze of meek question. "Come here, Viola," the woman on the porch said, and she came slowly.

She stopped at the foot of the steps, still mute and ques-tioning, her hands still at her breast.

"Come up here, Viola."

She came up the steps. "Good morning, Miz Allen," she said, and her fingers absently brushed the gray fur on the open coat collar.

"You've got a new coat, Viola."

"Yassum," the Negro said, letting her hands drop with a delayed empty gesture.

"It's a pretty coat, Viola."

"I fancied hit," the Negro woman said. "I seed a girl one time outer my winder and she had on a gray dress and gray shoes and a gray coat and hat . . . all gray. . . ." She lifted her pale copperish face, and gazed at the woman from out yellowish eyes which, though depthless like an animal's, ex-pressed a certain solicitude, a resignation. The woman met the gaze, put her cigarette to her lips, then puffed the smoke straight out into the air, with no pleasure. Suddenly she turned aside to the porch rail, leaning against it. "Viola," she said decisively, and hesitated. In a stiff-armed abrupt motion she flung the burning stub down to the yard, where it sent up a faint trail of smoke from the midst of new grass and the tattered winter-old spikes of sage. She swung round to face the Negro. "Viola, you said Jake's wife charged you nine dollars that week we went off."

"Yassum."

"That's what you said."

"Yassum, I did."

"Jake," the woman said, confronting the mild yellow eyes, "he's been up here and he said they didn't charge you nine dollars."

The face, the gazing yellow eyes, were unchanged and impassive.

"He said he charged you seventy-five cents a week for that room and thirty cents a day when you ate there. Is that right?"

"Yassum."

"You say 'yassum'!" A spasm of irritation swept over the woman's features, leaving them hurt and hard. "You lied to me. What made you lie?"

"That warn't no lie, Miz Allen."

"I don't know what else you'd call it. A lie's when you don't tell the truth." She fell into the patience of explanation, then pulled up sharply: "You lied."

"That warn't no lie, Miz Allen."

"Don't contradict me, Viola!"

The man at the table scraped the chair back, got up, bumping himself on the table, and went into the house.

"You lied," she continued, still hard, "because you wanted money out of me. Three dollars. You wanted to buy a coat. You stole three dollars."

The Negro woman began to move her head from side to side, not seekingly, but with an almost imperceptible motion, like a sick animal annoyed by flies. "I ain't never stole noth-ing," she said.

"You stole from me," the woman said, weakening a little, leaning against the porch rail. "After all I've done for you. After all the clothes I've given you. I gave you that dress you've got on, and it's a good dress."

"Yassum." She looked down at the green silk that hung in folds too big for her over the flat chest. "I kin give 'em back," she said.

"I don't want them back. I just want you to know I've been good to you and that you lied and stole, that's all the thank-fulness you've got."

"I'se got thankfulness," she said.

The woman took the cigarette from the pocket of the green gingham and tried to light it, plunging its end into the shak-ing flame of the match, putting the match out. She removed the blackened cigarette from her lips and held it in her hand, which trembled a little. "I can't find my blue cook book, Viola," she said. "Now I want you to go in there and find it." Her voice was certain now.

The Negro moved across the porch and into the house, her bowed legs setting the feet down on the boards with a sort of painful accuracy, so that the heels twisted over at each step. The woman watched her go in, then lighted the cigarette and spewed the smoke out grayly before her face.

The Negro came back, holding the blue cook book out dangling as if her wrist were too weak to support it. "Here 'tis," she said. "Hit war just where I done left hit. Where it belong," she added, and her small features twitched into some-thing near a tentative, deprecatory smile. Then the smile dis-sipated, and the features sank into their meekness.

The woman took the book. "Now, Viola, I want you to go away. You haven't treated me right. And you haven't treated right these Negroes round here who've tried to be nice to you, taking you in and inviting you to their parties and things." She looked off down the valley, speaking quickly and harshly.

"You go away. You better go back to Alabama to your own people."

"Wellum," she said without any tone, and turned down the steps.

The woman came to the edge of the porch. "Go away," she said. "I don't ever want to see you again."

Slowly the Negro went down the uneven brick part toward the gate. At the gate she stopped, fingering the weather-gray palings. Then she looked round. "I wouldn't never say that 'bout you, Miz Allen," she said. "I wants to see you." She went out the gate and methodically down the hill.

The woman sat on the top step sucking her cigarette. Her husband came out the door. "Fire her," he said unsympathetically.

"I sent her away. But you—" she looked accusingly—"you would go off and leave me to do the dirty work. You always do."

"I couldn't bear to watch you in action," he said amicably. "I've got a very sensitive nature." He tapped the typewriter several times aimlessly. "What did you say?" he said.

"It was awful," she said. "I acted awful." She got up and moved to the open door. "I just behaved like some old self-righteous Methodist slut."

"You went to Sunday School, didn't you?"

She smoked her cigarette down to the dead end, jerked the paper loose from the flesh of her lip, and crushed the ash out against the door frame. "And I ended up," she said, "saying I never wanted to see her again."

He spaced the sheet in the typewriter for another paragraph, then leaned back. He said, "Well, you don't have to, you know."

Going down the hill, the heavy old car groaned and slithered in the gravel ruts, where water ran down from level to level, yellow and flecked by whitish foam. It was still raining, hard and straight down, for there was no wind in the valley. The new leaves on the trees by the lane hung limp and beaten under the steady impact.

"I come home," he said bitterly, "and you drag me out in this again."

"I suppose you think I love it."

When he had steered the car, clattering, over the loose planks of the bridge, beneath which the creek boiled hollowly against the stone supports, he said, "I'm fed up with those niggers."

"Well, Jake sent a boy up there through all this rain to say to come down, it was important."

"All right, all right," he said, "we're going, aren't we?"

They drew into the highway, where the asphalt was slick and black, glittering dully. The rain had let up a little. Down the highway two hundred yards, the house stood, bare and boxlike on its tall stone foundations, the roof sodden black beneath two oak trees that were not yet leafing. The man and the woman picked their way across the yard, which showed no grass, only flat packed earth where the water stood in little pools, giving forth no reflection.

He knocked on the door, and stepped aside so that his wife occupied the space before it. The tall Negro, wearing overalls now and in sock feet, opened it. "Good evening, Miz Allen," he said. "I'se much obliged to you for coming, and hit raining like this."

"What is it, Jake?"

"Hit's that girl, Viola," he said. He moved back, and they followed him inside. A Negro woman, black and angular in the face, rose from beside the stove in the center of the room, nodded stiffly and pushed a pair of steel-rimmed spectacles up on her forehead. "Hit's that girl," she said.

"What is it?" the woman said.

"She's done got in the bed and she won't git up. I done tole her she's gotta go, but she won't say nothing. She just lays there. Going on three days." She paused a moment, breathless and truculent, then spoke more moderately. "You kin see how it is."

"I'll talk to her."

The Negro woman stood with her hand on the knob of the door to another room. "You tell her, Miz Allen, she's gotta go."

The curtains at the window were almost drawn, only a little light coming in to mark the rocking chair where clothes and the gray coat were piled, the table by the wall, and the bed. She lay in the bed, on her back, with the sheet pulled up to her chin. When they entered, her eyes rolled to fix on them for a second, then slowly again looked at the ceiling.

"Viola," the woman said.

The woman on the bed said nothing, her face with no expression.

"Viola, you talk to me now." She went closer, putting her hand on the straight chair by the bed. On the chair a bucket of water stood, beside it a piece of cheese and an open box of crackers. "Do you hear me? Answer me!"

"I hears you."

"Now, Viola, you get up. You're making yourself sick." She shook the chair impatiently. "Cheese and crackers for three days."

The old Negro woman came closer, sticking her knotty black face out oracularly in the dim light. "You tell her she's gotta go," she said.

"You hear that, Viola? You're not treating these people right. You've got to go."

"I hears," the woman on the bed said, still looking at the ceiling.

"I'll buy you a ticket home. On the bus. But you've got to go."

"I'se got money," she said.

The white woman looked down at her for a minute, at the body under the tightly pulled sheet. "You can't stay here," she added.

"Yassum," the voice said from the bed.

"Now you get up from there and go right away. You hear me!"

"Yassum."

"Good-bye, Viola," she said; but there was no answer. She went into the other room, where the two men waited.

"Is she gonna go, Miz Allen?" the Negro man asked.

"I think so. She said she would, Jake."

"She ain't going neither," the Negro woman interrupted savagely. "She just says 'yassum.' You tell her she's gotta go. I ain't having nobody laying up in the bed in my house like that. You gotta tell—"

"You be quiet, Josie," the Negro man ordered.

"I've done what I can," the woman said. She took a bill from her purse and laid it on the table. "That's for her bus," she said, and went out on the porch, where her husband already was. She laid her hand on his arm. The Negro man followed them, carefully shutting the door after him. "Miz Allen," he said, hesitantly, but not in embarrassment, "my wife didn' mean nothin' talking like that. She's just worrit, and all. That girl layin' up there."

"It's all right, Jake."

They went down the steps and got into the car. It had stopped raining altogether now, and to the right of the highway the rays of the sun, now almost at setting, lay over the field of young wheat. They turned up the lane and over the plank bridge, beside the tree, whose topmost leaves glistened in the level light. "It's right pitiful," she finally said, "thinking of her lying up there."

He slammed the gears into second for the grade.

"I'm fed up," he said.

"Then what the hell you think I am?" she said.

The Life and Work of Professor
Roy Millen

PROFESSOR ROY MILLEN had loved his wife devotedly, and now, in the spring of the year 1937, she was dead. He had not realized before how much she had meant to him, how his own life had described its orbit, as it were, within the steady and beneficent influence of her being. If she had dominated the course of his life, it had not been by isolated, individual acts of superior will, but rather by defining, subtly but more completely year after year, the very atmosphere he breathed. His position at the university, the long tranquil evenings at the bridge table with the light glinting subduedly on the exciting and rich designs of the royal cards, the friends at the table, the respectful greeting in the corridors and on the street, the very food he put into his mouth—all of these items had been defined by her. He had never protested against this, not even fleetingly, in the privacy of his own mind. Day after day, year after year, he had accepted it as part of the inevitable furniture of his life, just as he had accepted the sound of her voice and the expression of her face. If he felt anything, it was a kind of gratitude. Any little act he could do for her —and it comforted him now to remember that he had always tried to do the little things she wanted, especially after her health failed—had only been the proper manifestation of his gratitude, or at least of his candid admission that she had made him what he was.

The self which he now was—the man with the carefully brushed tufts of white hair on each side of the pink and hygienic-looking bald skull, the rimless pince-nez with the black cord, the well-pressed but somewhat worn suits, blue or medium gray according to the season, the cleanly cut nails, the thoughts that came into his head—that self, too, had been defined by her. And during the twenty-odd years of his life with her, he had remembered more and more rarely the other self which he had been before his marriage. He did not like to remember that other time, for those years had been painful and long, so painful that even in recollection something of the distress of the old reality could revive within him. He had bent over the long rows of cotton, with the sun bearing down on his shoulders and the humid air swimming around him. He had clerked in crossroads stores. He had taught in the country schools of his native section, listening all day to the sullen or droning voices of the children and then tramping down some muddy road to his rented room in a tumble-down farmhouse. Later, long after those years were past, he would occasionally wonder, when the unsought recollections came to him, what had sustained him, what hope had given him strength enough to go on. Looking back, he could not say. He could not remember what strength had been in him, or remember what he had hoped for, or expected. Certainly, he had not hoped for what he had actually found. Anyway, he told himself humbly, this was better than what he had hoped for. For he had scarcely known that there could be such a life as this.

By the time he was twenty-nine he had managed to get a degree from a small denominational college. For two years then, he had better teaching jobs, and saved enough to see him through a winter at the state university. When he was thirty-seven, he received a Ph.D. in English literature. That June day he stood on the platform of the auditorium, stooped and sweating under the black robe and colored hood, as though to their weight were added the weight of all the privations and distresses which had brought him to that moment, and his outstretched hand shook. That fall, quite unexpectedly, he got a small job teaching freshmen at the university. One of the regular instructors was ill, and the head of the department thriftily surmised that Millen would take the job for little or nothing. During the year the instructor died.

"Millen is a good steady man," Dr. Saunders, the head of the department remarked to his daughter one day toward the end of the year. "It looks as if we might just keep him on another year until we can make a permanent appointment."

"Yes," Mildred Saunders said dutifully, abstractedly. She was a tallish woman, a little past thirty, with a spindly figure and plain features. Her habitual expression was kindly, however, and she had a quiet nature. A few weeks after her father's remark, she saw Millen at a faculty reception, miserable and lonely in a corner, and talked to him, remembering what her father had said. In ministering to his embarrassment and shyness, she forgot something of her own habitual diffidence. The following year, early in the session, when Dr. Saunders had Millen to his house on some piece of academic business, Mildred Saunders saw him and asked him to come again. He came more and more frequently during the year, to sit in the shadowed and dingy parlor, his bony hands with the bitten nails moving uneasily on his knees. In May he received a permanent appointment to his job, and Mildred Saunders announced her engagement to him. She had married him, and he had been devoted to her, and now she was dead.

She had died quite suddenly and ironically, just at the time when, after years of ill health, she seemed to be getting well and strong again, and they were planning to go away on a year's leave. They were planning to go to England, where he could work in one of the great English libraries and finish his book. Six years before, he had had a leave, and they had planned to go to England to work on the book, but they had gone, in the end, to southern California. He had not protested, even to himself, at the change in plans; in fact he had suggested the change. The cold, damp climate of Millersburg in winter had always been bad for his wife's asthma and neuralgia, and England might be worse. And his wife's cousins in Los Angeles would be company for her while he worked on his book. And there were some very nice libraries in California. Everybody knew that.

She had seemed better at first in California, but then, despite everything, her health had taken a turn for the worse. She had been in the hospital, and the doctors had done all they could, and the cousins had been helpful and considerate. Some days they had even gone to the hospital and he had been able to stay at home and work or go to the library. But she had been very ill, and he knew what to do for her—better, he told himself, than the cousins or even the nurses. Even after she was able to leave the hospital and go back to Millersburg she was never really well. But she was very patient and rarely lost her temper with him. Sometimes, when he sat beside her bed—for during that period she was confined to her bed almost half of the time—she would reach out to touch his hand and say: "Just leave me alone, Roy, and go work on your book. You ought to work on your book, Roy. I don't mind being alone. I've gotten used to being alone." He would say that it didn't matter, or that it was moving along nicely, that he had done quite a bit lately. Or she would say: "I'm sorry we have to spend so much money on me, Roy, when you want to go away to work on your book." Then he would try to comfort her.

She was dead now, but there was the book left for him. I have my book to do, at least I have that, he concluded as soon as the first shock of grief had worn off and he had begun to search in himself for some center of meaning for his life. Then, day after day, as he came to accept the fact of his loss and his mind dwelt more and more on his book, a kind of modest excitement grew within him—an excitement so pleasurable that once or twice, remembering in the midst of it his wife's death, he was filled with a sense of shame and remorse.

He made his plans to go abroad, to England, to work in the libraries there, as he and his wife had planned. It was what she would have him do, he told himself. And the book would be a kind of monument to her. He would dedicate the book to her. As he walked slowly back from the campus to his house in the late afternoons or early evenings of spring, he would try to compose the dedication, saying the words aloud to himself as he looked up at the paling, peach-colored sky beyond the newly leafed branches. He had decided to sail in June, as soon as he could leave after commencement.

"I hear you're going away for a year, Professor Millen," Tom Howell said, standing respectfully before Professor Millen's office desk. Then he added, in a dutiful tone, "To work on your book."

"Yes," Professor Millen said, "to work on my book." Then, as though recollecting himself, he made a little gesture toward the chair in front of the desk, and said, "Won't you have a seat, Howell?"

"Are you going to finish it in a year?" Howell asked, and sat down.

"I still have a little research to do. I have to settle a few points—points which can't be settled in libraries in this country. I have to do some work yet in one of the great English libraries." Professor Millen paused, looking over the green lawn outside his office window. "But I'll get it written within the year. Practically everything is in order. Though, of course," he paused again, looking at Tom Howell, who listened respectfully and with what seemed to be interest, "I'll have to do a good deal of retouching—style and so on, you know—" he waved his hand modestly in the air, "when I get back."

"I'm hoping—" the boy hesitated, fumbling in his pocket to draw out a folded paper, "I'm hoping to be able to go abroad next year. If I can make it. That's what I wanted to see you about, Professor Millen."

"Anything I can do, I'll be glad to do."

"It's a scholarship. A French scholarship, and I was hoping you'd recommend me. I've had a lot of work with you, and all. The French Department will recommend me, but I've done my minor in English, you know. What you'd say would count a lot."

"Howell," Professor Millen said, judicially putting the tips of his fingers together and inspecting the boy, "I've never had a better student than you are. Possibly never one as good. I'll say that in my recommendation. I'll write a strong one."

He felt his enthusiasm mounting as he spoke, and a warmth suffused him as though at the prospect of some piece of happiness, some success, for himself.

"I certainly appreciate it," the boy said. "This is about the only thing I've got in sight for next year, and I'm graduating. Oh, I reckon I could get a little teaching job or something for a year or two to save up some money to go on. I don't think I ought to ask my family for any more—they've been swell, putting me through college and giving me that trip to France two years back—"

"Yes, yes," Professor Millen said abstractedly, "oh, yes, you did go over one summer, didn't you?"

"Oh, that was just for fun," Howell said, "but this time it would be for work. And when I get back I ought to be able to get a pretty good job so I could save enough to get my Ph.D. quick. Up East."

"A year of study in France will be a fine opportunity," Professor Millen said. That enthusiasm and warmth which had filled him like a promise of happiness was waning now, he did not know why. He wished the boy would get up and go and leave him alone.

"Oh, it'll be an opportunity," Howell agreed, "and I'm not going to waste it. The work'll be fun, and there ought to be a little fun besides. I was in Paris for two weeks—and you know how Paris is, it sort of knocks you off your feet. You've been there?"

"Yes, yes," Professor Millen said hurriedly, impersonally, almost impatiently, averting his face from the boy and looking off across the patch of lawn, wondering why he had lied, why he had told the boy he had been to Paris. He watched some students, two boys and a girl, who moved across the sunlit, open space. They moved lingeringly. It seemed that they would never be across that bright, open space of green where the sun was. Then they were gone, hidden by the screen of foliage.

Professor Millen turned and brought his gaze to rest again on the boy. The boy was leaning forward, his face smiling,

Professor Millen saw, as for the first time, the blond, crisp hair combed back from the square forehead, the confident gaze of the blue eyes, the comfortable, confident way the coat hung from the good shoulders.

The boy stood up. "I've stayed too long. I know you've got a lot of work to do."

"No," Professor Millen said.

"And I certainly appreciate your recommendation. The address of the scholarship committee is on here," he said, and laid a printed sheet on the desk. "That's the circular, and all the information."

"I'll attend to it right away," Professor Millen said.

"Thank you," the boy said, and was gone.

For a few minutes Professor Millen sat there, his eyes on the bare wall opposite his desk. Then he read the circular. He laid it back on the desk and pressed a button. When the secretary came in, he handed her the printed sheet. "The address is on that," he said, and waited while she copied it. Then he said, "I'll give you the letter." He studied the bare wall for a moment, then began: "Gentlemen. I can truthfully say that I take the most sincere pleasure in recommending to you Mr. Thomas Howell. In my long career as a teacher I have never had a better student. He has an acute and penetrating intelligence, and, as is so often not the case with young men of his capacity, the patience and honesty of a true scholar. I am sure that if he is appointed to—" He hesitated, looking at the wall. "I am sure that—" he said at last, then stopped.

The secretary, her pencil poised above her pad, waited while Professor Millen seemed to withdraw, to sink within himself. Her foot made a slight reproachful scraping sound as she changed her position in the chair. She, too, began to look out the window, where Professor Millen's gaze now was fixed.

"That's all—all for the present," Professor Millen said, suddenly. "Just hold that and I'll finish later. I've just thought—" he managed to look directly at her—"of something else I've got to do. There's something else."

After the secretary had left the office, closing the door softly behind her, he did not move for some time. Then he again looked out the window. The shadows were lengthening over the smooth lawn. The faintest premonitory flush was touching the puffs of white cloud visible toward the top of his window. Before long now he would be going home. He picked up the circular. He read it again, very carefully, dwelling on it almost painfully, as though he were an illiterate trying to extort some secret from the words. He lifted his eyes from the sheet and stared at the chair where the boy had sat leaning forward, the pleasure shining on his clear, handsome face, the good coat riding easy on his shoulders, saying, "—you know how Paris is, it sort of knocks you off your feet. You've been there?"

Professor Millen let the circular slip from his lap to the floor. Then, decisively, he reached into the drawer of his desk and took out a sheet of paper. He wrote rapidly in his large, firm script:

GENTLEMEN:

I have been asked to recommend Mr. Thomas Howell to you for a scholarship for study in France. As you will observe from a transcript of his academic record, with which no doubt you have been provided, he has made the grade of A in all of his work in the English department of this institution, and I understand that his grades in French (his major subject) have been very high. This achievement, of course, deserves consideration, but candor compels me to say that a superficial facility and cleverness seem to characterize his mind. I do not wish to prejudice the committee against his case, and I may be wrong in my estimate; certainly, I hope that the committee will consider him very carefully. But I do feel that he lacks solidity of character, the spirit of patient inquiry, and what might be termed the philosophical bent.

Very respectfully yours,
ROY MILLEN,
Professor of English.

Without looking up, he addressed an envelope hurriedly, the pen making a dry, scratching sound. Then he blotted and stamped the envelope, inserted the sheet, put the letter into his pocket, picked up his hat, and left the office. He would, he remembered, pass a postbox on his way home.

The Unvexed Isles

THE WHISKY—the best whisky in Russell Hill—sloshed with unthrifty golden opulence into the third and last of the glasses that stood on the lacquered tray. Professor Dalrymple, something of the crystal-gazer's pious abstraction in his regard, watched the spill and whirl of the liquor in the orbit of bright glass. Professor Dalrymple did not relish whisky, even the best whisky in Russell Hill, which, indeed, he dispensed. But he never entered the warm pantry on a Sunday evening, hearing the competent rustle of the electric refrigerator and the murmur of voices from a farther room, without feeling, as he lifted the decanter, a sense of decorous liberation. It was the same sense of liberation he sometimes felt when, looking at his own fine white hands, he recalled that one visit home and the sight of his brother's hands lying inert on the table-cloth in the lamplight: burned by sun, chapped by wind like rotten leather, grained irrevocably with black dirt from the prairie.

Sacramentally, the whiskey sloshed into the glass. Bubbles of air streamed upward, and at the surface minutely exploded.

Professor Dalrymple set the silver-mounted siphon on the tray beside the silver bucket of ice, picked up the tray, squared his shoulders as he did these days when he detected that unconscious droop, and proceeded through the door, across the dining room, where articles of silver discreetly glimmered in the dimness, across the hall, and into the room where they sat, waiting.

"Not the true, the blushing Hippocrene," he uttered, and approached the bright fire where they sat, "but 'twill serve."

"It'll serve all right, Doctor," Phil Alburt said. "It's as much of a beaker full of the warm South as I ask, even on as lousy cold a night as tonight." His voice filled the room with authority, a kind of aimless vitality that seemed to make the fire burn up brighter and the bulbs behind their parchment shades glow with more assurance. "It was snowing again when I came in."

"So that's what you got out of my English 40, sir?" the Professor demanded.

"Not exactly." His laughter was like his voice.

"Well, Phil, if you didn't get more than that, nobody did. I'll wager on that."

"Don't loiter, George," Mrs. Dalrymple commanded, a tinge of asperity licking along the edge of the pleasantry. "Mr. Alburt can wait for his compliment, but I don't want to wait for my toddy."

"Pardon me, Alice," he said, and with some formality presented the tray.

Looking at the ready tray, she commanded, "Squirt it for me."

Her husband set the tray on the little table, placed his long white thumb with its chalky nail on the siphon lever, and pressed. The liquor swirled, paled in the soft light, rose toward the brim.

"Ice," she said.

"On a night like this," Phil Alburt deplored.

"We always take ice back home in Baltimore," she said.

Professor Dalrymple handed his wife the glass.

"No ice for me," Phil Alburt said, "and not much water."

"I remember," the Professor said. "No ice. Result of your English visits, I suppose."

"Perhaps," Phil Alburt said, and laughed the vital, vacant laugh.

"Not the only result, I'm sure," the Professor said, and carried the tray across to him. The young man laid his cigarette on the receptacle beside him, looked up at his host with a smile of affable toleration, and reached for the siphon. "Thank you, sir," he said.

The Professor regarded the head with its dark hair which lay in neat gleaming curly folds as though carved. As the water hissed peremptorily into the glass, the smoke lifted from the idle cigarette on the tray under the Professor's eyes and swayed in its delicate substance. The Professor's glance rested on the cigarette. *It is most singular,* he thought, *that the tip of that cigarette should be stained with lipstick.* The words came through his head with such emphatic clarity and distinctness that, rattling the glasses, he started as though the sentence had been spoken by an unseen observer.

"That's fine. Thank you," the young man was saying.

Professor Dalrymple, with effort, disengaged his eyes from the cigarette to meet the large features turned up at him in the contortion of amiability. The features were large and suddenly naked: the strong lips, the even white teeth unbared, the thrust of the nose, the wide brown eyes in which swam flecks of gold, the heavy eyebrows where hairs arched sleekly out from some vigor at the root.

"You're welcome," Professor Dalrymple rejoined mechanically, then, aware of his words, flushed. As he turned about and traversed the excessive distance across the blue carpet, he felt that all these objects accumulated around him—table, chair, chair, blue carpet, rug, lamp—were unfamiliar to him, and now for the first time might, if he so chose, be construed in their unique and rich unities. After he had adjusted the tray, with special care, on the stand, he gave to its obscure design a lingering and analytic regard. Lingering, as if he were a schoolboy unwilling at the last moment to lay aside the book before entering the examination room, or as if his attention to the intricacies of the design might postpone the need to inspect those people whose voices, somewhat remotely, impinged upon him.

The liquid was cold and sweetish in his mouth. He set the glass back, and as he did so discovered with some surprise that the muscles of his cheek were warped upward in an attentive smile. He might have caught sight of himself in a random mirror, so surely did he see, not feel, the thin, long, over-sensitive lips lift and recede beneath the accurate line of black bristle in the ambassadorial mustache. *I am making a great fool of myself,* he reflected, *grinning like that.*

Alice Dalrymple had just said, "I guess old Prexy would turn over in his truckle bed if he knew we were plying one of his charges with toddy."

Professor Dalrymple, yet smiling, cleared his throat slightly. "You know, Phil, we are not able to follow the dictates of hospitality as a general thing. Offering refreshment to our undergraduates is, as a general thing, shall I say, tabu. But I feel, we feel, that we are at liberty to do so in certain cases where the undergraduate's background is more liberal—when the undergraduate is more mature, more, shall I say, a man of the world." The words slipped precisely over his lips, and he was aware, at their conclusion, of the lips still warped upward in the smile. He was aware of having uttered the words at some time in the past, of some quality and inflection that implied rehearsal. But as he said "A man of the world," he did not experience that feeling of inner security and relish which customarily was his on like occasions.

Phil Alburt lolled in dark well-tailored mass behind a glass, a look of bland inattention on his features. When he spoke, it was, likewise, with an accent of rehearsal. "I must say I'm mature enough to appreciate the quality of this hospitality," he said, and significantly fingered the glass.

Professor Dalrymple thought, *A man of the world.* He slipped the phrase about in his mind as a child sucks candy, but the words were hard and savorless like marbles. Quite suddenly it occurred to him that the young man opposite, who nodded his head in amused approbation at some remark from the pretty woman, fancied himself as a man of the world. *Because he is rich,* it occurred to him, *because he lives in New York and wears tailor-made clothes and goes to Europe and drinks whisky, and, in fact, has kissed Alice Bogan Dalrymple in my house, he fancies himself a man of the world. I was born in Nebraska in a house that stood on the bare ground with no trees.* Then with a feeling of distant fatality, his sense of warmth for Phil Alburt, somewhat modified but real enough, came back within him. In all perversity, it came back.

Alice Dalrymple gave her gaze to the fire, where flames scrolled ornamentally upward to the black chimney throat. The brass dogs gleamed, the hearth was swept to a sharp border, the flames sprouted upward like flowers from an accurate parterre. *She turns her head so,* Professor Dalrymple observed, *because she knows she looks best in profile. She is thinner these days, she looks tired.* Alice Dalrymple held her head at right angles to the young man's chair; her profile was clean and delicate, with a careful dyspeptic beauty. The young man himself was looking into the fire.

"So you are leaving Tuesday?" she said.

"Tuesday," Phil Alburt said with the air of one gently engrossed in the collaboration of fireside and toddy. "Tuesday, and I get home the next night just in time to hang up my stocking."

"And up early next morning," Professor Dalrymple said, "to see your new velocipede."

"Not to see my new velocipede, to take some Mother Sill's. You see, I've got to hang my stocking up over the wash basin on a boat to Bermuda. Mother is dragging me off down there."

Mrs. Dalrymple laughed, a quick accurate modulation. "And Old Santy comes down the hot water pipe and fills it with little guest cakes of Palmolive and Dr. West toothbrushes." She laughed. "Instead of ashes and switches."

"I won't care if it's full of horsewhips, I'll be feeling so bad that first morning. I'm a rotten sailor."

"Not horsewhips for a good little boy," Professor Dalrymple echoed, and, quite unexpectedly, laughed too.

"I've been planning to go East," Mrs. Dalrymple said in a tone of mild frustration. "To Baltimore."

"Home?" Phil Alburt said.

Home, Professor Dalrymple thought, *Mrs. George Dalrymple lives in Russell Hill in Illinois.* He tabulated the items of her address in his mind. *Mrs. George Dalrymple, 429 Poplar Street, Russell Hill, Illinois, U. S. A.*

"But George here can't go," she said, "and I'm going to be sweet and dutiful and stay right here."

"You ought to go, Alice," Professor Dalrymple said. And he said to himself, *She can't go because she can't buy a ticket on a train to Baltimore. Because she married a poor man.*

"George, you see, wants to finish up some research this vacation. He gets so little time during the year."

"What is it, Doctor?"

"Just a little Chaucer note I've been working on," the Professor answered, and thought for a minute that he might, after all, write a paper. Satisfaction and meaning filled him and velleities slipped away as he lifted his glass to his lips.

"So I'll stay here with him, a martyr to the noble cause of scholarship."

"A mild martyrdom, I would call it, to sit with my heels on the fender," the young man said.

"We used to have some pretty good Christmases in Baltimore, didn't we?" Mrs. Dalrymple gave her husband a full intimate glance, and he noted how the flesh dropped thinly away from the base of her nostrils. "I believe Father made the best eggnog I ever tasted. Everybody used to come in for eggnog on Christmas. Everybody. You ought to let your old research go hang this Christmas, George—"

"Yes, indeed," her husband said. He was conscious of the rhythm of forgotten voices, forgotten excitements, like the sea sound in empty whorls of a shell. Old Mr. Bogan's voice saying, "Gentlemen, gentlemen." Old Mrs. Bogan's voice with the shrillness all drained away in time. Form of voices with no sound.

"—but instead we'll just sit this Christmas."

Eggs. Dozens of eggs. Baskets of eggs. Whiskey, sweetish and gold. Hams. Arrogant turkeys. Wine. A steaming mess heaped and poured on the altar of Lucile Bogan's and Alice Bogan's need for a man to share the bed and pay the bills. A steaming, sweating altar, while smoke ascended from twenty-five cent cigars. *Ah,* he thought, and old Mr. Bogan's ritualistic white shirt front obtruded, a-glitter with starch and studs, in the midst of his fancy. *Ah, they spent a lot of money and the best they got was me. But that was when Alice wrote her little verses for the Junior League magazine and showed an English professor to her friends.* Then he concluded with a flat feeling in his head like a run-down clock: *She would know better now.*

"Well," Phil Alburt said, "just sitting has its points. I'm going to do a good deal of sitting myself this vacation. Taking my little school satchel along."

"To Bermuda," Professor Dalrymple said, dryly he hoped, and realized on the instant that he hated Phil Alburt, not because lipstick stained a dead cigarette butt in the ash tray across the hearth, but because Phil Alburt had said those precise words in that precise accent of comfort.

"To Bermuda," Phil Alburt agreed, and laughed without embarrassment.

Mrs. Dalrymple laughed, again the quick accurate modulation. Her husband stonily inspected her mirth: *She has no more self-respect than to laugh after what he just said to her. When she laughs now she holds her head up so the skin won't sag in her neck. Craning her neck like that, she looks like a cigarette advertisement.* He looked guiltily across at the tray by Phil Alburt, as if it were necessary to assure himself that the dead butt reposed there in its matrix of ash.

"However, I can't just sit any more right now," the young man said. "I've got to go now and do a little work before bedtime. I just came to say good-bye." He stood in front of his chair, not really tall but erect, broad shoulders appearing broader by the cut of his coat, his hair with a dark waxen gleam in the light, the double-breasted coat buttoned sleek and flat over his hips and belly.

Professor Dalrymple rose.

"Must you go," Mrs. Dalrymple asked, and likewise stood.

"Must," he said.

"Off to the happy isles," Professor Dalrymple said cheerfully. Then: "I'm thinking about a trip myself. I think I'll go home this Christmas." With a certain pleasure he noted his wife's faint movement of surprise—or was it annoyance?

"Fine," Phil Alburt said.

"You see," he continued, "I haven't been home in a long time. Not for nine years. I was born and reared out in Nebraska."

"On a ranch, I bet," the young man said hopefully.

"No. On a dirt farm, that's what they call them. Near a place named Sinking Fork Station. Just a wheat elevator and a siding. Did you ever hear of the place?"

Phil Alburt looked quickly at Mrs. Dalrymple, a glance of appeal for support or enlightenment. Then he managed a smile. "I can't say that I have," he said.

"I didn't really imagine that you had. My brother out there is still running the farm, I believe, unless they have foreclosed his various mortgages."

"Recent times have been difficult for the agriculturist," Phil Alburt said, somehow with a touch of piety.

"Indeed," Professor Dalrymple said, an ambiguous inflection to the word which he himself, for the flicker of an instant, tried in his mind to decipher. But he could scarcely decide what he had intended. He stood passively while his guest, a perturbed peevish light in his brown eyes, hesitated before taking comfort in the circumstance of farewell. Phil Alburt and Mrs. Dalrymple said good-bye. Good-bye and Merry Christmas.

In the hall, while he held Phil Alburt's coat, he felt like a fool. At the door, he shook, cordially as one trying to make amends, the hand offered him, refrained from looking at the face of the parting guest for fear he might find a smile on it, and said, several times, "Good-bye."

After Phil Alburt had gone down the steps, he yet stood in the open doorway, while the cold wind blew down the street and a few small flakes whipped past, and watched the figure proceed the length of the walk and climb into an automobile. He called once, "Merry Christmas," but his voice, he knew immediately, was lost in the easy, vicious whir of gears.

The wind which blew down the street tossed the decorative conifers by the walk so that they looked like two old women in tattered black shawls begging at his doorstep. He straightened his shoulders and experienced again, though but faintly, the accustomed sense of Sunday night complacency. Then his wife called, "Shut the door!"

He knew exactly how she would be when he entered the room. She would be standing before the fireplace, very still, as though spent by agitations of the evening; the black chiffon, in contrast to pale skin and pale hair, would hang to her slender figure with that extravagant flimsiness which once had made him suspect that a dress was borrowed for the occasion; and her breasts, defined but flattish, would lift, then decline, in a movement of disturbing, finicky respiration.

He closed the heavy door, took three paces down the hall, and entered the room.

There she stood.

"I think, Alice," he announced with a premonitory clearing of the throat, "I think that I shall do that paper. The subject has never been approached from precisely—"

She fixed her eyes on him; said, "What paper? . . . Oh, of course"; and relapsed into her stillness. The cigarette which hung, almost artificially, from her thin nervous fingers surrendered its trail of smoke to the air.

As he approached her across the carpet, warily as though he trod a treacherous surface on which he might slip and lose dignity, desire, an irritable but profound desire, took him. "Alice," he said, unsure of what words were to follow.

She again looked at him. "You were very rude to Phil," she said.

"Rude?" he echoed.

"What ever made you so rude to him?" Her voice was the voice of dutiful catechism.

He almost said: "Under the circumstances I had a right to be rude to him"; but did not. Then he thought: *She is angry because I said what I did to that fool. She doesn't believe I am really going home. I am going home.*

"What made you so rude?" she patiently demanded.

He was conscious of a small kernel of blind, blank rage deep in him. Its tentacles dumbly, blindly, groped within him.

"I never saw you act like that before."

"If I was rude to Mr. Alburt, I am sorry." He framed his words with care. "I assure you that my intentions were of the kindest."

The desire came back, profound and dangerous, but he preserved from it a strange detachment. He felt like a man about to pick a scab: that perverse curiosity, that impulse to view the object, to test his own pain. "Alice," he said, hearing the syllables distantly, and put his arm round her shoulder. His kiss did not reach her mouth; he felt the bristles of his mustache press into the yielding flesh of her cheek.

He did not know whether she had disengaged herself, or whether, in fact, his arm had simply fallen from her shoulders. There she stood, and she lifted one hand, palm against the temple, in that fatalistic gesture which now, as ever, filled him with a sense of insufficiency.

"I am very tired," she said.

"Yes," he agreed, "you look tired." And he felt with gratification that by not having said a moment before, "I love you," he had maintained his self-respect.

"Good night," she said.

She withdrew from him, past the chair where she had sat that evening, past the table where his own drained glass stood, and toward the door. With her movement the black chiffon fluttered and waggled.

He looked at the door through which she had just passed. Words took form in his mind with such special satisfaction that he was tempted to speak them aloud. *I would be doing my friend, Mr. Alburt, a favor if I should tell him that Alice Dalrymple is cold as a snake*. Then, as he surveyed the room, whose articles, now that she had gone, seemed out of focus, he could not help but wonder what she would have said, how she would have taken it, if, after all, he had said, "I love you."

He drifted toward the hall door, and out into the hall.

Somewhere on the upper floor a light burned, splaying shadow and angular patches of illumination into the lower section like a gigantic, ghostly pack of cards. Without looking up, he passed down the hall to his study door, opened it, and threw the electric switch. The big bronze lamp on the desk in the center of the room released its steady flooding light over the appointed objects: over the tray of pens which lay in meticulous intimacy side by side, the bronze inkstand, the leather spectacle case. In shadow, just beyond the rim of light, the books, tier on tier, mounted like masonry of some blank, eyeless structure.

He seated himself before the desk; removed the spectacles from the case; dutifully wiped them with a white handkerchief; hooked them over his ears. He opened the book in front of him. He was scarcely aware that he had performed that set of actions, so habitual to him; it was, indeed, with a subdued surprise that to him came recognition of the words on the printed page. It was as if, on relaxing his attention at the end of each sentence, he should say, "Well, well, here I am."

He tried to follow the words that marched cleanly from margin to margin, line by line; but the faces persistently came. He perceived Phil Alburt's naked face set in the rich flaring fur of an overcoat collar, and beyond it another face, undefined, unknown, anonymous, the face of a girl whose body, reclining, was lapped in silk and fur: faces fixed above the dash lamp and the little white unwinking dials that said all was well, all was well, while the bold-flung beams of headlights ripped the snowy road and the dark that whirled toward the faces.

Between the words on the page, between the sentences, he saw the faces appear and reappear as between the spokes of a slowly revolving wheel. *Necking,* he thought, *out necking.* He suddenly discovered as though he had been searching for it, that word he had heard the students use. *And he is going to Bermuda,* he thought, and into his mind crowded the pictures he had seen in travel advertisements, the man and woman on horseback, in bright coats, riding along the white beach by blue water. *To Bermuda,* he thought, *but I am going home. Even if Alice doesn't believe me, I am going home.* That satisfied him and he felt, somehow surprised at his emotion, a deep homesickness.

He tried to comprehend the words on the page, but his mind, like nervous fingers, dropped them. While the wind sweeping down the great valley of the Mississippi beat the town, beat the house, and hurled the sparse lost flakes through the upper reaches of darkness, he sat in the ring of steady light from the bronze lamp on his desk. At length before he possessed the calm, sufficient meaning of the words under his eye, he knew that he would stay here forever in Russell Hill, Illinois, at this sad, pretentious little college on the plain, in this house with the rustling electric refrigerator and the tiers of books; that this Christmas, or any other, he would not go home; that the woman now sleeping upstairs where the single light burned was perfectly his own; and that Phil Alburt, who had, really, nothing to do with them, with George Dalrymple and Alice Bogan Dalrymple, would ride away, forever, on horseback, his naked face smiling as he rode down the white beaches beside the blue water of the unvexed isles.

Prime Leaf

LORD, make us thankful for these blessings. Make our salvation commensurate to Thy mercy. Bless this food to the purposes of our bodies and us to Thy service. Amen." Little Thomas looked up promptly, just as the last word of the grace was uttered, and then seemed abashed when he met the incurious glance of his grandfather. His mother, at the foot of the big table, had not seen. Now she was turning with an appearance of hospitable interest to their guest.

"Did you have a good trip this time, Mr. Wiedenmeyer?"

"Vell, no," answered Mr. Wiedenmeyer. "I come on the steamboat up the river. Paducah to Clarksville I come. I vill tell you, Mrs. Hardin, not one wink of sleep did I get."

Little Thomas took the wide bowl of soup, which made his fingers quiver slightly with its weight, and passed it into his father's large hand.

"It was mighty hot here Thursday night," Mrs. Hardin was saying. "That was the night three nights ago—wasn't it?"

"Ja, Thursday night vas the night all right I guess, but that vas not the trouble." Mr. Wiedenmeyer's moist thumb with its broad, glistening nail closed over the edge of the second bowl. He settled it in front of him, very near to him. "But that vas not the trouble all right." He picked up the spoon and waggled it gently in Mrs. Hardin's direction. "Three drunks get on at Paducah and have the room next to my room. All night they sing, they yell, they stomp. One drunk, he has a harmonicer and he plays it all night. It vas terrible, Mrs. Hardin, I vill tell you. A man not so young any more like me not to get his sleep. Terrible. That so, Mr. Hardin?" he asked, turning to old Mr. Hardin and shaking his head with a vague air of self-commiseration.

"I reckon so. I'm sixty-nine—about twenty years older than

you—but two years ago this coming fall I went coon hunting with Big Thomas here and the niggers, and we didn't come back till half-past four. We got two coons," he added like an afterthought.

"Yes, and kept me up all night waiting for you men to come in," Mrs. Hardin said sharply, but with a smile. "And you, Papa, almost had a chill the next night and I had to sit up with that."

"Humph!" The old man half snorted, and then, catching himself, laughed.

"Edith." There was a note of rebuke in the young Mr. Hardin's voice. His father appeared to pay no notice and gravely tilted his bowl to get the last spoonful of soup and the bright disk of carrot submerged in its midst.

Mrs. Hardin tapped the brass bell in front of her. A large Negro woman padded in from the pantry passage and began clumsily to transfer the dirty china to the sideboard, where a scrawny and very black boy stacked it with more than necessary clatter. He started toward the door.

"Careful, Alec," admonished Mrs. Hardin.

"Yas'm, Miss Edith," the black boy said, and disappeared with the precarious load.

"I done tole him," the large Negro woman remarked to no one in particular, and she followed her son into the pantry passage.

"Shiftless, these neggers, shiftless," said Mr. Wiedenmeyer, and again shook his head with that vague air of commiseration. Mrs. Hardin looked up quickly at him and then fixed her eyes on the brass bell, as if she had been about to speak and then, in the nick of time, had recollected herself. There was silence, except for the faint, pleasant sounds from the kitchen, until the Negro woman reappeared with a platter. Her boy was behind her with two covered dishes.

"I hope your business has been good, Mr. Wiedenmeyer," Mrs. Hardin said. The tone seemed to imply that she had put away completely whatever other remark she had been considering a few minutes before.

"Ja, ja, but business is nefer too gud in this business."

"It ain't ever too good in any business," the young Mr. Hardin interrupted. "But how is the crop looking over in Tennessee? I haven't heard anybody say recently."

"Gud, gud enough if tings they go gud now."

"Do you reckon you'll get much buying done down there when buying time comes?"

"Vell, to tell the truth among friends, I don't know. It looks like a gud crop all right, all right. But it's a leetle early to be talking about the tobacco-buying business so soon in the season."

"If it turns out a good crop," said young Mr. Hardin, "I hope you all will be paying a price to match it. Do you think it'll fetch a good price this year, Mr. Wiedenmeyer?"

"Vell, it's a leetle early like I say to be talking about the tobacco-buying business yet a time. But it vill be a gud price, I bet."

The young Mr. Hardin laid down his knife and fork with deliberation and looked steadily across at his guest. "It wasn't too early to talk about the tobacco-buying business August last year when you were down here. You talked a right smart about it. And just like now you said, 'Oh, it will bring a good price, all right, all right.'" There was the slightest hint of mimicry in his tone. "I recollect well what you said. You said eleven cents, maybe twelve cents, for good prime leaf. All I wonder is if 1907 is going to be just like 1906. Eleven, maybe twelve cents, you said, and when you came around after and we did business with you it was prime leaf, eight cents, lugs, three cents. And we had a lot of good prime leaf. It was a fine crop. I reckon you were well pleased with that lot, weren't you, Mr. Wiedenmeyer?"

"Sure, it vas a fine crop you had. But the profit, there vas not much profit." Again he shook his head, but this time did not look up from the plate. "Eleven cents, I said. Maybe I said eleven cents, when I vas here last year August. If you say I said eleven cents, eleven cents is what I said. You always vas a careful man, Mr. Hardin. You got a long memory, Mr. Hardin."

"I reckon it pays to be careful, sometimes."

Old Mr. Hardin glanced at his son in the same incurious fashion, not quite a reproof, which had met Little Thomas after the blessing. Big Thomas ignored it completely. He continued with studied innocence.

"I'm mighty sorry to hear you don't expect to get your proper amount of buying done towards Clarksville."

"I vasn't saying I didn't expect to get no buying done towards Clarksville, Mr. Hardin. It is early a time yet to talk."

"Maybe. But then I sorter understand there ain't going to be much tobacco buying done down there, or anywhere much else. That is, there ain't going to be—yet."

"Ja? Ven the time come, they vill sell, all right, all right. The fellers I talked to down there ain't got a crop so far along like you. They didn't get a gud season in setting-out time like you got."

"Yes, sir, we had a good early season this last spring and there was mighty little resetting of plants to do. But I reckon folks won't be so quick to do business this year."

"Vell, I don't know. Ve all gotta do business. Some gotta sell, some gotta buy. Ve all gotta live, ain't ve? Ain't that true, Mrs. Hardin?" And he turned to her flatteringly and waited for the agreement which, as his posture seemed to imply, would settle the matter for good and all.

"You are right, of course, Mr. Wiedenmeyer. We all have to live."

The Negro woman removed the plates, and again Alec stacked them on the deep walnut sideboard. This time there was no rebuke from Mrs. Hardin, despite the careless clatter, and Alec went out, pressing the pile against the faded blue front of his Sunday overalls with one hand while with the other he opened the door. After he passed, it creaked shut with a slight musical whine from its heavy hinges.

"Lemon custard," old Mr. Hardin observed to his grandson. "Don't you like lemon custard, Tommy?"

"Sure I do," Little Thomas answered. And then almost pertly, "Don't you?"

"Sure," said Mr. Hardin, nodding with a fine show of gravity. The old man, his son, and his grandson ate in silence. Only Mrs. Hardin was still trying to keep up some sort of conversation with the guest. Then Alec burst open the pantry door, perspiring from the heat of the kitchen and very excited.

"'Scuse me, Mr. Hardin, but, Mr. Hardin, dere' one er dem hawks atter de chickens agin."

"I'm coming," said old Mr. Hardin. "Tommy, get me my gun, won't you?"

Thomas pushed back his chair with a rasp and ran into the next room. He found the gun in its corner, jerked off the oil-spotted paper envelope over the muzzle, and dropped it on the floor. He glanced over at another corner where a second shotgun and two rifles stood.

"Can't I use your gun just for one shot, Daddy?" he shouted.

"No," his father called back, "and how about hurrying a little?"

Thomas went to the writing desk under the window, opened one of the lower drawers, and fumbled in a box of shells. He dropped two shells into his pocket. Then he slipped one into each barrel of the gun and looked quickly at the safety-catch.

"Here it is, loaded," he said as he ran back into the dining room. His grandfather was already standing.

"Mr. Wiedenmeyer, why don't you come out back and talk to me while I wait for that God-damned hawk? Big Thomas hasn't finished his pie yet. But I still do most of the shooting around the house." He spoke between puffs while he lighted his pipe.

"All right." Mr. Wiedenmeyer got up very laboriously and leaned slightly over the back of his chair with his large stomach pressing against it. "You vill excuse me please, Mrs. Hardin."

"Yes, of course."

"Come on, Mr. Wiedenmeyer." Mr. Hardin was already at the side door which opened on a porch. "Come on, Thomas."

They went out to the broad porch and down the stone steps. A dirt path led back to the left, past the painted rain barrel which stood under the gutter, and through a wooden gate into the chicken yard. Alec came running out from the kitchen after them.

"Dat hawk done gone long ago. He done flew ten miles away by now."

"That's all right. He'll come back if he wants his dinner."

"If'n he wants our dinner," Alec replied and grinned at his own joke.

"Well, we'll wait for him then. We can sit over here, Mr. Wiedenmeyer, and talk till that hawk gets back." With his pipe he pointed to a wooden bench under the enormous maple which shaded a corner of the chicken run. They walked toward the tree, Alec and Thomas a little way in front. Alec paddled up the soft yellow dust with his bare feet, so that it rose in little clouds as high as his knees.

"For God's sake, Alec," Mr. Hardin mildly rebuked him.

"Yessuh."

Thomas looked at him slyly. "I told you so." This was spoken very low.

"Naw, you did'n." And Alec devoted his attention to making elaborate and perfect footprints in which the dust outlined the creases of the skin and stood up beautifully in the spaces between his toes.

There was no sign of the hawk. Already the full-grown white leghorns were picking about in the few patches of grass in the large yard. One hen with her brood still squatted anxiously just inside the door of the whitewashed chicken house, and another had sought safety close against the base of the big iron wash kettle. In a minute or so she came out and the awkward chicks began to stray over the yard. She looked very harassed and the soot from the kettle still clung to the white feathers of her back.

It was hot, even under the shade of the maple. Mr. Wiedenmeyer's ruddy forehead had tiny beads of perspiration, and he seemed to lack the energy to wipe it again. His damp handkerchief lay spread out over one knee, with streaks of yellow where the dust had settled. Obviously he was very uncomfortable. Mr. Hardin was not inclined to renew conversation, but held his pipe between his teeth and idly fingered the point of his trimmed gray beard. Now and then he looked at the expanse of bright blue sky above the cedar grove which began at the very edge of the woodlot to the north.

"Me, I guess that bird vill not come back maybe." Mr. Wiedenmeyer looked hopefully down the slope of lawn toward the deep cool porch, where the young Mr. Hardin and his wife could be seen through the vines.

"Let's wait."

Now Mr. Wiedenmeyer studied the sky, as if his added attention might bring the hawk a little sooner and end the unpleasant affair. After a time he spoke again.

"Didn't you, Mr. Hardin, think I'm right? Ain't ve all gotta live?"

"Sure," said Mr. Hardin. He did not take his pipe from his teeth.

"I hear about this pool, this tobacco fellers' association, a long time back—last spring, I guess. But I say to myself, It is all the same, some gotta sell, some gotta buy." He paused, waiting for an answer. There was no sign from Mr. Hardin.

"Me, I think this tobacco association is all foolishness. If a feller, he knows the honest man to buy his crop, he don't need this association business. Sometimes the price fall low, like last year, but nobody, he can help that. This association vill not help ven the end come. It vill ask a high price and nobody vill buy, and then somebody vill sell his tobacco, a little higher than most year maybe, and then somebody else and somebody else. Somebody in this association business, maybe, somebody out, maybe. Then everybody want to sell quick and get the price before it drop. People need money bad that time year. And the price vill drop—quick. You vill see. It vill end like that—cost everybody money and do nobody gud. You vill see."

"Some of us don't think exactly like that, Mr. Wiedenmeyer."

"You vill see, I guess." He picked up the damp handkerchief, pressed it into a dull-colored pad, and slowly wiped his forehead. With great care he spread it back on his knee and again looked at Mr. Hardin, waiting for his words to take effect. Then he continued less vehemently. "Besides, I don't see vy a feller like you want to be in this association for. You alvays got a gud crop if there is any gud crop in the country. You got gud land and you know how to verk it. And this year you got a extra fine crop, and it vill be early."

Mr. Wiedenmeyer turned around on his bottom and gestured vaguely off to the left, beyond the house. A half mile away, beyond the lawn, beyond the driveway and the irregularly spaced forest trees which bordered it, the fields began. They dropped away gradually to the south and east, ending in a point where the creek joined the river. On the other side of the brush and sycamores which followed the curve of the creek bottom was a pasture land. Some red cattle, very small and far away, were grouped at a gap in the line of sycamores where the ford of the creek was. The heat waves shimmered up from the broad ripe green of the tobacco, from the sycamores, and from the browning pasture land beyond.

Mr. Hardin had turned to follow the gesture, as if some new sight had been pointed out to him. For a moment he contemplated the fields, and then took the pipe from his mouth. Deliberately he knocked it out and laid it on the bench near the propped shotgun.

"It is pretty good, even if it ain't extra fine. And we got it in early. That's usually something."

"It is almost extra fine, but you alvays did have a gud crop. Sometime people say they don't see how you do it." He suddenly seemed to think of something else. "But if you are mixed up with this association business, getting a crop in early von't help much, vill it?"

"Getting it in early won't help one way, I reckon, but a man likes to have things over and done with. It's satisfying that way."

"That is all right, but you lost some money."

"Maybe."

"Maybe, but all the same I don't see why a feller fixed like you get mixed up for."

"Well, it's about like this. I'm not generally a man to join up with societies and associations and things. I think most of the time you have to stand on your own, and I like to pick and choose my friends some other way, too. I didn't take to the idea in the beginning. And Big Thomas was all dead set against it. He said pretty much what you've been saying, so I've heard all those arguments before."

"But Big Thomas don't talk that vay now, Mr. Hardin. You just seen him."

"But he did talk that way. And I thought about it a right smart. I had some long talks with Old Man Hopkins, over there across the river. He was strong for the association idea. Said all of us growers wasn't getting our due, even if one or two of us made good money now and then off a crop, and we couldn't do anything about it unless we stuck together. Old Hopkins is a mighty clever feller, and maybe he talked me into it. All the same I believe he's right now. And I talked Big Thomas into it. All the association is after is our due." He looked amiably at Mr. Wiedenmeyer, and then almost smiled as he added, "But I reckon some of us could be content with just a little bit more than our due. We're all human."

"You alvays got your due from me, Mr. Hardin. Alvays the top price for the season. Ja?"

"Sure, nobody's blaming you if the price is dirt sometimes."

"It vud not be dirt a year like this with a crop like that." And again he turned heavily about on his bottom and gestured toward the fields and the river.

"We ain't intending for it to be dirt this year. The price won't be dirt for this or any other crop. You see, we expect to fix that matter up ourselves."

Mr. Wiedenmeyer spread his hands out in the air before him, the soft fingers standing apart, and then brought them down with deliberate emphasis on his knees. "Ven the end come, don't say I didn't tell you. It vill be bad for everybody.

And it vill be mighty bad fer fellers like you vot didn't need to have nothing to do with the business."

"I reckon we'll all take our chances together on that."

"Together. You don't have to take chances together. I tell you it is nefer too late. Anyvay,. it ain't too late a time yet."

"Yes?"

"Ve have done a lot of business with each other, Mr. Hardin. Ve is like old friends, and it is like an old friend I talk to you. Understand me, Mr. Hardin?"

"I don't exactly know whether I do or not."

"De hawk, Mr. Hardin! Here come de ole debbil!" Alec was pointing off to the north.

The hawk floated very high over the hill crest and the cedar trees. It passed over, still very high, and then tilted into a long bank, slipping down like a leaf across the air.

"He shore is comin' back," Alec exulted.

"Alec, you and Thomas get back here under the tree or he won't come back. Come here, Thomas."

The boys stood behind the bench, very quiet, as if the least sound might carry far up into the air and frighten the hawk away at the last. Then Thomas whispered, "Can't I take a shot?"

"No."

"Just one. I'll hit him. Please." It was not quite a whisper now.

"No."

Thomas was quiet again. The chickens had not yet taken alarm. The old leghorn hen, the soot from the kettle still on her feathers, crouched in the yellow dust, ruffling it luxuriously with her wings. The chicks and a few young pullets wandered aimlessly. The hawk had drifted to the north again, over the cedars, sinking in a broad unhurried circuit.

"Thomas, you can have one shot," Mr. Hardin said. "Come around here on this side the bench."

Thomas made no answer. He came around in front of the bench, looking very grave under the new responsibility. His grandfather handed him the gun.

"The safety's off. Be damned careful. Don't shoot while he's circling around over the trees, even if he gets low. He's too far for the gun. Wait till he stops that foolishness and starts straight down at the yard. He'll come whizzing down, so shoot plenty in front. And don't try to follow him down with the sight. You'll sure miss him. Sorter let him and the sight almost meet. See?"

Thomas nodded. His knuckles were white from gripping the gun. The hawk still drifted lazily around the big spiral. The boy's gray eyes squinted at the sky, following its course. Now and then the tip of the hawk's wing caught the sun and glittered like metal.

"Funny the fool chickens ain't worried yet," Mr. Hardin remarked.

The hawk dropped suddenly, checked, tilted sidewise, and came swooping down across the tree tops. Thomas' gun rose to meet it. For a second it wavered, and then jerked back with the explosion. The lowest maple leaves shivered with the gust.

"Missed," said Mr. Hardin and seized the gun. The hawk, within ten feet of the ground and the terrified chickens, did not strike, but veered off and bounded upward with a deep beat of its wings. Mr. Hardin ran out from under the tree and fired at the high hawk. The wings beat again. The hawk seemed to rest on the air for a moment and glide hesitantly. Then one wing crumpled. The hawk tumbled on the hurt wing, downward, fluttering and turning, making no resistance. It struck on the other side of the wire fence in the wood lot.

Alec and Thomas ran toward the place like dogs.

"Shut that gate, or the chickens will get out," Mr. Hardin called, but the boys paid no attention.

He came slowly back to the bench and sat down beside his guest again. Very carefully he broke the gun and flicked the empty shells away.

"Fine," said Mr. Wiedenmeyer, "you got him all right. A

feller might know a boy like Thomas vud not get him. I knew he vud not get him."

"I knew it too."

"Vell," Mr. Wiedenmeyer began, and then thought better of it when he realized that Mr. Hardin was paying no apparent attention to his impending remark.

The boys came back, quieter now. Thomas was holding the hawk by its legs. The head swung listlessly in time with Thomas' quick step. The broken wing drooped forward and down, occasionally brushing the dust, while the other fluttered out stiffly and awkwardly.

"Here he is. He's a big one," Thomas said to his grandfather.

Mr. Hardin took the hawk and stretched out the broad wings to their full span. "More'n three feet. He is a mighty big one. A red shoulder. They get bigger than this though sometimes."

The hawk's small head had fallen forward. The beak, slightly parted, was pressing against the downy feathers of the breast where a few beads of blood stood.

"Dat hawk, he done had his las' dinner," said Alec, grinning at Mr. Hardin. "He wuz deader'n a door-nail when we fotched him."

Mr. Hardin handed the hawk to Alec. "Thomas, take the gun back to the house, and if you've got any more shells, don't forget to put them back in the box. And when Sam comes up after milking tonight, you might tell him to clean the gun if he's got time."

Thomas picked up the gun and followed Alec down the path toward the kitchen porch. He was furtively rubbing his right shoulder. Alec, turning, caught him at it.

"Dat gun done kick like a mule, I bet. You ain't helt it right."

"It didn't kick. I just itch. I reckon I held that gun all right."

Alec sniggered. "But yore gran-pappy, he got de hawk."

"Darn," said Thomas. "Can't I scratch myself where I itch without you going and giggling like Susie?"

"I bet you itch." And Alec began whistling.

Mr. Hardin was still sitting on the bench. He made no sign of going back to the house. "Where were we when the hawk came?"

"I vas saying ven it come that it might not be too late yet. It vill not be too late some time yet, for a feller like you to get vot is coming to him."

"I'm expecting to get what's coming to me."

"Maybe, you might not get it some vays. You got a gud crop, a gud early crop. Some vays you vill not get your right money out of it. It is like the old friend I vant to talk to you, Mr. Hardin."

"I reckon you're making me an offer, Mr. Wiedenmeyer?"

"I vas not making any offer yet. It is early some to be making offers. Soon maybe, ven the time come, I vill make you the offer. A extra gud offer, Mr. Hardin. Then ve vill talk business."

"We might talk a little business right now."

"Ja!"

"I just want to ask you one question. You knew when you came out here today that I was in the association. You knew that, didn't you?"

"Ja, I knew it. I knew it a long time before I come down here. It vas in the paper you vas a director."

"That's true, too. I'm one of the directors."

"Fine, fine. I give you my congratulations. It is a honor sure."

"That don't matter much. What I want to say is something like this. If you knew I was in the association, why, for the love of God, did you reckon I'd be open to any offers you might have to make? Why now, Wiedenmeyer?"

"I just thought maybe you vas not sure how ve stood. I just vanted you to know ve could still do business yet. I vanted you to know I do vot is right with you."

"If you've got any more right offers to make, it might be a pretty good idea, I guess, for you to make them a little later when the association starts fixing prices. And then you might just make them direct to the association. Don't you think it might be a good idea, Mr. Wiedenmeyer?"

"Plenty of fellers is not in the association."

"That's true too. Some of them will come in though. But it might be a good idea all the same to make any private offers just to those people. Some people in the association might not take it right. It's funny the way people take things sometimes, ain't it?"

"Ja." Mr. Wiedenmeyer paused for a minute. "You vud not be mad, vud you?"

"No, I'm not mad. It's only that I want us to understand each other."

Mr. Wiedenmeyer did not speak. He was studying his companion with a puzzled expression.

"And I reckon we understand each other well enough now. Let's go down to the house."

They got up and left the bench in silence. Mr. Wiedenmeyer walked a little bit behind, regarding the unstooped shoulders before him with the same bewildered look. When they were half way down the path, near the rain barrel, Mr. Hardin turned pleasantly.

"You might sit around a time and have supper with us. We always have early supper on Sunday. It'll be cold though."

"Thank you all the same, I vud have to be going. I'm crossing the river this afternoon."

"Dropping by to see Old Man Hopkins?"

"No."

Young Mr. Hardin and his wife were still on the side porch when the two men came up. She looked at them questioningly.

"Mr. Wiedenmeyer says he can't stay for supper, Edith. He's got to be crossing the river this afternoon."

"I'm sorry you're not staying."

"Thanks all the same. I got to go now. Good-bye. Goodbye, Mr. Hardin."

"Good-bye."

Mr. Hardin leaned against the trellis post and watched the

stocky man walking down the long path to the front gate. Mr. Wiedenmeyer went out, untied his horse from the hitching rack, and got in his buggy. He did not wave back, or even turn around, as he drove off under the trees by the edge of the nearest field.

"You didn't make him mad, did you, Papa?" asked Mrs. Hardin. "He acted a little funny."

"No," said Mr. Hardin cheerfully. "I didn't. He ain't exactly mad. He's just worried."

His son looked up suddenly. "I hope you gave him hell. I wish to God you had made him good and mad. What does he want coming around here for? The old Jew," he added.

"I didn't give him hell, I just gave him some advice. And you can't make a man like that mad anyway. And besides he ain't a Jew. He's just a German. A German who feels sorter sorry for himself."

"What did you tell him?"

"I just advised him if he had any more offers to make, to make them to the association direct or make them to people not in the association."

"Well, you wasted your breath."

"No doubt about it," Mr. Hardin complacently agreed. "But he's got something to figure about while he rides over to Hopkins' place."

"He better not. Hopkins'll just take one good look at him and then dump him in the river before he opens his damned mouth. Did he say he was going over there?"

"I asked him, and he said, as I recollect, that he wasn't. But he will." Mr. Hardin looked very cheerful about the whole matter. "It'll be good for both of them, too. Old Man Hopkins can get some steam worked off, and maybe Wiedenmeyer will learn something."

"Well, we should worry," and Thomas gave an elaborate late afternoon yawn and settled back in the swing.

"We've got considerable to worry about. The reason Hopkins will probably dump Wiedenmeyer in the river is because he's worried. If he weren't worried he'd listen to all Wiedenmeyer had to say, not saying anything, just sitting with that crab-apple grin of his on his face. That's the way with Hopkins. He's a clever fellow, a mighty clever fellow, but when he gets worried he's just got to do something all of a sudden. He's similar to you that way, Thomas. And Hopkins is worried pretty much right now. You know people ain't coming in the association like they ought. But do you know that if things don't pick up, we'll be short about a hundred-fifty or two hundred names when the fun starts."

"I didn't think it was quite that bad, Papa," said Mrs. Hardin. "What are you all going to do?"

"We can't do anything in the world right now but wait. There's a meeting of the board of directors in about a month. We can tell better then. But if we don't get a bigger membership, we can't make a real fight this year. And the only thing that'll get a bigger membership for next year is a real fight now. It looks to me the association is about the only chance of getting our rights, but some people can't see any farther than their noses. They think the dues are too high or, if they're real skunks, they figure that they'll get the good out of the association without it costing them anything. But in general it's just that people here don't like to join up with things much. That is, except the Baptist Church or a possum hunt."

He came up on the porch and stood, with legs apart, in front of the swing where his son and daughter-in-law sat.

"Lord knows we need money," he said, speaking directly to Mrs. Hardin, "but I reckon we can hang on another year. But don't fret yourself, Edith. It'll all come out right."

He turned and opened the big screen door of the dining room. Holding it back with his body, he stood there fumbling about in his pocket for his watch. He seemed to study its thick face as if he expected to find something there of more importance than the time of day.

"It's just about five o'clock," he said. "I'm going upstairs and take me a nap before supper. If you see Sam tell him to clean my gun, will you. I asked Thomas to tell him, but he'll sure forget."

"Close the door, Papa," said Mrs. Hardin. "You're letting all the flies in the county get in."

Without a word he stepped inside and the door slammed with a crash. Then from the dining room came his voice, half singing, half humming.

The old gray mare come trottin' through the wilderness, trottin' through the wilderness . . .

A minute later there was the sound of his step in the bedroom just over the dining room, and then, in the late afternoon quiet, the faint creak of the bed springs as he lay heavily down.

II

The meeting had just adjourned. Near the unlit grate at the side of the room, the directors were standing in a silent group. "It's about time for dinner," one man remarked tentatively, then turned to pick his hat from among those scattered on the threadbare sofa. "It's time," said Mr. Hopkins, who still sat in the chairman's place at the head of the long table. He did not even glance up when he spoke. He sat very erect in his chair, filling it. One heavy, sunburned hand lay flat out on the table before him, palm down, while the other plucked at a rip in the old, green-baize table-cover. The rest of the men, all except Mr. Hardin, moved toward the door. The last one hesitated a moment with his hand on the knob.

"You all will lock the door and leave the key downstairs, won't you? I'm not coming back this afternoon. I've got a case on."

"Listen, Sullivan," said Mr. Hopkins, "why don't you hang around a spell? Maybe you can have dinner with Mr. Hardin and me. We are going over to the Ellis House."

"I'll stay a few minutes, but I can't eat with you, I've got to hurry." He came over and leaned against the table, facing Mr. Hopkins. Mr. Hardin stood across the room looking out of the window. There were not many people in the street, even on Saturday, at noontime. A few buggies and a surrey stood on the far side; the horses were tied to iron rings set in the stone curb of the pavement, and their heads drooped down over their hoofs. Sunlight filled the narrow street, and glittered on the few puddles left by the rain of the night before. It was all very familiar to him. He was paying no attention to the low voices from the table.

"Hey, Joe, wake up," Mr. Hopkins called to him. "Sullivan can't eat dinner with us, but he's got time for a drink."

Mr. Hardin turned slowly. "All right, let's go to the Utopia."

While sitting, Mr. Hopkins looked like a very big man. A certain impression of size and endurance came from the heavy shoulders, the large bald head and deep-set eyes, the muscular wrists. But now, when he stood, his head came only a little above Mr. Hardin's shoulder. His thick legs were ridiculously short, and the boots which he wore almost gave the look of a deformity.

He led the way out. Sullivan pulled the door shut and locked it.

"A. M. Sullivan, Lawyer," Mr. Hardin read aloud the lettering on the frosted glass. "If I was you, Mike, I'd sell my farm and stick to the law."

"I sorter like my place though, even if it don't pay some years," answered Sullivan as he followed his friends down the dark stairs.

"Well, I just like my place the years when it pays," interrupted Mr. Hopkins sardonically.

"You sure muster hated it last year," Mr. Hardin said with mild good humor. "I like my farm well enough to keep it as long as tobacco buyers and banks will let me. All the same it might be good to be a lawyer in these days and times, if I was as young as you are, Mike. My father was a lawyer, but he had a place in the country, too, like you. It was all right then. In South Carolina—that's where I was born—they raised cotton and weren't bothered with this God-damned tobacco crop. I started out to be a lawyer myself."

"I didn't know that," said Sullivan.

"That was long before your time. It was before the war. Somehow I never got settled back to it after the war."

They came out on the street and turned to the left. Without speaking again they walked the hundred yards to the saloon. The lawyer paused in front of the swinging doors of the Utopia, and tapped the uneven crumbling brick of the sidewalk with his stick.

"They're going to put in a concrete sidewalk for seven blocks along here sometime next year. The contracts haven't been let out yet though."

"More damned foolishness," said Mr. Hopkins. "Better put that money in the schoolhouse or some place where it'll do some good."

"Or in the jail house maybe," Mr. Hardin suggested.

It was crowded inside the saloon. Dozens of farmers were about the bar, and others sat at the little marble-topped tables across the room. Some were wearing their good clothes —dark suits and collars very white against the red of their necks and faces. There were others whose trousers were tucked into mud-splattered boots and whose loose coat pockets bagged with small packages and freshly folded newspapers. These had ridden in on horseback. All of them leaned over their glasses, looked at each other or into the broad bar mirror which reflected the whole scene, and talked. When one of them picked up a glass or pipe, the ends of his fingernails showed white where they had been scraped carefully and deep with the point of a heavy knifeblade. The blue tobacco smoke rose slowly through the thick air and puddled against the painted ceiling.

The three men found a small space at the bar. "Hello, Jerry," Mr. Hopkins said to the sad-faced fellow who was fishing glasses from a basin and wiping them bright. "I see you've got a good run today."

"Good for cutting time. What'll you have?"

Mr. Hopkins turned to his friends. "How about three Jack Daniels?"

"No, I reckon not," said Sullivan. "I'll have a beer. I never drink whisky, not even a little whisky, before I have a case on. Some people don't like it for you to do their business when you've got whisky on your breath."

"The hell you say," answered Mr. Hopkins. "But you'll have your whisky, won't you, Joe? You haven't got any case on."

Mr. Hardin only nodded. Mr. Hopkins turned back to Sulllivan.

"Well, you can have my cases whether you're drunk or sober, Mike."

"Thanks, but I lost the only case I ever had for you."

"It wasn't exactly your fault. I ought never fought that case. I knew that son-of-a-bitch Mitchell had a lot of law on his side, but I was so mad at him that if I hadn't sued him I would have thought about the whole business till I cut his heart out. I saved his life maybe."

"All the same I'm sorry I didn't win for you." Then Sullivan grinned. "But I'm glad you didn't cut his heart out."

"Mitchell just had more law than I did. I reckon the rights were about even, but the rights and the law of things ain't exactly the same thing sometimes."

"We lawyers do the best we can. God-a-Mighty Himself frequently don't make things and the rights of things match up. We just do the best we can and try to make a living out of it at the same time."

"God-a-Mighty ain't even got that excuse." Mr. Hopkins picked up his full whisky glass and laughed. "Let's drink. Let's drink to the rights of things." He held up the glass and, still smiling, looked at the clear gold liquor. They drank quickly. He and Mr. Hardin set the empty tots back on the bar.

"Two more, Jerry," said Mr. Hardin, "and one for yourself."

Jerry brought the drinks and Mr. Hardin paid him. "Let's go get that table before somebody else wants it. It looks quieter over there."

They went over to the corner and settled themselves.

"I'm glad you made it up with Mitchell," said Mr. Hardin.

"I am too. I like to be at peace with my neighbors like the Bible says," Mr. Hopkins remarked and again laughed. "And

Mitch is a good neighbor, but he's a son-of-a-bitch. I like lots of sons-of-bitches though. If I went to law with all the sons-of-bitches I know, you'd have your hands full, Mike, fighting my cases. I've noticed that the sons-of-bitches have the law on their side right frequent."

"Mitchell ain't exactly a son-of-a-bitch," said Mr. Hardin reflectively, "but I know he's a pretty hard man to deal with sometimes. Thank the Lord he ain't on the board."

"I don't mind a man being hard and grasping, because you generally know what to do about that. What I mind is a man being hard and grasping and still telling you he wants to do what's right by you and that it hurts him more than it hurts you. I wouldn't be surprised if some day Mitch don't sit on my front porch and look down the road to that patch of woods that caused all the trouble and say, Well, Bill, I reckon it was God's will and mercy you lost that suit to me. . . . And just let him."

"All the same," said Sullivan blandly, "I hear you two spent a right smart time sitting on each other's porches this summer. I'll bet you didn't talk about lawsuits or politics. Or religion. You old infidel."

"Well, I don't know," Mr. Hardin suggested. "Being a good Episcopalian, I can see how an old infidel, like Bill here, and an old Baptist, like Mitchell, might get together on a good many points of common interest."

"Damn," Mr. Hopkins said. Then he winked at Sullivan.

Sullivan grinned and got up. "I've stayed too long now. Good-bye, gentlemen." He picked up his stick from the table and started for the doorway. He turned, fumbling in his inside coat pocket, and stepped back to the table. "I was about to forget something, Mr. Hopkins. Here's this little item I promised you for today. Good-bye." He laid an envelope on the table in front of Mr. Hopkins.

"Thanks, Mike."

"Good luck, with your case," Mr. Hardin called after him. Sullivan, already at the entrance, waved back and was gone. Mr. Hopkins half turned in his chair and stared at the doors as if to assure himself that his friend had really left the bar room. The doors swung lightly back and forth from Sullivan's passage, weakened in their irresolute arcs, and settled into place. Only then did Mr. Hopkins pick up the long manila envelope from the table. Mr. Hardin looked casually at it; it was unsealed and tied with a red band, and on neither side was there a word of writing.

Mr. Hopkins caught the look, and his strong forefinger slipped under the red tape as if he intended to snap its fold and satisfy whatever idle curiosity prompted that glance. Searchingly, but for only the fraction of a second, he hunched forward against the edge of the table and looked into his companion's eyes. Mr. Hardin deliberately met his gaze and then looked slowly down at the envelope. The strong forefinger relaxed and carefully withdrew from under the tape. Once or twice Mr. Hopkins turned the packet over in his hands and then, with the slightest air of regret, slipped it into his pocket.

"A little legal work Mike did for me. Sorter a last will and testament." He saturninely tapped the right breast of his coat which bulged slightly from the envelope. "I might fall off a horse some night in the dark of the moon and break my neck."

"Not much chance. A man that rides like you and holds his likker like you ain't going to fall off any horses," said Mr. Hardin. "But let's go get our dinner."

"Can I have one more drink? Besides, we'll miss the first rush at the Ellis House if you can hold out a little longer. This is Saturday and the town is stinking full."

"All right. I'm not specially hungry. But no drink."

Mr. Hopkins held up one finger in the air; Jerry caught the sign and came across the room with another whisky. Mr. Hopkins did not pick it up, but sat back in his chair with one hand flat out on the table before him, palm down, just as he had sat in the chairman's seat in Sullivan's law office. His large head hung a little forward, crinkling into deep furrows the strong red flesh of his jowls. The least breath of air from the saloon's half-doors disturbed the red fine hair which fringed his head, and fluttered the leaves of the calendar on the wall above. Mr. Hardin watched him calmly, waiting for him to speak. Finally he looked up.

"It's pretty bad, ain't it, Joe?" Though the voice was still harsh, it was somehow different, with a deeper and more resonant tone.

"It's bad, and there ain't a doubt. The worst is we can't do much about it. We didn't start organizing soon enough, and in a thing like this you haven't got anything really but the time between one crop and the next. If we lose out this year, we'll lose members instead of gaining them for next year. If people could only see what we're up against. I reckon people usually see things clear enough in the end but it sure takes a devil of a long time."

"We ain't going to lose this year," said Mr. Hopkins with the old voice. "I'll be damned to hell if we lose."

"Yes."

"People always see too late. A hell of a lot of good it'll do next year when prime leaf is six cents and dropping for people to say that maybe, maybe, the association was a good thing. See for them, and cram it down their throats. I know the association is a good thing, and you know it's a good thing, and there's dozens of men that know it's a good thing. See for the rest and cram it down their throats." He picked up his glass to drink. "And they'll like it in the end," he said.

"Things don't work that way, Bill. I sometimes wish they did," Mr. Hardin answered. "You can work them that way a little while maybe, but you lose something else. Too much."

"I know all about that, Joe. Hell, Joe, I've heard you talk like that before."

"And I reckon you're right apt to hear me talk like that again before I die."

"Sure. About once a month for the next twenty-five years. And I don't go so far as to say that you ain't right in a majority of cases. It wouldn't surprise me a bit if you are right. But you can't play that way when you're playing against time, and we're sure playing against time right now. If people won't see, we've got to make them see. Cram it down their throats. Do you know, Joe, that if we could get twenty-odd more names, the right names, in this county, and about the same number in a few other sections we might stand a chance of getting our figure when selling time comes?"

"I know it. The devil of it's going to be getting them."

"We're going to get them."

"I hope to the Lord we do, but I don't quite see how."

"I see one way. I grant you, Joe, it's a way I don't cotton to much, but it's a way. There's two things about people; one of them is that they won't see what's good for them till it's too late, and the other is they're always wanting to play safe. They're afraid, they're afraid of their shadow. They're downright timid, Joe." Again he hunched forward a little against the table and looked into Mr. Hardin's eyes, and again Mr. Hardin deliberately met his gaze. He shook his head before he spoke.

"It ain't that people are so much afraid. It's just that they're fuddled. Fuddled as hell right frequent. When they see straight they ain't generally afraid."

Mr. Hopkins said nothing. Motionlessly he still leaned forward and watched his friend's face.

"And, Bill, I sorter suspect," Mr. Hardin continued, "that you've already shown your hand."

"And you're dead right."

"I suspected it. I suspected it pretty strong just this minute."

"It was just a little private experiment I made. I wrote some friendly little letters to some people I ain't so fond of. That is, I signed them 'A friend.' You know this fellow Jerdan over in Trigg County, and you remember how he was almost stumping against the association. Writing damn fool letters to the papers and going on. Well, he stopped it pretty sudden, you remember, and it wasn't long before he signed up. I've tried it three or four times on the quiet, and, by God, it's worked. It's worked sweet. There ain't even a whimper, for if a man's afraid enough to mind a dirty scrap of paper, he's afraid to do much complaining. And nine out of ten are afraid."

"Well, Bill, number ten is going to take his letter out of his postbox some morning, and he's going to look at that little tin American flag on the box, and there's going to be hell breaking loose in Georgia."

"Look here, Joe. Damn your tin flags, Joe. A lot of good we get out of it. A farmer pays his taxes and gets a vote— and he's lucky if some fellow in shirt sleeves don't throw it in the paper basket instead of counting it. But does he ever get time on his loans, or roads, or a decent price for his crop? Give us a chance and we'll fix those things ourselves."

"I still think we'll get them fixed, but I don't believe your way can do the job. I don't claim all the tin flags either. I used to see that particular flag behind some guns pointing in my general direction, and Lord knows it wasn't my flag then. But I managed to keep a certain amount of respect for it." He surveyed Mr. Hopkins humorously. "A little more respect, I reckon, when it was on the other side of those dog-gone guns than now when it ain't."

"Well, just let number ten look at his little tin flag all he wants. But that's all."

"Um-huh." Mr. Hardin was leaning back and filling his pipe with an excess of care. No longer was he looking at Mr. Hopkins, and Mr. Hopkins seemed just a little disturbed by the fact.

"You know that when I write a letter, any letter," Mr. Hopkins went on, "I mean what I say. Of course now," and he seemed pleased with his whimsicality, "I'm pretty long-suffering."

"Um-huh."

"The only people we wouldn't be long-suffering with would be those that bolted the association. After they bolted, there won't be any tobacco for them to sell. Of course, they might collect a little insurance. No objection to that."

"I guess this project you propose couldn't be called exactly private?"

"No. I've talked it over with plenty—or rather I fixed it so they talked it over with me—and there's plenty people that hold my views. I didn't mention what made Jerdan change his mind though. That was just a little private experiment."

"Funny I didn't get wind of all these goings on."

"You see it wasn't like something official for the board. Some of the others sorter felt it might be better if you didn't get spoken to yet awhile. They sorter felt—" Mr. Hopkins hesitated vaguely.

"I get your point, Bill. They sorter felt I was getting old and set in my notions. They felt that if I happened to agree, I was too old to be much good to them, and that if I didn't agree, I'd better not be told. I'd better read it in a newspaper —after it was over."

"Well, Joe, that's putting it a little hard."

"Do you think so?"

"I do," Mr. Hopkins said. He seemed not to notice whatever sarcasm lay in the question. "And I'm telling you all this now on my own responsibility. Mike and me thought you ought to know."

"So Mike's in it too?"

"Sure, Mike's in it. In it up to the neck. Hell, Mike's a farmer before he's a lawyer."

"Thanks for telling me."

"We thought you had a right to know where you stood. Mike thought you might see like we do, but I never thought so. I hoped so a little maybe, but I knew you too well, and when I saw you sitting there in Mike's office today, I was dead sure of it. I ain't even asking you, Joe."

"You needn't. I'm against it on every point and every way you look at it. And the next board meeting I'm putting the matter on the table and we'll have it out in the open. If the board don't see sense and decency, they can have my resignation. I reckon from what you've just said that they don't need my efforts much anyway."

"You're crazy. You carry influence around here, and if you resign there'll be trouble."

"That don't matter. If it happens, I'm resigning, and on the morning when our friend number ten starts to collect insurance because somebody's decided that a tobacco crop had better be smoked up in one pile, I'm getting out of the association altogether."

"The hell you say, Joe! You can't get out."

"I can. I reckon you figure you're doing right according to your lights, but they ain't my lights."

"It's a question of getting our rights. Isn't that so?"

"It depends on how you get them. I've set a lot of store by the association, but if things go that way, I'm getting out. You see, I have to get out if things go that way."

"You're a fool, Joe. A perfect damn fool."

"Maybe. But I get out if things go that way."

"Well, Joe, I tell you this much. They go that way if they have to go that way to win. I'd see every leaf in two states burned up in a bonfire before I'd see one hand of tobacco sold half a cent under the association price. We'll fix a fair price and we'll have it. It ain't just the money—it's our rights in that and everything else."

"You'll need that sorter last will and testament Mike so kindly fixed up for you. You'll need it bad, maybe. But you won't fall off any horse in the dark of the moon. Some fool farmer that wants his rights will shoot you off in the light of the moon, Bill."

"The hell he will. There won't be any shooting done."

"There'll be a little shooting, one way and another. I reckon you know that you're proposing a sort of revolution. You say you usually mean what you say, and I guess you do. Well, in revolutions I've noticed that right frequent there's a little shooting."

Mr. Hopkins stood up with a violence that sent his chair spinning to the floor. The clatter of its light metal back against the tiles suddenly hushed all of the talk of the saloon as if it had been the crash of a gavel in the courtroom. Every man lounging along the bar or sitting at the other tables was now staring at Mr. Hopkins. Only Jerry, who had seen a good deal in his job, gave a glance and kept on polishing his glass. One fellow heard the clatter just as he passed the doors, turned and saw its cause, and then, with the easiest air in the world, sauntered back into the saloon. He leaned against the near end of the bar, watching. Mr. Hopkins neither stooped to pick up the chair nor paid the least attention to the score of farmers who were regarding him with covert curiosity. He stood very straight, with his legs wide apart, and he was white to the lips.

"I won't be threatened. I'll be damned if I'll be threatened." He spoke very low, almost in a harsh whisper. "Let them shoot and shoot their bellyful. We're going to beat them."

"I wasn't threatening you, Bill. I was just remarking."

"We're going to beat them. And you, you haven't got any right to get out. You won't get out!"

"I've had my say."

"You have?" He stepped back and took his hat from the hook on the wall. "Well, so long, Hardin." He smiled heavily, sarcastically down at him. "I'll see you in the board meeting."

He strode toward the door. His direct stare met the group about the bar, but gave them not a sign of recognition. They all might have been strangers to him.

"Good-bye, Bill," called Mr. Hardin. "Don't fall off any horses."

Mr. Hopkins did not turn to the joke, or to the farewell. The curious eyes watched his broad back and red creased neck under the brim of his black hat disappear through the swinging doors and out into the street.

"Well, I'll be damned," someone remarked in a reflective monotone. In the silence the words carried distinctly across the room.

For a little while Mr. Hardin kept his seat in the corner. He got up finally and, hat in hand, walked across to the bar.

"I'll pay for Mr. Hopkins' last drink, Jerry." He laid a silver dollar carefully on the bar. While Jerry got the change he turned to a man at the nearest table.

"Hopkins certainly gets heated up about his politics on one

or two points. You know, Mr. Jackson, I have times when I almost believe Bill is just a black Republican." He spoke carefully, putting his words out as he had put the silver dollar on the onyx top of the bar. Then he shook his head and, smiling, repeated, "Just a black Republican."

"Hopkins gets heated up pretty easy," agreed the man at the table.

"Good-bye, Mr. Jackson. Give my respects to Mrs. Jackson. You all ride over to see us sometime when the season slacks a little. Edith gets right lonesome, I guess, with just us men around. Good-bye."

He picked up his change and moved toward the door. To one or two familiar faces he lifted his hand gravely in a sort of salute, but he did not pause to speak again.

He stood for a moment irresolutely in front of the Utopia, and then looked at his watch. A little after one o'clock. He put it back in his pocket and turned to the right in the direction of Sullivan's law office. He passed the door to the dark stairs which led up to it without a glance. Farther down across the street stood the Ellis House. Along its front ran a two-story gallery, which sagged with decrepitude between the supporting posts and sloped perilously out toward the pavement. Men who had finished their dinner now lounged there on both levels and smoked and talked in the sunshine with their feet propped up on the green iron grillwork of the railing. Without quickening his pace Mr. Hardin walked past it, giving it no more attention than he had given to the dark stairs. A few blocks farther on he turned into a side street and entered a small restaurant.

"Hello, Mr. Hardin," said the fat little man who came over to his table. "I ain't seen you in town for a coon's age."

"I ain't been in much lately. We've been pretty busy getting the cutting done and the firing started."

"I reckon you're in over Sunday, ain't you?"

"No. Just for today. I'm going back tonight on the eight-fifty train."

"Just in for the 'sociation meeting, I reckon. I seen about

it in the paper, and there's been right smart talk about it, too."

"Yes, we had a meeting this morning."

"Well, I shore hope you git yore price. If tobacco gits right in this section, everything gits right, and when it gits wrong, they ain't nobody got any money."

"That's true," agreed Mr. Hardin. "But what's good to eat today, Jake?"

"We've got first class ham. A first class ham, Mr. Hardin."

"Give me some ham and vegetables then. You needn't hurry. I'm not in a hurry this afternoon. And a cup of coffee, Jake."

He climbed into a coach and found himself a seat near the end. Across from him sat an old woman dressed in a black silk dress. She did not notice Mr. Hardin, for she was already dozing with her head resting on the back of the seat and her respectable black hat just the least bit crooked. Looking at her, Mr. Hardin smiled, then he began to survey the station platform. Just by his window some people stood while they took their good-bye. Another old woman, very much like the one who slept so peacefully opposite him, kept leaning down to kiss a little boy who held the hand of a young woman. The young woman paid no attention, but talked busily to another young woman. Once the old woman blew the little boy's nose on her own small white handkerchief, wiping it gently as a sort of token of service and affection at parting.

Beyond them, almost in the shadow, two men conversed. Their backs were to the train, but one of them was a powerful man whose thick, booted legs almost gave the look of deformity. The other man, who waved his hands now and then as in argument, was tall and stooped. At last they walked over to the other side of the platform where the east-bound local waited. The powerful man fumbled in his coat pocket and produced a packet which he passed into the emphatic hands of the friend. The packet was a long envelope bound in two folds of red tape; in the light from the vestibule of the local it showed plainly. The friend mounted the steps of a

coach, leaned to shake hands with the powerful man, and
disappeared. Mr. Hopkins turned away and walked the length
of the platform and into the door of the waiting room. Then
the local drew out of the station, bearing Blake Mitchell and
the long envelope away to the east.

"Well, I'm damned," said Mr. Hardin aloud, and then
glanced across at the old woman. "Well, I'm damned. Old
Man Hopkins giving his last will and testament to Blake
Mitchell." He chuckled to himself. "His last will and testament."

The train pulled out with a jerk and left the station. Slowly
it passed a grade crossing on a street which led up into the
town where people walked about under the lights. Then
came the flour mill by the river, the warehouses, and then the
scattered Negro cabins where black faces pressed against
the windowpanes as the train went by. After that there was
the open country with the occasional gleam of a light in the
distance.

The conductor put his head in the door of the dim coach.
"Thomasville," he called, "Thomasville." Mr. Hardin stood up,
as the train swayed to a stop, and collected the packages beside him on the seat. Only the stationmaster and a few Negroes
were on the platform when he got off. The brakeman on the
rear of the last coach leaned out to wave his red lantern
and the train drew quickly away down the valley cut. Once or
twice the trail of smoke above the engine glowed with a soft
cumulous rose in the reflected light from the firebox door,
showing that the fireman was stoking for the grade ahead.
Just after Mr. Hardin had turned away from the station toward the town the full moan of the engine whistle blowing for
Johnson's Crossing came drifting back on the still night air.

"OO–oo, OO–oo," one of the Negroes behind on the platform mocked the echo. It was a deep and melancholy voice,
full like the distant whistle. "OO–oo, OO–oo." Then there
was the sound of laughter.

The door of the livery stable was locked when he got there,
but he could see the light of a lantern through the broad

cracks. He kicked the boards and, when that brought no one to open, he shouted. At last there was the rattle of the bolt and the big door grated outward, showing a stooped old fellow, who blinked in the lantern light.

"I'm sure sorry I didn't hear right off, Mr. Hardin. You been here long?"

"No, I just got here," Mr. Hardin said as he followed back to the box stall where his mare was. The keeper disappeared into it and his voice came vacantly from its gloom.

"Mr. Hopkins didn't come by like he said for his hoss after the early train so I says to myself, both you and him was staying over till tomorrow about that 'sociation business. So I shuts up and goes to bed."

"Mr. Hopkins didn't come on the last train either, so you can shut up for good this time. I reckon he's staying in on association business."

"Funny he didn't git back. He generally gits back soon's he can." He emerged from the stall leading the saddled mare, and stood there with the bridle ends dangling idly from his hand. He made no sign of turning Jenny over to her owner and saying good night. "Yeh, he generally gits back right prompt. He won't be away from that farm of his'n half a minute, if he can help. He sticks to his business, sure, and he always has. If I'd stuck to my business when I was young, I might a-had a fine place like him now. I just gallivanted when I'se young and look at me now. That's what I says to these shiftless boys around here. I says, Just look at me now." He spat into the dung and straw of the stable floor, and then put his broken shoe over the spot. A streak of tobacco juice clung on his long mustache, glistening like dew in the lantern light. His head hung forward and he looked up in an anxious dog-like way at Mr. Hardin, seeming to expect some answer that would set straight the shiftless years.

"Lord knows, John, you haven't got much to worry about." Mr. Hardin leaned down and took the bridle rein from the old man's loose hand as if he were lifting it from a peg. "You're pretty well fixed here for the rest of your life. Mr. Alexander's a good man to work for. You haven't got a thing in the world to worry about."

Mr. Hardin swung easily up to the saddle and Jenny walked toward the door. He lifted the bridle and turned. "John, I'm leaving some bundles over there on the bench. I'll get them tomorrow when we drive in for church. Good night."

"Good night," answered John, "good night, Mr. Hardin." The voice sounded impersonal and thin like the voice of a man coming from a trance. He stood in the middle of the wide doorway while Mr. Hardin trotted off down the street. Even after Mr. Hardin turned out of sight beyond the station, he still stood in the door, against the lantern light from the cavernous stable hall.

Beyond the station the road ran steeply up a hill, and there Jenny dropped into a walk. After the crest of the hill it was an easy ride of two and a half miles to the farm gate. By the time Mr. Hardin reached it the last bit of cloud had drifted away to the horizon on the north and the moon was clear. He took the long lane between the fields and grove, and Jenny, knowing that she was nearly home, went into a brisk canter. The shadow of the tall trees which bordered the fields lay blackly across the moonlit lane. The fields were bare now with only the regular stubs where the tobacco had been cut. Jenny's hoofs clattered hollowly over the wooden bridge where the lane crossed the creek, then, far away in the direction of the house, came the answering bay of a hound. Just beyond the bridge the house could be seen, and farther down the sweep of land toward the river, the bulk of the firing barn. The smoke stood up from its roof in thin unperturbed plumes and lay over the fields like the faintest strata of mist. In the middle of the nearest field stood a wagon, deserted after the day's work. Not a breath of wind stirred, and everywhere hung the scent of burning.

The house showed no light. Mr. Hardin took the branch of the lane which led toward the barn, and rode straight to it without going to the stable. He hitched Jenny to the prong of a peeled sapling near the barn and entered by a small side door. In the middle of the dirt floor two logs smoldered. Their smoke lifted heavily and spread out in the upper obscurity of the barn where the ripe tobacco hung in tier after tier. A Negro man lay on an old quilt near the stack of fresh logs on the other side of the fire, lying on his stomach with his head on his arm and his legs sprawled straight out. In the firelight the upturned soles of his feet showed a creased and ashen gray. His shoes were set carefully side by side at the end of the pallet.

Mr. Hardin stepped noiselessly across the powdery floor to the Negro. For a long time he looked down at him. There was no sound in the barn except the steady draw and whisper of the sleeper's breath and the occasional crackling of the logs as they dropped apart and settled into ash. Finally Mr. Hardin bent over and shook the Negro firmly by the shoulder.

"Wake up, Sam. Wake up."

The Negro rolled over and rose to a sitting posture and leaned back on both stiff arms like a clumsy child. Then he recognized Mr. Hardin. "I jes' gone to sleep," he said. "I jes' done napped off this minute."

"Well, you better not nap off any more. For God's sake, Sam, what do you think you're down here for?"

"Yassuh. I jes' napped off this very minute though."

"Get up and put Jenny in the stable. I'll stay here till you get back."

He sat down on the pile of logs and watched Sam as he laboriously pulled on his shoes. Sam stood up, stretched himself, and moved toward the door.

"Sam," Mr. Hardin said, "I'm not much sleepy, I reckon I ain't sleepy a bit. If you hurry and put that mare up, I'll be down here a time yet, and you can do some more of your damn-fool napping."

"Yassuh," Sam answered and closed the door behind him.

III

Mrs. Hardin laid her book down on the sofa beside her and looked up at the big clock above on the mantelshelf. As she looked, the minute hand twitched over a space and somewhere in the bowels of the clock began the whirr and catch which presaged the half-hour stroke. The two strokes came, muffled and deliberate, in the afternoon silence. The setter bitch on the hearth drowsily raised her head, blinked at the fire, and again settled the black nose between crumpled forelegs. It was half-past three.

Mrs. Hardin had no sooner begun to read once more than the dog scrambled up and stood with ears cocked. There was the sound of steps from the rear of the house and stamping as if a man were knocking the mud off his feet before entering. The dog ran to the dining room and whined to be let out.

"Thomas," called Mrs. Hardin.

"Coming!"

Big Thomas entered from the dining room, with clothes wet and his black hair a tangle of damp curls. He came over and kissed his wife, who ran her hands through his hair and then brought them down on his shoulders.

"You're mighty wet, Thomas," she said. "Maybe you better change."

"I guess not. I'll just dry off by the fire. I'm a little cold."

"Is it cold out now?"

"It's cold, but it doesn't get cold enough to stop this infernal raining. It's been raining all winter. It didn't really let up today till fifteen minutes ago. We may get an early spring out of it though. Where's Papa?"

"Papa went out when the rain let up. He said he was going down to the road and get the afternoon mail."

"I guess he wanted his paper. He gets mighty restless for his paper in the afternoon. But I could tell him what's going to be in it this time. Jones just told me when I went over to his place about that heifer."

He leaned from his stool, by the hearth, spreading his big hands to the fire, and gazing into its depth. He appeared to be disturbed, almost truculent. The vapor from the drying clothes ascended in thin clouds about his head, caught the drift of air to the chimney and vanished. Once or twice he flexed his hands; a few drops of water still clung to the black hairs on the back of his hands and wrists. Mrs. Hardin waited for him to go on, but he gave no sign.

"What was it?" she asked at length.

"What's been going on for some time maybe, but there can't be a doubt about it now. Nightriders."

"They're sure, Thomas?"

"My Lord, Honey, they burned up two barns full of tobacco, and then when old Mr. Salem's barn didn't burn proper, they used dynamite. People saw them, too, plain as day, riding down the pike this side of Hubertsville. There wasn't much secret about it.

"I hoped those burnings last fall were accidents, but I bet, by God, most of them weren't accidents. But those fellows were clever about it. Some people who bucked the association got letters, but the people who got the letters didn't get their barns burned; it was people who didn't get letters that had their barns burned. But almost every time the man who lost his barn wasn't in the association either, and the fellow who had the letter got the point right quick. But when the fire marshal came around about a burnt barn and asked if there'd been any threats, they had to tell him no. And there weren't any tracks. Last night's job was different; there were plenty of tracks and they burned the barns belonging to men who've had letters and been standing out against them since last fall. The fire marshal will sure find plenty of tracks this time, but he'll have a devil of a time finding the men who made them. And then he might not be so anxious to find the men that made them." He did not look at his wife as he talked; his eyes were still fixed on the depths of the burning coals. "If I happened to be the fire marshal or the sheriff and knew who made the tracks, I wouldn't be anxious to have the job of serving any warrants."

"I guess you would serve your warrants all right, Thomas, if you had them." She spoke sharply, in a voice that demanded reply. He did not answer or look up, but stretched his hands again before the fire. He seemed very cold and his eyes stared into the depth of the embers like those of a man who sees something he desires but may not have. Then his wife laughed. "But of course you aren't the sheriff."

"That's just one piece of luck and not enough. There's going to be a lot of trouble around here soon. I wish Papa would come on back to the house. I hope to God he doesn't get any more of his notions."

"He's already got them, Thomas. You know how he is."

"I can see how he felt about getting off the board. I reckon they sorter crowded him off maybe. The only thing I'm sorry about is his breaking up with Hopkins. I like Hopkins pretty well, and he's got lots of influence in this section."

"Papa's always been thick as thieves with Mr. Hopkins, and he still likes him. They just didn't think alike."

"I wish I knew just exactly what they had to row about. Papa just shuts up when I ask him and nobody else knows much about it. People just say that Hopkins jumped up and kicked his chair over and walked out the door. Then Papa went over and paid for Hopkins' drink. Did you know that, Edith? He just walked over in front of all those people and paid for his drink. He muster been crazy. I'd go to jail before I'd do a thing like that."

"I know, Thomas. You and Papa are mighty different. I don't know which one of you I like the best."

"I know which one. It's him."

"Maybe so, maybe you're right." And then she caught sight of her husband's face. "Why, Thomas! You crazy old goose. I do believe you're jealous of your own father. You ought to be spanked like Tommy."

He turned and stared directly at her with the same look in

his eyes as when he had been staring into the center of the fire. Startled, she met his eyes.

"Papa and I ain't a damned bit alike," he said in a quiet voice. "I take more after Mother's people. Papa and I don't think the same thing about anything in the world. Just wait about ten minutes till he comes up to the house and comes in here with his newspaper stuffed in his pocket and that set look on his face. Talking won't help any, for he just listens and then acts like he'd never heard a single word."

"Why, Thomas! You know that's not true. Thomas, I don't know what's the matter with you."

"Nothing is the matter. I'm just not going to be ruined now by any of Papa's damned foolishness. He never knows on which side his bread's buttered. I didn't want to get in this association mess in the first place. We don't make much out of our crop some years, but we manage better than most. We always manage to pull through with a little to show for it. Papa talked me into this and look what a hell of a mess it's turned out to be. What a hell of a mess. The only thing we can do now is to stick it out and get what we can from the association. I'm just not going to let any of Papa's damned highfaluting notions ruin us all. That's what's the matter."

His wife got up quickly from the sofa and went over to him. She put her hands on his forehead and then leaned down and kissed his hair.

"Thomas, I do believe you've got fever. You don't feel like a chill coming on, do you?"

"No. I don't. Didn't I tell you, Edith, that I'm all right? I haven't got any fever."

She drew his head back against her breast, her fingers still on his forehead. He sat erect on the low stool with his arms straight and his hands on his knees. His body was perfectly rigid, resisting, but his eyes were closed.

"Oh, Thomas," she whispered. Her mouth was almost against the damp black hair.

Again the dog stirred by the hearth. There was a sound of

voices from the outside and the dog went to the door that opened on the front porch.

"It's Papa. Get away, Edith, get away."

She moved to the sofa again without speaking.

"Tommy is with him," he said. "Back from school early today."

Mr. Hardin came in with Thomas at his heels.

"Hello," Mr. Hardin said, but before either of the others could answer, the boy ran across and stood in front of his father.

"The nightriders were out last night, Father. They were out for sure this time. They burned up three barns. They burned up old Mr. Grey's barn and Jack Grey said at school today that Mr. Grey said he thought Mr. Mitchell helped do it. He said he thought he saw Mr. Mitchell's horse and if he ever found out for sure he'd shoot Mr. Mitchell if it's the last thing he ever does. I'll bet he does, too. I'll bet Mr. Mitchell did it. I'll bet—"

"I know all about it," said his father. "I've heard the whole story already."

"Listen, Tommy," rebuked Mrs. Hardin, "you don't know whether Mr. Mitchell had anything to do with it or not. Don't you say one word about all this at school or anywhere else. Not a word. Do you hear?"

"But, Mother, everybody knows about it. Jack said his father said he bet Grandpa was kicked off the board just so they could put Mr. Mitchell on and the association could nightride all it wanted and he said he'd shoot every man on the whole board 'fore he'd ever join up with a bunch of skunks like that. And Mrs. Grey's mighty sick today. She's caught a breakdown."

"Tommy, I've told you. Don't say a single word to anybody. And your grandfather wasn't kicked off the board either. He resigned because he wanted to. Now go upstairs and change your clothes. You're wet as can be. Then go back and get yourself something to eat. It's a long time till supper."

"They say Grandpa had to resign and that he got kicked off. It's the same thing, Grandpa, ain't it?"

Old Mr. Hardin looked down at his grandson with puzzled eyes. "Do what your mother says, Thomas, before you catch cold."

"I'm not cold."

"Do what your mother says, son," Big Thomas threatened, "or you'll get your hide frailed off in about a minute."

The boy looked at his father with a sort of impudent amusement at the terror of the threat; then he turned and left the room. The noise of his feet, as he took each stair with a solid deliberate stamp, carried his protest back to the hearthside.

"He ought to be spanked," said Big Thomas, "I've got half a mind to spank him right now."

"I expect you've about forgotten how to spank him," smiled his wife, "it's been so long since you've spanked him." She paused a moment and studied him. "And besides, Thomas, it's you who need a spanking."

"He's a mighty bright little boy," old Mr. Hardin remarked, just as the feet reached the last stair with especial violence. "He's mighty clever. He understands everything as clear as can be."

"You didn't talk to him about the nightriding, did you, Papa?" asked Mrs. Hardin with a trace of anxiety in her tone. "You ought not to, you know."

"I didn't say a word about it to him. I just let him talk about it to me coming up to the house. I met him down at the big gate."

Big Thomas looked directly at his father for the first time since the old man had come in. "You mean he came while you were sitting on the gate reading your paper," he said. "I wish you wouldn't sit on the gate. It's ruining the gate."

"I sit up pretty near the post, son. It don't hurt the gate any more anyway. The gate's already solid down on the ground."

"Your sitting on it put it solid on the ground."

"I reckon so, even if I always do sit up pretty near the post, but the gate's the only place to sit down there. When the weather warms up maybe I'll put me a bench down there. There's a right pleasant place for a bench under that big white oak. Don't you think so, Edith? It'll be nice to sit down there some when summer comes. It's nice and close to the road."

"Yes, Papa," she answered, "it's nice and close to the road for you."

The old man came around by the fire opposite his son and took the big chair reserved for him. He propped his stick against the stonework of the fireplace, and began filling his pipe. When that was lighted and the first blue puff or two had been dissipated into the upper air of the room, he took the folded paper from his pocket. Slowly, he spread it on his knees.

"You seen this, Thomas?"

"No, I haven't seen it, but Jones told me all about it when I went over about that heifer. Jones sorter thinks it's a good thing, even if he is a friend of Mr. Salem's. He says he feels sorry for Mr. Salem because of Mr. Salem not having any insurance to speak of, but he says it's a time when you can't think too much about friends. You've got to think about the future for everybody. Let's see the paper."

Without a word his father passed him the newspaper. He began to read, holding the sheets firmly with both of his large hands and leaning forward over them. His father watched him; he still held the pipe fixed between his teeth while he watched, but no more puffs of smoke came from it. Mrs. Hardin's book lay open in her lap with her hand on it to hold the place, but she, too, was watching her husband. When he turned the sheet, hunting the rest of the story, the paper crackled sharply in the silence, like a new-lit log at night. He finished, folded the paper, and passed it back to his father.

"I suppose you've made up your mind," he said.

"That ain't exactly the point," the old man answered. "The point is, What do you think about it?"

"You won't see it the way I do. I don't see much use in talking about it." The voice was sullen, constrained. For a moment his wife seemed about to speak, and then, with an effort, turned her eyes from him.

"Son, that ain't the point either. What do you think about it?"

"I feel about like Jones, I reckon."

"You feel that the association's got to win, no matter how?"

"I reckon so."

"Not feeling that way made me get off the board. I can't feel that way now since it's come to this. Nothing in the world's worth winning or doing, no matter how. You always cut your own throat that way."

"I'd take a chance right now on cutting my own throat. We've got a crop on our hands and we've got to sell it. And next year we'll have a crop and we'll want to sell that for enough money to pay hands and pay taxes and pay this and pay that. And everybody's in the same boat. I'd take a chance all right."

"Well, I told Hopkins something when we had our little disagreement."

"I can guess what you told him."

"Maybe you can guess. You ought to be able to guess. I told him that the first time I was certain the association burned a barn, I was getting out and was going to stay out. I can't stop them being damned fools, but I can get out myself. I might've stayed on the board if I thought I had a chance of stopping it, but I didn't see a single chance. Now they've got that fellow Mitchell in my place, most likely they'll be singing a hymn before and after setting a fire to a barn. Well, I just don't see that singing one of Mitchell's hymns changes things. I'm getting out right away."

Big Thomas got up from the stool and stepped to the center of the hearth. His father, sitting in the chair with the newspaper on his lap, looked very small before him.

"You are going to ruin us, Papa. Just as certain as you get out, you are going to ruin us. But I'll not have it. I'm not going to be ruined now by any notion of yours. God knows

I've worked hard enough on this place, but always what you say runs it. But it's not going to run it this time. You helped start this association. You got us in it and you got a lot of other people in it. You've started something and you can't stop it, so you're getting out. You made your mistake when you got off the board. Papa, you're on horseback now, you're on horseback, and it's a wild piece of horseflesh. By God, Papa, it's you or the horse. A bad horse don't let you step down at the block, just because you've decided you can't ride him. He throws you. You just try easing out now and see what happens. It'll be ruin. And I'll not be ruined by you."

"It won't be ruin, son, but even if it is, I'm going to try to keep my hands clean as I can."

"Clean? Clean? Why, if you keep on this sort of thing your hands'll be dirty from grubbing in somebody else's tobacco patch. It's ruin, I tell you."

"You're crazy, Thomas."

"It's not me that's crazy. It's you. I've got other people to think about. I've got Edith here and Tommy. You're crazy, and you don't think about anybody in the world except yourself when it come to do something like this. Keep your hands clean? Why don't you think about the rest of us a little? Keep Edith's hands clean. Keep them out of somebody's dishwater."

"Thomas, Thomas," implored his wife, "don't be such a fool. Come over and sit down. Sit down over here with me."

He swung around toward her, his head drooping a little, but without shame, and his arms straight at his sides.

"Come here, Thomas."

He followed the direction of her extended hand and came to sit beside her on the sofa. Mr. Hardin regarded the proceeding with no apparent interest; he looked like one finally detached from it, a spectator who had no concern with its outcome. There was silence in the room. Each of the three seemed to be completely unaware of the others, and lost in thought.

"Why don't you say something?" Thomas demanded at last.

"I don't know if there's anything for me to say now."

"Are you getting out?"

"I might say this, Thomas, after all. I've broken horses since I was fifteen years old and I've been thrown by them, but I always rode them in the end. I guess I understand them all right. I thought I understood something about men, too. But I guess I don't understand a thing in the world about them."

"Are you getting out?"

"Yes. I'm getting out. No, don't say anything, Thomas." He lifted his hand, palm outward, toward his son. "That don't mean you're getting out at all. I can't see any reason why we ought to stay together on this business. I think one way and you think another. We've both got our reasons, but there's mighty little use in talking about them. We'll divide the crop up right now, and we can divide the land up for this year's crop before it's set out. We'll let people know right away too."

"But, Papa," Mrs. Hardin begged, "you can all fix it up. You don't have to do that."

"Hush, Edith," he said gently. "There's nothing to fix up. Thomas, are you satisfied?"

"I'm satisfied."

"We might even build a new barn. We need another barn pretty bad. That'll make things easier."

"Yes, I reckon we need another barn."

"Well, I'll write a letter to the board tonight and tell them I'm out. And I'll write to Wiedenmeyer tonight, too."

"To Wiedenmeyer?"

"Yes. I ain't going to try to ride in on the tail of the association price. The buyers are getting a good deal of tobacco round the country but maybe they'd be glad for a little more good prime leaf. We've got a right smart good leaf down there. I'll ask Wiedenmeyer for an offer right away tonight. He won't pay the association price, but his figure ought to do me."

"Do it quick. I'll feel better with your tobacco sold. The nightriders won't be wanting to see a good lot like that just put in the buyers' hands. I wish it was off the place right now."

"It'll be off soon enough. I'll get shet of it just as quick as I can, son."

"Well, hurry. I wouldn't write to the board just yet. I'd wait a day or two maybe, till I heard from Wiedenmeyer."

"No, I'm writing both the letters tonight."

Thomas got up and moved toward the door. "Suit yourself," he said. There was an air of victory, of business, about him. "Just suit yourself," he repeated, "but it's playing with dynamite to wait around."

"Where are you going?" his wife asked.

"To hunt Sam," he answered, with the air of achievement still about him.

"Just a minute," his father said. "I'd like to ask you a question. Don't you think the association'll think you're acting a little funny in just helping me to turn over a good crop to the buyers? You, a strong association man. Me, a man that's been kicked off the board and bolted the association?"

"You're my father." The answer was again sullen,

"Sure. I'd just forgotten that for a minute," the old man said reflectively. "I'd just about forgotten about that, thinking of this other."

"Why, Papa," Mrs. Hardin protested with genuine alarm. "You hadn't forgotten anything of the sort."

"Oh, yes, I had. But I just forgot for a minute. And, Thomas, I'd like to ask something else if you don't mind."

"Ask it."

"You're a strong association man. What are you going to do if they ask you to do a little nightriding? Being a strong association man, why don't you do a little nightriding? Most likely they're going to need a few more men that can ride and can shoot pretty well. That is, shoot if they have to shoot. What about Simmons over here? He ain't in the association. He's got a good crop over at his place. More'n likely he'll be ready to sell soon, and they won't want to see that much tobacco put on the market right off. Simmons is a friend of yours. What are you going to do if they ask you to ride with them? Are you going to ride? Or are you going to tell Simmons to get ready, Simmons being a good friend of yours?"

"I'm not telling anybody anything."

"Just going to wash your hands. Just going to call for the bowl and pitcher and wash your hands? Going to keep your hands clean?" The old man's voice was innocent of sarcasm. His question was almost gentle.

"I'm not telling anybody anything," Thomas repeated slowly, his hand on the knob of the door. "I'd be a fool to tell anybody."

"Why don't you ride? Maybe you ought to ride, son, feeling like you do."

Thomas hesitated a moment and then pointed at his wife. "I've got other things to think about. There's Edith, and there's Tommy for me to think about."

His wife looked at the hand outstretched toward her, the stubborn index finger and the black hairs on the back of the hand. "You needn't bother about me," she said.

"God damn it to hell!" said Thomas in a voice that filled the room. "Maybe I will ride."

He went out, slamming the door behind him; the heavy pictures, indistinct now in the late afternoon light, rattled on the walls.

Mrs. Hardin walked over to one of the deep windows and stood with her back to the room. It had begun to rain again. It was a slow, nerveless rain, dropping to earth like an embodiment of the winter twilight. Already the path to the gate was filled with a small riffled flood, and to the left, in the low part of the lawn, water stood almost over the grass. The water reflected nothing in such a light and at such a distance, but a gray splatter which the drops made in the east corner told that it stood there, like a miniature marsh, among the roots and unclipped stems of the grass. The nearer trunks of the leafless trees between the drive and the stagnant fields were visible, but the farther ones of the row gradually dissolved into the opacity of rain. To the left, toward the river, the firing barn was a scarcely distinguishable hulk; to the right, the cedar grove seemed a dim but solid body which pressed, nearer than ever, against the white palings of the lawn fence. The water dripped from the eaves of the veranda and rustled in the overflowing gutter, and immediately in front of the window where Mrs. Hardin stood it plunged in steady, swollen drops from a leak in the veranda roof. Their more regular beat, among the other noises of the weather, was audible in the still room.

"Papa," said Mrs. Hardin, "there's that leak again."

"Yes, Honey, it needs fixing soon. Maybe I better write it down so I'll remember it. I'll write it down when I start my letters."

"Why don't you do them now before supper? There won't be anybody in here to bother you now. I'm going back and start Sallie with supper."

"All right. I'll fix them now."

He got up from his chair and knocked his pipe out against the blackened stone of the inner chimney. Mrs. Hardin walked across the room to the sofa where her book lay face down. She picked it up and then closed it with a faint snap. The place was lost. Just as she turned to the door, Mr. Hardin spoke.

"Honey, I'm sorry I said that last to Thomas. I reckon I oughtn't. After all, it's his business."

"Nothing turns out to be just anybody's business all to himself, Papa. That's the trouble."

He made no answer, even though she stood there for a moment or two as if she expected one. She was a tall woman with loose dark hair which looked heavy above her white face. She stood, as her husband had stood, with one hand on the knob of the door, while with the other she held the red-backed book which she had been reading. "But it doesn't matter in the least," she finally said.

Not until after the sound of her steps on the uncarpeted dining room floor had died away did he go to the desk under the second window. The top rolled back with difficulty, for the wet weather had swollen it in the grooves and age had loosened the joints so that it no longer ran true. He sat in front of the desk, staring at the loose papers which cluttered its interior, the two tarnished silver inkpots, and the silver tray where the pens lay on a matrix of paper clips, pins, and faded stamps. It was a long time before he began to write. Then his pen moved slowly, almost painfully, to form the meticulous, small letters, whose outline wavered a little even though the fingers which held the penstaff seemed firm. Once he laid the pen back in the silver tray and looked out of the window before him. It was still raining and the light was dim.

Just as he finished the first letter and laid it aside, unblotted, to dry, the door of the dining room opened and Alec entered with an armful of wood for the fire.

"Better put some on the fire," Mr. Hardin said. "It's pretty chilly now. And don't put the rest in the box, Alec. Just put it out on the hearth to dry a little. It gets right wet in the shed."

The Negro boy stooped before the fire and lowered his arms slowly so that the sticks slipped off heavily to the stones of the hearth. Then he put two on the fire, dropping them quickly on the andirons to snatch his thin curled fingers back from the heat like a hurt animal. As he leaned forward the new flame lighted up his small, intent face.

"Alec, won't you bring me a lamp right away?"

"Yassuh, Mr. Hardin."

Mr. Hardin got another sheet of paper from one of the pigeon-holes before him and laid it on the desk. Across the top of the sheet ran the business caption: *Cedardale—J. C. Hardin & Son—Tobacco Growers and Stock Breeders.* Carefully he drew a single line through the "& Son" of the caption, but he did not begin to write again.

Alec did not bring him the lamp. It was Mrs. Hardin herself who came with it, holding it almost at arm's length before her in steady hands. The clear light fell on her arms and breast, but across her face was the shadow of the opaque roses which garlanded the lamp's frosted shade. With the burden of the lamp she moved slowly; there was a certain gravity, like that of a ritual, in her step and bearing as she crossed the room to Mr. Hardin. She set it on the upper part of the desk in front of the window. Immediately the world outside vanished, and the panes, which separated it from the room, went flat and black to reflect the glowing shade with its wreath of roses, her tall figure, and Mr. Hardin's bearded head.

"I've got something to tell you, Papa."

"Yes, Edith," he said.

"It's Thomas. Thomas just came up to the kitchen a minute ago and said to tell you that he thought he might sell his crop with you. And he wants to resign from the association. He said tell you that, too. Have you written the letter yet?"

"I'll write another one."

"Are you glad, Papa?"

"I can't tell, Honey, whether I'm glad or not, it's all so mixed up. But I'll write the letters."

IV

Mrs. Hardin rose on her elbow and then sat bolt upright in the bed. Somewhere, very faintly, a dog was barking. She got out quietly and went across the room to the dim square of the south window. For a minute or two she leaned over the sill while the slight wind ruffled her nightgown.

"Thomas," she called softly.

There was no answer from the dark side of the room where the bed stood. Very quickly she crossed to it and bent above her husband.

"Thomas," she said, but he only stirred in his sleep. She took him by the arm and shook him. "Thomas, wake up. Wake up. I think there's somebody down by the barn."

Suddenly he was awake and rising from the bed as if his deep slumber had only been a joke played on her.

"What is it?"

"Down at the barn. I heard the dogs. And I think the gate to the drive is open. I couldn't see plain."

Without a word he strode to the window and peered out.

"I can't see either. I'm going down. Don't light the lamp."

She stood at the window, while he fumbled with his clothes in the dark.

"Can you see anything?" he asked in a low voice.

"Nothing. You can't see the barn from here for the trees." And then, just as she spoke, the faintest glow like early dawn, spread above the tree tops.

"They are, Thomas! They are there!"

He was at the window beside her in a single awkward bound.

"Oh, the dogs! The dirty dogs! The dirty sons-of-bitches!" His voice was almost a sob. "Wake Papa," he called back from the door. And then there was the noise of his feet pounding down the stairs, in the living room, and across the hollow floor of the veranda.

She ran out of the room and down the pitch-dark hall to the last door. She beat on the panels with the flat of both hands, calling over and over again. Then his voice came from within.

"Hurry! Hurry!" she called. "Thomas has gone."

He found her in the hall, standing at the head of the stairs. She was quiet now, but she gripped him by the arm when he reached her side.

"Take care of Thomas," was all she said.

"I'll take care of him."

He hurried down, stumbling once in the dark. At the bottom he turned and looked up at the almost indistinguishable white figure at the head of the stairs.

"Dress, Edith," he ordered. "You'll catch cold."

A flickering light fell through the windows of the living room, more a reflection than a light, and the grass between the trees to the east of the lawn was faintly luminous with what seemed to be a light of its own. Just as Mr. Hardin reached the front gate, there came the protracted empty staccato of hoofs from the wooden bridge down the lane. By the time he reached the gate off the drive, the barn was in full blaze, and, as he turned there, an enormous flame spun up from the roof and plunged through the high drift of smoke above. The bulk of the cedars behind the barn leaped from black to green, and the wide expanse of the field shimmered like water as the innumerable small shadows cast by inequalities of its surface flickered with the flickering of the tall flame. Near the barn three or four men rushed about. Then the roof of the barn collapsed with the cracking of a broken bough. The single flame plunged again, a little higher, held for a moment, and dropped into the tangled blaze below. The barn and the tobacco in it had burned like tinder.

Mr. Hardin slowed his pace to a walk. His lips were open, and between his teeth the breath came in quick gasps. When he got to the barn the men were standing close together in silence. They were all Negroes.

"Where's Mr. Thomas?" he asked.

"I ain't seen him," said one.

"He ain't bin here a-tall," Sam interrupted. "I wuz here at de fust. I heared dem dogs and I say ter myself, Dey's at de barn. And dar dey wuz. I come up de back way and dey wuz ridin' off down tow'd de gate, jes' lopin' along, an—"

"You haven't seen him, Sam?"

"Naw, suh. Jes' as dey rode off—"

Mr. Hardin turned abruptly away. "Thomas! Thomas!" he shouted, and then hurried out across the rough earth of the field. He stumbled a little, caught himself, and ran on. He stopped, shaking as with a chill, and put his hands, trumpetwise, to his mouth. "Thomas! Thomas!" There was no answer. He ran again but more slowly. Again he stopped and lifted his hands to his mouth and called. "Thomas! Thomas! O Thomas!" There was no answer, not even an echo of his own voice in the broad field. For several minutes he stood there in the middle of the field. "God-a-Mighty," he said aloud, "what a fool I am." Then he began to walk slowly back to the barn.

The four Negro men stared curiously at him when he came up. Their eyeballs were white and wide, and their cheeks, on the side toward the fire, glistened dully in its light. None of them spoke. They seemed embarrassed, almost guilty.

"How many men were there, Sam?" Mr. Hardin spoke very

deliberately as if he were making an effort to control his heavy breathing.

"I doan know egzackly, Mr. Hardin. I reckin maybe fifteen. Maybe more'n fifteen. I jes' seen them hawses lopin' down tow'd de gate an' den dem nightriders muster seen me. Dey turn de gate an' den dey go jes' as fas' as dey can down tow'd de big-road. Den I go roun' ter de udder side de barn whar they lit de fire fust, but it wuz a big fire den. Dar wuzn' trompin' er nuthin' could put dat fire out den. Dar jes' wuzn' nuthin' I could do den, Mr. Hardin."

"I know it, Sam."

"I'd er done sumthin' ef'n I could, Mr. Hardin."

"Sure, Sam."

Again the Negroes relapsed into the vague embarrassment with which they had met Mr. Hardin when he came back from the field. He left them and walked as near as he could for the heat to the spot where the barn had stood. It was a glowing, oblong heap from which a perfunctory blaze now and then spurted. Some of the heavy beams still burned steadily with thin, clinging flames. It had been an old barn, and the frame timbers of the lower part had been cut with ax and adze, not sawed, from solid tree trunks. They would burn all night like backlogs in a fireplace. As he watched, the length of one which protruded from the mass broke off and dropped flatly to the glowing bed. The sparks spattered under the impact like molten iron and for a second the flame leaped again, higher than a man's stature, to light up the space around. But it sank quickly and again the darkness began its gradual encroachment from the field and from the cedars on the other side of the place.

"Look, Mr. Hardin, look yonder."

He swung about and peered in the direction of the Negro's pointing arm. A lank hound was sniffing at something over by the fence. Mr. Hardin ran to the spot, shouting at the hound as he ran. He dropped on his knees by the fence, while the hound stood behind him with lowered head.

"Come here," he called back to the Negroes.

They came, walking almost timidly in a close group, and gathered about him. The hound moved back behind them.

"It's old Bess," Mr. Hardin said slowly. "It ain't anything in the world but old Bess," he repeated half to himself, and rubbed the coat of the setter's back with a hand that trembled.

"She daid?" one of the Negroes asked.

Mr. Hardin did not answer. Sam stooped to feel with his hand over the bitch's head and throat.

"Yeh," he said. "She's daid. Daider'n a doornail."

One of the other Negroes had picked up a heavy stick of firewood from the ground at his feet. It was a short, gnarled stick, and at one end the bark was matted with blood and hair.

"Dey done it wid dis." He turned the stick over in his hands, looking at it stupidly, and then hefted it. "Yeh, dey done it wid dis. Dis stick enuff ter kill enybody." He hefted it again, and then struck a wide, sweeping blow in vicious pantomime.

"Dem houn' dawgs jes' barked," said Sam. "Dey didn' try ter bite dem nightriders. Dey ain't nuthin' but ole coon-dawgs. But ole Bess, I bet she try an' bite. Den dey kilt her."

Mr. Hardin rose from his knees and reached out for the stick. The Negro passed it to him. Without a word he laid it on the ground by the fence away from sight. He leaned against the top rail of the fence for a moment looking at the Negroes.

"I reckon you boys better go home to bed," he said. "Just take old Bess down to the stable first. We'll bury her to-morrow."

Two of the men picked up the dog, one with the fore and one with the hind legs, and started off with their burden toward the clump of cedars. Another walked beside them, talking in a low voice. Sam loitered behind. He stood a few feet away from Mr. Hardin as if waiting to speak.

"Better go to bed, Sam."

"I'se goin' ter bed."

"Good night, Sam," said Mr. Hardin and turned away.

"Mr. Hardin." He hesitated a moment. "Mr. Hardin, I bet

Mr. Thomas'll sure be all right. He's a pow'ful good man, Mr. Thomas. He kin take care uv hisself."

"Yes, Sam," agreed Mr. Hardin, and turned away, this time quickly, in the direction of the house.

A light was burning in the living room when he turned into the lawn. Halfway up the veranda he paused, put his hands to his mouth, and then withdrew them. He crossed the veranda in three long steps, flung the door open, and stood at the sill. A small lamp burned on the mantelshelf, near the clock, but in the big room its light was feeble. Some expiring coals had been raked together against the back log in the depth of the fireplace and blown to life in the midst of the bed of cold ashes. Very close, almost in the mouth of the fireplace, Mrs. Hardin sat on the low stool. She had not dressed herself but wore a blue flannel robe which dropped loosely from her shoulders to the stone of the hearth and crumpled there to give a strange impression of arrangement in the cold disorder of the room. The wide sleeves of the robe dropped from her bare arms, stretched out toward the fire, and her hands, which shifted above the flame with a tentative, weaving motion, showed a sudden whiteness against the sooty stone of the fireplace. They seemed almost too thin for the hands of a young woman. Her son crouched opposite her.

"Where's Thomas?" she asked.

Mr. Hardin did not answer.

"Come in, Papa. Close the door and tell me where Thomas is."

"Thomas is all right, Honey," he said, and he pulled the door gently into its place. "Thomas said tell you he'd be back before morning and for you to get to bed. He said he'd be mad if he found you up when he got back. He looked at the light up here and he said to me, I bet Edith's up catching her death of cold and her not strong this season. That's exactly what he said. Now, Edith Honey, you get to bed."

Mrs. Hardin's hands continued to weave their deliberate, invisible thread above the flame.

"Where is Thomas?" she said.

"Honey, he's ridden over to Simmons' place to tell Simmons the nightriders are out and to watch for them. He took my mare and went by the short cut so he'd beat them there if they aim to get Simmons' barn tonight. He had to go because of Simmons not having a telephone yet. He oughter almost be there now. He'll be back long before morning. Simmons has got three big boys and all of them can go out and lie behind that stone wall and when the nightriders come up they can call to them and say, We got you now. Then the nightriders'll go off. They don't want any stand-up fight and they'll know they're beat. But Thomas won't stay. He promised me not to stay. He knows he's got you to think about, Honey, and he won't stay a minute after he tells Simmons." His voice went on impersonally as if he were recounting a story that had happened long before. "Now, Edith, you just get along to bed and get some sleep."

She neither moved nor answered.

"Get up, Edith, and go to bed. Thomas'll be mighty mad if he comes back and finds you here. There ain't even any fire in the fireplace to speak of." He went to her and took her hands and drew her up beside him. "You're cold already, your hands are as cold as ice. Go to bed. Thomas just rode over to do something neighbor-like, being a good friend of Simmons. He'll be back long before morning."

He led her to the hall door and then in the darkness to the foot of the stairs.

"Good night, Edith," he said.

She climbed the stairs silently, faced about for a moment at the landing, and vanished. Mr. Hardin went back into the living room. Little Thomas was still crouching beside the fire.

"Get up, boy, and go to bed."

Little Thomas rose, but made no sign of going off. "I hope Mr. Simmons shoots a dozen nightriders. Red Simmons is a good shot, too, and I'll bet he shoots a nightrider. The dirty skunks. I'd like to shoot all those nightriders."

"There won't be any shooting, Tommy, because the nightriders will just go off when Mr. Simmons calls to them. People that ride around like that at night and burn other people's barns don't want to fight. They're just cowards, Tommy."

"I'll bet Mr. Mitchell's a coward. But Mr. Hopkins, Grandpa, if he's there, I'll bet he ain't a coward even if he is a dirty nightrider."

"No, I wouldn't call Bill Hopkins a coward. I guess I can't tell who's a coward. But you don't know whether he's a nightrider or not."

"He's on the board."

"Yes, he's on the board all right. But you, Tommy, you get to bed right now. You've got to go to school tomorrow, and if you don't get to bed you'll be sleepy all day like last Monday. I mean what I say, Tommy."

The boy walked toward the door and then turned. "Can't I just run down and look at the barn once? Mother wouldn't let me go. I'll be right back. Please?"

"No."

When his grandson had gone, Mr. Hardin went to the hall door and listened for a moment. He pulled it shut and then moved hurriedly to the far corner of the room where the rays of the lamp did not penetrate. There were the two shotguns propped in the corner with the white, oil-stained envelopes pulled over their muzzles. His foot touched something on the floor, and he stooped to pick it up. It was a rifle. He went to the other corner and looked. The second rifle was gone. The lower drawer of the desk beside him was half open. He pulled it out and peered inside. There were two solid square boxes with the picture of a shotgun shell on their tops, and beside them lay a smaller, oblong box overflowing with brass cartridges. His hand plunged in the drawer and withdrew, clenched full of them. He let the cartridges slip between his fingers into the palm of the other hand like heavy, swollen grains of corn. He inspected them as they lay in the cupped palm, stirring them gently with a forefinger as a farmer inspects seed corn, and then let them trickle through his fingers again and thump into the obscurity of the drawer.

He wandered aimlessly out to the porch and down the low

stone steps to the grass. To the left a light still glowed from the barn. The front windows of the living room did not reflect it now, but shone with the faint light from within, and the grass under the trees was dark. He walked to the gate and stood there, leaning over its top, while he regarded the lighter strip of the drive, which wound off between the cedar grove and the fields. A hound came cautiously out from the shadow of the trees on the east side of the lawn and approached him with tail wagging and head lowered. When the hound nuzzled at his knees he dropped his hand to fumble with its head and soft loose ears, but he did not look down. At length he turned from the gate and began to walk back up the path; the hound gave the dangling hand a clumsy final lick and was gone, sniffing the grass, into the shadows.

Back in the house Mr. Hardin took the lamp from the mantelpiece and went into the dining room. The unwashed dishes from the Sunday night supper were still on the table, waiting for Sallie in the morning, and about the table stood four chairs pushed irregularly back as they had been left the evening before. Mr. Hardin went to the sideboard and opened one of the panels. From the interior gloom he took a large square decanter and a tumbler. He slipped the tumbler into the pocket of his coat and, with the decanter in one hand, and the lamp in the other, returned to the living room. The whisky, sloshing about inside the cut glass, gave off thin prismatic gleams from the light of the lamp. When he had set the lamp carefully on the mantel and the decanter and glass on the stool he got down to his knees and began to blow Edith's remnant of coals back to flame; he fed it with shags of cedar gently, and at last trusted two heavier sticks to its heat. Only then he poured out a drink for himself, three fingers in the tumbler, and sat down in his chair. Once he got up to put more wood on the fire, which now leaped cleanly toward the chimney, and once to pour himself another drink, three fingers in the bottom of the tumbler.

Shortly after three o'clock there was a noise from the dining room. Mr. Hardin stood up from his chair and stepped for-

ward, but before he could reach the door, the knob turned
in the socket and it swung gently inward. Half concealed by
the shadow stood his son, filling the space of the doorway.

"Put out the light," he ordered. The voice was scarcely more
than a whisper.

Mr. Hardin turned about casually, took down the lamp,
and moved to the other side of the hearth. Then, cupping his
hand behind the glass chimney, he blew sharply, and the room
went dark except for the firelight. Thomas came in. He was
wringing wet and shivering with cold, but he did not approach
the lighted hearth.

"God-a-Mighty, son, what is it?"

"I got one of them, maybe two. I saw one fall off his horse.
I ran down across the field and cut them off at the pike and
when they rode by I got them. If my rifle hadn't stuck I'd a
gotten some more. The God-damned rifle stuck and I had to
run. They chased me down toward the river, but they didn't
have anything but pistols. I lost them in the cane down there
and swam the creek where it's deep near the river. God, if my
rifle hadn't stuck I'd gotten some more of the sons-of-bitches
when they came across the field toward the cane, running and
shooting off their pistols, and me in the cane. But I got one, I
know. I saw him fall off his horse in the road. I hope I killed
the son-of-a-bitch."

"Son, you fool, you fool."

"Maybe I am a fool, but I hope he's dead. Oh, the dirty
sons-of-bitches."

"You're cold, son." Mr. Hardin picked up the decanter and
poured a drink and took it across to him. "Drink it, son," he
said gently.

Thomas swallowed the whisky in two choking gulps. "We've
got to hurry," he said, and coughed. "I reckon they'll be here
any time now if they ain't here now."

"Get some clothes, Thomas. You'll find some in the closet
in the hall. Hurry. And, Thomas, in God's name don't wake
Edith up."

Thomas went out into the hall, leaving a trail of water drops behind him; on the wood floor the water looked dark. His father got the rifle from the corner and a handful of cartridges from the desk. When Thomas came back he was standing in the middle of the room loading the magazine of the weapon. Thomas pulled off the wet shirt, dropping it with a soft smack to the floor, and began to wipe his muscular chest and belly. He put on an old sweater and a coat and twisted a scarf about his throat. He watched his father slip the last cartridge in.

"God, I'm cold," he said, picking up the decanter. He drank directly from it, thirstily, without troubling to use the tumbler.

"Get some pants," advised Mr. Hardin.

"I couldn't find any pants, and I haven't got time."

Mr. Hardin passed him the rifle. "I don't reckon this one will stick. I used it just the other day and oiled it."

"You using the shotgun?"

"I won't need anything. Now you get along, son. Better get down to the woods by the river."

"The hell I will. I'm staying. This is my house."

"Tommy, you better get along."

"I'm staying. I'm not leaving you here."

Mr. Hardin regarded him for a moment with that incurious gaze. "All right," he said.

"I better go out back."

"Yes, you go out back. Get up by the chicken house and you can see all the backyard. I'm going down in the edge of the cedars by the drive. Go on. I'll get me another coat first. Go on, son."

As soon as Thomas left the room, Mr. Hardin went into the hall to return with a coat. From the corner he took a shotgun, dropped a shell into each barrel, and slipped out, closing the front door softly behind him. He did not go directly to the gate, but skirted the front of the house, close to the shrubbery, and crossed the lawn to the fence. He climbed it quickly and in two or three paces more was wrapped in the dense shadow of the cedars. He picked his way among them, his feet making no sound on the bed of needles which cloaked the wood earth. Some ten feet from the drive, beyond the gate which opened off toward the barn, he found a gap and settled himself with his back against a tree trunk.

The branches spread out flat and fanwise above him, drooping at the tips, but they were still high enough to give a view of the drive, the field beyond it, and the open space outside the lawn fence. The broad strip of white-washed paling made an excellent background for any object which might move between it and the cedars, but nothing, not even a prowling hound, came again into that obscure area which intervened. Once or twice some animal stirred in the grove, and once an owl called from the hill back of the house. Before dawn the slight wind, which had shifted the cedars to a pervasive whisper, died altogether, and there was perfect stillness. The glow from the barn declined with the first light, was lost in it, and then, long before the sun, the casual smoke took substance above the spot. Finally the sun lifted across the higher land beyond the river, the last rooster crowed and drummed his wings, and the whole scene, the river bottom, the fields, the house, and even the cedar grove, appeared again as a place of use and familiar habitation.

In the broad daylight Mr. Hardin walked up the little rise, through the gate, up the path to his house, and opened the door. He broke the gun, put the shells back in the drawer, and set the gun in its corner with the envelope again over the muzzle. Then he passed the length of the house, through the dining room where the unwashed dishes still cluttered the table, through the kitchen, and across the back porch. He was halfway to the chicken run when Thomas rose from hiding and walked down to meet him. The rifle dangled like an ineffectual toy, almost dragging the ground, at the end of his long arm. Mr. Hardin stopped and waited until his son approached.

"God, I'm cold," Thomas said. His face was very pale, and a black stubble of beard stood out against the white skin like the beard on a sick man's face.

"Hurry, son, and get dressed. Maybe a drink would help first."

"I don't want a drink."

Just inside the privacy of the kitchen they stopped.

"Thomas, you better hurry and get dressed. You want to be dressed like usual when Sallie comes to get breakfast and Sam comes up after milking. I've got to get dressed too."

Thomas made no move. "I don't know what I'm going to do," he said.

"Go on, son. We'll talk about that later. Maybe it ain't so bad."

"I don't much care how bad it is. God, the dirty bastards."

"Hush, son, hush. You go and get dressed proper."

In the living room he stopped and Thomas obediently went upstairs. Mr. Hardin rang the telephone, turning the little crank with a cautious hand while with the other he muffled the bells. For almost a minute he waited and then there came an answer.

"Central," he said with his mouth close to the transmitter, "this is Hardin speaking. I understand there was a little shooting down on the west pike last night. Can you tell me if anybody got hurt? . . . No, we didn't hear any shots. One of my niggers that lives on the river down closer to the pike says he heard a right smart shooting. . . . No, don't ring me up, I'll ring you up in a few minutes again. I'm much obliged, Miss Turner." And he, too, left the room.

It was Thomas who first reappeared, to kneel on the hearth and begin rebuilding the fire. When the door closed behind his father he did not even glance up from his task.

"I've told Edith," he said into the black hollow of the chimney.

Mr. Hardin stood behind him, staring down at his son's broad back. He did not answer.

"I've already told her," Thomas repeated.

"How did she take it, Thomas?"

"She's taking it bad," he said, with his face still averted. "I told her quick, and she didn't say anything to me. She just began to walk around the room, walking around in her nightgown, crying and brushing her hair. God, I couldn't stay up there and stand in the middle of the floor and watch her crying like that."

"Maybe you better go back up, son."

"I can't go back up there," he said, rising to face his father. "She didn't even say anything to me. She's just walking around, brushing her hair, and crying and crying. I don't know what to do."

"There ain't but one thing to do, that I can see. Call up the sheriff and tell him you shot somebody when they burned your barn and you're coming in to him. I'll call him. I know Jack Burton. He'll take my word and he won't come get you, son. It'll be all right, son."

Thomas looked at him steadily for a moment, and then spoke very slowly. "Papa, I'll be damned to hell if I'll go in. They know where to find me if they want me. This is my house. They can find me here."

Mr. Hardin reached out to touch him lightly on the arm. "Thomas, you can't do that, you just can't. You can't let them ride up here and let Edith see them take you. It would about break her heart, son."

For a long time Thomas stood there looking stupidly down at the fingers which touched his sleeve. "I reckon I'll go," he said.

Mr. Hardin moved to the telephone. "We better find out who got hurt. Miss Turner is going to tell me." Again he muffled the bells and rang. While he waited for an answer with his bearded lips close to the instrument, Thomas stood on the hearth, rigidly erect, and never shifted his eyes from his father's face. The face was inscrutable and tired.

"That you, Miss Turner? . . . Yes, this is Hardin." There was a pause, and then, "My God, you don't say! My God." Thomas started as if a bull whip had cracked about his ears. Mr. Hardin hung up the receiver and turned..

"It's Bill Hopkins, Thomas. But he'll live, Thomas. The doctor says he'll live. But, Thomas, it's old Bill Hopkins that you saw fall off his horse down on the pike."

"He'll live?"

"Yes, he's going to live. Dr. Jacob told Miss Turner that he's hurt bad, but he'll live. He'll live all right. But, Thomas, it's Bill Hopkins."

"It don't matter who it is. He rode, didn't he?"

"But, Thomas, you don't understand."

"It don't matter." The voice was stubborn. "He rode."

"All right, son. You go up and tell Edith quick. Tell her he'll live and she'll be glad and she won't take it so hard then."

Thomas stepped off the hearth toward the hall door and then paused at its edge. "It don't matter," he said, "but I reckon I'm glad he's going to live." He hesitated again. "Call the sheriff," he ordered and was gone.

"Central, give me Mr. Jack Burton's place, please." The only sound in the house while he waited was Sallie's voice singing in the kitchen as she got the breakfast. "That you, Jack?" he finally said. "This is Hardin, Joe Hardin. . . . The night-riders burned our barn last night, and, Jack, my boy shot one of them, down on the pike. . . . He muster been a little crazy and mad when they burned our barn. Yes, it was Old Man Hopkins he shot, but Hopkins'll live the doctor says. . . . Listen, Jack, I'm sending my boy in to you. I'll go his bail, I reckon I'll be good for his bail all right. Get him back quick as you can, because my daughter-in-law, Edith, she's in a bad shape about it. . . . Much obliged, Jack. . . . And listen, he belongs to you now, and if anybody tries to stop him on the road, he's coming on in anyway. Understand? . . . Take care of him. . . . And, Jack, listen to me, Jack, for God's sake don't go bothering Old Man Hopkins. He's hurt pretty bad the doctor says. And you know him, he wouldn't get away if he could. Much obliged." He hung the receiver up with awkward fingers.

They ate breakfast in silence, each in the usual place. Big Thomas was dressed in his good clothes, a blue serge suit and white stiff collar. His face was shaven now. Mrs. Hardin, at the foot of the table, poured the coffee and passed the large cups without a tremor, but she ate little. At length Mr. Hardin rose from the table and pushed his chair into place.

"I'll go see about saddling up," he said. "You, Tommy, you better get ready for school. Get along."

Almost with an air of relief the boy slipped down and left the room. Mrs. Hardin rose to go around behind her husband's chair. She put her hands on his shoulders and stood there.

"I'll go," said Mr. Hardin, and left them so, her hands on his shoulders and his reaching up to cover them.

On the back porch he found Alec sitting propped against the post with a nearly empty plate of bread and molasses on his lap. A cup of coffee was on the floor beside him. He looked up and grinned.

"Mawnin', Mr. Hardin."

"Hello, Alec. Alec, do you know where your pappy is?"

"He down at de cawn crib. He done et his brekfus'."

"Alec, I want you to go and tell him to saddle up for me and Mr. Thomas. I ain't feeling very well this morning."

"Yassuh, Mr. Hardin." Alec took one more mouthful and wiped his sticky hands on the trousers of his overalls. Whistling, he strolled off toward the side gate of the yard. Mr. Hardin sat on the floor of the porch, his back to the post against which Alec had been leaning, and watched him go. He was still sitting there when his son came to tell him that the horses were ready.

Mrs. Hardin stood at the gate while they mounted. "Come back, Honey, as soon as you can," she said to her husband. "I'll be worried till you get back."

"I'll hurry. I'll telephone from town, too, before I start."

"Good-bye," she said. Her eyes were dry but her lips trembled a little when she spoke.

"Good-bye, Edith."

"Good-bye," said Mr. Hardin and lifted the rein.

The two men rode easily down the slight dip of the drive. At the last bend before the bridge Thomas looked back to wave, but his wife had turned and was walking up the path to the house. The soft earth and gravel of the drive was scored with the deep hoof marks of galloping horses. Studying the surface, Mr. Hardin remarked, "Looks like there might have been nigh onto a score of them."

"No," said Thomas. "Just about a dozen. I watched them coming down the pike."

They rode slowly for another mile, and spoke no more; they were absorbed in their own meditation as if they were strangers riding the same road by the chance of travel who had talked out the commonplaces of greeting and crops and weather. At the branch of the road Mr. Hardin drew rein.

"I reckon I turn off here," he said.

"You ain't going in with me?"

"No, I reckon I better not. It might be better for you to go riding up to Jack Burton's office by yourself."

"Yes," said Thomas in a voice of some trifling bitterness, "it might look like you brought me in."

"It never crossed my head once that way. You know it never did."

"You going to Hopkins' place?"

"Yes, I'm going over and see how he's making out. There ain't anything else I can do."

Thomas hesitated a moment, seeming to suppress something. "I guess I better be getting on," he said finally and touched his heel to the horse's flank.

"I'll meet you in town before long," Mr. Hardin said. "Good-bye, Tommy, and take care of yourself."

"Good-bye," Thomas called. Again he gave his mount the heel and took the road toward town.

Mr. Hardin picked up the rein, and Jenny wheeled to the left branch. He rode off down the gentle grade to the river, sitting the trot like a cavalryman, and disappeared beyond a clump of sycamores which guarded the first bend of the road.

The schoolroom was warm even though the fire in the big iron belly of the stove had run low. The children bent above their books with a hint of restlessness of the impending season or stared with rebellious frankness out of the windows. The teacher, a young woman, was writing figures on the strip of blackboard which ran across the front of the room. There came a knocking at the door and she laid the bit of chalk on her desk and went to open it. A tall Negro man stood there, hat in hand. He spoke to the young woman in a voice which did not carry distinctly back to the curious children. The young woman turned and walked to her desk.

"Thomas," she said, "Thomas Hardin, you can get your books and go. Somebody has come for you."

She herself brought his cap and coat from the hook on the wall and handed them to him as he stood just inside the open door. He stepped out and Sam reached clumsily down to take the cloth satchel from his shoulder.

"What's the matter?" the boy asked.

"Nuthin'," answered Sam, "yore mammy jes' wants you home."

The Negro led the way to the buggy and unhitched the horse from the top bar of the fence. He got up to the seat, unlooped the reins from the splatterboard, and clucked to the horse.

"Sam, what's the matter? I know something's the matter."

The Negro did not look around but continued to stare toward the front, over the horse's jogging back, down the gray road between the fields and trees.

"Dey done shot yore pappy, son. Dey done kilt him down on de pike tow'd town."

The boy hid his face against the Negro's rough coat, which smelt of sweat and tobacco, and wept, weeping silently, as they rode along through the clear, premonitory sunlight of early spring.